Please return/renew this item by the last date shown

worcestershire
countycouncil
Libraries & Learning

Proudly Published by Snowbooks in 2011

Copyright © 2011 Alan K Baker

Snowbooks Ltd.
Tel: 0207 837 6482
email: info@snowbooks.com
www.snowbooks.com

British Library Cataloguing in Publication Data
A catalogue record for this book is available from the
British Library.

ISBN 978-1-907777-54-7
ISBN 978-1-907777-57-8

To the memory of Robert W Chambers (1865-1933), who first unleashed the King in Yellow upon an unsuspecting world

*The forthcoming end of the world will be hastened by the
construction of underground railways burrowing into
infernal regions and thereby disturbing the Devil.*

– Rev Dr John Cumming, 1860

From *The Times,*
14th November, 1899

GHOSTS BENEATH THE METROPOLIS

Uncanny Events on London's Urban Railway Network

For some weeks now, reports have been made of strange happenings on the capital's Underground Railway, which have left the authorities baffled and perplexed.

That these events are of a supernatural nature can scarcely be denied, even by the most sceptical of commentators, coming as they do from reliable witnesses of good character, many of whom are employed on the network in positions of considerable responsibility.

Ever since its inception more than thirty years ago, the Underground has played host to the occasional encounter with a wandering apparition or ghostly voice; however, in recent weeks those encounters have grown dramatically in number, most particularly in those parts of the network which were once occupied by cemeteries and plague pits.

Sir William Crookes, President of the Society for Psychical Research and one of the country's most respected scientists, stated that he is at a loss to explain the sudden upsurge in supernatural activity. 'Ghostly manifestations are often the result of anger or distress on the part of the spirits,' he said. 'That may be the reason for the recent sightings and encounters, although what may have caused such anger and distress is, at present, entirely unclear.'

PART ONE

The Madness from the Tunnels

CHAPTER ONE:
The Kennington Loop

Alfie Morgan hated being in this part of the network.

He had been a train driver on the Central and South London Railway for nearly ten years and had grown used to the noise and darkness of the Underground, the heat and the cramped conditions and the sheer strangeness of ploughing through the miles of deep-level tunnels which wound beneath the bustling streets of London.

He had grown used to all that… but he had never grown used to being in the Kennington Loop, and he suspected that he never would.

The Loop was at the southern end of the Central and South London line and was exactly what its name suggested: a loop of tunnel which enabled southbound trains to turn around past Kennington Station before entering the northbound Charing Cross branch platform.

There were several things which annoyed Alfie about the Loop, things which made him uneasy and jittery, so that he always found himself counting the minutes until he was out of it and back in the main tunnels. For one thing, its diameter was such that the tunnel curved tightly around, so that the wheels of the trains screeched loudly, almost plaintively on the tracks; for another, there were frequent delays, during

11

which trains were held in the tunnel for up to twenty minutes before being allowed to exit into Charing Cross.

At times like this, the drivers found themselves sitting alone in the subterranean darkness (for no train ever carried passengers into the Loop, and precious few inhabitants of the metropolis even knew of its existence), strangely mindful of the two hundred feet of London clay pressing down upon them, cutting them off from the light and air of the outside world.

It was nearly ten o'clock in the evening when Alfie pulled out of Kennington Station and headed into the Loop, leaving the subdued light of the station's gas lamps behind and plunging into a darkness only fitfully relieved by the lead carriage's electric headlights. The air was hot and close, and carried upon it a strange taint: a combination of machine oil and the musty ancientness of the surrounding earth.

The train's wheels began their expected screeching and squealing as they turned upon the tightly curving track, and Alfie tried to ignore the eerie sound as he gripped the engine throttle. The tunnel curved away into the pitch-black distance, the ugly ribbing of its cast iron reinforcement segments catching the light and giving Alfie the unsettling impression that he and his train had been swallowed up by some ravenous denizen of the earth's depths.

Alfie wished that he were anywhere on the Tube but here, and he envied the construction crews and maintenance men who were at present working elsewhere on the network, replacing the electrified tracks with the new atmospheric railway system. They still had to work in the tunnels, of course, but at least there were lots of them around; at least they had *company*, and Alfie imagined the good-natured banter that would lighten all the hard work.

The atmospheric railway was a technological marvel of the modern age. Alfie had wanted to take his family to see the working model of it that had been on display at the Greater Exhibition in Hyde Park the previous month, but that madman from Venus had put paid to that idea when he attacked the New Crystal Palace with a stolen Martian fighting machine. What a mess that had been! They were still picking up the pieces and rebuilding the sections of the palace which had been destroyed by the maniac. Alfie had read about it in the illustrated papers: it had all been part of some plan to get Earth and Mars to go to war with each other, and it was only by the grace of God that the villain hadn't succeeded.

Bloody Venusians, thought Alfie as he recalled how the life of Her Majesty herself had been under threat during the attack. *A load of bloody buggers, that's what they are! Why can't they keep to themselves without messing around in our affairs?*

Alfie cursed aloud as a red signal light came into view, like a baleful eye in the darkness. He applied the brakes and brought his train to a halt. *Must be clearing the platform at Charing Cross. Oh well, at least that damned screeching's stopped for a while.*

As he sat in the darkness and the silence, Alfie thought again of the maintenance crews and how he'd have given anything to join them. As far as he understood it, the atmospheric railway system worked by means of a sealed metal tube running between the tracks, to which each railway carriage would be attached. The trains would be propelled by compressed air generated by the new Vansittart-Siddeley Ultra-compressors, which were being installed at pumping stations throughout the network. The idea had been tried once before back in the 1860s, in the early days of the Underground, but it had been abandoned because of the problem of keeping the metal tube properly sealed so that the compressed air couldn't leak out.

That problem had now been solved, thanks to the use of Martian rubber of the same type that was used in the self-sealing neck rings of their breathing apparatus. It was amazing stuff, to be sure. Alfie had seen it being installed at Notting Hill Gate a couple of weeks ago. Strange stuff it was, completely sealing the pressure tube between the tracks, without even a seam visible – until a train passed over, whereupon it opened to admit the short pylon connecting the train with its drive cylinder. A clever bunch, those Martians, and no mistake!

A distant rumble sounded in the darkness, making the stationary train tremble very slightly, and Alfie cocked his head to one side, trying to gauge its direction and distance. Was that the train leaving the Charing Cross platform? Could he get going at last and take himself out of this infernal bloody tunnel?

The signal light remained on red, however, and so Alfie heaved a great sigh of nervous irritation and waited.

Presently, another sound disturbed the hot, heavy silence, and Alfie glanced over his shoulder in momentary confusion. It sounded like the *clack* of an interconnecting door shutting, back along the train. Alfie's experienced ear told him that the sound had come from one of the doors separating the last two carriages… but that couldn't be true. He was alone on the train: the guard, old Vic Tandy, had got off at Kennington. He had waved to Alfie from the platform as the train headed for the tunnel leading to the Loop.

Alfie sat still and listened...

A few moments later, there was another *clack* – closer this time. The sound *was* coming from the interconnecting doors. Alfie frowned. Perhaps Vic had jumped back onboard before the train entered the tunnel – bloody stupid thing to do, if he had. Vic knew better than to do something like that: more than one passenger on the Tube had met an untimely –

and very messy – end trying to jump onto a moving train via the interconnecting doors.

And why would he want to, anyway? Alfie wondered, as he gazed through the front window of the driver's cab, wishing that the red signal light would hurry up and change.

Another *clack*, a little louder still…

Alfie turned and peered through the window of the door between the driver's cab and the passenger compartment. The carriages curved away into the dark distance. Their gas lamps had been turned off; the only light came from the driver's cab, and it was barely enough to illuminate the lead carriage.

Clack.

Alfie stood up and leaned towards the door, pressing his face against the window. His hand trembled as he undid the latch and pulled the door open. 'Vic?' he called, his voice sounding flat and dull in the confined space of the carriage. 'Vic… is that you, mate?'

No answer came from the darkness.

It must *be Vic*, he thought. *Who else could it be… who else?*

Clack.

'Vic! Answer me, you old bastard!'

Why don't you answer, Vic?

Clack.

Alfie's mouth had gone dry, and his tongue felt like sandpaper as he licked his lips. His breathing sounded loud in his ears. The last sound had come from close by, between the second and third carriages, he reckoned. There was no doubt that whoever was on the train was making his way towards the front.

Alfie quickly closed the door again and glanced back through the front window at the signal. It was still on red. He thought of the stories he had recently heard, both at work and in his local pub afterwards ... stories of things being seen in the tunnels: strange things, horrible things. He'd laughed at them and paid them no mind, but now...

Clack.

That was from the doors connecting the first and second carriages.

'Go away!' The words sprang suddenly to Alfie's lips, almost as if they had been said by someone else. 'You shouldn't be here, whoever you are. I'll have the police on you as soon as I...'

Alfie stopped, for he could see no one in the half-light of the carriage. And yet... the door leading to the second carriage *had* opened and closed. It *had*...

He glanced back once again at the signal light and then at the throttle. It would be more than his job was worth to pass the light at red – but at least he'd be out of the tunnel. Suddenly, Alfie didn't care about his job. He'd get another one and never come into the bloody Tube Railway again.

I'll take it slow, he thought. *I'll stop just before Charing Cross, and then I'll jump out and go the rest of the way on foot. That's what I'll do.*

He was about to sit back down in the driver's seat and open the throttle when a sound from the carriage made him stop, a sound so strange that at first he was unsure that it *was* a sound. It was a grunt, a low moan, a sigh, a flapping of wings and a stirring of sheets, a movement in the air that was not quite movement and yet not quite stillness. Alfie stood there, frozen in place, not daring to move as he stared through the front window at the red signal light which shone dully like an ancient star in the blackness of space. He held his breath until it burned in his lungs and then slowly let it out.

Oh God... oh God.

The sound came to his ears again; it was directly behind him, on the other side of the door leading to the passenger compartment.

Slowly, Alfie turned around. He didn't want to, and yet he couldn't help himself. He had to see what was making that sound. He leaned forward towards the window and peered once again into the compartment.

And then Alfie Morgan began to scream.

Outside, the signal light turned from red to green, but the train remained where it was, in the Kennington Loop.

CHAPTER TWO:
Blackwood Receives a Visitor

From his vantage point above the valley, he can see the house and its annex. The house seems as ancient as the livid sky beneath which it broods, its stone mottled and crumbling with the weight of centuries and the frequent onslaughts of wind and rain. The storm clouds rush overhead with unnatural speed, blasting across the firmament like breath expelled from the mouth of a consumptive god. In the distance, beyond the western end of the valley, the grey North Sea groans and thrashes itself furiously, its writhing surface bruised by thick white foam.

The annex is as new as the house is ancient. Built less than six months ago, it is composed of nine large, corrugated-steel huts. Each hut is semicircular in cross-section, like a miniature zeppelin hangar, and even from this distance, he can glimpse activity inside through the glowing windows. According to the mission briefing he received in London, whatever is happening at the research laboratory has brought insanity and probably death to the scientists at work out here on the windswept west coast of Scotland. Her Majesty's Bureau of Clandestine Affairs believes that the tragedy must be linked to the research being conducted into the mysterious Vril energy that powers the interplanetary cylinders of the newly discovered civilisation on Mars.

Her Majesty's Government wants the secret of Vril; the British Empire requires it, for the ultimate consolidation of its military and economic power.

The last communication from the research facility – the last communication that made any sense, that is – claimed that the team were on the verge of a momentous breakthrough. A means had been discovered, through the combined application of occult and electromagnetic principles, to open a fissure between the physical world and the ætherial realm containing the Vril energy.

The last sane telegraph message had stated that the team were about to activate their equipment and open the portal between worlds, between universes. The machines were fully charged, the containment receptacle primed and ready to receive the first transmission of Vril energy. In London, the Government waited, with orders to inform the Queen the moment further news came through from Scotland...

But when it did come through, it was not what they were expecting. The next telegraph message was horrible to read, so obviously the product of a mind that had been completely undone. Clearly, some appalling event had occurred in the laboratory, something frightful and incomprehensible. So concerned was the Government that the Prime Minister had contacted Her Majesty's Bureau of Clandestine Affairs and ordered them to send an agent to assess the situation.

And so here he is, Thomas Blackwood, Special Investigator, descending quickly and stealthily into the valley, towards the ancient house and the brand new research annex. Later, he will appreciate the irony of his stealth, for the people inside the laboratory care little for what is occurring outside or who is approaching.

With the wind screaming around him and the icy rain stinging his face, Blackwood creeps towards one of the windows in the nearest hut and looks through. What he sees makes him want to cry out. His stomach churns, threatening to void itself of his last meal, and he averts his gaze quickly.

The memory of the scene burns in his mind like a white-hot brand. Blood... dismemberment... the scattered fragments of what had once been men, cleaved and divided in strange ways... and there, amongst the human wreckage... there...

*

In the darkness of his bedroom, Thomas Blackwood's eyes flashed open. He gasped and sat up suddenly, as if to do so might banish the memory of the nightmare, but the horrible images drifting through his newly-wakened mind would not be denied so easily. He gasped again, and a low moan escaped his grimacing mouth.

Alone in the darkness, amid the rumpled chaos of his bed sheets, he buried his head in his hands. 'Oh God,' he whispered. 'Oh good God!'

Slowly, he got out of bed and walked to the bathroom, where he looked at his face in the mirror, at features which were normally finely chiselled and pleasing to the eye, but which were now twisted by anguish and stark with the memory of what he had seen in that remote Scottish research facility five years ago.

What the scientists had done to each other in their violent insanity was bad enough, but what had *caused* that insanity had still been there, glowing and pulsating in the laboratory. There had been more than a dozen of them, placed at various points throughout the room... no, not placed, *laid*, by the thing that had seeped through the fissure in time and space connecting the sane universe with the realm containing the Vril energy: the extradimensional abnormality known as a Sha'halloth.

The thing had sensed the fissure at the very instant it opened, had deposited its eggs and then withdrawn back to its own realm. The eggs were shapeless globs of glistening jelly, glowing with colours never seen in this or any other world of the ordered cosmos. They were covered with writhing tendrils which seemed to fade in and out of visibility, and as Blackwood had entered the laboratory and stood gazing at them in horror and revulsion, he had felt something probing his mind: a mental molestation more devastating than anything that could have befallen his physical body.

Before the glowing tendrils had a chance to take root fully in his mind and drive away his sanity, Blackwood had unslung the carbine from his shoulder and sprayed them with bullets. So revolting was the way in which they burst, and so awful were their contents, that Blackwood collapsed to the floor and vomited before turning the gun on the three remaining scientists who had entered the laboratory and thrown themselves at him, screaming, their minds no longer remotely human.

Five years is a long time, but Thomas Blackwood remembered the events of that day as if they had happened only five minutes prior.

When the Prime Minister read his report, he had ordered an immediate and indefinite moratorium on Vril energy research. The secret of the Martian cylinders' propulsion would have to remain with them for the foreseeable future, and Blackwood was far from sorry.

He regarded himself in the bathroom mirror, then undid the buttons of his pyjamas and sighed as he looked at his chest and the large silver circle which was embedded in the skin. Its irregular pentacle with the wide, staring eye at the centre had originally been carved into an amulet given to him by the Comte de Saint Germain, who headed Station X, the Bureau's occult research and development branch at

Bletchley Park. The amulet had been a detector and a ward against various forms of Magick, but thanks to Blackwood's recent entry into the Realm of Faerie during the affair of the Martian Ambassador, the amulet had become fused with his skin, and he no longer had the option of taking it off: it was now a part of him, and would remain so for the rest of his life, like a tattoo etched in silver upon his chest.

Blackwood washed and dressed, went through to his study, filled his favourite Peterson pipe with cherry tobacco, struck a match and watched in contentment as the bowl began to glow a luxuriant shade of orange. Drawing in the fragrant smoke, he went to the mantelpiece and leafed through the morning's mail which his housekeeper, Mrs Butters, had placed there for him.

Only one item sparked his interest: an envelope which bore a Masonic seal. He tore it open and took out a card embossed with the same design and bearing the following message:

The Society of Spiritualistic Freemasons is delighted to
offer an invitation to
MR THOMAS BLACKWOOD,
to attend a lecture to be given at half-past eight on the
Seventeenth of November, 1899 by
DR SIMON CASTAIGNE
at the Society's Hall in Mayfair.
The subject of the lecture is
'The Plurality of Life on Other Worlds'.
RSVP

'Hmm,' Blackwood murmured, puffing on his pipe. The Society of Spiritualistic Freemasons was an offshoot of his own Lodge, and he was a little surprised to receive such an invitation. He guessed that it was because of his work with the Bureau, which was known to a select few high-ranking members. He briefly considered accepting the invitation, but then reflected that in recent weeks he had had his fill of 'the plurality of life on other worlds'.

Dropping the invitation onto his desk, he sauntered over to one of the tall bookcases lining his study and selected one of his favourite volumes, a treatise on the mythology of the Dogon Tribe of West Africa. He then sat himself down in the large, comfortable armchair that stood in one corner of the room, and poured a brimming, steaming cup from the pot of Jamaican Blue Mountain coffee which Mrs Butters had prepared for him. The rich aroma of the coffee filled the room and, combined with the scent of the tobacco, produced an atmosphere which seemed to Blackwood, who was still out of sorts from the nightmare, to be eminently conducive to the passing of a pleasant morning of intellectual recreation.

Outside, the streets of Chelsea thronged with people going about their business in the cold dampness of the morning air, and Blackwood, for his part, was quite happy to let them get on with it. He had earned a rest, had paid for the last week of relaxation with a shattered left forearm, several broken ribs and a concussion. The recently-concluded affair of the Martian Ambassador had left him in a rum state, and it was only thanks to the administration of Martian medicine that he was not still confined to a hospital bed.

The Martians had taken charge of his medical treatment as an expression of thanks for his work in averting war between the Red Planet and Earth – not that he had acted alone, of course: he had been ably assisted by Lady Sophia Harrington, Secretary of the Society for Psychical Research, whose own research into the mystery of Spring-Heeled Jack had first brought them together.

The doctors who had been overseeing his convalescence were astonished at the rapidity of his recovery following the application of the Martian medical treatments, as was Blackwood himself. Within a matter of days, his broken bones had almost completely healed, and he was well on the way to feeling his old self once again.

He knew that very soon he would be required to return to work and recalled with a smile the look on Grandfather's face when he had paid Blackwood a visit just prior to the latter's departure from hospital. He suspected that the Bureau's Director was more satisfied at the thought that he would soon have one of his best agents back in the field than at any emotion which might have been inspired by altruism or fellow-feeling. Grandfather, after all, had lost both his legs during the Second Afghan War, and now had to make do with a pair of steam-powered artificial ones; a few broken bones and a bang on the head were of little consequence to him.

Sophia was another matter: she had hardly left his bedside, once he had returned to consciousness following his final battle with Spring-Heeled Jack, who had been revealed to be a Venusian *agent provocateur* named Indrid Cold, and more than once she had succumbed to tears as she surveyed his injuries. She really was a most remarkable young woman – brave, resourceful and decent – and Blackwood, who normally preferred to work alone and to pursue a solitary life in his infrequent leisure time, found himself missing her company.

No matter, for he was quite certain that they would be seeing each other again soon, and as he heard a faint knock on the apartment building's front door below, he placed a little wager with himself that the reason for their imminent reunion had just arrived.

A few moments later, there came another knock, this time on his study door.

'Enter,' he said, having resigned himself to the likelihood that a pleasant day's reading was about to be curtailed.

Mrs Butters opened the door a little way and poked her matronly head into the room. 'Mr Blackwood, sir, you have a visitor.'

'Let me guess,' said Blackwood in a loud theatrical voice as he stood and placed the unopened book on his desk. 'My visitor is none other than Detective Gerhard de Chardin of New Scotland Temple.'

A loud, throaty chuckle from the corridor outside told him he was correct. Mrs Butters showed the detective in and nodded at Blackwood's request that she bring another coffee cup, before bustling away towards the kitchen.

'Sounds like you've been reading too much Conan Doyle,' said de Chardin as he stepped into the room and offered his hand, which the Special Investigator shook warmly. 'How are you, old chap?'

The detective was an inch or so taller than Blackwood's six feet, although both men were equally trim and well-proportioned. While Blackwood was clean-shaven, de Chardin sported a neatly trimmed goatee, which he was in the habit of stroking contemplatively.

'Never better, thank you.' Blackwood indicated the armchair which he had just vacated. 'Have a seat, sir.'

De Chardin nodded his thanks, while Blackwood pulled out his desk chair and sat down opposite his guest.

'How did you know it was me?' asked the detective. 'I doubt it was anything as simple as looking out of the window.'

'Not at all,' Blackwood replied with a smile. 'I've been expecting you.'

'Ah, then Lady Sophia has told you about the case upon which I'm presently engaged.'

Blackwood nodded, and the two men regarded each other in silence for a few moments, both vaguely aware of a subtle alteration in the atmosphere – brought on, perhaps, by mention of the young lady's name.

The spell was broken by Mrs Butters's return with the coffee cup, which she placed on the tray next to the pot.

'Thank you, Mrs Butters,' said Blackwood. 'I'll pour.'

'As you wish, sir.' The housekeeper left once again, bound for more pressing domestic duties.

Blackwood poured coffee and handed the cup to de Chardin. 'Well now, Detective,' he said, 'why don't you tell me about this case of yours? Strange disturbances on the Underground, isn't it? Something of a supernatural nature, I believe.'

'Indeed. And I don't mind telling you that I've never heard the likes of it before.'

'Really? In any event, I'd have thought that this type of thing was a little outside your purview; surely it's something that the SPR should be investigating, rather than the Metropolitan Templar Police.'

'Ordinarily, you would be quite correct – and in fact, the Society for Psychical Research *has* begun its own investigation. But the fact is that we're not dealing with some restless spook rattling his chains. This is far more serious than that.'

Blackwood leaned forward, intrigued. 'Please explain.'

'During the past few weeks, there have been a number of reports of strange events and encounters in the Underground system, mainly by maintenance workers, plate-layers and the like. These reports range from vague feelings of unease to outright sightings and encounters with things which can only be described as supernatural in origin.'

Blackwood nodded. 'I'm bound to say I'm not all that surprised.'

De Chardin frowned at him. 'How so?'

'We must remember that London is an ancient city, with a history that is often violent and tragic, and the men who have been engaged for the last forty years on the construction of the subterranean railroad have by no means been reluctant to disturb the ground in which they're building their tunnels and stations. Indeed, they have no choice.'

'You're speaking of the deep-level Tube lines,' said de Chardin.

'Precisely. Delving into the earth is like opening a book of history, and it is not always wise to do so, for there are things down there which should remain undisturbed.'

'What kind of things?'

Blackwood shrugged. 'It is a fact well known by some, for instance, that at least one plague pit has been discovered during the construction of the network. Between 1665 and 1666, the Great Plague ravaged London, killing a hundred thousand people – a fifth of the city's population. The cemeteries quickly became overwhelmed with the numbers of dead, and so enormous pits were dug to accommodate the unfortunate victims – so many, in fact, that to this day no one knows their precise number or their exact locations.'

'There was certainly one on the site of Aldgate Station,' said de Chardin.

'Indeed. That particular pit is mentioned by Daniel Defoe in his *Journal of a Plague Year*; he notes that a thousand bodies were buried there during a mere two weeks. It is an unwritten law of the universe that the dead should be left in peace; no good can ever come of disturbing them – especially a thousand at a time! But tell me, Detective, why do you mention Aldgate in particular? Has something happened there?'

'A couple of incidents, actually,' de Chardin nodded. 'Several line workers have witnessed disturbances in the ballast around the metals… as if someone were walking there, but of course no one was.'

'Of course not.'

'And a few days ago, a maintenance crew saw the apparition of an old woman walking along the northbound tunnel. They said they had the impression that she was looking for something…'

'Or someone,' Blackwood mused. 'Perhaps a loved one who had fallen victim to the Plague. Powerful emotions possess their own life, and live on long after the ones who experienced them have departed.'

De Chardin shifted uncomfortably in his seat. 'That's not the worst of it, though. Just last night, a train driver encountered something near Kennington Station which seems to have completely unhinged his mind.'

Blackwood hesitated, then stood up and moved to the drinks cabinet next to his desk. Opening the cabinet and taking out a decanter of brandy and a couple of balloon glasses, he said, 'Before you continue, I think we could both make good use of something a little stronger than coffee – in spite of the early hour.'

De Chardin gave a grim chuckle and replied, 'I won't decline *that* offer.'

Blackwood handed him a glass, took a fortifying sip and said, 'Do go on… about Kennington.'

'Have you heard of the Kennington Loop?'

'It's the means by which trains turn around at the terminus of the Central and South London, isn't it?'

'Quite correct. A driver named Alfie Morgan took his train into the Loop at around ten o'clock last night. There was a delay while the Charing Cross platform was cleared of another train, during which Morgan was obliged to remain within the Loop. When the signal changed and Morgan failed to emerge, a track-walker was despatched to investigate. He came upon the stationary train three quarters of the way around the Loop and climbed into the driver's cab, where he found Morgan… laughing, gibbering and, apparently, quite insane.'

'Good Lord,' Blackwood muttered. 'Where is this Morgan fellow now?'

'He was taken to Bethlem Hospital, where his condition is at present being closely observed.'

'I see. And what is the name of the man who found him – the track-walker?'

'His name is Oliver Clarke.'

'And did he see anything unusual – more unusual, that is, than an insane train driver?'

De Chardin shook his head. 'Unfortunately not – or perhaps fortunately, for Clarke at least.'

'I daresay,' Blackwood smiled. 'A most intriguing case, but I must say that I fail to see what it has to do with Her Majesty's Bureau of Clandestine Affairs.'

De Chardin returned his smile as he replied, 'As we have already noted, ordinarily it would be left to the SPR to investigate, but there are several factors here that place it very squarely in your lap. For one thing, the Underground is, as you know, being refitted with a new atmospheric railway – a monumental project which hasn't come cheap. The directors and shareholders of the various railroad companies are getting very jittery indeed over this affair, and the drivers and maintenance crews are even more jittery, since they're the ones who have to work in the tunnels, and many are talking openly about refusing to carry on with their work until something is done about it.'

'An attitude which will only become more entrenched once word of Mr Morgan's condition gets around.'

'Oh, you may rest assured that it has *already* got around. In fact, they're talking about little else down there!'

Blackwood pondered this for a few moments. 'I suppose you're right: this situation *could* have serious implications for the Underground...'

'That's putting it mildly,' de Chardin muttered. 'It could threaten the very future of the network, and Her Majesty is not best pleased at the notion. The London Underground was the world's first subterranean urban railway: we were first with the idea, and the first to put it into practice – and the Queen is of the opinion that it cannot be allowed to fail, for any reason.'

Blackwood drained his glass. 'There's certainly been an awful lot of money poured in over the years.' He smiled. '"Trains in drains", they called it in the early days; now it is seen, quite rightly, as one of the greatest achievements of the Empire.'

'Quite so,' agreed de Chardin. 'We have an awful lot to lose if this situation is allowed to continue unchecked. The investment made thus far in the new atmospheric railway is nothing short of staggering, but it will all count for nothing if we have no one to drive the trains or maintain the system. And there is another question to consider,' he added.

Blackwood arched an eyebrow. 'Which is?'

'Why now?' said de Chardin. 'Engineers and architects have been disturbing the ground beneath London for very nearly forty years, yet only in the last few weeks have serious incidents of this nature been reported. What has happened recently to give rise to them?'

Blackwood chuckled. 'I think, Detective, that we now come to the real reason for my involvement.'

'You guess correctly, sir; for Her Majesty wonders whether there is some greater and more sinister agency at work here. Perhaps it is supernatural… or perhaps it is all too human. In any event, she wishes the Bureau to join forces once again with the Society for Psychical Research and the Metropolitan Templar Police to investigate the matter.'

'Human or supernatural,' Blackwood mused. 'An intriguing question. And with the combined talents of the Bureau, the SPR and New Scotland Temple, I'm quite sure it is one to which we shall ultimately find the answer!'

30

CHAPTER THREE:
At Bethlem Hospital

The building was vast, grey and foreboding beneath the overcast sky. Above the tall, copper-covered dome which dominated the facade, a bank of livid, smoke-like clouds hung in the damp air of mid-afternoon, as though a great fire were burning somewhere in the heavens.

To Lady Sophia Harrington, the image which had suddenly struck her was an appropriate one, for were not the fires of insanity burning in the minds of so many poor men and women in that place? She glanced at Thomas Blackwood, who was sitting beside her in the hansom as it clattered along the great, sweeping drive towards the hospital's main entrance. His finely-drawn features were immobile; his eyes, the colour of the angry clouds above, were fixed straight ahead, and Sophia had the impression that he was just as reluctant as she to enter that place of misery and madness.

Blackwood had called for her at her Kensington apartments, and together they had gone to the Bureau's headquarters in Whitehall, where Grandfather had briefed them on their assignment. Sophia had been surprised at Grandfather's manner: during the affair of the Martian Ambassador, he had been his usual self – gruff and business-like, with a hint of exasperated impatience – but during their meeting he had displayed none of those characteristics.

Instead, there was a look of bafflement and even fear in his eyes, which she had never seen before, and which had unsettled her even more than the situation that had occasioned their presence.

Whatever was happening on the Underground clearly had Grandfather completely flummoxed, and it was equally obvious that he didn't care for the experience. Sophia supposed that this was natural: Grandfather was still a military man through and through and was used to dealing with situations which could be evaluated and responded to with cold, hard rationality and well-planned logistics. However, Sophia knew from personal experience that supernatural events rarely followed such rules: they obeyed laws of which humanity knew little or nothing, and when they impinged upon the human world, they did so on their own terms. That was what made them so dangerous.

The cab drew up alongside the massive portico with its six Doric columns, and without a word, Blackwood descended and turned to offer Sophia his hand. She took it and stepped down into the clammy air, shivering slightly as she did so.

This elicited a brief smile from the Special Investigator, who said, 'Appropriate weather, don't you think?'

Sophia didn't answer; instead, she looked left and right at the long, four-storied wings which extended in each direction out from the central block. Massive, monolithic and silent, they contained the patient galleries – the male patients on the right and the female on the left. The central block, before which she and Blackwood now stood, contained the administrative offices and the chapel. She shivered again, although this time it was not from the cold, dank air.

'Are you all right, Sophia?' asked Blackwood with a frown of concern.

She gave him a brief smile. 'Yes, Thomas.'

They climbed the wide steps leading up to the main entrance, which led in to a large foyer, panelled in grim, dark oak. The clerk at the reception desk, a man of middle years, dressed in a neat black suit, looked up and said, 'Good afternoon, sir, madam. How may I assist you?'

'Good afternoon,' Blackwood replied, showing the man his identification. 'My name is Thomas Blackwood, and this is Lady Sophia Harrington. We are here to see Dr Graham Davenport concerning a recently admitted patient.'

'Ah, yes. The doctor informed me that you would be coming. Would you please sign the visitors' register?' He indicated a large book that lay open on the desk.

While Blackwood and Sophia did so, the clerk hailed a passing orderly. 'Conrad, will you please escort this lady and gentleman to Dr Davenport's office?'

The orderly, a tall, burly man dressed in a white coat and trousers, nodded and came over. 'This way, if you please.'

Blackwood and Sophia followed him along a short corridor to the doctors' rooms, where he left them at the door to Dr Davenport's office.

Blackwood knocked, and a voice drifted out to them. 'Come!'

They entered a chamber which was every bit as dull and dreary as the foyer, although it was neat and clean and was dominated by a large rolltop desk, before which sat a young, prematurely balding man with a thin beard and an inquisitive expression. The man turned his penetrating blue eyes upon them and said, 'Can I help you?'

Blackwood introduced himself and Sophia.

'Oh, of course! Do forgive me,' said Dr Davenport, rising from the desk and offering them his hand. 'I'd quite forgotten our appointment. You're here to discuss Mr Morgan's case, aren't you?'

'Correct, sir,' said Blackwood with a smile. He took in the man's slightly flustered demeanour. 'It looks as if you have a great many matters to attend to, if you'll pardon me for saying so. I promise we shan't keep you long.'

'Not at all, Mr Blackwood – although you are quite correct, and I'm bound to say it's always the case.' Davenport gave a brief laugh of embarrassment as he brought the only other chair besides his own from a corner of the office and placed it before Sophia. 'Please, madam, do take a seat. I, er, I'll see if I can rustle up another chair from somewhere.'

Blackwood held up a hand. 'Please don't trouble yourself, Doctor. I am more than happy to stand.'

'Oh, well, if you're quite sure…'

'Quite sure, thank you.'

Davenport took his own seat. 'May I offer you some refreshment?'

His visitors shook their heads.

'Well then. Mr Morgan.'

'Mr Morgan.'

'Yes, he was brought to us in the small hours of this morning and admitted straight away. I conducted the preliminary examination.'

'What were your observations?' asked Blackwood.

'His symptoms are quite striking, especially in view of the fact that he has apparently never suffered a mental episode of any kind before. Yes… very striking indeed. A complete breakdown of all the higher brain functions. I must admit I've never seen anything quite like it.'

'What do you think caused it, Doctor?' asked Sophia.

Davenport hesitated before replying, 'I'm tempted to speculate, your Ladyship, that it was caused by shock.'

'Shock?'

'Indeed. An experience so extreme, so utterly terrifying, that it has caused his conscious mind to retreat within itself: a defensive measure, if you will.'

'Then you believe that his mind is still intact,' said Blackwood.

Dr Davenport sighed. 'It's difficult to tell at this stage, without further examination and evaluation.' He glanced from Blackwood to Sophia. 'But may I ask what interest the Crown has in this case?'

'Mr Morgan's experience, while apparently the most severe, is not the first to occur on the London Underground in recent weeks,' Blackwood replied. 'In view of the circumstances, a Crown investigation is warranted.'

Davenport raised his eyebrows. 'I see. I've read about the disturbances in the papers, of course – who hasn't? – but I hadn't realised the situation was as serious as that.'

Blackwood gave him a brief, grim smile. 'I assure you, it is.'

'May we see the patient?' asked Sophia.

Davenport shrugged apologetically. 'I'm really not sure what good it would do, your Ladyship. Mr Morgan is quite uncommunicative.'

'I understand, Doctor,' she replied. 'Nevertheless, Mr Blackwood and I would be remiss in our duties were we to leave without at least attempting to speak with him.'

Davenport considered this for a moment, and then nodded. 'Of course. You have my assurance that I will cooperate fully with your investigation.'

Sophia smiled at him. 'We appreciate it, sir.'

Davenport rose from his desk. 'Well then, if you'd like to follow me...'

*

'If you'll pardon the observation,' said Sophia as they walked along the wide gallery which ran along the entire length of the male wing, 'I'm surprised at how comfortable your institution appears to be.'

The gallery was indeed most elegantly furnished with leather sofas and chairs, cheerful paintings, numerous pots of brightly-coloured flowers and birds in large, ornate cages. The carpet was richly patterned and of good quality, and the air was comfortably warm. One side of the gallery was lined with doors leading directly to the patients' rooms, while the other contained windows which looked out upon one of the two large airing grounds, where the more manageable patients were taken for fresh air and a little exercise.

'Thank you, Lady Sophia,' Dr Davenport replied. 'We are very proud of Bethlem Hospital, and the treatment it provides to the unfortunate people who find themselves our guests. I'll grant that it wasn't always like this, but progress in the treatment of mental infirmity is swift and ongoing. About ten years ago, for instance, the heating system was updated, and now all of the bedrooms are served by hot water pipes, which keep them pleasantly warm.'

'Most civilised, Doctor,' said Blackwood approvingly.

'Indeed. Although you can't see it from here, we also have an extensive garden. We find that it is most important to occupy our patients' time with wholesome and interesting activities, thus preventing them from brooding on their condition. Many male patients lend a hand with the upkeep of the garden, while the female patients help with the laundry and in the kitchen. We find it helps to maintain their connection with the outside world and to prepare them for their return.'

'Their return,' Blackwood echoed. 'May I ask what your success rate is in the treatment of mental disorders?'

'It's approximately thirty percent – not particularly high, I grant you, but as I mentioned, progress is ongoing. Ah! Here we are.'

Davenport stopped at a door which, like the others, contained a large spy hole. He slid aside the brass plate, looked into the room, murmured in evident satisfaction and inserted a key in the lock. He glanced at the two orderlies who were accompanying them and told them to wait outside the room. The men nodded.

The door swung open soundlessly, and Davenport beckoned to his guests to follow him inside.

The room was sparsely furnished but was clean, bright and comfortable. Upon the bed lay Alfie Morgan. He was awake and staring straight up at the ceiling, his eyes blinking perhaps twice a minute. Blackwood noted that his breathing was shallow but regular. In fact, there was no outward sign that anything untoward had happened to the man, apart from the fact that his shoes and belt were nowhere to be seen.

Dr Davenport stepped forward. 'Mr Morgan,' he said. 'Alfie, you have visitors; this lady and gentleman have come to see you. Won't you say hello?'

There was no response: Morgan simply lay there, staring up at the ceiling, his face completely blank and impassive.

Sophia took a couple of paces towards the bed. Blackwood followed her, ready to pull her away should the man perform any violent or threatening movement. 'Mr Morgan... my name is Sophia Harrington. I'm very pleased to meet you. May we speak with you for a few moments?'

The shallow breathing halted for a second or two and then resumed.

'Interesting,' whispered Davenport. 'A reaction – minute, but a reaction nevertheless. Keep trying, your Ladyship.'

Sophia nodded and took another step towards the bed. 'We are here to help you... but before we can do so, we need you to help us. We need you to talk to us about what happened... about what happened last night in the Kennington Loop.'

Morgan began to blink more rapidly. Davenport clutched Blackwood's arm and whispered to him, 'I don't know how, but it's working. Perhaps the sound of her

Ladyship's voice…' He glanced over his shoulder at the spy hole in the door, and saw the eyes of one of the orderlies looking intently in at them.

'Alfie,' said Sophia, 'what happened to you last night?'

Morgan's mouth began to move strangely, as if he were trying to say something, but had forgotten how to speak.

'What is it, Alfie? What do you wish to say?'

'Train,' he said in a thin, ragged whisper.

'Yes,' said Sophia in an encouraging tone. 'You were driving your train… through the Loop. You had to stop…'

'The signal,' Morgan said, his breath quickening.

'That's right. The signal was on red; you had to stop.'

'Stop… in the dark… in the silence.'

'Excellent,' said Davenport quietly into Blackwood's ear.

'Red… in the darkness… why won't it change? I want it to change. The sounds…'

'Sounds?' Sophia leaned closer, and Blackwood felt his muscles tense.

'Noises in the dark.'

'What noises?'

'Doors opening… closing… coming closer.'

'Someone was on the train?'

Morgan shut his eyes and emitted a thin, high-pitched moan. The sound made Sophia's blood run cold.

'Alfie,' she said. 'Who was on the train?'

'Who was on the train?' he echoed. 'Who was on the train?'

Sophia leaned closer still. 'Please try to tell us.'

'Sophia,' said Blackwood, stepping forward.

Suddenly, Morgan opened his eyes and looked at her, and his face became contorted in such an expression of feral horror that she gasped and took an involuntary step back. In an instant, Blackwood was at her side, his hands on her shoulders.

'Wait!' she said in an urgent whisper.

'Nothing from the world,' Morgan cried. '*Nothing from the world!* Oh no, not from here. Everything wrong… everything about it… *all wrong!* Carcosa… Carcosa.'

'What?' said Blackwood. 'What did you say?'

Sophia glanced at him. 'Thomas…?'

'I think that's enough for now,' said Davenport. Without looking back, he beckoned with his hand. Immediately, the door opened, and the two orderlies came in.

'Another few minutes, Doctor,' said Blackwood. 'Please.'

'I'm sorry, Mr Blackwood, but I must think of my patient. He is becoming far too agitated. He needs to rest.' He indicated the open door. 'If you please.'

Blackwood sighed. 'Very well.'

'If you would kindly wait for me outside, I shall be with you presently.'

Blackwood and Sophia left the room. Before one of the orderlies closed the door, they heard Alfie Morgan crying out again and again, 'Don't go down there! *Don't go down there! Carcosa! CARCOSA!*'

*

Ten minutes later, they were once again in Dr Davenport's office. His secretary brought in some tea, which they all sipped in nervous contemplation.

'Most remarkable,' said Davenport.

'That poor man,' said Sophia. 'His mind has been quite undone by his experience.'

'And yet, we did glean something of use,' observed Blackwood. 'Whatever he saw in the Loop, it was not some run-of-the-mill phantom.'

'I should say not,' Davenport agreed. 'Although as to what he *did* see, I wouldn't like to speculate.'

'Something not of this world,' Sophia murmured. 'Which could mean… something not *native* to this world, something that does not belong here and has never belonged here. And what was that strange word he uttered? Carcosa… what does that mean?' She looked at Blackwood, but he did not offer any answer.

'I have no idea,' said Davenport. 'Gibberish, I shouldn't wonder: a random product of the turmoil in his mind. As to what he saw… well, *perhaps* an apparition of some kind, but as to its nature and origin, I'm afraid that's outside my area of expertise.'

'But not ours,' said Blackwood.

Davenport glanced at him. 'You have experience of such things?'

'Most assuredly,' the Special Investigator replied, setting his cup and saucer upon the desk. 'Dr Davenport, I would like to thank you for your time. Now we must take our leave, for we have much to do.'

Davenport stood up and shook hands with his visitors. 'You're welcome. And if there are any further developments with Mr Morgan, I will be sure to let you know.'

*

As their carriage drew away from the hospital, Sophia gave a small sigh of relief. 'I'm glad to be out of there,' she said.

'As am I,' Blackwood agreed.

'I wonder if poor Mr Morgan will ever recover.'

'Whatever the prognosis, there can be little doubt that he is in good hands.'

Sophia nodded, and then turned to her companion. 'That word he said… Carcosa… in his room, you looked as though you recognised it. Did you?'

Blackwood hesitated. 'I'm not entirely sure: it had the ring of familiarity to me… I'm sure I've heard it – or read it – somewhere before. But I can't for the life of me remember where.'

'I've certainly never heard of it. I wonder what language it is. Is it a place? A person's name? Was it, perhaps, the name of the thing he saw?'

Blackwood remained silent as the hansom made its way through Southwark. Away in the distance, a pair of Martian omnibuses could be seen striding above the rooftops, heading north, their spindly tripod legs stepping delicately upon the shallow trenches of the purpose-built omnibus lanes which threaded the city. The sight brought back unpleasant recent memories, and he looked away, returning his attention to Sophia.

'Do you think it would be worth trying some psychometry on that train?' he asked.

'An intriguing thought,' Sophia nodded. 'I'll go to the SPR headquarters and enlist the aid of our best psychometrist.'

'Excellent.'

'And what about you, Thomas? What are you going to do next?'

Blackwood gave her a brief, troubled smile. 'For a start, I'm going to try and see if I can remember where I have encountered the word *Carcosa*. I've a strong suspicion that it will shed some much-needed light on this case.'

CHAPTER FOUR:
The Screaming Spectre

Seamus Brennan crouched down beside the steel pressure tube and placed the curved plate over the inspection opening. Holding the plate with one hand, he inserted the six locking bolts around the edges and tightened them with a large spanner.

His friend and co-worker, Barrymore Tench, walked across the railway line and stood beside him. 'All right, Seamus?'

'Sure, I'm done now,' Brennan replied.

'About time,' said Harry Fraser, the site foreman, who was standing on the platform looking down at them, fists balled on his hips like he owned the place.

'Ah, stick it up yer arse,' Brennan muttered.

'What was that?' Fraser snapped.

Brennan smiled up at him. 'Nothing, sir! I'm just sayin', job done.'

Fraser nodded. 'Good. Now clear the line both of you, and we'll start the test.'

The two maintenance workers climbed onto the platform and looked down at the tracks. Now that they had stopped working, they began to feel the deep chill of the night air. Farringdon Street Station had originally been the terminus for the Metropolitan Railway, the first of Central

London's urban lines; as such, it was above ground and open to the elements. It now had the additional honour of being the first section of the Underground to be fitted with the new atmospheric railway. The pressure tube, twelve inches in diameter, ran between the rails from Farringdon Street to Baker Street and was fed with compressed air from the great pumping station at Bethnal Green.

Further along the platform, the test train stood waiting. It was comprised of a single carriage fitted with an atmospheric drive cylinder, which was bolted securely to the underside. The cylinder was enclosed within the pressure tube, the pylon which connected it to the train passing through the single slit in the top of the tube. A strip of Martian rubber sealed the opening, preventing the escape of the compressed air and only parting to allow the passage of the pylon while the train was in motion.

After making certain that the line was completely clear of workers, Fraser nodded to a man who was standing in the doorway of the ticket office. The man went inside and sent a brief telegraph message to Bethnal Green. At the pumping station two miles to the east, the powerful Vansittart-Siddeley Ultra-compressors were switched on and began to pump air at fantastically high pressure into the system.

Less than a minute later, there was a barely audible hiss, and the test train began to move forward, gradually gaining speed as it passed the observers on the platform. As he passed them, the driver, Bert Smallwood, gave them the thumbs up, a wide grin on his stubbly face.

'Nice one, Bert!' called Tench, giving him a wave.

'See you at Baker Street!' he called back.

Tench looked down at the pressure tube, which had instantly resealed itself behind the train. 'How do you think that stuff works?' he asked Brennan.

'Buggered if I know,' the Irishman replied. 'Them Martians, sure they know a lot o' things we don't.'

'You're right there, mate,' said Tench, glancing up at the black sky and the tiny pinpoint of ruddy light that was Mars.

'All right men,' said Fraser in his officious bark. 'Let's pack up here and get over to Baker Street.'

'Right you are, sir!' said Brennan and added under his breath, 'Arsehole.'

'Ex-corporal,' whispered Tench. 'What d'you expect?'

Brennan sniffed. 'Corporal? He acts more like a general. Look at him there, swaggerin' around. Bastard.'

Tench chuckled as he leaned over the edge of the platform and looked into the tunnel. The lights of the test train were growing steadily fainter as it headed towards Baker Street. 'Come on, mate,' he said. 'This bloody cold's gettin' into my bones.'

They were about to leave the platform when a sudden squeal echoed back along the tunnel. Both Tench and Brennan instantly knew what the sound was. It was the squeal of brakes: for some reason, Smallwood had brought his train to a halt.

Fraser turned away from the platform exit. 'What was that?'

'Brakes, Mr Fraser,' Tench replied.

'The test train?'

'Yes, sir.' *Bleedin' idiot*, Tench thought. *What other train would it be? It's the only one running on the whole bloody network.*

Fraser came back from the exit, and together the three men leaned over the edge of the platform and peered into the tunnel. In the distance, they could see the train's lights. They were not getting any smaller or dimmer: the train was indeed at a standstill.

'What the devil is he playing at?' demanded Fraser. 'Brennan, Tench, go and see what the matter is.'

Brennan looked at him askance. 'Us, sir?'

'Yes, you sir! There might be a blockage on the metals. Go and see – and if there is, get it cleared immediately.'

Tench sighed. 'Yes, Mr Fraser.' He jumped down from the platform and looked back up at Brennan. 'Come on, mate.'

Brennan hesitated, and Fraser turned to him. 'Well go on, man! What's the matter? Afraid of the dark?'

'No, sir,' muttered Brennan as he climbed down to join his friend on the tracks.

'Off you go, then, and be quick about it,' snapped Fraser. 'I'm going to telegraph Bethnal Green and see if there's a problem at their end.'

Brennan and Tench looked at each other, picked up their Tilley lamps from the edge of the platform and headed off into the tunnel.

*

'You ain't afraid of the dark, are you Seamus?' said Tench as they trudged along the tracks, holding their lamps out before them.

'Of course not!' Brennan snapped. 'And I'll knock down any man who says I am.' He paused before adding, 'It's what's *in* the dark that bothers me.'

'Oh, shut yer bleedin' mouth!' Tench chuckled. 'You don't believe any of that, do you?'

'Any of what?'

'You know... what they've been sayin' lately. About things... *happenin'*... down there.'

'And what things might they be?'

'You know what I'm talkin' about. Ghosts and things...'

Brennan said nothing for a moment. Their feet crunched loudly on the ballast as they walked through the pitch-darkness, the light from their lamps playing strangely upon the walls of the wide tunnel.

'Ghosts? That wasn't no ghost that Alfie Morgan saw.'

'How do *you* know what he saw?' demanded Tench. 'Maybe he didn't see anything... maybe the Loop just got to him.'

'*Got* to him!' Brennan gave a short, derisive laugh. 'Jesus, Mary and Joseph, no one likes the Loop, but bein' in there doesn't drive you *mad*! No, poor old Alfie saw somethin' – and it wasn't no ghost.'

'What was it, then?'

'How should I know?'

'Well, if you don't, then –'

Brennan cut him off suddenly. 'Shh!' He stopped and took hold of Tench's arm.

'What?'

'Listen...'

The two men stood still in the darkness, their lamps held out in front of them. They were now more than halfway to the train. Its lights burned like bright stars in the near distance.

'What is it?' asked Tench.

'I heard something.'

'It's your imagination.'

A sound drifted along the tunnel to them, faint but unmistakable. It was a voice; the voice of a child.

'Saints preserve us,' whispered Brennan.

Tench felt his skin crawl. 'It can't be...'

'Listen to it!'

The voice sounded again, a tremulous moan which echoed delicately through the tunnel. Tench peered into the darkness, swinging his lamp this way and that, searching for the source. 'Must be some poor little street urchin who's got into the network... probably looking for a place to spend the night.'

'Bert!' shouted Brennan. 'Are you all right there, fella?'

There was no reply.

'Come on,' said Tench.

They hurried along the tracks until they had reached the train. The driver's door was open, and they climbed into the cab to find Bert Smallwood sitting there, staring straight ahead into the darkness.

'Bert,' said Tench. 'Are you all right?'

Smallwood shook his head slowly.

'Come on, mate. Fraser's going to have our guts for garters if we don't get moving. What is it?'

'Can you hear her?' Smallwood asked in a thin, strained voice.

'Who?'

'The child.'

'We heard her,' said Brennan.

'I thought I'd hit her. She was on the line, right in front of me. That's why I stopped.'

Smallwood gasped and put his hand to his mouth as the thin, tremulous little voice echoed again through the tunnel.

'I don't like the way that sounds,' whispered Brennan.

'Shut yer gob, Seamus!' said Tench. 'If there's a child on the metals, we'll have to tell Fraser and do a tunnel search – and I don't like the way *that* sounds.'

'It isn't a child,' said Smallwood.

Brennan and Tench looked at him, and then at each other. 'What are you talkin' about, Bert?' asked Tench.

'It isn't a child,' Smallwood repeated. 'Not anymore.'

At that moment, the light from their Tilley lamps faded, as if they had suddenly run out of fuel, and then the train's lights went out, plunging them into impenetrable darkness. Smallwood moaned in terror.

'What the bleedin' hell's going on?' whispered Tench.

The darkness did not last, however, for presently the three men became aware of a faint blue glow which seeped into the driver's cab, evidently from somewhere up ahead.

'What's that?' said Tench. 'Another train? Can't be.'

'It isn't,' said Brennan, pointing through the cab's front windows.

There was a shape on the railway tracks, made hazy and indistinct by distance and the glow which surrounded it… or which perhaps emanated from it, and as the shape drew nearer, the men saw that its outline was that of a human being, small and frail.

It was a little girl.

The silence in the cab was broken only by the ragged breathing of the three men, who watched in disbelief as the glowing figure drew up to the front of the train and looked up at them through the windows.

'God,' whispered Brennan. 'Oh God…'

The girl was perhaps twelve or thirteen years old and was terribly thin. The long gown that she wore trailed behind her, and Brennan quickly realised that it was a burial shroud. Her pale blue face was drawn in anguish, or perhaps fear, or perhaps a mixture of the two, and her eyes were wide and filled with the darkness of the grave as she looked up at them.

The men were terrified, of course, but it was not fear which smote their rough hearts as much as sympathy, a searing compassion which flooded their entire beings at the sight of this poor, benighted, lonely little creature.

'Who is she?' whispered Tench.

His companions did not answer.

'Is she… alive?'

The waif looked up at him, and then at Brennan, and then at Smallwood, her face bathed in the blue glow.

And then she opened her mouth and let out such a piercing scream that the railway men clapped their hands to their ears and shut their eyes, thinking that their eardrums would burst. She screamed again and again, and such was the loudness and the anguish of it that they thought they would go mad. The screams echoed back and forth along the tunnel, filling the darkness...

Across the city in Chelsea, Thomas Blackwood's eyes flashed open, and he sat up in bed. His mind, drifting on the edge of sleep, had suddenly revealed the source of his vague memory of having read a strange word somewhere...

'Carcosa,' he said into the darkness of his bedroom. 'Oh, good God!'

CHAPTER FIVE:
The Fantasmata of Simon Castaigne

When Sophia called at Blackwood's rooms the following morning, she found Mrs Butters in a state of some agitation. 'Oh, do come in, your Ladyship!' exclaimed the housekeeper as she threw the door wide and beckoned Sophia inside.

'Whatever is the matter, Mrs Butters?' Sophia asked as she stepped into the hall and took off her hat and coat.

'It's Mr Blackwood, ma'am; I don't know what's the matter with him. He won't come out of his study – didn't even want his breakfast. And he hasn't even got dressed yet, and here it is, past nine o'clock! It's most unlike him, your Ladyship.'

'I see. That does sound a little odd…'

'Odd? Oh yes, ma'am; Mr Blackwood is always early to rise and get his ablutions attended to. But he's still in his dressing gown – hasn't even combed his hair! I don't know what's the matter; I'm *sure* I don't!'

Sophia laid a comforting hand on the housekeeper's shoulder. 'Don't worry, Mrs Butters. I'll go and see him. After all, we've got a busy day ahead of us.'

'Oh, *thank* you, your Ladyship. Might I bring you some refreshment?'

'Perhaps a pot of coffee for Mr Blackwood and me, if you'd be so kind.'

Mrs Butters nodded vigorously and took herself off to the kitchen, while Sophia went to Blackwood's study and gave a loud knock upon the door.

'I told you I don't want any breakfast!' came the response.

'And I assure you I have no intention of making you any!' Sophia replied.

There was a pause, and then the door opened to reveal Blackwood. His grey eyes were wide and intense, and, just as Mrs Butters had indicated, he was clad only in his dressing gown, his dark hair wild and dishevelled.

'Thomas! Whatever is the matter?'

'Come inside,' he said and quickly drew her into the room, closing the door firmly behind them. 'I must apologise for my untidy appearance, Sophia, but I've had neither the time nor the inclination to attend to it.'

Sophia glanced around the room. This was where she had first met Blackwood (was it really only a fortnight ago?) and had saved him from the ætherial virus that had infected his cogitator and very nearly devoured his mind. A rather odd way to make each other's acquaintance, to be sure, and things had only become odder during the subsequent affair of the Martian Ambassador. Sophia noted that Blackwood had yet to replace the cogitator, and decided that she couldn't really blame him.

A number of books lay scattered about the room, on the couch and chairs, and also on the desk. Blackwood hurried over to it and picked up one of the books, which he waved at Sophia with an evident mixture of fear and triumph. 'It's all in here,' he said.

'What is?'

'That strange word which Alfie Morgan uttered when we went to see him yesterday. Carcosa – you recall?'

'Of course I do,' Sophia replied in surprise. 'You have found a reference to it?'

'I *knew* I recollected it from somewhere,' said Blackwood excitedly. 'And this is where.'

'What *is* that book?' Sophia asked.

'It's called the *Fantasmata of Simon Castaigne*.'

Sophia frowned. 'The *Fantasmata*... I've heard of it, and of Dr Castaigne. But I regret to say I haven't read it.'

'There are few who have,' Blackwood smiled. 'It is not easy to come by, and were one to do so, one would find that it does not make for particularly light or comfortable reading. Please, Sophia, do have a seat.' He gathered up the books from the armchair and dumped them onto the desk.

'Thank you.' Sophia sat down and waited for Blackwood to explain.

He began to pace back and forth in front of her as he said, 'Dr Castaigne is a well-known figure in certain esoteric circles. He has led a strange life, even by the standards of the occultist and delver into the arcane arts. He was born into a wealthy family of financial brokers, and so was guaranteed a sizeable income. However, the world of finance held no allure for him, and instead he devoted himself to the study of the occult and supernatural. His brilliance is undeniable and was evident from an early age. He studied Mythology and Anthropology at Cambridge and had gained his doctorate by the age of twenty-three. Not long after, he took himself off to the Far East where he travelled widely in China, Mongolia and Tibet. It is rumoured that he even discovered – or was guided to – the fabled city of Shambhala...'

'Shambhala?' exclaimed Sophia. 'But that's incredible! The city can only be reached by the most knowledgeable and pure-hearted of mystical adepts. I know of no outsider who has ever managed to reach it – except for Madame Blavatsky, and I'm not entirely sure I believe her.'

'Quite so: but then, it *is* only a rumour, and Castaigne has never written or spoken of the matter. What is undeniable is that he returned to Great Britain after ten years away, bringing with him an astonishing depth of knowledge regarding the mystical practices of the Orient, knowledge which he set down in this book, the *Fantasmata*. It was privately printed and circulated only amongst those groups whom Castaigne considered worthy of receiving it.'

'How did you obtain a copy?' Sophia asked.

'It was given to me by a friend in my Masonic Lodge a good while ago. I must admit that I gave it only a cursory inspection, for at the time I was engaged upon a particularly complex case which had nothing to do with the occult, and I never went back to it in depth.'

'May I examine it?'

'Of course.' Blackwood handed the book to Sophia. It was a handsome volume, produced with great finesse and attention to detail. It was bound in Moroccan leather of a deep, rich purple, which was tooled with fantastically intricate intaglios outlined in gold. The paper was of the highest quality: creamy and smooth, and delightful to the touch.

'And what, precisely, is the nature of the knowledge Dr Castaigne set down here?'

'Ah! That is what I have been examining since the early hours of this morning. I was in bed, on the very edge of sleep, when my mind performed that curious trick which minds are wont to do in moments of great relaxation: it revealed itself to have been working on the problem of that half-remembered word without my conscious knowledge, and I suddenly remembered where I had read it.' He indicated the book.

At that moment, there was a knock on the door, and Mrs Butters entered carrying a tray with a large silver coffee pot, two cups and saucers, a jug of cream and a bowl of sugar. Before Blackwood could say anything, Sophia smiled and said, 'Thank you, Mrs Butters. Would you please set it down here?' She indicated the occasional table beside the armchair.

'Of course, your Ladyship,' the housekeeper replied. She put the tray down, gave her employer a disapproving glance and quickly left, closing the door behind her.

Sophia poured coffee for them both. 'You were saying, Thomas...'

'It seems that Castaigne learned a great many things during his lengthy sojourn in the Orient.'

'Such as?' Sophia handed him a cup, which he accepted with a nod of thanks.

'Such as the means by which the human mind can travel unaided into the depths of the Luminiferous Æther.'

Sophia gave him a shocked look. 'Are you serious, Thomas?'

'Quite serious, I assure you.'

Sophia shook her head. 'That's incredible.'

'May I?' Blackwood took the book from Sophia and opened it to a place he had bookmarked. 'Listen to this.' He read aloud.

The Æther – how should we describe it? Word and phrase, thought and experience crumble to useless dust in the face of what lies outside the ordered realms of the times and spaces we know. We look up at the black seas of Space, yearning to depart like hopeful adepts in the wake of some cosmic Poseidon. We are unable to release ourselves from the shackles of our quotidian existence, but were we able to do so, we would be gone in an instant, into the depths of the great night which surrounds us.

'A little florid for my taste,' Sophia observed.

Blackwood grinned at her as he turned to the next page. 'And here.'

Take a handful of sand, the tiny grains glittering and golden. Cast it where you please, like a child at play by an innocent sea; count the grains, hold that vast number in your mind, and know that it is but a fraction of the worlds that exist throughout the Æther. How far may the human mind reach, once freed from the base flesh of the body? I have asked myself many times, as if the very act of repetition might forge an answer from the question. How far could one voyage? How far?

Blackwood flipped through to another page and continued reading.

Of all the worlds I have seen, the strangest is Carcosa in the Hyades: strange, paradoxically, because it is so similar to our own in so many ways. But in other ways, it is horribly, frightfully different! I have watched the cloud waves breaking upon the shores of the Lake of Hali; my mind has hovered above those strange waters and has wondered what lies beneath. I have wandered through the melancholy streets of Carcosa's last cities, Alar, Hastur and Yhtill...

'So, Carcosa is a planet!' Sophia exclaimed.
'Indeed,' Blackwood smiled grimly. 'But listen.'

I have heard the last inhabitants sing the Song of Cassilda: a strange, sad song which struck my heart with fear, so clearly does it express the terror of existence – for the universe is emotion, and that emotion is fear. I have heard the last people of Carcosa sing:

Along the shore the cloud waves break,
The twin suns sink beneath the lake,
The shadows lengthen
In Carcosa.

Strange is the night where black stars rise,
And strange moons circle through the skies
But stranger still is
Lost Carcosa.

Songs that the Hyades shall sing,
Where flap the tatters of the King,
Must die unheard in
Dim Carcosa.

Song of my soul, my voice is dead;
Die thou, unsung, as tears unshed
Shall dry and die in
Lost Carcosa.

As she listened to Blackwood recite these verses in his deep, resonant voice, Sophia felt the strange sadness of them seeping into her mind and felt her heart beat faster as a subtle, nameless fear gradually enveloped it. 'Who... who is the King of which the song tells?' she said, her voice barely more than a whisper.

'I have scoured the *Fantasmata* for further mentions of him, for there is something in Cassilda's Song which strongly hints at his importance.'

'Did you find anything?'

'Oh yes, I came upon several references. He goes by many names: the Feaster from the Stars, the King in Yellow, the Unspeakable One, and some others. He appears to be a figure of ultimate evil in the eyes of the people of Carcosa, who seem to be on the very edge of extinction. And there is a strange symbol which seems to be associated with him, something known as the "Yellow Sign".' Blackwood turned to another page, and held out the book for Sophia to see.

The symbol was indeed strange, and as she gazed at it, Sophie felt her unease grow.

'And what of Carcosa itself? Do you think it really exists? Do you think that Dr Castaigne's mind really voyaged there?'

Blackwood shrugged. 'Well... the Hyades certainly exist. They were first catalogued by the Italian astronomer Giovanni Battista Hodierna in 1654. It's a large cluster of stars, very distant from the Earth – trillions of miles – in the constellation of Taurus. Astronomers believe it to contain several hundred suns, all moving through the Æther in the same direction. Whether any of them possess habitable worlds... well, that's another question.'

'But you believe it to be so, don't you?' said Sophia.

Blackwood was silent for a few moments before replying, 'Alfie Morgan believes it to be so. Whatever he encountered on that train while in the Kennington Loop left him with a shattered mind and the desire to repeat a word which, according to Dr Castaigne, is the name of a planet many trillions of miles from Earth.'

Sophia shook her head. 'This is utterly bizarre. It makes no sense whatsoever.'

'I agree,' Blackwood sighed. 'It's completely outrageous; nevertheless, we must get to the bottom of it. We must find out what the connection is between the London Underground and a planet drifting through the fathomless depths of space!'

CHAPTER SIX:
What Was Left on the Train

The psychometrist from the Society for Psychical Research was already waiting on the street outside the train depot at Golders Green when Blackwood and Sophia arrived.

'Thomas, this is Mr Walter Goodman-Brown of the SPR,' said Sophia. 'Walter, this is Mr Thomas Blackwood, Special Investigator for Her Majesty's Bureau of Clandestine Affairs. I must apologise for our lateness...'

'The apology should be mine, sir,' Blackwood interrupted with a smile as he and Goodman-Brown shook hands. 'I was following a new lead in this case and rather lost track of the time.'

'A new lead already?' said Goodman-Brown. 'I can see that your reputation is well-deserved, Mr Blackwood.'

The Special Investigator gave a brief nod of thanks and took in the psychometrist. The man was of slightly-below-average height and was dressed conservatively in a suit of dark tweed. He had a pleasantly studious look about him that was emphasised by the apparently ill-fitting spectacles he wore, which he kept readjusting on the bridge of his nose. In fact, he looked more like a librarian than a talented psychic with the ability to divine an object's origin and history merely by touching it.

'Shall we?' said Blackwood, indicating the entrance to the depot.

'This is where the train is being kept?' said Goodman-Brown as he and Blackwood followed Sophia inside.

'It is. The Bureau gave instructions to the Central and South London Railway to bring it here and leave it completely untouched until we've had a chance to examine it. No one has been aboard since it arrived from Kennington.'

Goodman-Brown nodded his approval.

As soon as they entered the foyer, a harassed-looking man in an ill-fitting suit that had clearly seen better days approached them. Blackwood showed him his credentials and introduced his companions.

'Good day to you all,' said the man. 'I'm Derek Sullivan, manager of the Golders Green Depot.'

'A pleasure,' said Blackwood.

'You've come to examine the train?'

'If you'd be so kind.'

'I'm glad you're here, I don't mind telling you, Mr Blackwood. I'm at my wits' end with these fellows…'

'Which fellows?' asked Blackwood, as Sullivan led them across the foyer and through a door leading to the main depot.

'The maintenance gangs. Your orders to leave the train untouched were rather superfluous, I'm afraid: no one wants to touch it, anyway. In fact, they're refusing to go anywhere near the blessed thing! You can't have a train running unchecked and unmaintained, so at present it's all but useless.'

'I see,' said Blackwood. 'Have they really been that unnerved by the Kennington Loop incident?'

'Oh yes, sir. Word of the incident has spread like wildfire right across the network. Potentially, we're looking at a very serious problem. Lots of workers have been missing their shifts, claiming to be sick – drivers *and* maintenance men. But just between us, I believe I know the real reason...'

'They just don't want to go down into the tunnels.'

'Exactly. Here we are...' Sullivan opened a door and led them out onto a short metal catwalk overlooking the maintenance shop.

It was a huge space, spread out beneath a shallow-arched ceiling of glass and wrought iron girders, filled with light and noise. At least a dozen carriages were undergoing maintenance at that moment, and men were hurrying to and fro between them, carrying tools and components and shouting information and instructions to one another over the general din of hammering and welding.

Blackwood was about to ask where Alfie Morgan's train was, but he quickly realised that the question was unnecessary. Away in the distance, on the far side of the maintenance shop, a single carriage stood by itself. No one was paying it any attention; no one even looked in its direction. Blackwood pointed to it and glanced at Sullivan, who nodded grimly.

'All right, Mr Sullivan,' the Special Investigator said. 'I think we can take it from here. We'll be sure to let you know when we've finished.'

'I shall be in my office,' said Sullivan, and with a nod to Sophia and Goodman-Brown, he took his leave of them.

They walked along the catwalk to the stairs leading down to the shop floor. As they descended, Blackwood said, 'How long have you been practising the art of psychometry, Mr Goodman-Brown?'

'I prefer the term "contact analysis", Mr Blackwood.'

'Forgive me.'

'Not at all. I first realised I had the gift when I was a small boy. My father was a carpenter, and he would make me toys – ships, railway locomotives, that type of thing.

And while I was playing with them, I would become aware of certain mental impressions: internal visions, if you will, of my father actually constructing the toys – fashioning the components, assembling them and so on.'

'Fascinating.'

'Oh, that's not all. Not only was I aware of the toys' immediate history, but also of the trees from which the wood was hewn. With my mind's eye, I saw where they had grown; I could pinpoint the time at which the saplings first sprouted and the time at which the trees were cut down. Their entire history was spread out before me while I was in contact with my toys, somewhat in the manner of a landscape glimpsed in dream.'

'You have a singular ability, sir,' said Blackwood as they reached the bottom of the stairway and began to walk across the rough concrete floor towards Alfie Morgan's train. As they passed, the workers momentarily stopped what they were doing and looked at the visitors. Some spoke to each other in low tones, while others grinned at Sophia and extended invitations for her to join them in the local pub later on. Sophia ignored them, although she found their attentions rather amusing in the manner of an off-colour joke, while Blackwood resisted the urge to walk over and thrash the lot of them.

The maintenance men fell silent, however, when they saw where the three newcomers were headed.

When they reached the carriage, Goodman-Brown took off one of his gloves and touched the front bogie. 'Hmm,' he said. 'Brand new... wooden-bodied composite motor coach... built by the Brush Electrical Engineering Company in Loughborough.'

Blackwood smiled. Goodman-Brown was clearly anxious to display his 'contact analysis' skills without delay – although his preliminary observations were hardly world-shaking. Nevertheless, he wished to encourage the psychometrist as much as possible, and so he nodded approvingly and said, 'Excellent. I can see we've got the right man for the job.'

Goodman-Brown glanced at Blackwood and gave him a broad smile. 'You misunderstand, sir. I wasn't performing a contact analysis; I'm something of a railway enthusiast and was merely expressing my admiration for this particular model.'

Sophia giggled, and Blackwood grinned ruefully. 'I see. I beg your pardon.'

'What a fine beast,' sighed Goodman-Brown as he walked back towards the carriage's midsection, which contained a pair of sliding doors. 'Wonderful!'

'Shall we climb aboard?' asked Sophia.

'Yes, do let's!' replied Goodman-Brown, looking around until his gaze alighted upon a set of steps, which he pulled over and placed before the doors; without a platform, they were more than four feet above the ground. He then mounted the steps and pulled the doors open manually. Blackwood and Sophia followed him into the carriage.

The interior was silent and dimly lit: the gas jets had been switched off, so that the only light came in fitfully through the windows from the maintenance shop. Although most of the workmen had recommenced their activity, the sounds were oddly muted, as if coming from a very great distance. Sophia looked up and down the carriage, at the empty bench seats lining each side, and shuddered. 'Something *was* here,' she said quietly. 'One does not have to be a psychometrist to feel it.'

Blackwood had to agree. There was a very strange atmosphere in the carriage, and although he was tempted to put it down to imagination, he couldn't quite bring himself to dismiss it so easily. 'Mr Goodman-Brown,' he said. 'First impressions?'

'Lady Sophia is quite right: there is a residue here… something… I'm not sure what…' He took off his other glove and sat down on the right-hand seat, placing his hands palm down upon the fabric. He took a deep breath and closed his eyes. As he sat there, perfectly still, his breathing grew deep and steady, in the manner of one asleep.

'I can see the train,' he continued presently. 'It's moving into the tunnel…'

'The Kennington Loop?' asked Blackwood.

'Yes.' Without opening his eyes, Goodman-Brown turned his head to the right, in the direction of the driver's cab. 'Mr Morgan is there… he is not pleased… he doesn't like the Loop – none of the drivers do. I can see him now. The train is following the tracks into the tight curve of the Loop… the wheels are squealing on the metals… Morgan is wincing at the sound. I can see the light…'

'The light?' said Blackwood.

'The signal light; it has changed to red. Morgan is bringing the train to a halt. The air is hot, stifling… uncomfortable. No… Alfie doesn't like it down here. He's counting the seconds until the light turns to green.'

Suddenly, Goodman-Brown's head snapped around to the left. 'What was that?'

Blackwood leaned towards the psychometrist. 'You can hear something?'

A frown crept across Goodman-Brown's forehead. 'Yes… a noise. It sounds like… yes, the connecting doors between the carriages… far back, at the rear of the train. They have opened… and closed. But that can't be: Alfie is alone on the train.' Goodman-Brown's voice had become a whisper. 'There is no one else. There it is again! Alfie is wondering whether the train's guard came back aboard, but he doesn't think that's very likely.'

Blackwood and Sophia looked towards the rear of the carriage. The other carriages were of course no longer there, having been decoupled from the motor coach and transferred to other trains. Through the connecting door at the rear end, they could see the wall of the maintenance shop.

'There it is again!' said Goodman-Brown. 'Closer now… a little closer. Alfie is listening in the silence… the signal is still on red. He has no choice but to wait here.'

'Do you know what's making the sounds… what's moving through the connecting doors?' asked Blackwood.

Goodman-Brown shook his head. 'It doesn't work like that, Mr Blackwood. I am in physical contact with this carriage only – not the others. This is where the contact analysis must be performed; this is where my psychic awareness resides.'

'I understand. Take your time, sir.'

Goodman-Brown smiled. 'I have no choice. I must wait, as Alfie waited, to see what comes through those doors.' He winced. 'Another one… Alfie is looking back along the train from his driver's cab… but he can't see anything. Another! Click-clack! Closer still. Whatever it is… it's moving along the train.' The psychometrist shook his head. 'Poor Alfie. He's afraid now. He's calling out, asking who's there. I can feel his fear… growing… growing! It's in the carriage directly behind this one. The door is opening…'

Blackwood, Sophia and Goodman-Brown were all looking at the connecting door at the rear of the carriage.

'The door is opening,' Goodman-Brown repeated, his voice suddenly strained, as if he were finding it difficult to breath. 'Something is coming through. Oh God… *oh God!*'

'What is it Walter?' Sophia cried, her gaze still fixed upon the door.

'It's in the carriage!' he hissed. 'I can *see* it! Oh, dear God. It's like nothing…' His voice trailed off, so that the only sound in the carriage was his ragged breathing.

And then Walter Goodman-Brown screamed, just as Alfie Morgan had done. He screamed until there was no breath left in his lungs, and then he inhaled and screamed again, and again.

Blackwood lunged forward, grabbed him by the shoulders and hauled him out of the seat.

'Thomas, we have to get him out of here, now!' said Sophia.

'Understood. Give me a hand.'

With Goodman-Brown between them, they staggered back to the doors at the centre of the carriage and hurried down the steps to the shop floor. The psychometrist was virtually insensate now, his body a dead weight. Blackwood and Sophia laid him down upon the concrete.

'Walter,' said Sophia, bending over and examining his contorted face. 'Walter, can you hear me?'

Some of the workmen who had been alerted by Goodman-Brown's screams hurried over. 'What's goin' on?' demanded one. 'What the bleedin' hell do you people fink you're playin' at?'

'Go and fetch Mr Sullivan,' said Blackwood.

'Hold on,' the man said. 'Who the bleedin' hell are you lot, anyway?'

'Shut up and do as you're told!' thundered Blackwood, standing up to face the rapidly growing group. Withdrawing his identification from his coat pocket, he added, 'We are Crown investigators, and you will follow my orders or pass the night behind bars.'

Startled, the workmen glanced at each other, and one of them hurried off towards the offices.

He returned less than a minute later, accompanied by Derek Sullivan, who looked down at Goodman-Brown. 'Good God! What's happened to the fellow?'

'We need to take him to a place of peace and quietness

immediately,' said Sophia.

'There's… there's a couch in my office,' Sullivan replied.

'Good,' said Blackwood. 'Give me a hand to get him up; there's a good chap.'

Together, they carried Goodman-Brown across the shop floor and up the stairs into the section of the building containing the administration offices. Sophia followed them to Sullivan's office and closed the door behind them, while Blackwood and Sullivan carefully placed the psychometrist on the couch. Deeply shaken and muttering to himself, the depot manager went across to a small cabinet and withdrew a bottle of whiskey and a glass. 'Will this be of benefit, do you think?'

'Yes, bring it over,' Sophia replied, crouching down beside Goodman-Brown and undoing his shirt collar.

Sullivan poured a measure of whiskey and handed it to Sophia. Goodman-Brown appeared to be regaining his senses a little, and Sophia put the glass gently to his lips. He grimaced as he swallowed. 'I'm all right,' he whispered. 'I'm all right.'

'What the devil happened in there?' demanded Sullivan.

Blackwood held up a hand, ordering him to silence. 'What was it, Goodman-Brown?' he asked quietly. 'Can you tell us what it was?'

'It was… like nothing I've ever seen before,' the psychometrist replied, taking the glass from Sophia and downing the rest of the whiskey. 'It wasn't a ghost – nothing so mundane! It was alive, I'm quite sure of that: a living, conscious thing, possessed of awareness and purpose.'

'What purpose?' asked Blackwood.

'I'm not sure… its thought processes were… *utterly* non-human…'

'And its appearance?'

Goodman-Brown laughed harshly. 'The only reason I am still sane, Mr Blackwood, is that I was not actually present when it appeared – unlike poor Mr Morgan. It was most assuredly not of this world! It was something fantastically, *hideously* alien.'

'But what did it *look* like, Goodman-Brown?' Blackwood persisted.

The psychometrist shook his head. 'You may have difficulty believing this, Mr Blackwood, but I can't describe it. Its shape… will not fit into my memory, just as it did not fit completely into my awareness while I was looking at it. It was simply too *other*. I don't know how else to explain it.'

'Forgive me, sir,' rejoined Blackwood, 'but your use of the word "explain" is far from justified.'

'Believe me, I'm all too well aware of that, and I offer my apologies…'

'We won't hear a word of it, Walter,' said Sophia gently. 'You did your best, and we are most grateful.'

'There was one thing…' Goodman-Brown continued hesitantly.

'Yes?' said Blackwood. 'Go on; any impression you can recall will be of use, I'm sure.'

'Well… there was something about the thing… a part of it which gave the impression of *not* being alien.'

Blackwood and Sophia glanced at each other, while Sullivan looked at all three of them and shook his head, wondering what kind of lunatics he had allowed into his depot.

'I had the impression of tendrils of some kind…'

'Tendrils?' said Blackwood.

'Or perhaps filaments is a better word. Very fine filaments… like wires, almost. I think it used them to open the connecting doors between the carriages, but I don't think they were actually a *part* of it.'

'Most intriguing,' murmured Blackwood. 'Did you gain any impression as to why it attacked Alfie Morgan?'

'It didn't attack him,' Goodman-Brown replied. 'It was merely observing him, perhaps out of curiosity... or perhaps for some other reason I cannot fathom. At any rate, it didn't touch him – although its mere presence was sufficient to completely undermine his sanity!'

'So, where does this leave us?' wondered Sophia.

'It leaves us with more questions than answers, I'm afraid,' Blackwood replied with a faint, rueful smile. 'And a rather fine mess in our laps. Mr Goodman-Brown's experience proves that there's something far stranger than mere ghosts abroad on the Underground. Something that is definitely not of this world.'

Goodman-Brown shook his head. 'I'm sorry, Mr Blackwood, but it's even worse than that. The thing I saw, the thing which drove Alfie Morgan insane... not only is it foreign to this world, I believe that it is foreign to our very universe!'

PART TWO

Mysteries of the Worm

CHAPTER ONE:
A Conversation with Mr Shanahan

Blackwood and Sophia offered to take Walter Goodman-Brown home to recuperate from his dreadful experience on the train. He declined, however, saying that he had already recovered sufficiently, and would appreciate it if they could take him back to the SPR headquarters, where he intended to write a full report of the morning's events.

'I must say I admire your fortitude, sir,' said Blackwood, as the hansom entered Marloes Road in Kensington and came to a halt outside Number 49.

'Thank you,' the psychometrist replied. 'In fact, it's imperative that I record my impressions of the contact analysis without delay. I'm sure it will make a most interesting and valuable piece for the SPR *Journal* – in addition, I hope, to aiding with your investigation.'

'You may have no doubt of that.'

'Perhaps you and I could retire to my office, Thomas,' said Sophia. 'I believe we need to discuss these developments further.'

'Of course,' Blackwood replied as he stepped down from the cab and offered his hand to Sophia.

The headquarters of the Society for Psychical Research were housed in a large, elegant but rather nondescript

Georgian building with four stories and a whitewashed facade. Once inside, Goodman-Brown took his leave of Blackwood and Sophia, who climbed the stairs to Sophia's office, which was located on the first floor.

This was the first time Blackwood had visited his colleague's professional domain, and he was both amused and delighted at the feminine touches which had been applied to the room's otherwise drably academic mien. There were large vases filled with flowers set on tables before the two tall sash windows, and several photographs upon those sections of the walls which were not obscured by heavily-stacked bookcases and file cabinets. He noted that the photographs were mainly of family gatherings, which were taken on a beautifully tended lawn in front of a large manor house.

There was another photograph on Sophia's desk. It was of a handsome, distinguished-looking man in an immaculate evening suit. His expression was rather stern at first glance, but there was a sparkle in his eyes which hinted at great humour. He reminded Blackwood of a young Thomas Carlyle.

'My father,' said Sophia, who had noted Blackwood's interest in the photograph.

'He was a fine-looking gentleman.'

'Indeed,' Sophia said, very quietly.

She had told Blackwood, not long after their first meeting, of the strange and terrible fate suffered by Lord Percival Harrington during a hunting trip in the wilds of Canada. Sophia, then a girl of eighteen, had been with her father when he had been snatched from their camp by the mysterious and lethal entity known as the Wendigo and carried off into the sky, never to be seen again. His loss had nearly destroyed both her and her mother, and it had left Sophia with a burning desire to investigate and understand the supernatural in all its forms and manifestations.

Sophia offered Blackwood a chair and took her own seat at her desk. 'Well, Thomas,' she sighed. 'What do you think?'

'I think that Mr Goodman-Brown was very lucky to leave that carriage with his mind intact. It's quite obvious that we are not dealing here with some run-of-the-mill phantom or discarnate spirit – at least, not in this particular instance.'

'What *are* we dealing with? A demon? Something unspeakable from the world's remote and unfathomed history?'

'I'm not sure. Goodman-Brown seemed to be quite certain that the thing was *alien* – not of Earth at all, and not even of this universe. And it strikes me that it does not seem to be corporeal, either – at least, not in any understandable sense.'

'It could be connected with Carcosa in some way,' Sophia suggested.

'Quite possibly.' Blackwood hesitated before continuing, 'I think it might be a good idea to get a fresh perspective on this.'

'What do you mean?'

The Special Investigator smiled and said in a loud voice, 'Mr Shanahan! Are you there?'

A few moments later, there was a puff of lilac smoke in the air directly above Sophia's desk, and a tiny man appeared before them. He was about an inch tall and dressed in clothes which might have been fashionable a hundred or so years before. A pair of iridescent dragonfly wings sprouted from between his shoulders; his hair was an untidy, sandy-hued mop, and his green eyes were like tiny, glittering jewels.

'Here, sir!' said the little man. 'How are you and her Ladyship today?'

'Well, thank you.'

'And your injuries… they're almost completely healed, I'm glad to observe.'

'You're very kind to say so,' said Blackwood, unable to keep a tone of reverence from his voice, for well he knew that the image of the tiny faerie before them was merely a disguise, and that Shanahan was, in fact, none other than Oberon himself, King of the Faeries. Blackwood had first met him when Shanahan was masquerading as the Helper from his cogitator, and had only later learned of his race's interest in protecting Earth from the attentions of its dying sister-world, Venus.

In truth, Blackwood felt extremely awkward at the need to maintain this pretence. He and Sophia had seen Shanahan as he really was: tall, powerful and terrifying in his beauty and magnificence, and he fought against the urge to bow down before the little man. Oberon was well aware of this, and found it both amusing and slightly tiresome, and so he preferred to maintain the appearance and persona of an amiable and not-very-important little faerie when visiting his human friends.

'And what can I do for you, sir?' Shanahan enquired.

'Lady Sophia and I are at present engaged upon a rather peculiar case...'

'The disturbances on the Underground Railway,' said Shanahan.

'Quite so. Are you aware of the background?'

'I am, sir.'

'Well... I was wondering whether you could shed any light upon it.'

'Ah,' said Shanahan, shaking his tiny head sadly. 'I wish I could, sir, believe me I do. But I can't.'

'May we ask why, Mr Shanahan?' said Sophia.

'For the reason I spoke of not long ago, your Ladyship. We of the Faerie Realm are limited in our actions by our Covenant with the universe, which we made in ages long past, when we decided to leave the Earth and allow Humankind to assume stewardship of the planet. We must keep our interventions in human affairs to a minimum, and then only in small ways. Besides which, there are certain pressing matters in the deep Æther which require my attention, and I cannot linger here for long, much as I would like to.'

'Really?' said Blackwood. Playing a sudden hunch, he added, 'These matters wouldn't have anything to do with a planet named Carcosa, would they?'

'Carcosa?' Shanahan repeated with a chuckle, and flew several tight little circles in the air. 'And what would you know of Carcosa, Mr Blackwood? Humans will not reach that world for many hundreds of years – and not with Æther zeppelins either, I might add!'

'I'm afraid I know very little,' said Blackwood, with a shrug. 'It's just that two nights ago, a driver on the Underground was driven insane by something he saw down there. And when Lady Sophia and I went to see him, he kept repeating the word "Carcosa".'

'And how do you even know what Carcosa is?' asked Shanahan. 'Where have you heard of it?'

'I read of it in a work written by an occultist named Dr Simon Castaigne.'

'Indeed! Now Dr Castaigne is a *fascinating* gentleman. Very well versed in all manner of esoteric subjects.'

'Including, apparently, the forms of life and intelligence on distant planets,' said Sophia.

'Oh yes, your Ladyship!' exclaimed Shanahan, flitting over and alighting on the desktop in front of her.

She leaned forward and smiled at him. 'Do you know how he does it?'

'Does what, ma'am?'

'How he is able to send his mind into the Æther, to visit other worlds.'

'Just between us three and the walls,' he said in a loud, theatrical whisper, 'he has chemical assistance.'

'What kind of assistance?' asked Blackwood.

'A powerful narcotic, known as Taduki.'

'I've never heard of it.'

'There are very few who have, and fewer still who are able to use it safely, for it has a profound effect on the human nervous system and allows the consciousness to depart from the body and roam about at will.'

'So Carcosa does exist, and it really is inhabited?' said Sophia.

'Oh, indubitably,' replied Shanahan, with an odd smile which she found difficult to interpret.

'Are you absolutely sure you can't tell us anything more... please?' she said.

'Would that I could,' the faerie sighed. 'But unfortunately, this is one of those occasions when I must be extremely careful what I say. I'm sure you understand.'

Sophia smiled. 'Yes, Mr Shanahan, we understand entirely.'

Shanahan regarded her in silence for a moment and then said, 'There is one item of information I can provide to you.'

Both she and Blackwood leaned forward. 'Yes?'

'I believe that Dr Castaigne will be arriving in London tomorrow. He is giving a lecture to the Society of Spiritualistic Freemasons in Mayfair; the subject is the plurality of life on other worlds.'

'I know,' said Blackwood. 'In fact, I received an invitation to attend in yesterday's post.'

Shanahan turned to him. 'Good for you, sir! Dr Castaigne's lectures are very few and far between, and I believe it's considered quite an honour to be invited to one.'

Blackwood smiled. 'I wasn't going to go, but the events of the last few hours have most certainly changed my mind.'

'I should strongly advise it, Mr Blackwood. I'm sure that you and Lady Sophia will find much to ponder on if you do attend.'

'But how can I attend?' asked Sophia, 'if the venue is a Masonic Lodge?'

'The Society of Spiritualistic Freemasons is not like other Lodges,' Blackwood explained. 'They have devoted themselves to the study of Spiritualism, and since women make far better mediums than men, they have secured a special dispensation from the Grand Lodge to allow female participation in all of their activities. I think that you will find the audience to be divided more or less equally between men and women.'

'A most enlightened attitude, I must say,' said Sophia.

'As must I,' agreed Shanahan. 'But now I must reluctantly take my leave of you, for as I said, I have pressing matters to attend to elsewhere.'

'Well,' said Blackwood, 'whatever they are, I wish you the best of luck with them.'

'Thank you, sir!' Shanahan replied as he rose into the air on his dragonfly wings. 'And good luck to you, and to your Ladyship. Farewell!'

And with that, he was gone in a puff of lilac smoke.

CHAPTER TWO:
The Fluffers

Seamus Brennan and Barrymore Tench climbed down from the platform at Aldgate Station and looked into the pitch-black tunnel.

'This ain't fair,' muttered Brennan. 'This just *ain't fair*.'

Tench said nothing; he merely gathered his broom and canvas sack from the edge of the platform, threw the empty sack over his shoulder and picked up his Tilley lamp.

'I mean,' Brennan continued, 'this is women's work. Fraser's a prize bastard, and no mistake!'

'Yes, but he's the boss, and he's the one who caught it over the business at Farringdon Street. Are you surprised he took it out on us? We're the ones who saw the girl. It's 'cause of us that there was a track search and the test had to be postponed.'

'And what about Bartie Smallwood? He saw her too!'

'Well, matey, I suppose that just proves they need drivers more than they need blokes like us. Now, shut yer mouth, pick up your lamp and broom, and let's get started.'

'Fluffers,' said Brennan. 'Bloody fluffers. It's... it's *demeanin'*, that's what it is.'

'Oh, I don't know,' Tench replied philosophically as they headed into the tunnel. 'It's still important work, you know...'

'What, picking up bits o' rubbish from the lines? Dust and dirt... and *hair*? God almighty, what a job!'

Tench shrugged. 'Well, if you let all that stuff build up, it gets dangerous. The lines have to be kept clear all the time. It can cause accidents if they're not kept clean.'

'Women's work,' said Brennan.

His friend sighed. 'Look, Seamus, I'm just tryin' to make the best of it, all right? I don't like it any more than you do, but we've got no choice: we either do it, or we're out on our arses. You want that?'

Brennan sighed. 'No... but why did it have to be Aldgate, of all places?'

'I'd rather be here than in one of the deep-levels.' Tench glanced at his friend, who was looking back longingly at the mouth of the tunnel, which was gradually growing smaller as they trudged on. 'What the bleedin' hell's the matter with you, Seamus?'

'This is where they found one o' them plague pits.'

'That was years ago, when they first built this place.'

'A thousand bodies, they found. A thousand skeletons, all flung on top of one another. No proper Christian burial... just flung into the ground and covered up.'

Tench was getting fed up with Brennan. He was his mate, but sometimes he really got on his nerves. The truth was, Tench didn't like being underground either, not anymore – not since the previous night, when they'd seen the girl and been sent fleeing by her terrible screams back out into the station. Fraser had looked at them like they were mad and had ordered a track search. 'If there's a child in the tunnel,' he'd said, 'we'll have to stop the test.' When they'd told him exactly what they had seen, he had looked at them in disgust and said he didn't go in much for ghost stories (apparently, he had not heard the screams), and when the track search had revealed nothing – and no one – out of the ordinary, Fraser had told them that if they did anything like this again, the only way they'd ever be allowed onto the Underground would be as third-class passengers. He had then assigned Brennan and Tench to fluffer duty, clearly to teach them a lesson.

'All right,' said Tench. 'Might as well start here.' He set his lamp down on the stones of the ballast between the rails, took his broom and set to work sweeping up the assorted pieces of debris and dust which had collected there.

It was amazing how much of this stuff found its way into the tunnels of the Underground over time. The strands of human hair, especially, were tedious and unpleasant to gather up. Above ground, you didn't even notice this kind of thing – or if you did, you paid it no mind... but down here, it looked like it didn't belong; it looked... *unnatural*, somehow. All the little bits and pieces of rubbish, scraps of litter, small items dropped or mislaid, the hairs which fell from people's heads without their realising – everything found its way from the platforms into the tunnels sooner or later, blown in by the breezes caused by the movement of the trains. It was as if the tunnels were the mouths of some vast and ancient beast, some long-buried scavenging thing that swallowed whatever it could from the human beings who passed obliviously through it.

Tench shook his head to banish the thought as he swept the lines with his broom. It was a stupid thought – a stupid, horrible thought which had sprung into his mind without warning. Most people using the Underground Railway spent little time in the tunnels, and when they did, they were inside trains... protected... not like this, standing on the lines, exposed, lingering in the darkness and the silence.

He hated Fraser for giving them this job. Was it their fault that they had seen the girl? Was it their fault that they had had to perform a track search and postpone the testing of the atmospheric train? Tench sighed loudly as he swept the bits and pieces of rubbish and hair into his sack, and he glanced at Brennan, who had moved a little further up the line.

And then Tench frowned, for something was not right... not right at all. He had looked up at his friend because he had heard the sound of footfalls on the stones of the ballast. In fact, he could still hear them.

But Seamus was standing still.

The Irishman stopped what he was doing and looked back at his friend. Tench could see his face in the fitful light of the Tilley lamps; he looked anxious and confused, an uncomprehending frown creasing his brow.

The footfalls continued... crunch... crunch... on the ballast, echoing strangely in the still air of the tunnel.

Tench grabbed his lamp and thrust it into the darkness. 'Who's there?' he demanded in a quavering voice. 'Who is it?'

The crunching ceased.

'Someone's having a laugh,' said Brennan.

'What?'

'Someone's playin' a joke on us!' Brennan picked up his own lamp and spun around on his heals, peering frantically in every direction. 'Where are you, you bastards? Come out. Come out, and I'll knock you down!'

Could that be it? Tench wondered. Could it be one of their workmates, crouching somewhere in the darkness and making noises to frighten them?

The crunching of the ballast resumed, and as he swung his lamp around, Tench realised that no workman was causing it. He hurried over to Brennan, seized his arm and pointed. Brennan looked and drew in his breath sharply.

There, beside the line, the stones were moving, as if heavy steps were falling upon them.

'There's no one there,' Tench whispered in disbelief.

83

'Yes there is,' Brennan replied. 'But we can't see them.' There was a tone of anguished defeat in his voice; he had hoped with every fibre of his being that the sound *was* being made by a colleague with a malicious sense of humour, but that hope was now dashed by the clearly visible movement of the ballast – movement which was being caused by someone or something *not* visible.

'Jesus, Mary and Joseph,' whispered Brennan. 'Who is here with us?'

'Let's get out of here, Seamus,' said Tench urgently. 'Let's get out, right now! Fraser can give us our marching orders – I don't care. I'm not stayin' here anymore – here or anywhere else on the Underground. I've had enough!'

'Wait,' said Brennan. 'What's that?' He held out his lamp towards the depths of the tunnel, which wound off into the darkness towards Liverpool Street.

Something was moving in the darkness – or was it the darkness itself which was moving? Brennan couldn't tell, but *something* was there. The workmen felt the tug of a slight breeze, and their ears caught a faint sound, like a distant sigh.

'Come *on*, Seamus!' whispered Tench.

'What *is* that?' The Irishman's voice was filled with fear, and yet he could not turn away from the strange movement in the dark distance. It captivated him, snaring him in a terrible curiosity. It was like wind… like wind that you could *see* – that was the only way he could describe it to himself.

Brennan moved to the side; his foot caught on one of the rails, and he stumbled. He dropped his lamp, which struck the rail and smashed. Now, the only light in the tunnel came from Tench's lamp, and the darkness surged around them, like a predator sensing a meal.

The strange movement-that-was-not-movement drew closer to Brennan, and by the inadequate light from Tench's lamp, they saw what it was, and Seamus Brennan and Barrymore Tench moaned aloud in horror and disbelief.

It was hair... human hair, hovering before them in a cloud of writhing filaments.

Tench began to edge backwards, away from the thing. 'Come on, Seamus,' he whispered. 'Come *on!*'

But Brennan remained where he was, horribly entranced by the slowly shifting mass, which seemed to be regarding them, as if possessed of some hideous, unnatural awareness. 'So much,' he said, shaking his head. 'Why so much?'

'I don't know. Please come on.'

'Must have come from everywhere... everywhere on the Underground. Why?'

'I don't want to know. Come on.'

Tench edged back further, and as he did so, his foot caught the edge of a sleeper, and he fell backwards with a loud cry.

Whether it was the movement or the sound of his voice, he didn't know, but the mass of hair suddenly surged forward, and in an instant had enveloped Brennan, its gossamer strands twining repulsively around his face and neck. He screamed and staggered, his hands clawing at his face, trying to rip the stuff away. But it was no use: there were thousands of hairs – *hundreds* of thousands, and they were like a great, dark cobweb as they clung to Brennan.

Tench looked on in abject terror as the writhing hairs entered Brennan's screaming mouth, while others wrapped themselves around his ankles and tipped him over onto the ground. He lay there, thrashing wildly, his cries choked off as the hair squirmed into his throat.

If his friend had been set upon by men, Tench would have ploughed in with fists flying to aid him, but he knew that there was nothing he could do here, not against *this*. If he went to Brennan now, he risked being ensnared by the filthy, unnatural thing. He burned with shame to think of it, but it was clear that his only chance for life was to flee this very minute, to escape the tunnel and re-emerge in the sanity and safety of the outside world.

If there was any doubt in his mind, any last vestige of courage and desire to help his friend, even at risk to his own life, they were utterly annihilated by the thing which began to smear itself into visibility in the hot, dank air above the frantically struggling Irishman.

Tench only caught a glimpse of it before he twisted his head away in panic, knowing instinctively that to gaze upon it for any length of time would be the end of him. He whimpered like a terrified dog as he dragged himself over the sleepers, then got to his feet and began to run.

'I'm sorry, Seamus,' he whispered as he fled back along the tunnel towards Aldgate Station. 'I'm so sorry!'

CHAPTER THREE:
Tench's Revenge

'Blackwood, Lady Sophia,' said Detective de Chardin. 'Good of you to come so quickly.'

'We came as soon as we received your message, Detective,' Sophia replied, as de Chardin beckoned them into his office at New Scotland Temple.

'What's happened?' asked Blackwood, who had instantly noted the harried expression on the detective's face.

De Chardin motioned them to be seated. 'Another incident on the Underground – this time near Aldgate Station...'

'Aldgate?'

'Yes.' De Chardin took his own seat at his desk and regarded his visitors with a worried frown. 'I asked you to come because I would like you to be present when I question the prisoner.'

Blackwood and Sophia glanced at each other.

'You have someone in custody?' asked Sophia. 'Someone who might be responsible for these events?'

De Chardin smiled grimly and shook his head. 'If only that were the case, your Ladyship. The man we have is a maintenance worker, accused of inflicting grievous bodily harm upon his foreman. His name is Barrymore Tench, and the foreman is named Harold Fraser. This morning, Tench went to Fraser's office and gave him a thrashing the likes of which I have rarely seen. Fraser is at present in hospital, with a jaw broken in three places and more broken ribs than sound ones.'

'Good Lord!' said Sophia. 'And why did he commit such a vicious assault?'

'That's the reason for my asking you to come. According to witnesses, Tench was screaming about something that happened last night, in the tunnel between Aldgate and Liverpool Street. He said that something had attacked his co-worker, a man named Seamus Brennan, and that it was all Fraser's fault for sending them down there. It took three men to pull him off Fraser, and when the police were called, they could get nothing more from him. We're holding him now, in the lower cells.'

'What were they doing in the tunnel?' asked Blackwood.

'They were on fluffer duty.'

Blackwood raised an eyebrow. 'That's not the sort of work maintenance men are usually asked to do.'

'Excuse me,' said Sophia. 'Fluffer duty?'

'Fluffers are people who go through the tunnels at night and clear the lines of detritus, such as litter and hair,' explained Blackwood.

'*Hair?*'

'Yes. Everyone sheds a few hairs every day, including the thousands of people who use the Tube Railway. The breezes from the passing trains blow the hair into the tunnels, where it collects on and around the lines. The fluffers go in and sweep it all up. But as I say, maintenance men are not usually assigned to such duty.'

'Correct,' said de Chardin. 'We have taken statements from several people, who say that Tench and Brennan were demoted by Fraser to the status of fluffers as punishment for their involvement in another incident the previous evening.

'*Another* incident?' said Blackwood. 'What happened?'

'Tench and Brennan were part of a crew preparing the line between Farringdon Street and Baker Street for a test of the atmospheric railway. Apparently, they encountered the ghost of a young girl on the line. Fraser didn't believe that she *was* a ghost and was forced to initiate a lengthy track search, which resulted in the postponement of the test.'

'Do you think this might be a straightforward case of revenge?' asked Sophia.

'It's possible,' de Chardin replied. 'Tench might have concocted his story about Brennan being attacked as a mitigating circumstance, so that it would go easier for him in court. And yet, that doesn't quite ring true. Tench could easily have pounced on Fraser in the streets at night, not allowing his victim to see who was attacking him. To walk into his office in broad daylight and have at him... well, one is forced to ask why? And there's something else which lends a certain weight to Tench's story, and which forces me at least to consider taking his claims at face value.'

'Which is?' said Blackwood.

'No one has seen or heard from Seamus Brennan since last night. He has a family, to which he is devoted, and his wife says that his disappearance is completely out of character.'

'You think he may still be somewhere on the Underground?' said Sophia.

'It's possible, and in fact that section of the network has been closed while a search is made for him.' De Chardin heaved a great sigh. 'This business is getting completely out of hand. I'm going down to see Tench now, to try and get some more information out of him, and I'd be grateful if you both would accompany me.'

Blackwood nodded. 'Of course, de Chardin. In any event, I think it's high time we went down into the tunnels ourselves, and had a good look at the locations of these disturbances. Aldgate is as good a place to start as any.'

'Excellent. In that case, if you'll follow me...'

*

'Might I ask if you have made any headway in this business?' asked de Chardin as he led Blackwood and Sophia through the warren of corridors leading to the Temple's main staircase.

'A little,' Blackwood replied. 'But I fear it has revealed more questions than answers.'

De Chardin chuckled. 'I do so dislike those cases. But you saw Alfie Morgan...?'

'Indeed. Lady Sophia and I visited him at Bethlem Hospital a couple of days ago.'

'And did you glean anything useful?'

'Perhaps.'

De Chardin glanced over his shoulder at the Special Investigator. 'Would you care to elaborate?'

Blackwood hesitated while a pair of constables passed them. The men wore the dark grey uniforms of the Metropolitan Templar Police, with the characteristic cross pattée stitched in crimson silk upon their left breasts. The men nodded to de Chardin. When they had passed, Blackwood replied, 'I'm not at all sure where this will lead, but Morgan kept repeating an unusual word, "Carcosa", which I have since established is the name of a distant planet.'

De Chardin glanced at him again, this time in undisguised incredulity.

Blackwood smiled. 'I know how that sounds, Detective, but it has been corroborated by Mr Shanahan. Whatever is happening on the Underground seems to be connected in some way with that mysterious world.'

'Shanahan,' said de Chardin. 'I didn't know he had become involved.'

'He hasn't, not really. Lady Sophia and I had a brief conversation with him yesterday morning, during which he verified the existence of Carcosa. He said that he had pressing business to attend to elsewhere and wouldn't be able to offer us much help on this case, although he did advise Lady Sophia and me to attend a lecture to be presented by an occultist named Simon Castaigne here in London – a lecture to which I have already received an invitation.'

'I've heard of Castaigne,' said de Chardin.

Blackwood gave him a surprised look as they followed the detective down the wide marble staircase towards the ground floor. 'You have?'

'Oh yes. He wrote a treatise on the early history of the Knights Templar a few years ago. We have it in our library upstairs. It makes for entertaining – if rather lurid – reading.'

'Then it isn't accurate?' said Sophia.

'Well, let's just say that he fills in the gaps in his knowledge of our early years with some rather wild speculation.' He glanced at Blackwood. 'I'm not sure how much credence I would place in the claims of Dr Castaigne.'

'He knows of Carcosa,' Blackwood replied, 'and now, so does a common train driver. And it seems that that knowledge has cost the poor man his sanity.'

'Well,' shrugged the detective, 'I'm sure you know what you're doing. This whole business is so unconscionably bizarre that I suppose we should take our leads wherever we may find them.'

They continued down past the ground floor to the basement, where the holding cells were located. Although the place was clean and well-lit by gas lamps ranged at equal distances upon the whitewashed walls, it still held an oppressive atmosphere which hinted at violence and wasted lives. There was a faint odour of unwashed bodies, and when an occasional shout emerged from behind one of the doors lining the main corridor, it was harsh, guttural and filled with rage.

At the far end of the corridor, a constable sat at a desk. He stood up when he saw them approaching. 'Good morning, sir,' he said.

'And to you, Constable,' de Chardin nodded. 'I'd like to speak with Barrymore Tench.'

'Yes, sir.' The constable led them to one of the doors, withdrawing a set of keys from his pocket as he did so.

'How has he been?'

'Quiet as a mouse, sir. I was expecting a bit more trouble from him than we've actually had, I must say.'

De Chardin slid aside the observation panel set into the door and looked into the cell. He frowned.

'What is it?' asked Blackwood.

De Chardin didn't reply as he motioned for the constable to unlock the door. Blackwood and Sophia followed him into the cell, where they immediately saw the reason for the detective's expression of concern.

Barrymore Tench was sitting on the edge of the narrow metal bed on the far side of the room. His head was bowed, and he was weeping quietly.

Blackwood closed the door behind them as de Chardin said, 'Mr Tench, we've come to ask you some questions about what happened. I advise you to answer immediately and honestly: I hardly need remind you of how much trouble you're in.'

Tench looked up at them, and his tear-filled eyes were clouded with fear and horrible memories. 'Not as much trouble as poor Seamus,' he said in a quiet, defeated voice.

'Why did you beat Harold Fraser in such a vicious manner?'

'I was angry,' Tench replied without hesitation. 'I wanted to make him suffer the way my mate suffered.'

'You maintain that something… unnatural happened to Mr Brennan?'

'Oh yes… oh yes. Something unnatural happened, and no mistake!'

'What was it?' asked Blackwood, stepping forward.

Tench looked up at him. 'You're no copper. Who are you?'

'Never mind who he is, Tench,' said de Chardin. 'Just answer his question.'

'What difference does it make, what happened?' Tench said, his voice filled with bitterness. 'Seamus is gone, and I'm goin' to gaol… and maybe that'll be the safest place to be, so I ain't bothered.'

'Tell us what happened, Mr Tench,' said Sophia. 'We need your help to understand what's happening down there, in the tunnels.'

The prisoner looked at Sophia in surprise, as if he had only just noticed her presence. 'You can't understand what's happenin' down there, miss. No one can. They should shut down the Underground… fill in all them tunnels an' leave it alone! We're not meant to be down there; we don't belong, don't you see? There's somethin' down there that wants to be left alone!'

De Chardin took another step forward. 'Tell us what happened.'

Tench gazed up at him, and his eyes filled anew with tears.

'*Tell us what happened!*' the detective thundered.

Tench recoiled, shutting his eyes. Sophia jumped and put her hand to her mouth. Blackwood gave her a warning look, for he could see as well as de Chardin that Tench was on the verge of breaking down completely, and that a shouted order would certainly be obeyed. The man was clearly approaching the end of his tether, and in no mental state to offer any resistance to his questioner's demands.

De Chardin spoke again, but this time his voice was soft, almost imploring. 'Tell us, lad…'

And Barrymore Tench told them everything. He told them what they had seen in the tunnel, what it had done to Seamus Brennan, how he himself had escaped, and how the shame had burned in his heart as he staggered in panic and confusion to the nearest public house, when in fact he should have alerted his supervisor that something had happened in one of the tunnels. He told them how he had got drunk to ease the pain and the memories which swam before his eyes, of Brennan writhing and thrashing on the ground, covered in a moving mass of human hair, and the brief glimpse he'd had of something indescribable hovering in the darkness; he told them how he had woken up this morning feeling nothing but the desire to thrash Fraser, to cause him all the fear and pain that Seamus had felt…

And so that was what he had done: he'd made the bastard pay for sending Seamus to his death. 'I'm not sorry,' he said. 'You needn't think I'm sorry! I'd do it again, I would!'

'All right,' said de Chardin. 'What about the previous night? What about the girl?'

Tench lowered his eyes and shuddered. 'Yes… the girl. We saw her – Seamus, Bertie Smallwood and me. On the line… poor little thing, she was. Thin, afraid-lookin', surrounded by a blue light. She was walking in the tunnel, along the metals. Bertie stopped the train when he saw her, and when Seamus and I went to see what was the matter, we saw her too.'

'What did she do?' asked Sophia.

Tench turned his haunted eyes to her. 'She screamed, miss. She screamed and screamed, and we ran…'

'And Mr Fraser put you on fluffer duty as a result,' said Blackwood.

Tench ignored him. 'The look on her little face,' he said. And then he looked again at Sophia and whispered, 'Even the dead are afraid of what's down there.'

Blackwood touched de Chardin's arm and nodded towards the cell door.

'All right, Mr Tench,' said the detective. 'You've been very cooperative. We'll talk again.'

They left the workman and stood in the corridor while the constable closed and locked the door once again.

De Chardin glanced from Blackwood to Sophia. 'Well... what do you think?'

'I think,' Sophia replied, 'that there is a force at work on the Underground that is capable of manipulating objects for its own ends. I also think that this may well be what Mr Morgan saw in the Kennington Loop.'

'Manipulating objects?' said de Chardin. 'You mean the human hair which Tench mentioned?'

'I do,' she replied, and she described Walter Goodman-Brown's impressions during his contact analysis of Alfie Morgan's train. 'The thing used what Walter described as fine filaments to open the connecting doors between the carriages; he also believed that they were not actually a part of the thing. It's my suspicion that whatever this entity is, it can only interact with the material world in limited ways. And yet...' She paused and put an index finger to her chin in contemplation, a gesture which both Blackwood and de Chardin found rather charming, in spite of the macabre nature of the conversation.

'And yet?' said the detective.

'If it can manipulate something like human hair to perform actions, such as opening a carriage door, then why not simply open the door itself?'

'Perhaps there's some quality to the hair,' suggested Blackwood. 'Its lightness and tensile strength, perhaps. It may be easier to manipulate that than the metal of a door latch.'

Sophia nodded. 'You may well be right, Thomas. It could be using the hair in a similar manner to that in which a spirit uses ectoplasm to interact with the physical world.'

'And what of its origin?' asked de Chardin. 'Could it really be a visitor from a distant planet?'

Sophia gave a grim smile. 'Or perhaps a distant universe.'

'A distant *universe*?' De Chardin shook his head. 'Good grief.'

'In any event, detective,' said Blackwood, 'I still think it's time you and I went down into the network to have a look for ourselves.'

'I'll join you,' said Sophia.

Blackwood shook his head. 'I don't think that will be necessary.'

Sophia frowned. 'Why ever not?'

'It's far too dangerous. We don't know what we may encounter down there; I would be much happier if you remained on the surface.'

Sophia's face flushed with sudden anger. 'Thomas, I really think –'

Blackwood held up a hand. 'I'm sorry, but I am responsible for your safety...'

'I am responsible for my *own* safety, sir! Might I remind you that as Secretary of the SPR, I have conducted numerous investigations of supernatural events? I can assure you that I am quite capable of looking after myself.'

Blackwood glanced at de Chardin, who had lowered his eyes in embarrassment and appeared to be inspecting his shoes. 'Perhaps we could discuss this later, Sophia,' he said quietly.

'Later? You mean, after you and the detective have returned! Thomas, we have not known each other for very long, but even so, I would not have expected this of you.' She shook her head and regarded him with hurt and angry eyes.

Blackwood sighed. 'Please forgive me, Sophia, but this is my final word on the matter.'

'As a Special Investigator for the Crown,' said de Chardin, 'Mr Blackwood does have seniority.'

Sophia glanced at de Chardin, and then at the constable, who had returned to his desk and was now looking at them, having heard the exchange.

There was more she wanted to say, much more, for she was angry and embarrassed, and the embarrassment made her even angrier. How dare Blackwood tell her where she could and couldn't go! She was at least his equal in her understanding of the supernatural, and another pair of eyes down on the Underground network would only increase the speed and efficiency of their investigation.

However, she could see that she had already shocked Detective de Chardin with the vehemence of her reaction, and she had no desire to make a scene in front of him and the constable. And so she took a deep breath and said as calmly as she could, 'Very well, Thomas. I will accede to your... seniority. Is there anything you would like me to do while you and the detective are down in the network?'

'As a matter of fact, there is,' replied Blackwood, clearly relieved that Sophia had chosen not to give full vent to the irritation and resentment she so clearly felt (and which, he had to admit, was entirely understandable). 'Mr Charles Exeter is the Chairman of the City and South London Railway, which includes the Kennington Loop. The CSLR is at present continuing with its programme of excavating new deep-level tube lines. In view of what Mr Goodman-Brown described, I think it would be a good idea to request an interview with Mr Exeter and see whether his company has uncovered anything unusual recently – anything which might conceivably have caused the entity's appearance.'

'What do you mean "unusual"?' said de Chardin.

Blackwood shrugged. 'At this stage, I don't know.'

'A hunch?'

'Call it that. But there must be a reason why these disturbances have begun only recently.' Blackwood turned to Sophia. 'It would be very helpful indeed if you could talk to Exeter and see if there *is* a connection.'

In spite of herself, Sophia was intrigued by this idea, and so she nodded and replied, 'Very well, Thomas. I shall ask Sir William to draft a letter of introduction without delay.'

Blackwood smiled and nodded. With an introduction from Sir William Crookes, the President of the Society for Psychical Research, she would have no trouble gaining access to the CSLR Chairman. 'In that case,' he said, 'I suggest that we fall to our tasks without delay.'

CHAPTER FOUR:
An Excursion and an Interview

While Blackwood and de Chardin headed off to Farringdon Street, Sophia returned to the SPR headquarters and went immediately to Sir William Crookes's office, where she found him poring over an assortment of newspaper clippings arranged neatly upon his desk.

'Hello, Sophia,' he smiled. 'Do come in.'

'Thank you, Sir William.'

'Have a seat, my dear. You look a little flustered, if I may say so.'

Sophia smiled at the observation. Although he was approaching his seventies, Sir William Crookes's mind was as keen as ever. He had been a close friend of the Harrington family for many years and had been instrumental in helping her to come to terms with the loss of her father during their hunting trip in Canada ten years before. Indeed, he had been the only person with whom she had felt able to discuss their encounter with the Wendigo.

Sir William had observed, and understood, the resultant yearning in Sophia's heart to investigate the mysteries of the supernatural world, to discover ways of guarding humanity against the darkness while also seeking out the light in order to learn and gain strength from it. Later, he had invited her to join the Society for Psychical Research and had persuaded her to share her singular experience with other senior members, who had had no objections when he suggested that she be appointed Secretary following the departure of Dr Henry Armistead to pursue a lecturing opportunity at Brown University in Providence, Rhode Island.

Sophia owed Sir William a great deal, and now, as she regarded the elderly scientist with his high, noble forehead, neatly-trimmed white beard and carefully-waxed moustache, she found herself wondering, as she often did, whether her father might one day have looked a little like this, had he been allowed to grow old...

'I suppose you could say I *am* a little flustered, Sir William,' she sighed.

'Why? Whatever is the matter?'

'Mr Thomas Blackwood is the matter,' she replied.

Sir William caught the huffy tone of her voice and chuckled. 'And what has he done to annoy you?'

'He has forbidden me from accompanying him and Detective de Chardin into the tunnels of the Underground. He says that he is responsible for my safety, and that the potential danger is too great. I mean... *really.*'

Sir William's chuckle became a soft laugh. 'Well, I suppose that's understandable...'

'Sir William!'

He held up his hands in a gesture of placation. 'I merely meant that he does not know you as well as I do, and he has yet to appreciate the great resilience and resourcefulness which you possess.'

'I would have thought that my contributions during the affair of the Martian Ambassador would have convinced him of that.'

Sir William gave her a warm, sympathetic smile. 'Sophia, we are living in a remarkable age: an age of astonishing advancements in virtually every field of human endeavour, and yet, there are certain aspects of the human personality, the *emotional* aspects, which sometimes have trouble keeping up with those of the intellect. I'm quite sure that Mr Blackwood has every confidence in your abilities, both in your capacity as an investigator of the supernatural and as his colleague. But that confidence does not yet have the power to overcome his innate desire to protect a young lady from harm and to recoil from the idea of placing her in a potentially dangerous situation unnecessarily. It is an attitude I wholeheartedly disagree with, since I know you so well, but it *is* one which I can understand.'

Sophia sighed as she took his words in. 'I suppose you are right,' she said.

Sir William's smile broadened. 'But you remain unconvinced: a properly scientific attitude in the absence of further supporting evidence.'

They both laughed.

'In any event,' he continued, 'how is the investigation going?'

'We have made some headway,' Sophia replied, and she proceeded to summarise what she and Blackwood had learned and theorised so far.

'Good,' Sir William nodded. 'I have been doing a little investigating of my own. Come around and take a look at this.'

Sophia joined him and saw that underneath the newspaper clippings there was a large map of the Underground network. Sir William moved the clippings aside to reveal an irregular pentagon which he had drawn on the map and which encompassed a substantial swathe of Central London. The five corners of the pentagon were at Farringdon Street, Paddington, Aldgate, Kennington and South Kensington Tube Stations, while the lines connecting them passed through Bond Street, Covent Garden, Bank, and Elephant & Castle.

'These are the locations of the disturbances,' Sophia observed.

'Indeed they are.'

Moving in a clockwise direction, Sir William pointed to each of the stations he had circled.

'Farringdon Street, where the ghost of a thirteen-year-old girl has been seen and heard screaming. It is widely believed that she is Anne Naylor, who was brutally murdered by her seamstress in 1768.

'Paddington. Strange noises have been heard in the tunnels here, by fluffers and maintenance workers, apparently coming from behind the walls.

'Bond Street. Something pale and shapeless has been seen moving along the metals at night. It vanishes when approached.

'Covent Garden. A tall man in a frock coat has been seen walking along the tunnels. He bears a striking resemblance to William Terriss, the actor, who was stabbed to death near the Adelphi Theatre in the Strand a couple of years ago.'

'I remember that,' said Sophia. 'A terrible, tragic business.'

'Well, it appears that Mr Terriss has yet to take his final curtain call. But to continue: Bank. This is where Sarah Whitehead, the so-called "Black Nun", has been seen on several occasions. Sarah's brother Philip was a cashier and was executed for forgery in 1811. Up until a few weeks ago, she was only seen very rarely, but now workmen encounter her virtually every night, wandering the platforms, apparently searching for her lost brother.

'Aldgate. The site of one of the largest plague pits ever discovered in London, and now the scene of several disturbances, including something invisible moving the ballast around the metals and an old woman who walks along the tunnels, apparently looking for something or someone.

'Elephant and Castle. Here we have the testimony of several witnesses who claim to have seen a young woman walking at night through the carriages of trains at the terminus of the Baker Street and Waterloo Railway. When she is pursued – for we know that passengers are not allowed on the network once it closes for the evening – she cannot be found. Her presence has triggered several track searches, but no trace of her can ever be discovered.

'Kennington. The site of the recent disturbance, to which poor Mr Morgan was a witness. He is still under observation at Bethlem, you say?'

Sophia nodded.

'And finally, South Kensington, where a ghost train has been seen on several occasions. The train is of the steam-driven type and has been seen pulling into the station, accompanied by an ear-piercing whistle. The driver, in reefer jacket and peaked cap, can be seen leaning out of his cab, before he and his train vanish into the tunnel.'

'Fascinating,' Sophia nodded. 'But why have you drawn these lines connecting the sites of the disturbances?'

'I was trying to see if I could discover some kind of pattern to the geographical locations…'

'It looks like you have: the pentagon is quite clearly defined… but what does it mean?'

'I doubt that the pentagon itself is significant on this occasion – its occult connotations notwithstanding.' Sir William traced an invisible line with his finger in a south-easterly direction, from Bond Street to Westminster. 'This is the route of the new deep-level Tube line currently being excavated by the Central and South London Railway. As you can see, it passes directly through the centre of the area enclosed by the five stations I have indicated.'

'And since the disturbances have recently increased, both in number and intensity,' said Sophia, 'you're wondering whether there is some connection.'

'Indeed I am – although at this stage I have no evidence.'

'Do you think that the excavation might have... disturbed something?'

Sir William turned his kindly eyes to her and shrugged. 'Perhaps.'

Sophia considered this. 'You may well be right,' she said presently. 'Walter sensed something during his contact analysis of the train which went into the Kennington Loop. It seems that nothing like it has ever been seen before.'

'I know. He gave me his report late yesterday evening.'

'Thomas was right: I *should* pay Charles Exeter a visit.'

'The Chairman of the Central and South London.'

Sophia nodded, suddenly recalling the reason why she had come to see Sir William. 'I need a letter of introduction from you, so that I may be assured of an interview with him.'

'I shall provide you with one, of course... although I'm not sure whether it will be entirely necessary.'

Sophia gave him a quizzical glance. 'What do you mean?'

Sir William smiled. 'If this business really is the result of their excavation, Mr Exeter may welcome a visit from the SPR.'

*

Blackwood and de Chardin took a police carriage to Aldgate. During the journey east, the Templar detective glanced at his silent companion several times, aware that the Special Investigator was out of sorts. He guessed that the heated exchange with Lady Sophia was still playing on Blackwood's mind and was unsure whether to broach the subject. He was certain, from Blackwood's taciturnity, that he would rather not discuss it... and yet, de Chardin found himself intrigued – and, truth to tell, not a little impressed – by Sophia's indignation, by the forthright manner in which she had expressed her displeasure at being overruled.

As the carriage turned into Wormwood Street, de Chardin finally gave in to his temptation, and said, 'A most remarkable young lady.'

'What's that?' said Blackwood distractedly.

'Lady Sophia. I have seldom met a woman of such intelligence and determination – not to mention courage. Have you known her long?'

'A fortnight,' was the laconic reply.

De Chardin nodded. 'I have known her somewhat longer: we have collaborated on several cases in the past... cases with a supernatural element, you understand.'

'Indeed,' said Blackwood, who was still gazing through the window at the heave and bustle outside.

'However, I have never seen her act like that before; she really was most put out...'

'Your point, de Chardin?' said Blackwood, glancing at him.

The detective shrugged. 'I have none... beyond the observation that you might have allowed her to come. This is, after all, her forte.'

'Are you so sure?' the Special Investigator asked quietly.

De Chardin regarded him in silence.

'We have no idea what's *really* down there,' Blackwood continued, returning his gaze to the street scene beyond the carriage window. 'All we know is that it has driven one man insane and may have killed another. That it is supernormal, there can be no doubt, but as to its actual origin, whether supernatural or materially scientific... well, I would rather get hold of some more facts before allowing Lady Sophia to face it.'

'I understand, of course,' de Chardin nodded and gave a brief smile, which Blackwood did not notice – and probably wouldn't have liked much if he had.

As the carriage approached Aldgate Station, Blackwood winced and put a hand to his chest.

'Are you all right?' asked de Chardin.

'Yes, I'm fine. It's nothing.'

In fact, the Special Investigator had felt a strange twinge which seemed to vibrate in his breastbone, as though he were clutching a stringed instrument to his chest and a note had been played upon it, powerful and melancholy.

The source of the curious sensation was the amulet: it was warning him of the presence of powerful supernatural forces. As if to drive the point home, the carriage clattered to a halt outside the entrance to the station.

The two men descended and made their way inside, where they asked to speak with the Stationmaster, who came across the ticket hall immediately, having noted their entrance. He was a tall, thin, slightly cadaverous-looking man with sallow skin and thinning hair. His heels clicked on the tiled floor, disturbing a silence which usually only descended upon the station when it was closed at night.

The Stationmaster introduced himself as William Jones and asked them their business. Blackwood and de Chardin showed him their credentials. 'We are here on orders of Her Majesty,' said Blackwood, 'with the purpose of investigating the recent events.'

William Jones raised his eyebrows at this, and Blackwood had the impression that he was not a little dismayed at what he evidently perceived to be a new inconvenience in an already complicated day. 'I see,' he said, an ungracious tone in his voice. 'And may I enquire what interest Her Majesty has in this?'

De Chardin glowered at the man. 'Her interest is the same as yours should be, sir: to get to the bottom of the curious events which have been occurring throughout the Underground network. Now, if you don't mind, Mr

Blackwood and I would like to examine the tunnel in which last night's occurrence took place.'

Jones's tone turned to one of defence. 'I assure you, Detective, that I'm doing everything in my power to resolve the situation – at least, here at Aldgate.'

'Is there any sign of Seamus Brennan?' asked Blackwood.

'Not as yet. I have track-walkers making their way along the lines in both directions out of the station, but so far, there is no sign of him.'

'I take it you are aware of Barrymore Tench's claims,' said de Chardin.

'I am.'

'What do you make of them?'

Jones hesitated. 'If this... incident... had happened in isolation,' he said, 'I would have had a very clear theory as to what actually happened. I would have suspected that Tench and Brennan had an argument of some kind while in the tunnel, that Tench killed his friend and hid his body somewhere, and that he concocted this story to get himself off the hook. But after everything else that has been happening on the Tube network over the last few weeks... well, I am not normally given to ghost stories and the like...' Jones's voice trailed off, and he gave Blackwood and de Chardin a troubled look. Presently, he continued, 'I apologise for my earlier impoliteness, gentlemen. The fact is, I'd greatly appreciate any help you might be able to provide.'

'Apologies are quite unnecessary, Mr Jones,' said Blackwood, with a smile. 'We understand that you must be at your wits' end with this business – after all, shutting down an entire section of the Tube is no trifling matter.'

'Indeed not,' Jones sighed. 'Well, please feel at liberty to look around. I am needed elsewhere, so if you will excuse me...'

'Of course,' Blackwood nodded, as William Jones headed off across the ticket hall.

De Chardin watched him leave, then turned to the Special Investigator. 'Let's get down to the platform,' he said.

*

Sophia's carriage came to a halt outside the offices of the Central and South London Railway in Piccadilly. She looked up at the facade of the five-storey building, which looked drab and a little grimy in the watery yellow light of early afternoon. The impression was more than a little at odds with what she had learned of the powerhouse of a man whose office lay within.

She had returned to her own office while Sir William wrote her letter of introduction, had switched on her cogitator and connected it to the Æther with the intention of getting hold of some information on Mr Charles Exeter, Chairman of the CSLR, in preparation for their meeting. The machine had scoured the Akashic Records, the semi-material, plastic field of energy which surrounds the Earth and retains an impression of every event, thought and action that has ever occurred, and had displayed the results in the cogitator's scrying glass.

Exeter, she learned, had been born in Philadelphia in 1837, and his early life was overshadowed by tragedy and ostracism: his mother died of puerperal fever when he was five years old, and his father was expelled from the Society of Friends as a result of his remarriage to a non-Quaker. This did nothing to dampen Exeter's thirst for power and success, however, and by the time he was twenty-two, he had established a successful brokerage office, which secured for him a large fortune, thanks to his innate shrewdness and ability to read the bond market.

His success was not to last, for the financial panic caused by the Great Chicago Fire of 1871 left him insolvent and unable to repay the $400,000 of public money he had used to fuel his financial speculations. Convicted of embezzlement, Exeter was sentenced to thirty-three months in the notorious Eastern State Penitentiary. However, he was released after only seven months, having secured an official pardon in return for his silence regarding the affairs of two influential Philadelphia politicians.

Exeter then left Philadelphia and moved to Chicago, where he immediately took an interest in the city's public transportation network. Through a highly complex (and not entirely ethical) financial arrangement of construction companies, operating companies, holding companies and interlocking directorships, he managed to gain control of a large proportion of Chicago's street tramways.

His dubious business methods, reported on more and more frequently in the American press, eventually damaged his reputation to the extent that Exeter realised he could no longer function profitably in that country, and in 1896 he had sailed to England, where he focussed his attention on London's public transportation system, and, using the methods familiar to him, set about building a new empire in the ancient city. Once again, his ruthlessness and audacity served him well, and during the last three years he had risen to a position of great power and influence.

Sophia had read all this quickly and with a keen eye, and by the time Sir William had drafted the introductory letter, she felt that she had gained a fair measure of the man.

She stepped down from the carriage and asked her driver to wait for her there, before climbing the steps to the building's entrance and slipping quickly inside.

She went to the reception desk, introduced herself and briefly explained the reason for her visit. The clerk, a young man who appeared to be in his early twenties, flushed as he took in her beautiful face and elegant bearing, and he asked her to wait while he sent someone up to Mr Exeter's office with her letter of introduction. Sophia thanked him with a warm smile, which only served to increase the colour in the lad's cheeks.

As she waited, she took in her surroundings. The large foyer was filled with activity: neatly-suited clerks hurried here and there, clutching papers and whispering excitedly to each other, as though they had just heard of some great, or perhaps calamitous, event. Sophia regarded their faces and decided that their frenetic animation was born more of worry or fear than anything else. She was hardly surprised: if half the things she had read about Charles Exeter were true, he must be climbing the walls of his office at this moment, fulminating against the turn of events which threatened his latest business interests. For a moment, she wondered whether her journey had been wasted. Would he agree to see her, with such weighty concerns on his mind?

The answer came a few minutes later, when the messenger returned to the foyer and asked Sophia to follow him. Mr Exeter, he said, had agreed to spare her a half hour out of his busy schedule. The expression on the messenger's face told her that this was not a common occurrence.

Sophia followed him up three flights of stairs and along several corridors before arriving at a door bearing Exeter's name on a polished brass plaque. The messenger knocked, bid Sophia good day and quickly withdrew, as a voice from within barked, 'Enter!'

She opened the door and stepped into a large and luxuriously appointed office. Exeter, clearly, was a man who liked to display his success. As she crossed the thick-piled carpet towards the vast oak desk behind which the director sat, she took in the valuable antiques displayed atop elegant tables lining the walls, the leather-bound volumes ranked, sentinel-like, within tall, cherry bookcases, and the large conference table, surrounded by beautifully upholstered leather chairs, which dominated one half of the room. To the right of Exeter's desk was another table, on which stood a highly-detailed model of a curious cylinder-shaped contraption. The air was heavy with the scent of expensive cigars.

Charles Exeter stood up and moved out from behind his desk as Sophia approached. Balding, heavy-set, with neatly-trimmed whiskers and a penetrating gaze, he looked every inch the successful entrepreneur, and Sophia had the profound sense that to get on the wrong side of him would be a very bad mistake indeed.

'Your Ladyship,' he said, bowing formally and, Sophia thought, a little ridiculously, 'welcome.'

Normally, Sophia disliked her title – or rather, she considered it irrelevant to her life and the pursuit of the interests which mattered to her – and frequently asked new acquaintances to dispense with it when addressing her, but with Exeter and people like him, she found herself more than happy for her social status to be acknowledged. In fact, she insisted upon it.

'Thank you for agreeing to see me at such short notice, sir,' she replied, taking the chair he proffered.

'May I offer you some refreshment?'

'Thank you, no.'

Exeter seemed relieved at this, although at that moment, Sophia couldn't decide whether it was because he was anxious to get the interview over and done with and be rid of her, or because he wished to avail himself of her help without delay.

She suspected it was the latter and was gratified when he retook his own seat and said, 'I'm real glad you decided to pay me a visit, your Ladyship.'

Sophia suppressed a smile at the American's curious mode of expression, at once formal and casual, and replied, 'It's my pleasure, Mr Exeter. As you may know, we at the Society for Psychical Research take a keen interest in the kinds of phenomena that have recently been reported on the Underground. Our knowledge and experience in such matters has been sought on many occasions by Her Majesty's Government, and we have worked closely with various official departments.'

'And you've been asked to look into this affair by Her Majesty as well, haven't you?'

Sophia raised an eyebrow at this, and Exeter gave a low chuckle. 'I have no special wisdom, your Ladyship, but I *do* have many sources of information, and I'm aware that the government has got itself mighty worked up over this – as well they should. What's going on down there is crazy, beyond belief, and I want an end put to it as soon as possible.' He lifted Sir William's letter of introduction from the blotter on his desk and waved it as if it were a banknote of a particularly low denomination. 'That's why I agreed to see you. I'm running out of options, see? Pretty soon, the world's first and most extensive underground railroad system will be empty: there'll be no trains running, because no one will want to drive them, and the system will fall into ruin because no one will want to maintain it. That's a problem for all of us.'

'And for you especially, Mr Exeter,' Sophia could not resist observing. 'Not only do you own the Central and South London, you also have invested heavily in the new deep-level line from Bond Street to Westminster. You stand to lose a great deal if the Tube Railway should fail.'

'You've done your homework,' said Exeter with a thin smile. 'But the fact remains, we're all in this together. I'll lose a heck of a lot of money, sure, but Great Britain will lose

a heck of a lot of prestige if the Underground goes belly up...
a *heck* of a lot.'

'Then I suggest we get down to business,' said Sophia.
'What can you tell me about the new deep-level line?'

Exeter gave her a puzzled look. 'Why do you want to
know about that?'

'It may be relevant to the current situation.'

'In what way?'

Sophia gave him a smile every bit as thin and humourless
as the one he had given her. 'I don't know until you tell me.
But I must ask you to be completely honest with me and to
withhold nothing.'

Exeter was silent for some moments, and Sophia took
in his expression. She had clearly hit a nerve: she could see
it in his eyes, and in the apprehensive drawing together of
his lips. *You may be a good businessman*, she thought. *But I
suspect you're a terrible poker player.*

'Something happened down there, didn't it?' she said.
'During your excavation of the new tunnels... you found
something.'

She watched as Exeter's expression darkened, and she
continued to meet his gaze until, presently, he dropped his
eyes to the desk and gave a low chuckle. 'You certainly *have*
done your homework, ma'am. I congratulate you.'

Sophia shrugged. 'We at the SPR *also* have our sources
of information, Mr Exeter.'

His well-manicured fingers drummed upon the ink
blotter for a few moments, as if he were debating with
himself whether to accede to Sophia's request that he share
all relevant information concerning the new excavation.
Sophia waited patiently, for she knew that, ultimately, he had
no choice.

Presently, Exeter stood up and moved to the table beside
his desk, on which sat the model of the curious contrivance.

'Let me show you something, Lady Sophia.' He indicated the model. 'This is a Greathead tunnelling shield – a remarkable piece of equipment. The ground beneath London is mostly clay, relatively easy to tunnel through, but not particularly good for it.' He glanced at her with a half smile. 'Too soft, has a tendency to cave in. The shield prevents that. It's an iron cylinder, twenty-four feet in diameter and sixty feet long, and fitted with pneumatic jacks which allow it to be propelled forward an inch at a time.'

Exeter pointed to the front of the model, which contained two levels nestling within a complex arrangement of iron braces and girders; each level contained a number of tiny human figures representing workmen. To Sophia, who was not an engineer, it was a hideously ugly thing, which looked like some loathsome, fat mechanical worm with a gaping maw in which the figures seemed trapped.

'It's an elegant solution to the logistical and engineering problems of tunnelling through clay,' Exeter continued. 'The men at the front of the machine excavate the working face as the shield is moved forward, supporting the newly-cut tunnel, while behind it the lining of cast iron segments is fitted into place.'

'You make it sound easy,' said Sophia.

Exeter laughed. 'It's anything but that. It's slow, dirty, dangerous work, but the tunnelling shield is the only practical means we have of excavating the deep-level Tube lines. We have three of them – one of which began work on the new line between Bond Street and Westminster three months ago.' He hesitated, as if he were recounting the events from an unreliable memory. 'We… did find something. Yes… we *did* find something.'

Sophia leaned forward in her chair. 'What, Mr Exeter?'

The director shrugged and heaved a deep sigh. 'At first, we thought it was a plague pit… you know about them?'

Sophia nodded.

'There are lots of them – more than I would have imagined.' He shook his head. 'What a strange and tragic history this city has! So much death and misery, as if the city itself were built from them.'

Sophia was surprised at Exeter's turn of phrase. Men like him were not usually possessed of such darkly poetic imaginations. 'You found a chamber filled with bodies,' she said. 'Like the one at Aldgate, perhaps?'

'No,' he said. 'Not like that. One of the first things I did when I embarked on this venture was to acquaint myself with the history of London – and in particular the history of the Tube Railway. I read about the discovery at Aldgate and the others. But this was – *is* – different.'

'How so?'

'It's… more like a proper burial chamber… like the ones you read about in Egypt or Rome, I guess. It was decorated…'

'Decorated?'

Exeter nodded. 'Like it was planned a long time in advance. The floor, ceiling and walls are covered with thousands of tiles – I believe they are terracotta. Whoever built it did so for a purpose other than disposing of the bodies of plague victims, I'm quite sure of that. At first, I thought it might be a mine left over from the Roman period.'

'It's true the Romans did mine for silver and other precious metals during their occupation of Britain,' said Sophia. 'But if you found human remains in there… perhaps it was discovered during the Great Plague, and used as a makeshift mausoleum.'

Exeter offered her a grim smile. 'I doubt that, your Ladyship.'

'Have you been there, Mr Exeter?'

'Yes. As soon as the discovery was made, I went down there to take a look for myself. I noted two things which undermine the theory that it had anything to do with the plague.'

'And what are they?'

Exeter didn't answer immediately. Instead, he turned to a large metal file cabinet which stood beside his desk. He unlocked the cabinet with a key taken from his pocket, pulled open the top drawer and withdrew something wrapped in a length of chamois. He placed the package carefully (as if, Sophia thought, it contained an object of great value or fragility) on the desk between them.

'The first thing I noted was that none of the twenty-three skeletons we discovered in the chamber had a skull. They had all been decapitated; their heads are nowhere to be found.'

Sophia swallowed. 'And the second thing?'

Exeter unwrapped the package. '*This* is the second thing,' he said.

Sophia looked at what the package contained, and saw that it was a tile, evidently terracotta, about six inches square and an inch thick. She felt her breath quicken as she saw the symbol which was carved in bas-relief upon its surface.

It was identical to the one which Blackwood had shown her in the *Fantasmata of Simon Castaigne*.

It was the Yellow Sign.

*

The platform was deserted and eerily silent as Blackwood and de Chardin descended the stairs from the ticket hall. Aldgate was one of the earlier Tube Stations; built in 1876, it had been constructed by means of the original cut-and-cover method, by which a trench was excavated and then roofed over. The skylights overhead shone with the dull lemon colour of the overcast sky, their feeble light augmented by three large gaslights spaced along the platform. As the Special Investigator and Templar Detective walked, their heels clicked upon the paving stones, sending faint echoes flitting into the tunnels.

'Feels odd, doesn't it?' said Blackwood quietly.

'A little,' de Chardin replied, glancing around the deserted platform. 'They must have every available man in the tunnels.'

'I daresay.' Blackwood walked to the edge of the platform, leaned over and glanced into the northbound tunnel. The darkness was broken only by a single red signal light and a couple of pale tunnel lights whose glow was quickly overwhelmed and swallowed in the surrounding gloom. With a single, lithe movement, he stepped off the edge and dropped to the ballast with a loud crunch. Turning, he threw a grim smile at de Chardin. 'Shall we?'

The detective took an electric flashlight from his coat pocket and jumped down to join Blackwood, who took out his own light, and together they began to walk along the line into the northbound tunnel.

The darkness was thick and oppressive and seemed to take on a life of its own. Blackwood could feel it upon his skin, touching his face: a repulsively warm caress. The strange tingling in his chest grew more intense as the amulet responded to the presence of... something.

From what seemed like an infinite distance, phantom voices drifted along the tunnel to them. They assumed the voices belonged to the track-walkers and other searchers who were looking for the missing maintenance man. At times, Blackwood thought he could make out Brennan's name being called.

Presently, they came to the place where, according to Tench, Brennan had met his singular end. Blackwood paused and played his flashlight beam over the rails. He bent down and, between thumb and forefinger, plucked a single hair from the metal. As he did so, he felt the amulet stir very slightly in his chest, a curious and unpleasant sensation. 'Something *did* happen here,' he said. 'Something very unusual.'

A sudden breeze took hold of the hair and snatched it away into the darkness.

'Where did that come from?' asked de Chardin. 'There are no trains running in this section of the Underground.'

'The ventilation system?' Blackwood wondered.

As if in answer to their questions, a faint moan drifted along the tunnel towards them. In an instant, Blackwood was standing straight and casting his beam into the darkness.

'Brennan?' whispered de Chardin.

'I rather doubt it.'

The moan sounded again.

'Come on.' Blackwood began to walk along the tunnel again, casting his beam to right and left, the light reflecting periodically from the rails. 'We're getting closer,' he said.

'How can you tell?'

Unconsciously, Blackwood touched his chest. 'I just know.'

De Chardin caught the movement and frowned at his companion. 'And do you know what we're getting closer *to*?'

'I'm not sure... but I'll wager it's something extraordinary.'

De Chardin sighed, and Blackwood could practically hear him thinking, *There's something you're not telling me.* He felt a brief surge of guilt, but he was not about to unbutton his shirt and bear his chest to the detective at this particular moment, nor was he inclined to explain verbally what had happened to him while in the Realm of Faerie. He would share his 'alteration' with de Chardin soon enough, but now was not the time.

They walked a few yards further, and then Blackwood stopped, for the strange tingling in his chest had begun to grow fainter, as though they were now walking away from whatever was causing it. Turning, he played his flashlight beam across the tunnel walls.

'There,' he said, indicating the entrance to a small access tunnel, which they had not noticed as they passed. Without waiting for a response from de Chardin, he moved towards it. As he did so, the tingling returned with renewed intensity, so much so that he had the feeling that the amulet was trying to release itself from the skin in which it was embedded. Blackwood wondered whether it was trying to flee from him or trying to lead him into the deeper darkness ahead.

'Is that where it is?' de Chardin whispered.

'I believe so.'

They stopped at the entrance to the access tunnel, which was barely broad enough to accommodate them side by side, and which was steeped in a darkness more profound than either of them had ever encountered. 'Do you know where this leads?' de Chardin asked.

'I'm not sure. Perhaps it leads to maintenance areas or other Tube tunnels…'

'What an ugly place it is,' said the detective.

Blackwood glanced at him, surprised at the utterance. Nevertheless, he was right: the curved walls of the little tunnel glistened with a mucus-like condensation, and the narrow ribbon of the concrete floor was strewn with black puddles. Ahead, the hungry darkness swallowed their flashlight beams so completely and utterly that they might as well have been trying to illuminate the interplanetary Æther itself.

It was indeed an ugly place, repulsive in its dampness, in the depth and totality of its gloom. It was an affront to the centuried earth through which it had been dug, and for the first time, Blackwood felt with his instinct rather than his conscious intellect that man was not meant to delve too deeply into the great realm of the subterranean.

Nevertheless, the amulet spurred him to movement, although whether its strange stirring was an encouragement or a warning, he couldn't tell.

Slowly and carefully, he entered the tunnel, and as he did so, there came another faint moan from the far distance ahead.

'What do you hope to achieve by this, Blackwood?' de Chardin asked quietly as he followed the Special Investigator through the entrance.

'Why did we come down here in the first place?' Blackwood responded with a grim smile which was invisible to his companion. 'To find answers.'

'And do you think we'll find any in here?'

'That is my intention, but if you'd rather wait outside, I'll quite understand.'

De Chardin grunted. 'You do me a disservice, sir! I'll see this through; you may have no fear on that score.'

It was only then that the detective realised Blackwood's true intention: he meant to gather information not from an examination of the scene at which Seamus Brennan had met his end, but from one of the ghostly creatures who inhabited it. With this realisation, de Chardin's respect for the man grew yet greater, although he could not help but wonder as to the wisdom of Blackwood's strategy. They might learn much from one of the lost souls who dwelt here, but they might just as easily encounter the filthy abnormality that had put an end to Brennan. Nevertheless, it was apparently a risk the Special Investigator was willing to take, and de Chardin had no intention of letting him take it alone.

They moved on through the darkness, the damp walls of the tunnel closing around them in a massive yet tentative embrace. The voice came to them again, a little louder this time, and with its increased volume they became more strongly aware of the plaintiveness of it, the despair, the misery, the terrible loneliness of it.

'I pity the creature that is making that sound,' de Chardin whispered.

'As do I,' Blackwood replied.

Presently, they became aware of a subtle alteration in the quality of the darkness ahead, as if someone or something were stirring there. Blackwood doused his light and asked de Chardin to do the same. After a moment's hesitation, the detective complied, and the darkness became complete... or *almost* complete, for up ahead there came to their eyes a faint glow which painted the distant walls a pale watercolour blue.

'Great God!' said de Chardin. 'There's something there!'

Blackwood had already taken the measure of the floor ahead and had seen no obstacles, and so he continued walking through the thick blackness, his light extinguished, bidding his companion to follow.

Whether the blue glow was stationary or was moving towards them they couldn't tell; it was not long, however, before it filled the tunnel ahead of them, and they were able to discern, at its centre, a tiny, frail figure.

'Who is it?' asked de Chardin, his voice trembling with terrible awe.

'I believe,' Blackwood whispered, 'that it is the ghost of Anne Naylor, also known as the Screaming Spectre.'

*

Sophia felt a curious sense of isolation as her carriage made its way through the noisy, bustling streets towards Whitehall. Her interview with Charles Exeter had concluded shortly after he had shown her the curious terracotta tile containing the Yellow Sign. She had asked him if she might take it with her for further analysis, and, somewhat to her surprise, he had agreed: she had half expected him to be reluctant to part with it, but then there *were* thousands of others in the recently-discovered chamber.

The strange artefact now lay beside her on the seat, wrapped in its chamois. Having also secured his permission to visit the chamber to conduct further investigations (Exeter, indeed, had practically insisted upon it), she had left his office with a strange combination of great elation and profound apprehension clutching at her heart.

Her feeling of isolation grew more intense as she watched the people outside, in the streets, in carriages and omnibuses, all going about their daily business with no inkling of the mysterious drama being played out beneath their feet – a drama which Sophia herself had yet to understand. She had little doubt that the supernatural disturbances in the tunnels of the Underground had their origin in events which had happened a long time ago, perhaps thousands of years, when London was little more than a village, if it existed at all. As to the nature of those events, she could only speculate, and Sophia recognised the danger of speculation when one had so few facts to hand. She needed more information... no, she corrected herself: she and Blackwood needed more information...

She felt a brief flaring of the resentment and indignation which had earlier risen in her, until she recalled Sir William's words: the Special Investigator had merely acted out of concern for her safety, which had nothing to do with his opinion of her abilities. She supposed she was flattered by the gallantry of his concern, however misplaced it might be, and yet, she desperately wanted to face the mystery directly, to confront the origin of the awful strangeness which seemed to have infected the very ground beneath the metropolis, to gain an understanding of it and, if necessary, to vanquish it. The Queen herself had ordered the involvement of the Society for Psychical Research in this affair... and after all, who was Thomas Blackwood to decide how she contributed to the investigation?

Sophia gave a miserable sigh: try as she might, she could not rid herself of her resentment: it smouldered in her heart like the embers of a fire which should have died but refused to do so. She checked her watch: it was nearly half-past four. She hoped that Blackwood and de Chardin had returned from their excursion into the tunnels around Aldgate Station, for, in spite of everything, she found herself looking forward to presenting the Special Investigator with this new and intriguing piece of evidence which she had managed to secure. She glanced again at the chamois-wrapped object on the seat beside her and gave a brief involuntary shudder.

What was the meaning of the Yellow Sign?

The carriage came to a halt outside the grand arched entrance to the Foreign Office. Sophia gathered up the package, stepped down to the street, and, asking her driver to wait for her, walked swiftly up the steps and into the building. With barely a glance at the clerks and other functionaries populating the vast foyer, she strode to the non-descript door in a far corner, which led to the Foreign Office's most secret section.

Very few people possessed a key to this particular door, and of the entire staff of the Society for Psychical Research, only Sophia and Sir William Crookes did so. Sophia quickly unlocked the door and stepped through into a small landing from which an ancient stone staircase descended into the ground. Clutching the package to her breast, she tripped lightly down the stairs, her shadow dancing upon the curving wall in the subdued glow of the gaslights.

In a matter of moments, she had reached the bottom of the staircase and was hurrying along a corridor, at the far end of which a black-uniformed guard stood before a single door. Without a word, the guard glanced at the identification Sophia showed to him and stepped aside to let her pass.

As Sophia entered the outer office of Her Majesty's Bureau of Clandestine Affairs, its sole occupant looked up from her cogitator and smiled. 'Why, good afternoon, Lady Sophia. A pleasure to see you again,' said Grandfather's secretary.

'And for me, Miss Ripley,' Sophia replied, returning her smile. 'I wonder if you could tell me whether Mr Blackwood has returned yet.'

'I'm afraid he hasn't. Would you like to wait for him?'

Sophia sighed. 'Yes, I suppose I should, rather.'

At that moment, the communication funnel on Miss Ripley's desk whistled. 'Yes, sir?' she said into it.

Grandfather's gruff voice issued from the funnel. 'Is that Lady Sophia Harrington there with you, Miss Ripley?'

'Yes, sir, it is.'

'Good. Ask her to step in, would you?'

'Of course.'

Miss Ripley gave a shrug and indicated the door behind her desk.

Sophia walked past the heavy oak file cabinets that lined the outer office and stepped through the door into the office of the head of Her Majesty's Bureau of Clandestine Affairs, the man who was known only by his codename, Grandfather.

As Sophia closed the door behind her, Grandfather stood up from his desk with the faint hiss and clank of his steam-powered artificial legs and strode forward to greet her. As he walked, tiny white clouds emerged from the knees of his trousers, and like everyone else who knew him, Sophia studiously avoided looking at them.

'Good afternoon, your Ladyship,' said Grandfather, extending his hand.

Sophia shook it. 'Good afternoon, Grandfather. I take it you would like an update on my investigations.' She could not resist omitting Blackwood's name from her observation.

'If you'd be so kind. By the way, where is Mr Blackwood?'

So much for that, she thought. 'He is at present examining the scene of the latest encounter at Aldgate Station, in the company of Detective de Chardin of New Scotland Temple.'

Grandfather gave a humourless snort, and his handlebar moustache twitched derisively. 'Encounter, you say. That's a pretty euphemism indeed.' He turned, and clicked and wheezed back to his desk. 'Do have a seat, your Ladyship.'

Sophia sat in one of the two burgundy leather chairs facing the desk and placed the package on her knees.

'Would you care for some tea?' Grandfather asked.

'No, thank you.'

He indicated the package. 'May I ask what you have there?'

Sophia unwrapped the terracotta tile and placed it on the desk for Grandfather to see, explaining how she had come by it. Pressing a monocle to his eye, he leaned forward to examine it. 'What's this symbol?' he asked. 'I've never seen anything like it. What does it mean?'

'It is known as the Yellow Sign. We believe it is associated with a personage known as the King in Yellow, among other things.'

'Never heard of the fellow. Who is he?'

'We're not entirely sure, but we believe that he lives on a distant world called Carcosa.'

'Indeed! And what's his sign doing a hundred feet below the streets of London?'

Sophia sighed. 'I'm afraid we're not entirely sure about that either, sir.'

'And what does Mr Charles Exeter have to say about all this?'

'I believe he is most anxious that we should get to the bottom of the affair as quickly as possible.'

Grandfather snorted again. 'I don't doubt it. The Queen shares his desire for a speedy resolution – as do I. What's your next step?'

'I have requested – and received – Mr Exeter's permission to investigate the chamber in which this object was found. Sir William believes it to be the focal point of the disturbances, their origin and nexus, if you will.'

'Hmm… do you trust Exeter?'

Sophia blinked at the question, her surprise clearly evident upon her face. 'Sir?'

Grandfather leaned back in his chair and regarded her. A faint, aqueous gurgle sounded from beneath the desk. 'I don't like him – don't like the sound of him or the way he's come by his money.'

'It's true his business methods have occasionally been… less than ethical…'

'That's one way of putting it. I don't much care for the cut of his jib; we have more than enough sharp practice going on in London without some Johnnie American sticking his oar in. In your dealings with Mr Exeter, Lady Sophia, I advise you to use the utmost caution. Men like him are never what they seem.'

Sophia considered this in silence for a moment. Was Grandfather simply displaying the British traditionalist's dislike of American extravagance and aggression in matters of finance and commerce? Or was his intuition telling him something of which Sophia was unaware?

He interrupted her thoughts with another question. 'Mr Blackwood mentioned Simon Castaigne, the occultist. Do you know anything about him?'

Sophia hesitated, feeling suddenly helpless. 'I... regret to say that I do not – aside from his apparent connection with Carcosa. He claims to have travelled there – non-corporeally, that is. This sign,' she indicated the tile, 'is reproduced in a book he wrote, called the–'

'The *Fantasmata*; yes, Blackwood told me.'

Grandfather regarded her, and Sophia had the sudden feeling that he was less than impressed with her contribution to the investigation. Again, she felt indignation rising in her; after all, it was she who had secured the tile, she who had discovered the direct link between Carcosa and the disturbances on the Underground. And yet, she realised miserably, that was not really true. Exeter's workers had been the ones to discover the artefact and the chamber in which it had lain for untold centuries; she had merely asked to borrow it! And it had been Blackwood who had made the connection between Alfie Morgan's ramblings and the distant, mysterious planet...

She felt a flush of embarrassment blooming upon her cheeks, which only served to increase her annoyance. 'Dr Castaigne is delivering a lecture this evening at the Society of Spiritualistic Freemasons in Mayfair,' she said. 'It is Mr Blackwood's and my intention to attend and to speak with him afterwards, if possible.'

Grandfather chuckled. 'Blackwood will *make* it possible, my dear – have no fear on that score.'

Of course, Sophia thought bitterly. *Blackwood will make it possible.*

'Well,' said Grandfather, pushing the tile towards Sophia. 'I'm sure Blackwood will get to the bottom of this – with your able assistance, of course, your Ladyship. I don't think I need detain you any longer.'

Sophia forced a smile as she replied, 'Thank you, sir. We will of course keep you informed of further developments.'

'You're most kind.'

Sophia re-wrapped the tile and returned to the outer office, where she sat down in a chair to wait for Blackwood.

I'm sure Blackwood will get to the bottom of this, she thought. *With my able assistance indeed! Why, he is quite incorrigible in his condescension!*

Miss Ripley glanced at her occasionally as she continued with her own work but said nothing. She had taken in the look on Sophia's face and decided that silence would be far more prudent than any attempt at conversation.

Sophia tried to gather herself and calm down a little and then a thought came to her... and that thought was comprised of three names: *Exeter, Carcosa, Castaigne.*

She repeated them under her breath. 'Exeter... Carcosa... Castaigne.' Was there a greater, more profound connection between them than she had hitherto supposed? Grandfather had intimated that Exeter was not to be trusted and that recollection had set off in Sophia's mind a curious train of thought which she was at present unable to formulate properly, but which nagged at her consciousness, refusing to be ignored.

In an instant, the decision was made, and Sophia felt a thrill of fear and excited anticipation as she hastily bid goodbye to Miss Ripley and hurried from the office and the Bureau.

'Where to, your Ladyship?' asked her driver.

'To Mr Blackwood's apartments if you please, John,' she replied. 'I need to leave a message for him with his housekeeper.'

*

The small girl approached Blackwood and de Chardin – although neither man could be entirely sure whether she was walking or gliding over the floor of the tunnel. In any event, they were unaware of any movement on the surface of the puddles as she moved over them. The blue glow that emanated from her frail body now filled the tunnel, so that they could see both her and each other quite clearly. She came to a halt and looked up at them in silence.

'Hello, child,' said de Chardin very quietly, his voice nevertheless echoing along the narrow tunnel.

The little ghost simply gazed up at him.

'Your name is Anne, isn't it?' said Blackwood gently.

She offered him no verbal response; instead, her eyes became fixed upon his chest, and a frown spread across her pale blue face. Slowly, she raised a slender arm and pointed to his heart, and Blackwood felt the tingling sensation, which had begun as soon as he entered the station, surge like a cold rain through his body.

The amulet, he thought. *She's aware of it and wants to see it*.

Slowly, he undid the top buttons of his shirt and drew aside the fabric to reveal the metal tracery embedded in his skin. De Chardin watched him and drew in his breath when he saw the irregular five-pointed star with the staring eye at its centre. 'What the deuce...?' he whispered.

'I'll explain later,' said Blackwood, his gaze still fixed upon the child.

'That is something of our world,' said the ghost of Anne Naylor, her voice heartbreaking in its ethereal fragility.

'Yes, Anne,' Blackwood replied. 'It is.'

'Are you of our world?' she asked.

'No, I am not, but I have friends who are. One of them gave me this gift.'

'Who?'

'Oberon, King of the Faeries.'

'Oberon...' whispered Anne Naylor. 'I have never seen a faerie. Are they as beautiful as people say?'

'Yes, they are.' Blackwood buttoned up his shirt again, and the ghost's outstretched arm dropped once more to her

129

side. 'Why are you here, Anne? You're far from the place where you normally linger.'

The child frowned up at Blackwood again. 'The place where I linger?'

'Farringdon Street Station.'

'Is that what it's called? I didn't know. What I am is like a dream. I don't like it there anymore.'

'Why not?' asked de Chardin.

The ghost regarded him with eyes that were dead and yet alive: eyes that were looking back from the other side of the veil which hides the ultimate mystery of human existence. Her voice became yet more tremulous as she replied, 'There is something there which I don't want to look at.'

Blackwood and de Chardin glanced at each other. 'What is it, Anne?' said Blackwood. 'What's there?'

'A monster,' she whispered. 'A horrible monster.'

'Can you describe it?' asked de Chardin.

Anne Naylor closed her eyes and sighed. 'Where would I be if Sarah hadn't killed me? I wouldn't be here... where would I be?'

'Who is Sarah?' de Chardin whispered into Blackwood's ear.

'Anne was an orphan. She was adopted by a seamstress named Sarah Metyard,' Blackwood explained. 'She was most cruelly treated by Metyard, who eventually murdered her. She cut up her body and disposed of it in the sewer at Chick Lane, but parts of the body were later discovered. Metyard's daughter turned her in, and she was convicted at the Old Bailey in 1768 and sentenced to death. As was the practice then, her body was given to the Surgeons' Hall to be dissected by medical students.'

'A fitting end,' de Chardin observed, 'given the appalling nature of her crime.' He regarded the little ghost, whose eyes were still closed, as if she were struggling to imagine a gentler history for herself. 'Poor little devil,' he whispered.

'Anne,' said the Special Investigator. 'We need your help to rid this place of the... the monster.'

Her eyes opened.

'Can you describe it to us?'

'Nobody likes it,' she said. 'None of us who linger here like it. It frightens us... makes us want to go away. But we can't... it won't let us. It gathers us.'

'Gathers you?' Blackwood recalled the words of Barrymore Tench in the police cell. *Even the dead are afraid of what's down there.* 'What do you mean it gathers you?'

Anne Naylor began to weep.

Blackwood sensed that she was preparing to flee, back into the labyrinthine darkness of the Underground. 'Listen to me, Anne,' he said, quietly yet urgently. 'If you help us, we can rid this place of the monster, and I promise that when all this is over, I will do my best to help you.'

She shook her head. 'How can you help me?'

'You do not belong here, in the grime and the darkness. I promise I will help you to enter the other world, the place which is hidden from you by the fear and despair of your earlier life, and by the dreadful way in which that life ended.'

'I want to leave,' she whispered, 'but the monster won't let me. It won't let *any* of us.'

'I will help you, but first you must help us. What do you mean when you say it won't let you leave, that it *gathers* you?'

'It takes us inside – thousands of us, the ones who died of the big disease in the olden days. It's got them all inside itself – they can't get out...'

'Good God,' said de Chardin with a shudder. 'Sounds like the thing has *eaten* them.'

The child seemed to consider this for some moments and then said, 'No, not eaten. It *gathered* them. That's why we're all so afraid.'

'And why is it doing that, Anne? Do you know?'

Anne seemed about to answer: she opened her mouth to speak but then stopped and began to glance fearfully around.

'What is it?' Blackwood asked.

'Something is coming.' She turned her terrified gaze upon them, and as she did so, Blackwood felt the amulet in his skin begin to throb urgently. 'Oh, sirs, you must flee, for *it is coming!*'

As if in response to her cry, there came to their ears a low, rumbling, echoing moan, as of something vast and powerful and unthinkably malignant moving through the earth.

'Great God, what is that?' said de Chardin.

'Whatever it is, it's coming towards us,' Blackwood replied, glancing each way along the tunnel.

'Back the way you came, sirs!' cried Anne. 'Back the way you came!'

The concrete floor beneath their feet began to tremble with the passage of the unseen thing, the black oily puddles rippling with the vibration. The guttural moan sounded again. Damp, obscene and utterly blasphemous, it gave the impression of having been produced by something which had never walked – *should* never walk – upon God's Earth.

'It sounds massive,' said Blackwood. 'But how can that be? Such a creature would destroy the entire Underground!'

'This is no time for analytical thinking, sir,' declared de Chardin. 'Let's take the waif's advice and get the deuce out of here!'

Blackwood glanced at the ghost child. 'Come with us, Anne.'

But it was quite evident that Anne Naylor had no intention of doing so. She opened her mouth, gave a single, piercing scream and vanished, plunging the tunnel into darkness.

Both Blackwood and de Chardin had their flashlights out in an instant, as the tunnel floor began to buckle as if in the grip of some horrible, unnatural earthquake. The moan sounded yet again, much closer now, and in spite of his terror, Blackwood marvelled at the sheer, incredible *power* of it. As he and de Chardin ran back along the tunnel towards the main Tube line, he thought again that whatever was making the sound must be truly gigantic – the size of a whale, or bigger. How could such a creature exist down here?

Unless it were not corporeal in any sense which was described or accepted by science; in which case, it would not be confined to the tunnels, but would be capable of moving through the ground as easily as a man walks through the air…

In a few moments, they gained the main line running out of Aldgate and took some comfort from the fitful glow of the lights mounted upon the walls. But that comfort was short-lived indeed, for away in the distance in the depths of the tunnel, another sound came to them: the sound of men screaming.

'It's the search party!' de Chardin cried. 'The fiend has got them!'

He made to run towards the sound, but Blackwood grabbed his arm. 'No, de Chardin!'

The detective turned to face him. 'What do you mean "no"? Those men are in dire peril. We must help them!'

'And how do you propose to do that? Think about it, man! Whatever the thing is, we'll be just as powerless against it as those poor wretches.'

'Do you suggest we run? Save our own skins?'

Blackwood caught the tone of disgust in de Chardin's voice, and felt a sudden wave of anger rising in him. 'Do you suggest we sacrifice ourselves in some stupid gesture of futile gallantry? And what then? The thing will still be there to wreak whatever havoc it wishes!'

For how much longer this argument might have lasted, neither Blackwood nor de Chardin could have said, but as they stood glaring at each other, the awful sounds emanating from the depths of the tunnel ceased: the screams of the men and the vast, wet moans of their unseen and unthinkable tormentor, fell away into complete silence.

CHAPTER FIVE:
A Lecture and a Revelation

It was a little after eight o'clock in the evening when Sophia's carriage brought her to the Langham Hotel in Marylebone. The late afternoon had been a busy one. From the Bureau, she had gone first to Blackwood's apartments in Chelsea, to leave a message with Mrs Butters that she would be unable to accompany him to the lecture they had planned to attend (she knew that he would go home at some point to dress for the evening). Then she had returned to the SPR headquarters in Kensington, where she had switched on her cogitator and connected to the Æther.

Her intention was to discover where Simon Castaigne was staying while in London. Blackwood, of course, could have found out for her, but she'd had no intention of asking him. She wanted to do this by herself, and she certainly didn't want to risk his vetoing her plan.

'With my able assistance,' she muttered, while she waited for the astral connection to be established between her machine and the Akashic Records. 'Pah! I'll show both him and Grandfather how ably *I* may assist!'

The cogitator's scrying glass glowed with a faint, pearly luminescence, and a message appeared in elegant characters:

You are now connected to the Æther.
Please type in your next command.

Sophia typed:

I WOULD LIKE TO KNOW WHERE DR SIMON
CASTAIGNE IS STAYING WHILE IN LONDON.

The characters dissolved, and were replaced with another message.

Please wait while a search is made of the Akashic Records.

Sophia's fingertips drummed impatiently on her desk while she waited for the information. Presently, it appeared.

Dr Castaigne has reserved a room at the
Langham Hotel in Marylebone.

It is noted that the hotel is equipped with a cogitator.
Would you like to send a message to him?

Sophia typed:

NO, THANK YOU.
I WOULD, HOWEVER, LIKE TO KNOW WHICH
ROOM HE IS STAYING IN.

Another few moments passed, and then the cogitator responded:

He is staying in Room 304.

Sophia smiled in satisfaction as she switched off the machine and left her office.

Now, as she descended from her carriage and stood before the imposing edifice of the Langham Hotel, she felt both her resolve and her self-satisfaction waver a little. Somewhere in her mind, a voice said, *This is really no way for a lady to behave.*

No, she supposed, it really wasn't.

And what will Thomas say when he finds out?

She really didn't care what Thomas would say: if he had not the good manners or wherewithal to congratulate her on her initiative, that would hardly be any concern of hers! And would his scruples prevent him from acting on any information she managed to secure this evening? She rather doubted it.

Nevertheless, the little voice would not be silenced and continued to admonish her even as she ascended the wide steps and entered through the massive portico.

Sophia was well acquainted with the Langham Hotel: the restaurant boasted one of the greatest chefs in the world (the man had trained with Escoffier himself), and she had dined there on a number of occasions. As she entered the vast and opulently appointed foyer, the hotel's manager, who happened to be passing, noticed her and came over.

'Lady Sophia,' he said. 'A pleasure to see you.'

'Good evening, Mr Broughton,' she replied, feeling her heart begin to beat even faster. 'I trust you are well.'

'Never better, your Ladyship. Are you dining here tonight?'

'Ah, no. I am visiting an old friend who is staying here.'

'I see. If you would be so kind as to tell me the room number, I shall arrange for champagne to be sent up with the compliments of the Langham.'

Sophia's heart jumped in her chest. 'You are most kind, Mr Broughton, but that will not be necessary. We have made arrangements to attend the theatre, and so we cannot linger.'

Broughton smiled and gave a brief, shallow bow. 'Of course, I understand. In that case, I shall wish you a pleasant evening.'

'You're most kind.'

Sophia walked on across the foyer towards the bank of pneumatic elevators lining a far wall. *You fool!* she thought. *Why did you say that? Now, if he sees you leave, he'll wonder where your imaginary friend is!* In fact, Broughton had caught Sophia completely off guard. She normally took a very dim view of lying and was not used to uttering untruths herself, and for this reason her own lie had been a clumsy one. Fortunately, Broughton's impeccable manners had prevented him from pressing her further on the location of her 'friend', and she could only hope that, once her mission was complete, she would manage to leave the hotel without him seeing her.

Her face flushed with embarrassment, Sophia entered an elevator and asked the boy for the third floor, reflecting that she really wasn't cut out for this kind of thing.

*

Blackwood was feeling wretched for several reasons. He and de Chardin had made a search of the tunnels but had found no trace of the search party whose screams they had heard, nor of the unseen thing which had apparently attacked them. As they probed the darkness, he had felt a burning shame at his reluctance to seek out and face the thing directly, to offer whatever aid might have been possible to the poor wretches who were now nowhere to be found. He had continued to sense de Chardin's antipathy, and the fact that he knew himself to be right did nothing to alleviate his sense of embarrassment at having spurned the idea of rushing headlong to meet the aggressor. *If de Chardin thinks me a coward, then de Chardin is a fool*, he told himself, for he had no doubt that it would have been suicide to do battle with the massive abnormality whose abhorrent moaning they had heard.

In fact, something else was weighing on his mind much more heavily than his spat with the Templar detective. While Alfie Morgan had apparently not been touched by the fiend, Seamus Brennan most certainly had been, and now the party of men who had been looking for him were nowhere to be found. Walter Goodman-Brown had opined that it had been merely curious about Morgan, but it had certainly gone on the offensive with Brennan and the others. What was the reason? Did it consider them a threat? Was it acting offensively... or *defensively*, like an animal protecting its territory?

If that was the case, Blackwood asked himself, what was the thing defending?

Now that he and de Chardin were safely out of the tunnels, he began to regret not having allowed Sophia to join them. With the benefit of hindsight, that decision now seemed rather callous, for it was clear that she desperately wanted to make a contribution to the investigation. Indeed, the Queen had made it quite plain that she desired the involvement of the SPR in this affair, and after all, who was Blackwood to prevent Sophia from doing her part?

He brooded uncomfortably on the matter as his hansom approached Chelsea in the gathering dusk. That Sophia was more than capable of holding her own, he had no doubt, and yet, the fact remained that she was a woman, and Blackwood could not free himself of the conviction that physical danger should be the province of men alone.

He was aware of another reason for his reluctance to expose Sophia to peril, but he much preferred not to dwell on that. He was sure de Chardin knew, or suspected, and he could only hope that Sophia's anger had clouded her vision enough to prevent her from realising the truth. It was, after all, most inconvenient: an annoying and potentially hazardous distraction which he would do well to put aside.

It was important that their relationship be placed once again on a firm professional footing, based on mutual respect and trust. As the cab came to a halt outside his apartment building, Blackwood decided that the best course of action would be to offer Sophia a sincere apology and promise not to pull rank on her in such a belittling way again. All the same, it would be difficult, for Thomas Blackwood was not a man used to apologising.

It was therefore with no small measure of relief that he received the news from Mrs Butters that Lady Sophia would be unable to attend the lecture with him this evening. Under other circumstances, he might have felt some irritation with her, but he found himself far from averse to the idea of postponing the apology he had decided to offer. Blackwood was not normally a man to put off until tomorrow what he could do today, but on this occasion, he felt a certain satisfaction in being able to do so.

He thanked Mrs Butters and went to his dressing room to prepare for the evening.

*

Sophia emerged from the elevator on the third floor and walked along the corridor to room 304. She knocked on the door and waited, this time with a better-prepared lie at the ready in case Simon Castaigne should still be there. There was, however, no answer: he must already have left for his speaking engagement. Checking that the corridor was still empty of guests or hotel staff, Sophia withdrew her lock-pick from her purse and quickly inserted it in the keyhole. A brief twist and the door was open. She stepped swiftly inside, closed and locked the door behind her.

Her heart was now racing wildly with a combination of excitement and apprehension that, she had to admit, bordered on the intoxicating. Who would have thought that breaking and entering could hold such a strange allure?

She turned up the gaslights and quickly took in her surroundings. Castaigne had spared no expense on his accommodation while in London. She was standing in the sitting room of a large suite; through an open door she could see the bedroom, while another door, closed, presumably led to the bathroom and water closet. The sitting room was decorated with all the sumptuous elegance for which the Langham was famed, and Sophia recalled Blackwood's description of Castaigne as a man of independent and substantial means.

As she looked around, her eye was immediately caught by a large Gladstone bag, which was standing on the floor next to a Chippendale escritoire on the far side of the room. Putting on her gloves (and congratulating herself that such a precaution had even occurred to her), she hurried over and placed the bag on the escritoire. She tried the clasps. It was unlocked. She opened it and looked inside.

The bag contained a large sheaf of papers, bound together with a ribbon of red silk, and a Moroccan leather box, similar in appearance to a shaving case. Sophia took out the papers and quickly leafed through them. They contained notes handwritten in a small, meticulous script. As her eyes skimmed the sheets, she noticed references to Carcosa, to the King in Yellow, and also to something called the Lake of Hali. She recalled that the Song of Cassilda, which Blackwood had read to her from Castaigne's book, contained reference to a lake…

As she examined the notes, it occurred to her that the title of his lecture was *The Plurality of Life on Other Worlds*… and yet she could find no mention of any world other than Carcosa in the notes. She set the sheaf of papers aside and turned her attention to the leather box, which she opened slowly and carefully, unsure of what she would find inside.

The contents consisted of a dozen glass ampoules, an inch or so long, which contained a fine, dark powder. Sophia took out one of the ampoules and held it up to the light. *And what is this, I wonder?* she thought.

The answer came to her almost immediately. *Of course! It must be the Taduki drug which Mr Shanahan mentioned – the means by which Castaigne is able to send his mind voyaging through the Æther.*

As she held the tiny ampoule in the palm of her hand, gazing at it in fascination, another thought occurred to her, and she caught her breath at the danger and audacity of it. Without allowing herself time to reconsider, Sophia thrust the ampoule into a pocket of her coat.

She was about to return to the notes and go through them in greater detail, when there was a metallic click behind her.

She spun around, her heart jumping wildly. The door to the suite was being unlocked. *Oh good heavens!* she thought, as panic seized her. *Castaigne has returned!*

Glancing this way and that, her eyes fell upon the door to the bathroom, and in another moment she had flown across the room and into her makeshift hiding place, closing the door behind her just as the door to the suite opened.

Panting with fear, Sophia stood in the darkness, for she dared not turn up the gas. She heard the door being closed again. Her only hope was that Castaigne had forgotten something and had returned only briefly to retrieve it. With any luck, he would be gone in a trice... but then Sophia realised that he would see his bag open and the contents placed on the escritoire. He would know that someone had entered without his permission and gone through his things, and without a doubt he would wonder if the intruder were still in the room.

What would he do then? Would he call for the hotel's security? Or would he make a search of the suite himself? Either way, she would be discovered, and she could imagine the look on Blackwood's face when he found out.

Standing there in the darkness with her heart pounding in her chest, Sophia realised that her only chance of escape would be if Castaigne went into the bedroom: then she might just be able to leave the bathroom and slip out of the suite unobserved.

She crouched down, silently withdrew the key from the keyhole and peered through the tiny opening.

What she saw made her gasp.

There were two men in the sitting room, wearing dark suits and grim expressions. They glanced around the room and, without exchanging a word, moved quickly and silently to the escritoire, where they began to examine the contents of Castaigne's Gladstone bag.

Oh good Lord! Sophia thought. *They are intruders, like me!*

*

Blackwood's hansom stopped outside the Hall of the Society of Spiritualistic Freemasons in Mayfair. He had never visited this Lodge before, and his face twisted in distaste at the grim ugliness of the building's edifice, with its fat grey columns and square windows.

He paid the cabbie and hurried through the chill evening air to the entrance, where he showed his invitation to the doorman and was ushered inside.

The entrance hall was decorated in typical Masonic fashion: the floor was of blue and white marble in a chequered pattern, while the walls held numerous paintings and symbols, each of which had a particular and arcane meaning. There was, of course, the principal symbol of the Square and Compass, common to all Masonic Lodges; in addition, however, there were symbols with which Blackwood was unfamiliar, at least in the context of Freemasonry. On one wall, for instance, there was a large engraving of the letters of the alphabet, which surrounded an arrow-like feature. Blackwood surmised that it represented a Ouija Board. Another wall was dominated by a rather well-executed oil painting of a man lying prone in bed, his form duplicated in a figure composed of smoke-like wisps hovering above, their heads connected to each other by a thin, silvery strand. This clearly represented the astral self, separated from the physical body, perhaps preparing to journey into the realms of the spirit...

Blackwood's inspection of the decor was curtailed by the approach of a stout man with thinning grey hair and a magnificent handlebar moustache. Over his evening suit, he wore a pale blue sash, upon which several Masonic symbols were stitched in gold.

'Mr Thomas Blackwood?' the man said.

'I am he.'

The man offered him a broad smile. 'I bid you good evening and welcome, sir. I am Cuthbert Fforbes-Maclellan, Worshipful Master of the Society of Spiritualistic Freemasons.' He offered his hand, which Blackwood shook in the Masonic fashion.

'An honour, Worshipful Master.'

'We were hoping you'd be able to make it,' said Fforbes-Maclellan. 'This evening promises to be a most fascinating and educative one.'

'I don't doubt it. In fact, I wouldn't have missed it for the world.'

'Splendid! I trust you are familiar with the work of Dr Castaigne?'

'Intimately,' Blackwood lied, hoping that his frenzied reading of the *Fantasmata* two days ago would see him through. 'I'm looking forward to hearing his theories on the plurality of inhabited worlds...'

Fforbes-Maclellan frowned. 'Theories?'

Dash it all! Blackwood thought. *My first* faux pas *of the evening.* 'Forgive me, Worshipful Master, I'm still wearing my Special Investigator's hat. I was merely speaking in those terms with which I am most familiar in the pursuance of my day-to-day duties on behalf of the Crown.'

Fforbes-Maclellan beamed at him once again. 'Not at all, Mr Blackwood. I quite understand, and I would be the first to express my thanks and admiration for the fine work you and the Bureau do on behalf of Her Majesty and the Empire. It is important to remember, however, that Dr Castaigne has seen with his own eyes the wonders he will share with us tonight. His work is based much more on direct observation than abstract theory.'

'Quite so, and I stand corrected.'

Fforbes-Maclellan deftly lifted two glasses of champagne from a tray carried by a passing Apprentice and handed one to Blackwood, who nodded his thanks and said, 'Tell me, sir: have you known Dr Castaigne for long?'

'Oh my, no! In fact, I barely know him at all. It was a most unexpected honour when he contacted us and asked us if we would like to host his lecture.'

'Then his reputation for reclusiveness is well-founded?'

'I should say so. From what I can gather, his journey through the Orient affected him most profoundly. He has few friends and seems to have divorced himself almost completely from the run of humanity, preferring to devote himself exclusively to his research.'

'An unusual fellow. Does anyone know how he manages to send his mind through the Luminiferous Æther?'

'I don't believe he has ever divulged that particular piece of information.' Fforbes-Maclellan gave him a sudden, keen look. 'I don't suppose *you* know...'

'I'm afraid not,' Blackwood replied. If Dr Castaigne wanted the source of his singular ability to remain a secret, Blackwood would oblige. It had already occurred to him that the Taduki drug could become a powerful tool of espionage for the Empire. Properly trained in its use, a spy could send his mind to any part of the globe without detection; the potential for information gathering was boundless – if the secret of Taduki could only be discovered...

'Where is your illustrious guest at present?' Blackwood asked.

'In the quarters we have prepared for him. In fact,' Fforbes-Maclellan added, taking out his fob watch and consulting it, 'I believe it is time we made our way to the lecture theatre.' He turned away from Blackwood and addressed the other guests, some of whom were milling around, while others gathered in small groups, conversing quietly yet excitedly with each other. 'Ladies and gentlemen, if I may have your attention. Dr Castaigne is due to begin his lecture in five minutes. If you will kindly follow me...'

With the other guests in tow, Blackwood followed Fforbes-Maclellan along a wide, brightly-lit corridor towards a set of double doors, which gave onto the lecture theatre. As he entered the room, Blackwood saw that the word 'theatre' was something of an exaggeration. In fact, the forty or so guests had trouble fitting into what was in reality little more than a large drawing room crammed with uncomfortable-looking high-backed chairs. A glance at several depressions in the carpet told Blackwood that the normal furnishings had been removed to make room for the gathering. On the far side of the drawing room, a plain wooden lectern stood like a lonely sentinel.

At Fforbes-Maclellan's invitation, Blackwood seated himself beside the Worshipful Master in the front row, and a few moments later, a door behind the lectern opened, and Simon Castaigne entered the room.

As he joined in the polite applause, Blackwood took in the man's appearance, which was in fact quite impressive. He was a shade under six feet in height, and although he appeared quite thin, it seemed to Blackwood's well-practiced eye that this was due more to a healthy asceticism than poverty of diet. In fact, Castaigne moved with a lithe and languid elegance which hinted at considerable physical power held in check. If the stories which were told of his exploits in the Far East were even half true, it was a fair bet that he could acquit himself favourably in a scrape. His high-cheekboned face was as thin as his wiry frame, but his skin glowed with health and vigour, and his neatly-trimmed goatee was of the same raven hue as his thick, slightly unruly hair.

Castaigne gave a slight bow in acknowledgment of the applause, which died down as he reached out and laid his hands upon the lectern, assuming a relaxed pose. For a recluse, thought Blackwood, he appeared remarkably at ease in front of an audience.

'Ladies and gentlemen,' he began in a quiet yet subtly commanding voice. 'May I first of all thank Worshipful Master Fforbes-Maclellan for allowing me to visit this most august society, and for extending to me the hand of friendship and hospitality. The title of my presentation to you this evening is "The Plurality of Life on Other Worlds", and yet I must confess that the title is not entirely accurate, for it is not of worlds in the plural I wish to speak, but one world in particular. And the name of that world is... Carcosa.'

*

Crouched beside the bathroom door, hardly daring to breathe, Sophia continued to press her eye to the keyhole.

One of the men had produced a camera from a small valise he was carrying and was taking photographs of Dr Castaigne's notes, while his accomplice held one of the ampoules up to the light and peered at it.

'What do you think this is?' he asked quietly. 'Opium?'

The other man stopped what he was doing and gave the ampoule a cursory glance. 'Don't know,' he replied in an equally hushed tone. 'Looks a bit like it. We'll take one of those with us. Whatever the stuff is, Exeter will want a sample.'

Exeter! thought Sophia. A wave of realisations flooded her mind. Grandfather was right: clearly, there was much more to the railway magnate than met the eye. In fact, she now realised, he obviously knew the identity of the strange symbol embossed on the terracotta tile, even though he had not mentioned it to her. Exeter had made the connection between the events on the Underground and Carcosa; he knew of Castaigne's knowledge regarding the distant planet, and had sent two lackeys to gather some more information. The question was: why be so underhand about it? Why not simply approach Castaigne openly? Sophia was quite certain that, despite his reputation for reclusiveness, the occultist would not forego the opportunity to investigate the recently-discovered chamber for himself. If Exeter wanted information on what his workers had inadvertently discovered, there could have been no more qualified man to talk to than Simon Castaigne.

And yet, he had not done so. Instead, he had sent two of his own people to *steal* that information.

Why?

The man with the camera continued to take pictures of the notes, while the other placed the ampoule in a pocket and looked around the room. 'I'm going to check the rest of the place,' he said. 'There may be something useful in his luggage.'

'Good idea,' said the photographer, without pausing in his task.

Sophia felt her fear tighten its grip upon her heart as she watched the man walk across the sitting room. 'The rest of the place' consisted of the bedroom – and the bathroom in which she was hiding. It would only be a matter of moments before the intruder discovered her, and then...

She glanced around wildly, her eyes darting here and there in the gloom, but there was nowhere she could go – apart from a small window with frosted glass which was set high in the wall next to the bath. She hurried to it and reached up towards the latch, but it was too high, and so, gathering her skirt, she climbed onto the rim of the bath and tried again.

Balanced precariously, the heels of her boots hardly suited to such a position, Sophia managed to undo the latch and pull the window open. Gripping the sill with both hands, she then hauled herself up until she was halfway through, but then she looked down, and stopped, panting, her heart withering with despair.

She had hoped and expected there to be a ledge beneath the window, onto which she could lower herself. But there was nothing of the kind on this side of the building: it was a sheer drop of sixty feet or more to the street below.

Suddenly, the idea of being discovered by the hotel manager seemed like the most blessed of reprieves.

Sophia lowered herself from the window and turned to face the bathroom door. There was no escape. In another few moments, the intruder would complete his search of the suite by coming in here. What would happen then, she dared not contemplate.

She crouched once again and looked through the keyhole. She saw the man approaching the bathroom door. Desperate to delay her discovery by even a few moments, she instinctively thrust the key back into the lock, quickly turned it and withdrew it again so that she might continue to view what was happening on the other side of the door. The man stopped suddenly and turned to his accomplice.

'Great God!' he exclaimed. 'There's someone in the bathroom.'

'What?'

'I tell you there's someone in the bathroom!'

Sophia backed away from the door, looking wildly around for something, anything, which she could use as a weapon. Her eye fell upon Castaigne's shaving case, which lay upon a shelf above the sink. She opened it with trembling hands and seized the straight razor which she found inside. It would be little help against two large male adversaries, she knew, but it was something.

The doorknob rattled as one of the intruders tried it.

'What should we do?' asked a voice.

'We should get the door open and see who's in there,' replied the other in an exasperated tone.

Sophia gave a silent gasp, and took a step back from the door.

'Castaigne?'

'It's not him. He'll be at his lecture by now.'

'A chamber maid, perhaps?'

'Perhaps... or perhaps not.'

'What do you mean? We should leave.'

'Not yet.'

'You're not thinking of...?'

'Whoever's in there heard you use his name. We'll have to take them with us. There's a fire escape at the end of the corridor outside; we'll take them that way.'

'And then?'

'We'll get rid of them. We can't risk exposing him. Damn it, you shouldn't have used his name!'

'I didn't know there'd be someone here!'

'Never mind that now.'

'What are you doing?'

'What does it *look* like I'm doing? I'm picking the lock.'

As the voice said this, Sophia heard a soft scratching and clicking coming from the keyhole. She took another step back, clutching the handle of the razor and looking down at it, wishing it were a revolver.

'Got it,' said one of the men, and Sophia's heart jumped into her throat as the doorknob turned once again.

*

'I see by your expressions that you are familiar with the name Carcosa,' Simon Castaigne said, as he regarded his audience. 'No doubt because you have done me the honour of reading my privately-published treatise describing my travels through the Luminiferous Æther, during which my mind voyaged to many worlds. I need not dwell on the means by which I am able to effect this singular mode of travel, nor will I waste time describing the worlds I have seen – save Carcosa... for it is of Carcosa alone that I wish to speak to you this evening.'

Castaigne hesitated, and Blackwood noted that the blood seemed to have drained from the occultist's face, while a dark and pensive frown crept across his brow. *What's up with the fellow?* he wondered, glancing at Cuthbert Fforbes-Maclellan, who merely offered him a small shrug.

'Ladies and gentlemen,' Castaigne continued, 'I beg your forgiveness, for this is not easy for me to talk about – and yet talk about it I must, to the only people in the country who will believe me, and who will take heed of the warning I bring tonight.'

A warning? thought Blackwood. *A warning about Carcosa?*

'I am certain that you came to this gathering with the expectation of hearing of the new wonders I have encountered during my latest travels,' the occultist said with a great sigh. 'And while it is true that I *have* seen much to wonder at, I have seen a great deal more to make the heart tremble – the very *soul*, in fact!

'To begin with, allow me to reacquaint you with Carcosa. It is a world which orbits not one sun, but two, in the group of stars known by astronomers on Earth as the Hyades. Its parent stars form a binary system known as Theta Tauri and are more than nine hundred trillion miles from Earth – an unthinkable distance, to be sure, but one which, as I hope to demonstrate to you this evening, is in reality as insignificant as the distance between each of you and your neighbours.

'Theta Tauri are ancient stars, of far greater age than our own Sun, and Carcosa is therefore an equally ancient world. It is mentioned occasionally in some of the less reputable of humanity's myth cycles, and has even made an appearance in modern literature. Those of you who are familiar with the work of that admirable curmudgeon Mr Ambrose Bierce will be aware that he could not resist penning a fragment, in which he hints at Carcosa actually being an ancient city on Earth, but that was only because even that great disliker of humanity could not bring himself to utter the truth: that Carcosa is in reality an entire world drifting through the dark depths of space, and that it contains secrets that no sane man or woman would do well to contemplate.'

Castaigne paused to pour himself a glass of water from a small jug which had been placed on the lectern for him. Blackwood leaned forward in his seat, fascinated. As he waited for the occultist to continue, he mused briefly that it was a shame Sophia could not be present, and then all thoughts of her and their unfortunate disagreement left him as Castaigne continued.

'Ladies and gentlemen, I have come here this evening to tell you of the last journey I made to Carcosa and of what

I learned there. It was just a few days ago that I made the usual preparations for the voyage and then lay upon my bed while my consciousness made ready to leave my physical body behind.

'I closed my eyes, and almost immediately became aware once again of my surroundings, with the eyeless sight of the unfettered mind. I rose from my body towards the ceiling of my bedroom and then *through* it and upwards through the roof of my house and into the boundless sky above.

'Unencumbered by physicality, my mind soared away from the Earth, leaving our beautiful blue-green world far behind and plunging into the star-strewn void of the Luminiferous Æther. According to the means by which I am able to induce my mental travels, I found the route to the Hyades with great swiftness and felicity and passed across the countless leagues of space as easily as one passes from one room of a house to another.

'I watched the flight of the stars in rapture, for you may believe that one never gets used to the vastness and ineffable splendour of this universe of ours. Like fireflies in the darkest night they hurtled past me – or rather, *I* hurtled past *them*, on and on through the great Æther, overwhelmed by my contemplation of the vast spray of light which extended in every direction, on and on into eternity beyond eternity.

'And then, presently, I came to my destination: the giant twin suns of Theta Tauri, smouldering baleful in the infinite night, seething and muttering in their unthinkable age, and there beside them, Carcosa, with its four strange moons, which do not behave as moons should.

'I entered the atmosphere and descended towards the great Lake of Hali, vast and mysterious, whose surface is covered with the clouds which break like waves upon its shores, where stand the last of Carcosa's cities, Alar, Hastur and Yhtill, and I watched the moons rise *in front of* the cities' towers, for those moons are bound by no physical law which pertains to the ordered cosmos.

'I swept across the surface of Hali, not daring to contemplate what lay beneath, towards Yhtill, the largest city, while above me the stars shone blackly in the dead grey sky and the mad moons circled, at once far away and near. I rode the cloud waves as they surged towards Yhtill's vast ramparts, which are featureless and windowless, for no one who lives in the last cities of Carcosa ever looks willingly upon the Lake of Hali.

'And as I flew on, I noted a curious difference in the quality of the lake's surface. It roiled and bubbled in a way I had never seen before, as though some great and powerful disturbance were occurring far below in its profoundest depths. That roiling and bubbling terrified me, and I increased the speed of my flight so that I might leave the lake and its secrets behind as quickly as possible.

'As the cloud waves broke upon the ancient stone walls, I flew over them and down into the streets of Yhtill, where I wandered among the cheerless, ragged people, unseen, my existence unsuspected, and I listened to what they said, as I have always done in the past. I have visited Carcosa on many occasions, and over time have managed to learn a great deal of their language, but it was not their words which first alerted me to the fact that something was amiss: it was the expressions on their faces. Every man, woman and child I encountered in the streets of Yhtill looked... *terrified*.

'For many hours I wandered amongst the people of Yhtill, through the city's winding streets, into houses and to the tops of its windowless towers, eavesdropping on conversations, trying to uncover some clue to the cause of this new terror which had augmented their general despair. Eventually, I discovered it. "The time of his emergence is approaching," they said. "He is preparing to come out of the lake, and when he does, our final doom will be upon us. The lake can no longer contain him. It knows that he is preparing to leave his castle and wishes to be rid of him. He will emerge soon, and all who look upon him will die!"

'For many hours I lingered in Yhtill, listening to the words of its people, and from their conversations I was able to piece together the facts about the King in Yellow and the final doom which now hovers like a carrion bird over the ruined world of Carcosa. Indeed, that doom is not theirs alone, but ours also, for when the King in Yellow emerges from the Lake of Hali, the Earth will fall beneath his power just as surely as Carcosa!'

*

Sophia drew in her breath and tightened her grip on the razor as the bathroom door began to swing open.

And then, without warning, there was a great whirring and flapping, and something began to bang loudly and repeatedly against one of the tall sash windows in the suite's sitting room. Sophia heard it clearly and nearly dropped the razor in her surprise.

'What the devil's that?' cried one of the intruders.

Sophia could hear the window rattling in its frame under the onslaught. So loud was the banging that she thought it must surely shatter.

'What *is* that?' the man repeated.

'I don't know, and I don't *want* to know,' his accomplice replied. 'Hang this. Come on, let's get out of here!'

'But…'

'Come *on!*'

As the great flapping and whirring continued, the intruders fled the suite, slamming the door behind them. As soon as they had done so, the mysterious cacophony ceased as abruptly as it had begun.

Sophia could feel her heart thumping in her chest in counterpoint to her laboured panting. Even in her terror and confusion, however, she realised that the noise must have been noticed, that at this very moment people were almost certainly rushing to investigate.

She dropped the razor in the sink, threw open the bathroom door and rushed into the sitting room. Sparing only the briefest glance at the windows, which were now still and silent, she moved swiftly to the suite's outer door, opened it a crack, and peered into the corridor outside.

It was empty, but she could hear voices approaching, and so she slipped out and headed quickly for the nearest stairwell. As she walked, she thrust a hand in her pocket, to make certain that the ampoule containing the Taduki drug was still there...

*

Blackwood regarded Simon Castaigne, taking in his drawn features, his wild eyes and furrowed brow, and tried to decide whether the man was raving mad. He was reluctant to consider him so, for he had seen the effects produced on weak minds which had delved too deeply into the mysteries of the occult, and he had little doubt that Castaigne's mental faculties were both powerful and entirely intact.

Castaigne took another sip of water, his hand trembling very slightly, and continued, 'Who or what is the King in Yellow? Let me be completely honest with you, my friends: he is the very embodiment of evil, its distillation and personification. Where his origin lies, I cannot say; perhaps it lies in the ultimate, uncharted gulfs of the Æther, or perhaps it lies beyond the bounds of our universe, in a dimension whose very existence is unknown and unsuspected by Earthly science. What I do know, from my many visits to Carcosa, is that he came to that unhappy world in the distant past, a blight from the nethermost reaches of space and time, a living nightmare from the ultimate Æther which infected the world with its hideous alienness.

'For centuries, the King in Yellow has ruled over Carcosa, feeding on his living subjects in atrocious and unfathomable ways, his form undiscernable save for the seething mass of tattered yellow in which he clothes himself, his true face forever hidden behind the terrible mask he wears.

'And throughout those long centuries, Carcosa has writhed beneath the Yellow Sign; the stars have turned black in the sky, and its moons have gone insane; its parent suns have withered, while the Hyades sing mournfully in the infinite night.

'Thus in ages long past did Queen Cassilda compose her singular lines:

> *Along the shore the cloud waves break,*
> *The twin suns sink beneath the lake,*
> *The shadows lengthen*
> *In Carcosa.*

> *Strange is the night where black stars rise,*
> *And strange moons circle through the skies*
> *But stranger still is*
> *Lost Carcosa.*

> *Songs that the Hyades shall sing,*
> *Where flap the tatters of the King,*
> *Must die unheard in*
> *Dim Carcosa.*

> *Song of my soul, my voice is dead;*
> *Die thou, unsung, as tears unshed*
> *Shall dry and die in*
> *Lost Carcosa.*

'Strange lines indeed, and I believe that a similarly strange and terrible fate awaits the Earth, once the King in Yellow has emerged from his castle at the bottom of the Lake of Hali. If that is allowed to happen, then he will travel to the Earth, and our world and Carcosa will become twins in despair and doom!'

A loud murmur of shock and consternation spread through the audience. Cuthbert Fforbes-Maclellan rose to his feet and said, 'But how do you know this, Dr Castaigne? And why does the King in Yellow have our own world in his sights?'

Castaigne's gaze fell upon the Worshipful Master as he replied, 'I know because I have watched the cloud waves roil upon the waters of Hali, indicating a great disturbance in the depths of the lake. And I have heard the people of Carcosa affrightedly whispering that the King in Yellow is about to emerge, releasing himself from his vast and horrible castle on the lakebed.'

'And what about the Earth?' said Fforbes-Maclellan. 'What interest could such a creature have in our world?'

'For a detailed answer to *that* question, Worshipful Master,' replied Castaigne, 'you would have to ask Mr Charles Exeter.'

Another murmur spread through the audience, but this one was louder, more confused and, Blackwood noted, more indignant.

'Charles Exeter?' repeated Fforbes-Maclellan. 'The railway magnate?'

'The same,' Castaigne nodded. 'I have been paying close attention to Mr Exeter's activities for some time now… ever since I was alerted to his existence by an acquaintance of mine, who is a collector and dealer in antiquarian books. My acquaintance told me that Mr Exeter had purchased from him a fantastically rare book written in the sixteenth century by the great mathematician and occultist Dr John Dee. The book's full title is *A True and Faithful Relation of What Passed for Some Considerable Time Between Dr John Dee and the Planetary Angels of the Distant World of Carcosa*; however, it is more commonly known as the *Carcosa Fragments*.'

In spite of his own surprise, Blackwood couldn't help but smile at the uproar this latest revelation caused amongst Castaigne's audience. The man certainly knew how to work a crowd, and if he were telling the truth, then his theatricality was more than justified. He was undoubtedly correct when he described the *Carcosa Fragments* as 'fantastically rare': it was a record of the astral visions described by Dee's assistant, the scryer Edward Kelley, who claimed to have visited the distant world in non-corporeal form and conversed with Carcosa's Planetary Angels, beings which were comparable to the faeries of Earth.

According to occult rumour and legend, Dee was so terrified by what he had written that he burned the manuscript; Kelley, however, had already made a copy, which he secretly kept. Through the centuries, several other copies had been made – one of which Exeter had apparently purchased from Castaigne's acquaintance. Those individuals who had been lucky – or unlucky – enough to read the *Carcosa Fragments* had refused to divulge what they contained, so horrifying were the contents, and Blackwood assumed that Exeter must have offered an irresistible price to secure his copy.

'I hardly need remind you,' Castaigne continued, 'of this book's fearsome reputation. After all, it is still listed in the Vatican's *Index Librorum Prohibitorum*, and all Catholics risk excommunication if they should be discovered to have read it. Of its contents much is whispered, the most persistent rumour being that Carcosa is home to a horrific entity, a being whose very existence is a blasphemy, an affront to the natural order of the universe. This being, known as the

King in Yellow by the people of Carcosa, lives in the remains of the Castle of Demhe, which was once home to the royal family of Carcosa, and which sank into the Lake of Hali shortly after his arrival. There he broods and bubbles, slowly absorbing the life of Carcosa and its people and warping the very laws of physics with his loathsome presence.

'This, my friends, is the being which Charles Exeter wishes to contact. This is the reason I have come before you tonight, for he must be stopped, before he brings down a terrible blight upon the Earth.'

Stunned, Fforbes-Maclellan sat down, shaking his head in disbelief and throwing a haunted glance at Blackwood. With a grim expression, the Special Investigator stood up and said, 'Dr Castaigne, how do you *know* all this? Where is your proof that Exeter is mad enough to try to contact this being? And how do you know what will happen if he succeeds?'

Castaigne looked at Blackwood and heaved a great sigh. 'I know, sir, because I am one of the unlucky few who have read the *Carcosa Fragments*... and as a result, I know exactly how and why Exeter is going to try to summon the King in Yellow to Earth!'

*

Sophia's carriage stopped outside her Kensington apartments, and she lost no time in bidding her driver goodnight and hurrying indoors. She gave her housekeeper the rest of the evening off and sent her away, before shrugging off her coat and retrieving the little glass ampoule from her purse.

As she held it up to the gaslight and peered at the ash-like powder it contained, Sophia felt both her breath and her heartbeat quicken. She could hardly believe what she was about to do: how reckless it was! How dangerous! *I should give this to Thomas*, she thought. *I should surrender it for chemical analysis and wait to see what he decides should be done.* She frowned. *But then again, why should I? I may well be holding in my hand the means to solve this mystery. I could have been killed tonight… how stupid it would be for my courage to fail me now!*

As she thought of how narrow her escape had been, she wondered again what had caused that loud whirring, flapping sound at the window…

'It was me,' said a voice behind her.

Sophia whirled around to see a tall, graceful, fabulously beautiful young woman standing in the doorway leading to the sitting room. She was dressed in a long tunic of bright emerald green which shimmered in the gaslight, as if it really were made of jewels. From behind her shoulders, four delicate dragonfly wings extended, their glittering surfaces like glass stained with mother-of-pearl. She smiled at Sophia and arched one perfect eyebrow beneath her long mane of shining, chestnut-coloured hair, and Sophia felt her pulse quicken yet further.

She recognised her instantly.

It was Titania, Queen of Faerie.

CHAPTER SIX:
Sophia's Journey

'You?' said Sophia when she had caught her breath and composed herself. 'You made the sound which forced those ruffians to flee?'

'Yes,' replied Titania, her voice at once as soft as a breeze and as powerful as a thunderclap. 'I must admit that I had expected more time to pass before our next meeting.'

Sophia resisted the urge to bow before the Faerie Queen, for she knew that Titania and her husband King Oberon did not care for such theatrical demonstrations of respect.

'It has been but a handful of days since you and Mr Blackwood were our guests in the Fortress of Apples. I congratulate you, by the way, on the manner in which you resolved the affair of the Martian Ambassador.'

'Thank you,' Sophia whispered.

'We have been watching you with great interest,' Titania continued. 'That is how I became aware of the danger in which you placed yourself this evening, and that is why I was able to come to your aid.'

'Thank you again, Your Highness,' said Sophia.

Titania laughed, and Sophia found herself simultaneously delighted and terrified by the sound. 'Your human salutations are most amusing, Sophia,' she said. 'And

I acknowledge your gratitude… yet I fear that you are still in danger, and still in need of my help.'

'I… I'm quite sure I don't know what you mean.'

Titania glanced down at Sophia's fist, which was curled around the ampoule. 'I think you know *exactly* what I mean.'

She turned and walked into the sitting room, and Sophia hurried after her. 'Would… would you care for some refreshment? A cup of tea, perhaps?' she asked.

Titania laughed again by way of reply, and Sophia felt her face burn with embarrassment as the silliness of the question. It had jumped to her lips automatically, although she excused it as merely the instinct of a young lady to be hospitable towards a guest – however unexpected or singular that guest might be.

The Faerie Queen sat down on the burgundy *chaise-longue* which dominated one wall of the little sitting room and watched in silence as Sophia tentatively lowered herself into an armchair across from her.

'I take it you know what that is,' Titania said, indicating Sophia's hand.

Sophia uncurled her fingers and looked down at the ampoule. 'It is a drug known as Taduki.'

'And you know the effect it has upon the human mind.'

'Yes… I know.'

'And still you intend to imbibe it.'

Sophia looked up and met Titania's gaze. 'I must.'

'Why?'

'To prove my worth.'

'To Mr Blackwood?'

Sophia didn't answer, and Titania smiled broadly, revealing small teeth, perfect as alabaster. 'He understands your worth, Sophia…'

'No… he does not, despite his protestations to the contrary.' She sighed and held the ampoule up to the light. 'But with this, I can make a real contribution to this investigation; with this, I might gain knowledge enough to allow us to solve the mystery of the Underground quickly, and without causing further suffering to the people who must work there.'

Titania regarded her in silence for a few moments. 'Is that the only reason?' she asked presently.

'Of course it is.'

'There is no other? Not the insatiable desire you have to plumb the deepest mysteries of the universe? To give some meaning, perhaps, to your father's death?'

Sophia jumped to her feet and glared down at Titania. 'This has nothing to do with my father!' she cried.

The Faerie Queen's eyes grew wide, and the smile which curved upon her perfect lips was no longer exquisite to behold, but dark and frightening and filled with incomprehensible power. 'Sit down, Sophia,' she said, and in her voice was a tone of command which Sophia could not refuse. Her knees buckled, and she sank quickly into the chair. 'Do you think I offer insult to your father's memory by describing the true nature of your motivations?'

Sophia sighed again. 'No.'

'And well you should not. We of the Otherworld have always taken an interest in those humans who take an interest in us, whatever their reasons. You strive to understand the supernatural, because the supernatural entered your life when you were little more than a child, and it took away your parent. You transformed your loss, your terrible despair, into a quest for knowledge, and that is what saved you. But the quest for knowledge can be dangerous: it can lead the seeker into places where one does not belong, places where nothing may be found but madness and death.' Titania indicated the ampoule. 'That is what you risk if you take the Taduki drug.'

'Have you come here merely to dissuade me from doing so, or to physically prevent me?' asked Sophia.

Titania held Sophia's gaze, unblinking. 'It is true that I *could* stop you... but I will not.'

'Why not?'

'For the reason Oberon explained to you when you were our guests in the Fortress of Apples. We cannot intervene directly in human affairs – at least, not those of greatest import. In fact, I have come close to breaking the Covenant by visiting you this evening, and yet I decided to do so, because I care for you, Sophia, and I would not see you destroy yourself.'

'I have the impression, Your Highness, that you know much more than you are letting on,' said Sophia. 'Do you know what will happen to me if I take the Taduki?'

'I... have an inkling.'

'Tell me.'

Titania shook her head. 'I cannot.'

'In that case, I don't understand why you came here at all. You can stop me, but you choose not to, and yet you *are* trying to dissuade me. If you are prevented from interfering in human affairs by the Faerie Covenant with the universe, then what's the difference?'

'The difference is that the choice must be yours. I can advise you, but no more. And, gentle Sophia, I advise you not to take the Taduki drug.'

Sophia looked again at the little ampoule nestling inoffensively in the palm of her hand. 'I must,' she whispered.

When she looked up again, she saw that she was alone in the room: the *chaise-longue* was empty. 'Queen Titania?' she said.

A voice sounded softly close to her ear. 'I have done what I can, Sophia,' it said.

As she sat alone in her sitting room, Sophia felt a great, seething wave of loss sweeping through her, freezing her heart and making her gasp. She dropped the ampoule to the carpet, buried her face in her hands and wept bitterly, her entire body shaking with each sob.

*

Eventually, the pain subsided, the tears stopped flowing, and Sophia took a handkerchief from the sleeve of her blouse and wiped her eyes. For what seemed like a long time, she stared at the ampoule lying on the carpet at her feet, then she reached down and picked it up and took it into the kitchen.

She ran herself a glass of water and snapped the top off the ampoule. She stopped, frowning, realising that she had no idea how the drug should be taken. She had intended to pour it into the water... was that the way to do it? *Well*, she thought, *I can't think of any other way...*

Taking a deep breath, she poured the powder into the water and gave it a stir. To her surprise, it dissolved almost immediately, imparting a murky grey colour to the liquid. Without hesitating, she drank the entire glass. It had a curious taste, a combination of sweetness and saltiness that was not entirely unpleasant, and which reminded her somewhat of Eno fruit salts.

What should I do now? she wondered. *Perhaps it would be best to lie down and wait for the...*

The room began to spin, slowly at first and then in a wild, nauseating gyre. *Oh good grief!* Sophia thought as she grasped the working top for support. The polished wood felt soft and mushy in her hands, and she realised that her senses were beginning to betray her under the unexpectedly sudden influence of the Taduki. What a fool she was! The ampoule might have contained a hundred doses, for all she knew, and she had swallowed the lot!

The kitchen floor seemed to pitch and roll beneath her feet, as if it were the deck of a foundering ship. She sank to her knees, her breath coming in shallow little gasps, her stomach gurgling in protest at the alien substance which had been so unceremoniously poured into it.

Sophia crawled on her hands and knees out of the kitchen, but as she watched, the corridor leading to the other rooms of the apartment warped and stretched away into an impossible distance, and her inner ears told her – quite unreliably, she felt – that she was clinging like a fly to the wall of an infinitely deep shaft. In panic, she thrust her fingers into her mouth as far as she could, trying to make herself vomit, but it was no use. It was as if her stomach were telling her that since she had seen fit to impose the filthy stuff upon it, she would now have to live with the consequences.

The corridor was rotating faster and faster, and Sophia became aware of a sound: a high, keening wail that seemed to come to her from a very great distance, and then she realised that it was she who was wailing…

…and then all was stillness and calm. Sophia was lying on her back. The corridor had stopped spinning and had returned to its proper horizontal orientation, and as she opened her eyes, she saw the gas lamps on the walls glowing warmly and reassuringly. The nausea had completely abated, and with it her fear. She took in a deep breath and slowly let it out and smiled. *I'm alive*, she thought. *Splendid.*

Well, so much for Dr Castaigne's Taduki drug. It was obviously quite useless – apart from as a means of torture! She got to her feet, amazed at how easily she was able to do so after such a ghastly and debilitating experience. In fact, she realised with great surprise, she felt positively wonderful – better than she had ever felt in her entire life: stronger, healthier, more vibrant, more *alive*.

What a strange concoction, she thought. *Why, I could easily imagine it becoming all the rage as a cure-all. Even better than laudanum…*

She turned back towards the kitchen, intending to pour another glass of water, for she was thirsty and had a peculiar tickle in the back of her throat. She stopped and put a hand to her mouth in shock.

There, lying on the carpet, face up, her eyes closed, her face as immobile as if in deep sleep or death, was... *she*. In an instant, Sophia realised the truth: that the drug *had* worked, and the physical body of the person known as Sophia Harrington lay motionless upon the carpet, while the personality, the essence, the thing she called *I* had emerged intact, independent and capable of thought and movement. No wonder she had been able to get to her feet so effortlessly, for she was utterly unencumbered by gravity.

My apologies, Dr Castaigne, she thought. *I misjudged both you* and *this remarkable substance.*

She looked at her hands, felt her face and limbs and clothes, and was surprised to see that she appeared to be just as solid and material as before. Was that an illusion, some form of mental residue of her sense of physical self-identity? She guessed that it must be – although she would find out soon enough, for she intended to leave her apartment and head for the Underground without delay. There she would do a little investigating of her own. Perhaps she would be able to speak with some of the ghosts who inhabited the network and gain some information from them. Perhaps they would recognise her as one of their own – or at least something very close – and confide in her, telling her of the true nature of the disturbances which had been plaguing the railway network...

She willed herself towards the front door, surprised anew at how easily movement was accomplished in this non-corporeal form. She could, of course, have simply flown out through the window and floated down to the street, but there was something about that idea which struck her as rather unseemly, and so she opted for the traditional method of doors and staircases.

In the corridor outside her apartment, she encountered her neighbour Mr Gardner, who was returning home after another late night at his office. Instinctively, she bid him good evening, but he did not answer, did not even glance in her direction.

So it is true, then, Sophia thought. *The form I perceive is nothing more than an illusion, a psychic memory of what I was. No*, she corrected herself, *of what I still am… back there in my chambers*.

She watched Mr Gardner enter his apartment and then drifted down the stairs to the ground floor, through the front door and out into the street. She took a deep breath of the night air, but it did not feel cold; in fact, it did not feel like anything at all, and she realised that the need to breathe was but another memory of her physical existence.

As she stood at the head of the short staircase leading from the front door down to the street, Sophia took in the scene. A few people were hurrying past, hunched against the evening's chill in their overcoats, while the occasional hansom or four-wheeler clattered along the cobbled road, the horses' breath issuing like steam from their flaring nostrils.

I no longer feel a part of this world, Sophia thought, and she was surprised at the sudden upwelling of sadness which greeted the realisation. *I am in an in-between state: neither of this world, nor the one to come. I am alone.* She looked up at the stars shining brightly above the city. *Father… where are you?* She closed her eyes and felt tears upon her cheeks. She reached up and touched one and looked at the liquid on her fingertip… but that too was only a memory of the form she had left behind.

At that moment, she felt a sudden breeze upon her face, and looked around in confusion. She had thought herself incapable of feeling the atmosphere of the physical world, and yet…

There it was again, stronger this time, bitingly cold, making her skin tingle. It grew rapidly in intensity, making her sway, so that she tried to take hold of the stone banister at her side to steady herself. But of course it was no use: her hand moved as easily through the stone as if it were made of smoke.

She tried to keep her balance as the breeze grew stronger, rapidly becoming a wind that howled like a wild animal and snatched her from her feet. She cried out in sudden terror as she was propelled from the staircase up into the air. Whirling upwards, Sophia caught glimpses of the street below, of the carriages and pedestrians, none of whom were affected by the great, invisible tornado that had her in its clutches. Instinctively, she cried out to them, but they did not even glance up at her.

A terrible memory flashed into her awareness, of a night ten years ago in the distant wilderness of eastern Canada, of a hunting trip with her father, Lord Percival Harrington; a memory of an eighteen-year-old girl roused from her slumber by the desperate cries of her father as he was lifted into the cold, merciless night air by the horrifying entity known to the people of that region as the Wendigo, the Walker on the Wind, never to be seen again.

Her father's cries had haunted Sophia ever since, and now, as she hurtled upwards into the night sky above London, she thought that the Wendigo had returned to claim her, perhaps drawn by the new supernatural state which she had so recklessly induced in herself.

Sophia watched helplessly as the streets of Kensington whirled away from her, diminishing rapidly in the distance. Then London itself became little more than a luminous tracery, surrounded by the lights of the outlying towns, scattered across the dark countryside of the South East. She expected to be carried across the globe, perhaps to the

Canadian hunting grounds of the Wendigo, there to suffer the same fate as that which had befallen her father...

But her terrified assumption was in error, for Sophia continued her upward flight, until she saw the outline of the British Isles and realised, as her fear increased a hundredfold, that the howling wind was carrying her into outer space...

*

The Earth became lost in the immensity of the star-scattered Æther, and then the Sun diminished to but one amongst the countless millions of diamond-bright pinpoints which surrounded her.

Once again, Sophia's instincts came to the fore, and she tried to draw breath, knowing full well that there was no air out here, that the rarefied substance of which the Luminiferous Æther was composed would not feed her lungs. Only after several horrible moments of mad thrashing was she reminded that in her present non-corporeal state, she had no need of air.

And so she waited, for there was nothing else she could do.

She waited, while the strange wind blew her soundlessly across space, a lonely being composed entirely of confusion and terror, whose mind was a wide, staring eye that watched the stars flashing past against the black backdrop of infinity.

Where am I going? Where am I going?

The question repeated itself over and over in her mind, as the stars approached and receded, revealing themselves to be of different colours – red, blue, yellow, white – and dark orphan planets, worlds which might once have belonged to solar systems, but which now wandered alone, perhaps as the result of some ancient catastrophe, turned beneath her, revealing their wrinkled, blackened surfaces.

On the shrivelled, icebound face of one such world, she thought she could discern the outlines of buildings, vast and strange and fallen into aeon-long ruin, before the wind carried her onwards into the gulfs ahead, and on another, she glimpsed something which made her scream silently and frantically turn her head away.

As she continued past the stars, Sophia realised where she was going... or rather, she realised that she had known all along, ever since leaving the Earth's atmosphere. The Taduki drug was indeed working, and she now suspected that the strange wind which was blowing her from star to star was not really a wind at all, but the drug's method of working upon her psychic awareness, and guiding her towards her destination.

Towards Carcosa.

But how can that be possible? she wondered. *The universe is vast beyond comprehension. How can the drug guide me to one particular place amongst countless other places? Perhaps Taduki can be made to guide the mind to any place one chooses... perhaps it is something to do with the proportion of ingredients – whatever they may be.*

That explanation seemed to Sophia as good as any other, and at any rate, it was the only one of which she could conceive. Chemistry, after all, had never been her strong point – still less chemistry based on arcane occult principles.

The stars continued to flash past, trillions of miles falling in her wake as quickly as footfalls during a brisk walk... until a brace of stars drifted into the centre of her field of vision and grew steadily until they seemed to fill the sky: vast, red orbs, seething violently in the eternal night. Around the red stars, hundreds of others clustered, and it seemed to Sophia that they were so near, she would only have to reach out in order to touch them.

The Hyades.

As she approached the giant red stars, Sophia became aware of a much smaller sphere, dwarfed utterly by its parents, a tiny fleck of dust against the fiery crimson, and it was towards this that she felt herself being guided.

Carcosa, she thought, the word conjuring images of strange mystery and nameless terror. *How many human beings have made this journey, besides Dr Castaigne and myself? How many would choose to?*

As she descended towards the dark surface of the alien world, she marvelled at the desolation, at the almost total lack of vegetation and water. This was a dying planet, a place that had been...

Consumed.

The word sprang suddenly to her mind, but she knew that it was the right one.

Yes, consumed by... something.

Dying Carcosa turned beneath her, and as it revolved, a great misshapen patch of white emerged from the horizon, glowing faintly in the light from the red suns. It appeared to be composed of slowly moving clouds, and as she watched, Sophia thought of the first line of Cassilda's song, which Blackwood had read to her just a few days ago, on the other side of space:

Along the shore the cloud waves break...

This, she knew, was the Lake of Hali.

She drew closer and saw three great cities spaced around the shore. What were their names? Yhtill, yes, that was one... and... Alar... and Hastur. Were these the last three cities on the face of Carcosa, the last outposts of a race which must once have spread across the entirety of their world?

Sophia drifted above the lake and watched the cloud waves breaking upon the distant shores, against the great stone ramparts of the last three cities, beyond which great windowless towers rose into the sky, as if seeking to flee their own imminent ruin. She watched Carcosa's four moons hovering above the roiling clouds of Hali, against a backdrop of stars which shone impossibly with rays of darkness, and she gasped as she saw the moons moving *in front of* the cities' towers.

Strange is the night where black stars rise,
And strange moons circle through the skies…

As she watched these marvels, Sophia gradually became aware that she no longer seemed to be under the control of the Taduki drug; she could move of her own volition, and in whichever direction her will decided upon. *It has fulfilled its function*, she thought. *It has brought me here, and now it's up to me where I go.*

She briefly considered exploring the cities and moving amongst their people, but then she looked down at the cloud waves swirling upon the waters of Hali directly beneath her and felt an irresistible urge to descend into the heart of Carcosa's mystery. She knew how reckless it was, how unutterably dangerous, but she could not help herself. She recalled the delicious feeling she had experienced when she broke into Castaigne's hotel room. This was a thousand times more intense – a *million* times! The temptation was maddening, the sense of transgression like a powerful intoxicant pounding through her veins.

Whatever is in there will not see me, she told herself. *I will see it, but in this astral form I will remain invisible to it.*

She descended towards the milk-white clouds which swirled and bubbled upon the surface of the lake. The red-tinged sky with its black stars and mad moons disappeared, and all around her was whiteness, blank and featureless. She had no idea how thick the layer of cloud was, nor how long it would take her to reach what lay beneath.

Down, she thought. *Down… down.*

And then the whiteness was transformed into murky darkness, broken only by the occasional dull glint of a stream of ugly, misshapen bubbles rising slowly towards the surface.

Sophia continued her descent, heading towards the lakebed and whatever lay there.

Gradually, she became aware of movement in the water around her: great dark shapes that flitted on the very edge of perception. Whether they were the natural inhabitants of the lake or something far from natural, she had no idea, for she had nothing with which to compare this experience. Her fear, however, was mitigated somewhat by the conviction that her presence remained undetected; in fact, there was a powerful dreamlike quality to all this, as if she were not really here at all, as if she had merely to will herself awake in order to find herself back once more in her Kensington home.

And so she continued her descent through the thick, dark waters of the Lake of Hali on the planet Carcosa…

*

Initially, Sophia couldn't quite decide what she was looking at, for the shapes emerged only dimly at first, gradually resolving themselves out of the surrounding gloom into vast slabs of stone which rose at improbable angles from the black mud of the lakebed. It looked like a castle… but it was like no castle Sophia had ever seen or imagined. For one thing, its size was beyond all logic or earthly reasoning: it stretched into the distance, wall beyond wall, tower beyond tower, rampart upon rampart, all warped and twisted in ways which left Sophia dumbfounded, appalled and terror-stricken.

At first, she had wondered whether it might be a natural formation, something akin to the vast coral reefs of Earth's oceans, but she had been quickly disabused of that notion when she saw what was undoubtedly stonework: massive, primordial masonry and lightless windows.

She also had the impression (although she could not fathom the reason) that the castle had not always looked like this, that its walls had once been regular and perpendicular

– that it had once been sane. But sanity had long ago fled this place, and whatever had usurped it had deformed and distorted everything Sophia could see, as if the very laws of physics had been undermined, perverted, destroyed.

Sophia decided that she had seen quite enough of this place. She would return to the surface immediately and explore the cities until the drug took her home, for she had already begun to suspect that once it began to leave her physical system back on Earth, she would automatically return – at least, that was what she fervently hoped.

She willed herself upwards towards the surface of Hali, but she had not gone more than a few feet when she felt something pulling at her, as if she were a swimmer who had caught her foot in a rock or a strand of seaweed on the ocean floor. She willed herself upwards again… and again she was halted and pulled back down towards the warped and twisted castle.

Panic flooded her awareness as she realised that the unseen force was dragging her towards a vast doorway which yawned like a misshapen mouth in one of the higher walls. She struggled frantically and uselessly as the force pulled her inside the castle, along miles of twisting corridors whose walls glistened with the pulsations of nameless things, and then down wide, broken staircases which plunged into fathomless darkness. Through networks of crumbling corridors and high-ceilinged, dungeon-like chambers she was dragged, like a tiny fish that had been snared by the tendril of some atrocious cave-dwelling predator.

When the force finally released her, Sophia found herself in a gigantic circular chamber, whose domed ceiling was barely discernible in the watery murk. Strange shapes, like the ones she had half glimpsed in the lake's open waters, flitted amongst the titanic columns which marched around the perimeter of the room. Upon each of the columns, which must have been at least a hundred feet tall, was carved the Yellow Sign:

Each symbol glowed dully with a slow, rhythmic pulsation, casting a diseased yellow light into the chamber and upon the thing which squatted at its centre.

At first sight, it appeared to be an enormous mountain of rags, of the same filthy yellow hue as the light emanating from the symbols. The rags fluttered and undulated obscenely in the currents caused by the movement of the nameless things which swam between the columns, and at once Sophia knew that this livid, putrescent mound was alive.

Where flap the tatters of the King...

No, Sophia thought. *Oh, no, no, no!*

As if in response to her wild, unspoken denial, the fluttering of the rags increased, and the vast mound began to heave and sway. The nameless swimming things fled the chamber, and the water became still, but the heaving and fluttering of the rags continued, growing yet more fevered.

Sophia tried to back away, but the invisible force that had brought her here seized her again and held her fast.

And then the great mass of fluttering rags parted like an infected wound, and when she saw what lay within, Sophia began to scream.

The shadows lengthen
In Carcosa...

CHAPTER SEVEN:
A Séance

'Dr Castaigne,' said Cuthbert Fforbes-Maclellan, 'may I introduce Mr Thomas Blackwood, Special Investigator for Her Majesty's Bureau of Clandestine Affairs.'

'A pleasure, sir,' said Castaigne, shaking Blackwood's hand.

The occultist's talk had ended. The lodge's Apprentices had removed the high-backed chairs from the drawing room and were now circulating amongst the guests with trays of drinks and canapés.

'Although,' Castaigne continued, 'I had the impression from your question that you are more than a little sceptical of my claims.'

'Not at all, my dear chap,' Blackwood replied. 'Quite the contrary.' He lowered his voice as he added, 'In fact, I'm very glad I accepted the invitation to attend this evening. There is something I'd like to discuss with you, something of extreme importance, which bears markedly upon your current concerns.'

'Really?' said Castaigne.

'Really?' echoed Fforbes-Maclellan.

Blackwood glanced around the crowded room. 'Gentlemen, I would prefer the three of us to discuss this in private.'

'My office,' said Fforbes-Maclellan instantly. 'Follow me.'

The rest of the guests stared at them with bemusement as they left the drawing room. The Worshipful Master led them along a corridor and into his small but immaculately (and somewhat arcanely) furnished office. Blackwood ignored the complexities of the Masonic decor as he and Castaigne took a couple of armchairs.

'How about a brandy and soda to kick things off?' said Fforbes-Maclellan.

'Capital,' Castaigne replied, and Blackwood also nodded. 'Well, Mr Blackwood,' he said when they had their drinks. 'What is it you wish to discuss?'

'The King in Yellow,' the Special Investigator replied. 'You are probably aware that there have been a number of disturbances reported on the London Underground recently – disturbances of a supernatural nature.'

Castaigne nodded. 'I read something of it in the *Times* this morning. Most curious, I must say... but I'm not sure what it has to do with me.'

Blackwood leaned forward suddenly, placing his brandy untouched on a small table beside his chair. 'My dear sir, it has *everything* to do with you, if what you have said about the events on Carcosa is true.'

Castaigne took a long swallow of his brandy and soda, and said, 'Go on.'

'For some weeks now, drivers and maintenance crews on the Underground system have been complaining of strange things happening. Ghosts, for the most part. It seems that the spirits of those who have met tragic and untimely ends, and which linger on the network, have been stirred into unusually high levels of activity. And then, three nights ago, a train driver named Alfie Morgan encountered something which completely unhinged his mind. I went to see him at

Bethlem Hospital with a colleague of mine, and during our visit he uttered the word "Carcosa" several times...'

At this, Castaigne jerked forward in his seat. 'You don't say!'

'Then, two days later, my colleague and I engaged a psychometrist from the Society for Psychical Research to examine Morgan's train. The poor man very nearly suffered the same fate as Morgan: his mind was all but shattered by the psychic impressions he received – impressions, he said, of an utterly alien being which is roaming the Underground.'

'By Jove!' said Fforbes-Maclellan, and drained his glass in a single gulp.

Castaigne was silent for some moments. 'I take it that you haven't encountered this entity yourself.'

Blackwood shook his head. 'No, but I have heard it while I was on the network with a Scotland Temple detective, who is also investigating these events. The creature – whatever it was – attacked the members of a search party out looking for a man who recently vanished. We... heard their screams, and also the sounds the thing made.' Blackwood hesitated before continuing, 'I must confess that I prevented the detective from going to their aid.'

Castaigne leaned forward and placed a hand on Blackwood's arm. 'Rest assured, sir, that you made the right decision. There was nothing you could have done, and had you given chase, you and your colleague would most certainly have perished.'

Blackwood sighed. 'Thank you, but I have to say that it was a most difficult decision.'

'I understand entirely.'

Blackwood turned haunted eyes on the occultist. 'Have you any idea what the thing was?'

'My guess is that it was a Servitor of the King in Yellow, mindless yet immensely powerful and dangerous. I suspected that at least one existed on Earth, but I had no idea that it was here in England, beneath the metropolis. I thank you, sir, for bringing this to my attention. This is further proof that the King in Yellow plans to leave Carcosa and take up residence on Earth...'

'With the help of Charles Exeter,' said Blackwood.

'Precisely.'

'But why would Exeter give aid to such a monstrous being? Surely he must know what it would mean for our world – especially if he has obtained a copy of the *Carcosa Fragments*.'

'I suspect that he is not doing so entirely voluntarily,' Castaigne replied with a sad shake of his head. 'One of the things Edward Kelley learned during his scrying experiments was that the entity is capable of contacting other beings in their dreams, and influencing their thoughts and actions. This must be what has happened to Charles Exeter.'

'And how is he going to carry out the entity's wishes? You said in your talk that you know the how and why of it.'

'I do. But tell me: have you read the *Carcosa Fragments*, Mr Blackwood?'

Fforbes-Maclellan gave a small start, as if Castaigne had uttered a profanity.

'No, I have not. I've never come across a copy... I suppose there is a limit even to the Bureau's resources.'

Castaigne gave a grim smile. 'Indeed. I take it, however, that you have heard of the ancient tribe known as the Catuvellauni.'

Blackwood frowned, at a loss as to where the conversation was going. 'Yes I have. They lived in the South East of England before the Roman conquest.'

'Quite so. According to the *Carcosa Fragments*, the Catuvellauni were visited by a man who came from the sky, and who arrived in the far south of their territory, near their border with the neighbouring tribe of the Regnenses. But that man was not really a man: he was an avatar of the King in Yellow, a kind of thought-form, similar to the tulpas of Tibet, which was capable of interacting with its environment. The avatar brought with it an object, which it showed to Tasciovanus, ruler of the Catuvellauni. This object, the avatar said, would bring good fortune and victory in battle to Tasciovanus's people, as long as it remained buried in an underground shrine which the avatar would instruct the Catuvellauni on how to build.

'Tasciovanus agreed; the shrine was constructed, the object buried, and the Catuvellauni subsequently enjoyed a period of great expansion. But the avatar had lied: there was no connection whatsoever between the object and the fortunes of Tasciovanus's people; the increase in their power was merely a coincidence, and was reversed with the arrival of the Romans.'

'Astonishing,' said Fforbes-Maclellan. 'But why is there no record of this in our histories of the British Isles?'

'The avatar swore Tasciovanus to secrecy on pain of death for the entire tribe, and so obvious was the being's power that the king agreed. In fact, once the underground chamber had been completed, the twenty-three men who had constructed it were sacrificed, so that they would never be able to tell of what they had seen and done.'

'And what, exactly, was the object which the avatar brought to Earth?' asked Blackwood.

'Edward Kelley uses a curious word to denote it,' Castaigne replied. 'He calls it the "Anti-Prism".'

'What the deuce is that supposed to mean?' wondered Fforbes-Maclellan.

Castaigne drained his glass. 'It is, essentially, a piece of technology – but a technology that is utterly beyond human understanding, based partly on a profound knowledge of physics and partly on an unknown form of extra-dimensional Magick.'

'What is its function?' asked Blackwood.

The occultist hesitated before answering, 'Nothing less than the opening of a gateway between worlds...'

'A gateway?'

'A means of travelling rapidly between different locations in the universe – in this case, between Carcosa and Earth.'

'Presumably, this... device... is not active right now,' said Blackwood.

'Indeed not.'

'Exeter needs to activate it before the gateway can be opened and the King in Yellow can come to Earth.'

'Precisely.'

'And how will he do that?'

'By channelling prodigious amounts of psychic energy into the Anti-Prism,' Castaigne replied. 'The King in Yellow must have known that human civilisation would develop and grow, and that great cities would arise across the landscape, filled with thousands of people. And, of course, people die, oftentimes violently and in great anguish, and become trapped in the twilight world between this life and the next. It is that energy, the energy of trapped souls, which is used to power the Anti-Prism.'

'Great God,' said Fforbes-Maclellan. 'What a fiendish device!'

Blackwood recalled what Anne Naylor had told him and de Chardin in the maintenance tunnel that afternoon, about the 'monster' which was haunting the Underground, gathering the souls of those who had died in the area, including the ones who had been killed by 'the big disease in the olden days'.

He told Castaigne and Fforbes-Maclellan what the little ghost had said. 'It's obvious,' he added, 'that she was talking about the Plague. Thousands upon thousands of victims, all having died in horrible circumstances, their souls trapped between this world and the next – a vast reservoir of psychic energy.'

'Good Lord, man, you've got it!' cried Castaigne. 'The Servitor of the King in Yellow has been gathering the souls of the anguished dead, preparing to discharge them into the Anti-Prism, thus powering the device and allowing it to open the gate between worlds.'

'It goes without saying that we must stop that from happening,' observed Blackwood. 'But the question is *how*?' He thought of Sophia and the interview she should have conducted with Charles Exeter that afternoon, and he wished that he had had a chance to speak with her before now. It was clear that the first thing to do was to bring Exeter in for questioning, but when Blackwood mentioned that, Castaigne shook his head.

'I'm afraid that wouldn't do any good, Mr Blackwood.'

'Why the devil not?'

'Because if the King in Yellow is influencing Exeter's actions, you won't be able to get anything useful out of him.'

'Dash it all!' Blackwood muttered.

'There is another way of getting hold of some information,' ventured Fforbes-Maclellan.

Blackwood glanced at him. 'And what is that?'

'You're forgetting that Madame Henrietta von Schellenberg, the finest spiritualistic medium in the country, if not the world, is one of our guests this evening,' the Worshipful Master replied. 'We don't have to ask Charles Exeter exactly what he's doing and where he's doing it; we can ask the spirits of those who have had first-hand experience of it.'

Blackwood regarded his host in silence for a moment. 'You're suggesting that we hold a séance?'

'Yes, Mr Blackwood, that's precisely what I'm suggesting.'

*

'Ladies and gentlemen,' said Fforbes-Maclellan, 'if I may have your attention...'

The guests, who were still assembled in the drawing room, their conversation having turned to the possible reason why their host had disappeared along with the guest of honour and the Special Investigator, turned towards the doorway where the Worshipful Master was standing.

'I beg your forgiveness for this unexpected change to the evening's proceedings, but we find ourselves confronted with the urgent need to conduct an impromptu séance for reasons of national security. Madame Henrietta, would you please come with me?'

A tall woman of statuesque build and aristocratic bearing glided across the room, the iridescent silk of her crimson evening gown making a subtle and delicious swishing sound which cut through the silence.

'I am at your service, Worshipful Master,' she said in a voice which was perhaps just a shade too deep for a woman, but which nevertheless succeeded in expressing all the power and mystery of her sex and the greater mystery of her vocation.

Fforbes-Maclellan gave a slight bow. 'I am much obliged to you, Madame. If you will follow me to the Séance Room...'

Before leaving the drawing room, he turned to the other guests. 'My apologies once again, ladies and gentlemen. We shall return to you presently. This shouldn't take longer than half an hour or so.'

Fforbes-Maclellan and Madame Henrietta von Schellenberg went to the Séance Room, where Blackwood and Castaigne were already waiting. After hasty introductions, they all seated themselves around a circular table covered with a rich burgundy baize.

'May I enquire as to the purpose of this séance, Worshipful Master?' said Madame Henrietta.

'Mr Blackwood,' said Fforbes-Maclellan. 'If you'd be so kind.'

Blackwood, who was sitting between the medium and the Worshipful Master, nodded. 'We need to contact at least one spirit from the London Underground. We require certain information, which only they are able to provide – information which may well prevent a terrible catastrophe. Can you help us, Madame?'

'I will certainly try, sir,' Madame Henrietta replied. 'Have you ever taken part in a séance before?'

'I have,' Blackwood said.

She placed her hands palm-upwards on the surface of the table. 'Then we all know what to do.'

The four of them joined hands in silence. Madame Henrietta von Schellenberg closed her eyes and began to demonstrate why she had become famous in London society and beyond. She bowed her head, and by the subdued light in the room, Blackwood could see the blood drain gradually from her face. Her features became utterly still, as if she were in a deep sleep. This was the self-induced trance which would allow her mind to reach out into the netherworld beyond material life, and to speak to the beings who dwelt there.

'I wish to speak with one who lingers beneath the city,' she intoned in a voice which was even deeper than normal. Blackwood felt the hairs on the back of his neck rise at the strangeness of it: there was something deeply unnatural in the timbre – no, he corrected himself: something *super*natural. There were many mediums plying their trade throughout Great Britain, and most of them were charlatans with little or no ability to apprehend the world beyond. Madame Henrietta, however, was not one of them: she was the genuine article.

Blackwood felt the temperature in the Séance Room drop by several degrees as the gaslights began to flicker upon the walls.

'Will no one speak with us?' said Madame Henrietta. 'We beseech you to help us... Who of you will come forward? There is something we desperately need to discuss with you – something of very great importance.'

Madame Henrietta lifted her head and looked at Blackwood. 'I sense fear, *terrible* fear. They are most reluctant to speak.'

'Anne,' said Blackwood.

'I'm sorry?'

'Anne Naylor, the Screaming Spectre.'

Madame Henrietta winced at the crude appellation.

'You are aware of her history,' he persisted.

'I am.'

'Call for her. She may come.'

Madame Henrietta nodded. 'I am speaking to the one called Anne Naylor, to the poor child who was taken from the world long before her time. Hear me Anne... and come to us!'

After some moments had passed in silence and stillness, the flickering of the gaslights increased, as if a strong breeze were blowing through the room, although none of the sitters felt the slightest stirring in the air...

And then the lights went out, plunging the room into total darkness.

The darkness, however, was short-lived, for the sitters quickly became aware of a faint blue glow which appeared in a far corner, and which gradually grew in intensity until it illuminated every part of the room.

They all turned to see a young girl standing in the corner, looking at them.

'Anne,' said Madame Henrietta. 'Thank you, child... thank you for coming to us.'

Wordlessly and with evident reluctance, the little ghost stepped forward until she was standing between Blackwood and the medium. She gave the Special Investigator a long, curious look, and said, 'I know you, sir.'

'Yes,' said Blackwood very gently. 'We met on the Underground Railway. Do you remember?'

Anne Naylor nodded.

'There is information of which we are in dire need, and we believe you may be able to help us obtain it.'

'Information?'

'The monster of which you spoke when we met, the thing whose approach we heard... we know what it is and where it came from. But there are other things which we need to know. Will you try and help us?'

The ghost regarded Blackwood uncertainly and then glanced at Madame Henrietta, almost, Blackwood thought with a stricken heart, in the manner of a child seeking approval from a parent. He supposed that it was logical, for it had been the medium's questing mind which had contacted her, and some form of bond must instantly have been forged between them.

Madame Henrietta nodded encouragingly.

Anne looked back at Blackwood. 'What do you want to know?'

'There is something on the Underground network which we need to find. An object. It is something very dangerous.'

'An... object?'

Blackwood nodded.

'What does it look like?'

Blackwood was about to speak and then realised that he had not the slightest idea.

He glanced at Castaigne, who leaned forward. 'It is essentially a hexagonal trapezohedron.'

Anne gave him a quizzical look.

Madame Henrietta sighed. 'Dr Castaigne, the child has no idea what a hexagonal trapezohedron is.'

'Oh, forgive me. It's… it's like a jewel, with many facets. Large. Perhaps ten feet in length…'

Anne's eyes widened at this description, and the sitters glanced at each other.

'She recognises it,' whispered Blackwood.

'You've seen it, haven't you?' said Castaigne.

Anne shook her head and took a step back from the table, her blue face twisted in an expression of abject fear.

'Yes,' said the occultist. 'You have seen it. You cannot lie to us, Anne.'

'I don't want to talk about that,' said the ghost.

'You must…'

'No, I mustn't!'

'Anne,' said Blackwood, and the ghost turned her frightened eyes to him. 'We need to find this thing. We need to know where it is. Please help us.'

'It's a horrible thing,' she whispered. 'None of us like it… none of us know where it comes from, but it doesn't come from the world… *this* world. I don't want to talk about it, sir!'

'You don't have to, child. All we need to know is where it is.'

Anne lowered her head and appeared to give a great sigh. 'It is beneath the new place, which the big machine has opened up.'

The sitters glanced at each other.

'The new place?' Blackwood said.

Anne nodded. 'The one that the big machine has opened up… the machine that makes tunnels.'

'What's she talking about?' wondered Fforbes-Maclellan.

'I believe she's describing one of the Greathead shields which are used to excavate new tunnels,' Blackwood replied.

'I don't want to talk about it anymore, sir,' said Anne plaintively.

Blackwood smiled at her. 'You don't have to. You've given me enough, and I thank you.'

'There's something else,' said Anne.

Blackwood leaned forward. 'What?'

'You have a friend... a lady.'

The Special Investigator frowned. 'A lady? Are you speaking of Lady Sophia?'

Anne nodded. 'Yes, that's her name.'

'What about her?'

'She is in great danger, sir.'

'What do you mean?'

'We felt her leaving...'

Blackwood felt something cold and dark clutching at his heart. 'Leaving?'

'Yes, sir. We all felt it – at least, those of us who remain, the ones who have not been gathered by the monster.'

Oh, good God, Blackwood thought, feeling the blood drain from his face. 'Do you mean to say that... she is dead?'

'No, she is not dead... but her mind is no longer here, in this world.'

'If her mind is not in this world... then where is it?'

The ghost of Anne Naylor looked up to the ceiling, but it was quite plain that her attention was focused on something far beyond. 'It is out there, sir... out among the stars.'

PART THREE

The Void Chamber

CHAPTER ONE:
Lady Sophia is Embarrassed

Castaigne's grand four-wheeler raced through the streets of Kensington, scattering the few late-night pedestrians who were unwise enough to attempt to cross the road in front of it. Blackwood and Castaigne were onboard, having left the Lodge as soon as Madame Henrietta had concluded the séance and broken her psychic connection with Anne Naylor.

Blackwood was beside himself with worry. What had happened to Sophia? A vague suspicion had begun to form in his mind as he leaned forward with furrowed brow and watched the streets rushing by, but without more facts, he was reluctant to believe it.

Before the driver had even brought the carriage to a halt outside Sophia's apartment building, Blackwood threw open the door and hit the pavement at a run, with Castaigne hard on his heels. He glanced up at the first floor windows, which were lit, and then bounded up the stairs to the front door. Knocking would clearly be of little avail, so Blackwood whipped out his lock-pick and had the door open in short order. Followed closely by Castaigne, he rushed up the stairs and repeated the operation on the door to Sophia's apartments.

The first sight which greeted them as they entered was Sophia's prone form in the corridor leading to the kitchen.

'Oh, good God!' Blackwood cried, rushing to her. 'Castaigne, give me a hand to get her to her bed.'

The occultist complied, and together they carried Sophia's unconscious body into the bedroom, where they laid her gently upon the bed.

Castaigne examined her face closely, and then opened her mouth and scented her breath. He gave Blackwood a confused look. 'She has taken Taduki.'

Blackwood sighed. He had suspected as much.

The occultist noted his lack of surprise and the fact that he did not ask what Taduki was. 'I take it you know what I am talking about.'

The Special Investigator nodded. 'The drug which enables the human mind to depart from the body and roam at will through the Luminiferous Æther. The means by which you have visited Carcosa.'

Castaigne was impressed. 'I see that there is more to you than meets the eye, sir,' he said. 'But I don't understand... how did she manage to obtain it?'

'Do you have any doses of the drug at your hotel?'

'Yes, I have a few doses amongst my personal effects.'

Blackwood smiled grimly. 'In that case, I have a strong suspicion as to her methods, Dr Castaigne, and I suspect equally strongly that you are not going to like them. Sophia was supposed to attend your lecture with me this evening, but she left a message with my housekeeper that she would be unable to come. She gave no reason, but I think I know what it was. She must have gone to your hotel room and availed herself of a dose of the Taduki...'

Castaigne shook his head. 'Good Lord, but those doses were specially formulated to guide the human awareness to Carcosa!'

'Is there an antidote? Is there any way we can bring her back quickly?'

'Physical consciousness is itself the antidote: all we have to do is bring her around, and her mind will fly back through the Æther instantly. Smelling salts should do the trick.'

Blackwood nodded. He ran to the bathroom and rummaged through the medicine cabinet until he had found a bottle of salts, which he took back to the bedroom and held under Sophia's nose.

Almost immediately, she groaned and arched her back. One hand flew up to her face and pushed the bottle away.

'Sophia,' said Blackwood, leaning close. 'Can you hear me?' He breathed a sigh of relief as her eyes opened and she looked at him. 'Do you know where you are?'

She looked around, breathing in shallow little gasps. 'My bedroom,' she whispered, and then winced and put a hand to her throat.

'It's all right,' said Castaigne to both her and Blackwood. 'A slight soreness in the throat is a side effect of the drug; it will pass quite quickly.'

'Who might you be, sir?' said Sophia, who appeared to have noticed him for the first time. 'And perhaps you can explain to me why I have the honour of receiving you in my bedroom!'

Blackwood smiled. 'Sophia, may I present Dr Simon Castaigne, the gentleman from whom you stole the Taduki drug.'

'The... what? Oh!' Slowly and with evident difficulty, Sophia sat up. Blackwood took a pillow and propped it against the headboard behind her. 'I, er, I'm very pleased to make your acquaintance, Dr Castaigne,' she said, rather timidly.

By way of reply, the occultist stepped back and indicated the door. 'The water closet awaits, your Ladyship.'

'I beg your pardon?' Sophia said, and then she placed a hand against her mouth. 'Oh dear!'

Without another word, she jumped off the bed and flew out of the room. A few moments later, some rather unfortunate retching sounds were heard to emanate from the bathroom.

'Another side effect of the Taduki drug,' Castaigne said in reply to Blackwood's concerned look. 'That too will quickly pass.'

*

While Sophia was gathering herself, Blackwood went to the kitchen and made some tea. She insisted on leaving the bedroom and continuing their conversation in the sitting room, and both Blackwood and Castaigne readily agreed, relieved to vacate the young lady's *sanctum sanctorum*.

Blackwood handed her the tea, which she sipped pensively while he and Castaigne seated themselves a little awkwardly on the *chaise longue* across from her armchair.

'I must apologise to you, Dr Castaigne,' she said presently, placing the cup and saucer with a shaking hand on the little occasional table beside her. 'What I did was unforgivable. I knew it was wrong, and yet I did it anyway.'

'Think nothing of it, madam,' he replied. 'I'm just glad that you have returned safely. You *did* voyage to Carcosa, did you not?'

Sophia nodded and turned haunted eyes upon her guests, eyes that quickly filled with tears. She placed a trembling hand to her mouth and began to sob quietly.

Blackwood went to her immediately, perched himself on the arm of her chair and placed a comforting arm about her shoulders. 'It's my fault,' he said.

'How so?' asked Castaigne.

'I prevented her from accompanying Detective de Chardin and me on our excursion into the Underground this afternoon. I thought I was acting correctly, protecting her from unnecessary risk...'

'I was angry,' Sophia managed to say through her tears. 'Humiliated... so I...' ·

'So you decided to take matters into your own hands,' completed Castaigne. 'You decided to gather some information for yourself. Well, I must say I admire your initiative, Lady Sophia. Most impressive.'

'What did you see on Carcosa?' Blackwood asked.

Sophia took a deep breath before replying, 'I saw what lies at the bottom of the Lake of Hali.'

At this, Castaigne jumped out of his seat and stood, regarding her with wide eyes. 'Great Scott! Not even I have entered the lake!'

'I wanted to see what was in there, and so I descended beneath the cloud waves, into the waters, but then something took hold of me and pulled me inside a vast and horrible building which stood on the lakebed.'

'The ancient Castle of Demhe,' said Castaigne, 'which sank into the lake shortly after the arrival of the King in Yellow on Carcosa. It is now his home. But tell me, your Ladyship: did you... did you *see* him?'

Sophia nodded, and Castaigne sank back onto his seat.

'I saw something that looked like a vast agglomeration of yellow rags, but each of them appeared to be like a creature in its own right: they moved and writhed around the centre, in which there was something that looked like a horrible mask. And then the mask fell aside, and the mass of rags unfolded...'

'What did they reveal?' asked Castaigne, his features drawn in horror and fascination.

Sophia shook her head and buried it in her hands. 'If you hadn't brought me back when you did...'

'It's all right Sophia,' said Blackwood, casting a glance at Castaigne which told the occultist that now was not the time to press her.

'There's something I have to tell you,' Sophia said presently. 'Two other people broke into your hotel room this evening.'

'What?' said Blackwood. 'Did they see you?'

'No: I hid in the bathroom. They were Charles Exeter's men; they mentioned his name while they were going through Dr Castaigne's things. They also took some of the Taduki drug.' Sophia did not mention the involvement of Queen Titania, since she felt that at this stage it would only complicate matters.

'Then Exeter is onto me,' said Castaigne. 'He knows, or suspects, that I'm aware of his activities and his intentions.'

'Then what are we to do?' asked Sophia.

'We must find the Anti-Prism and prevent Exeter from activating it,' Blackwood replied.

'The Anti-Prism?'

'A device of alien origin, which will enable the King in Yellow to come to Earth. We have a clue as to its location.'

So traumatic had her experience been that it was only now that Sophia recalled the events of earlier in the day. 'Thomas!' she said, jumping up from her chair and hurrying across the room to her desk. 'I went to see Charles Exeter this afternoon, as you suggested. He gave me this...'

As Blackwood stood up, she unwrapped the terracotta tile and handed it to him.

'Exeter *gave* you this?' he said, as Castaigne got to his feet and joined in the examination of the artefact.

'He did. It was strange... he seemed genuinely unnerved and gave every indication that he wanted you and I to get to the bottom of this business.'

'He's a sly one,' Castaigne muttered as he took the tile from Blackwood and peered at it closely. 'The Yellow Sign. Where did he say it was discovered?'

'In an ancient chamber, about two-thirds of the way from Bond Street to Westminster...'

'On the new deep-level Tube line?' said Blackwood.

'Precisely,' said Sophia.

'Did he tell you anything else about this chamber?' asked Castaigne.

Sophia nodded. 'He said that it is like a burial chamber – purpose-built, designed for that very function; the walls are covered with tiles just like this one. And he also said that a number of skeletons were discovered – minus their heads.'

Blackwood and Castaigne gave each other a long look. 'That must be the place,' said the occultist grimly. 'That must be the Void Chamber.'

'The Void Chamber?' said Blackwood.

'That's the name given to it by John Dee in the *Carcosa Fragments*, the place where the Anti-Prism is located.' Castaigne's brow grew furrowed, and his gaze grew fierce as he added, 'We must go there without delay and destroy it!'

Blackwood thought about this and then said, 'You're right when you say that the Anti-Prism must be destroyed… but I'm not so sure we should jump in immediately.'

Castaigne gave him an incredulous look. 'Why not? For Heaven's sake, man, the fate of the entire world is at stake!'

'I'm well aware of the danger, Dr Castaigne,' Blackwood replied levelly. 'But an assault on enemy territory is never likely to succeed when the lie of the land is unknown. We've never seen this Void Chamber, as you call it; we have no idea as to its layout, or even precisely where the Anti-Prism is located within it. What's more, we have the perfect opportunity to ascertain both of these things. Charles Exeter is unaware that Lady Sophia and I are onto him: he believes we are merely investigating the disturbances on the Underground and still have no clue as to their ultimate origin. That's very much to our advantage. Exeter has agreed to allow us to inspect the Void Chamber, and in the first instance, we should do so…'

'By way of reconnaissance,' said Castaigne.

'Precisely.'

The occultist considered this, and then nodded. 'I suppose that makes sense,' he conceded.

Sophia regarded Blackwood silently for a moment. 'You said "we", Thomas.'

He gave her a thin, rueful smile. 'Yes, Sophia. You and I.'

She gave him a smile of her own, satisfied and, he thought, a little mischievous. 'It may be dangerous, you know. It may even be a trap. Exeter is an intelligent, resourceful man. He may know more about us than he's letting on.'

'We'll take that risk,' Blackwood replied. 'Together.'

'When are you going in?' asked Castaigne.

'Tomorrow,' said Blackwood.

'Excellent. I wish I could go with you, but that's clearly impossible. Will you let me know what you find?'

'Of course.'

'In that case, I will take my leave of you.'

'I shall see you out, Dr Castaigne,' said Sophia. 'And once again, please accept my apologies for...'

Castaigne held up his hand. 'None are necessary, madam, I assure you. In fact, I had anticipated that much more effort would be required on my part to bring all this to the attention of the authorities. It is a great relief to know that both Her Majesty's Bureau of Clandestine Affairs and the Society for Psychical Research are already involved.'

'You may rest assured that we'll do everything in our power to meet this threat,' said Blackwood, 'and to neutralise it.'

Castaigne nodded, and, with a wry glance at Sophia, said, 'Well, at any rate you know where to find me.'

He picked up his hat and cane from the table where he had dropped them, and while Blackwood waited in the sitting room, Sophia saw him to the door.

When she returned, Blackwood asked her how she was feeling.

'Much better, thank you, Thomas,' she replied, but as she said this, Blackwood noted the fragility of her smile.

'You need rest. I'll be on my way.'

'Very well. What time shall we meet tomorrow?'

'I'll call for you at ten.'

In fact, Blackwood would have liked to stay a little longer to make absolutely sure that Sophia had fully recovered, but for him the evening was not yet over: there was something else he had to do before taking to his own bed.

Outside, he hailed a cab and told the driver to take him to Farringdon Street Station.

CHAPTER TWO:
Mr Exeter's Dream

'Someone was in Castaigne's hotel room?' said Charles Exeter.

The man standing before him nodded. 'Yes, sir. In the bathroom. We didn't manage to see who it was.'

'Why not?'

'They'd locked themselves in. I picked the lock and was about to open the door, when...'

'When what?'

The man shrugged helplessly. 'Something happened. There was a loud flapping and banging against the window. We knew it would attract attention, and we already had what we'd gone there for, so we left without seeing.'

'Did either of you mention my name while you were there? Take care now! Don't lie to me.'

The man hesitated, and Exeter shook his head in disgust. 'You goddamned idiot.'

'I'm sorry, Mr Exeter.'

'Get out.'

The man didn't need to be told twice. He turned on his heels and fled the room and the apartment without a backward glance.

Exeter stood up from the ornately-carved armchair and walked across the study to a table by the window, where he poured himself a large brandy and, sipping it contemplatively, looked out across the rooftops of Knightsbridge. Like many powerful, self-made men, he believed himself to be surrounded by fools and incompetents, the evidence being that he was the boss and they were not. The two cretins he had sent to Castaigne's hotel were a case in point. And yet, he doubted that much damage had been done; whoever had been skulking in the occultist's bathroom would, ultimately, be powerless against him and the being whose influence he could feel in his mind, even now.

That awareness brought with it the thought that he also was a lackey... but he quickly banished it, for like many lackeys, he believed that he had the potential to become the equal of his superior.

The strange sounds his men had heard were a different matter. They had evidently occurred at precisely the moment when they were about to open the bathroom door, which led Exeter to suspect that whoever had been hiding there had been aided by some supernatural agency.

There was an additional coincidence which gave Exeter pause for thought. That pretty young thing from the Society for Psychical Research had come to see him that very afternoon... and a few hours later, his men had found that someone had beaten them to Castaigne's hotel room. Was there a connection there?

Coincidence? he asked himself as he drained the last of his brandy. *Ain't no such thing, Charlie boy.*

As he undressed and made ready for bed, Exeter felt the familiar apprehension rising in him, as if he were a phobic who was about to be confronted by the object of his terror. He had felt this way ever since the King in Yellow had first made contact with him, shortly after his arrival in England. He knew that the being was manipulating him, bending him to its will in mysterious and subtle ways, and he recalled the waves of unutterable terror which had flooded through him that first time, when he heard its voice echoing through his dreaming mind. He had known immediately that the voice was not part of his dream; it was real and belonged to something that seethed and brooded an unthinkable distance away in the depths of space.

Part of Exeter's mind recoiled from the influence of the King in Yellow, but there was another part which had grown intoxicated by the vast power of the entity and welcomed it. Of course, Exeter was not sure that the feeling was his own, and sometimes he suspected that it was merely another element of the creature's control over him: a form of psychic venom which pacified his mind and made it yearn for further contact.

As he lay back in bed and turned out the oil lamp on his bedside table, Exeter's breath quickened momentarily, and then, just as swiftly, subsided. The muted sounds of the street outside likewise became misted by sleep and then vanished altogether from his awareness. He felt the first stirrings of a dream: disjointed images skittering like water on a hotplate, readying themselves to coalesce into a form of narrative... but the dream he might have had was stillborn, brushed aside by the thing which was now entering his mind.

<EXETER.>

It was not a voice, but rather a breath of thought from across the Æther, an exhalation that carried with it the sense impressions of words.

I am here, Exeter's sleeping mind replied.

<TELL ME OF YOUR PREPARATIONS.>

I have done as you instructed. I have activated the Servitor.

<IT IS GATHERING THE ONES WHO LINGER?>

Yes, just as you said it would. Their energy is contained within it. Soon it will reach a sufficient level to bring the Anti-Prism to life. And then...

<AND THEN I WILL COME.>

How does the Anti-Prism work?

Exeter sensed amusement from the thing in his mind as it replied, <THAT KNOWLEDGE IS NOT FOR YOU, EXETER. DO NOT ASK ME AGAIN.>

Forgive me.

<YOU ARE FORGIVEN.>

What will you do when you have come to Earth?

<I SHALL DRINK OF IT, AS I HAVE DRUNK OF CARCOSA AND ITS PEOPLE,> replied the voice of the King in Yellow. <BUT THAT WILL TAKE MANY YEARS – FAR LONGER THAN THE SPAN OF YOUR LIFE, EXETER, AND FOR THAT REASON YOU MAY REST ASSURED THAT YOU WILL ENJOY TO THE FULL THE REWARDS I SHALL BESTOW UPON YOU FOR YOUR LOYALTY.>

Why should you reward me, when I have no choice but to obey you?

There was amusement again as the voice replied, <A WELL-TRAINED DOG HAS NO CHOICE BUT TO OBEY ITS MASTER, AND THE MASTER REWARDS IT NONETHELESS. IT WILL GIVE ME SATISFACTION, AS IT HAS ALWAYS DONE IN THE PAST. BUT YOU HAVE MANY QUESTIONS THIS EVENING. WHAT HAS HAPPENED TO INFLAME YOUR CURIOSITY SO?>

Nothing.

<YOU LIE. YOUR PITIFUL MIND IS LAID BARE BEFORE ME. I CAN SEE YOUR MEMORIES, EXETER. I CAN SEE EVERYTHING. A HUMAN FEMALE – SHE CAME TO YOU TODAY.>

Exeter felt a surge of power in his mind – or rather, a *gathering* of power, as of some predator preparing to strike at its prey. He tried to withdraw from it, but of course, there was nowhere to withdraw *to*. He recalled the days of his boyhood, when he and his friends would go out and shoot bullfrogs in the forests of Pennsylvania during the summer; he recalled the sense of power when he had one of the creatures in his sights, and he wondered whether the King in Yellow felt the same satisfaction in its utter control over his life and destiny.

Sophia Harrington. Her name is Sophia Harrington.

<HER NAME IS UNIMPORTANT. I CAN SEE HER IMAGE IN YOUR MIND. SHE IS THE ONE WHO CAME BEFORE ME, ON CARCOSA.>

On Carcosa! How?

<SHE TOOK THE SUBSTANCE KNOWN AS TADUKI, THE SUBSTANCE WHICH ALLOWS MINDS SUCH AS YOURS TO VOYAGE THROUGH THIS UNIVERSE, UNENCUMBERED BY PHYSICAL MATTER. I WOULD HAVE FED ON HER, HAD SHE NOT BEEN SNATCHED AWAY AT THE CRITICAL MOMENT.>

The meddling wretch!

<SHE IS FULLY YOUR EQUAL, FOOL. SHE KNOWS I EXIST… AND SHE KNOWS THE LOCATION OF THE ANTI-PRISM.>

But she cannot know its purpose, Exeter replied desperately. *And besides, the knowledge will do her no good. I have invited her to inspect the Void Chamber…*

<I KNOW. THAT WAS A STUPID DECISION.>

On the contrary, it's the best way of getting her where I want her. Once she is in the Void Chamber, I'll get rid of her – kill her… or maybe give her to the Servitor, more fuel for the Anti-Prism…

<SHE IS NOT ACTING ALONE. IF SHE DISAPPEARS, OTHERS WILL COME.>

And if they do, they will suffer the same fate. And in any event, the psychic energy in the Servitor is approaching the critical level. It will soon be sufficient to activate the Anti-Prism. The time of your advent on Earth is fast approaching.

The voice in Exeter's head was silent for some moments. Presently, the King in Yellow said, <VERY WELL, EXETER. ALLOW HER TO ENTER THE VOID CHAMBER, BUT DO NOT KILL HER OR GIVE HER TO THE SERVITOR. TAKE HER AND KEEP HER SAFE, FOR I WILL WANT TO REACQUAINT MYSELF WITH HER WHEN I ARRIVE ON EARTH.>

CHAPTER THREE:
In the Chamber

'I'm glad to see that you have fully recovered, Mr Goodman-Brown,' said Blackwood, as the four-wheeler clattered through the mid-morning bustle towards Bond Street.

'Thank you, Mr Blackwood,' replied the psychometrist, who was sitting beside Sophia on the seat opposite. 'I must admit I received a pretty severe shock on that train – quite the most intense I have ever experienced during a contact analysis, I must say – but I am indeed ship-shape once again.'

'Splendid.'

'And you, Lady Sophia,' Goodman-Brown continued, turning to her. 'Are you quite sure that you are up to this? It sounds like you had a most dreadful experience last night.'

'Oh, I'm quite all right, I assure you,' she replied with a smile. 'Apart from a slight headache, of the kind which one experiences when one has had a little too much wine the previous evening, I feel surprisingly unscathed.'

Goodman-Brown smiled. 'I'm glad to hear it.'

Blackwood, however, could tell that Sophia was lying. As soon as he had laid eyes on her that morning, he knew that she had been severely wounded by her experience. The delightful glitter had gone from her brown eyes, her features were drawn and pale, and there was a subtle yet peculiar cadence of anguish in her voice which Blackwood had not detected even when she had spoken to him of the greatest tragedy of her life, the death of her father.

As to the depth and precise nature of his young companion's psychic wounds, Blackwood found it difficult to speculate. He would have to pay close attention to her, and try to ascertain what, precisely, her encounter with the King in Yellow had done to her. That *something* in her had changed, he had no doubt, for as soon as she had opened the door to admit him to her apartment that morning, he had felt the amulet embedded in his chest begin to tingle faintly...

'So... what are we looking for today?' Goodman-Brown asked.

'Any impressions you might be able to receive from the chamber which Exeter's men have discovered,' Blackwood replied. 'Anything at all which might be of use, including, if possible, the location of the Anti-Prism.'

'Ah, yes... the Anti-Prism. I wouldn't have thought that such a fantastic object could exist. Do you have any idea as to how it works?'

Blackwood shook his head. 'I'm afraid not, save that it utilises a combination of physics and Magick...'

'What form of Magick?'

'I'm afraid we don't know that either, Walter,' said Sophia. 'All we know for certain is that it may be instrumental in facilitating the arrival on Earth of an unspeakable abomination from the depths of space.'

Goodman-Brown paled a little at this. 'I see... well, I shall certainly do my best.'

'We can ask no more,' said Blackwood. 'Ah! Here we are.'

The carriage came to a halt and they stepped down to the street. Several passersby gazed at Sophia in unabashed surprise when they saw her outfit, which consisted of a dark grey blouse and jacket, trousers and sturdy walking boots, and more than one couple fell to whispered conversation and frequent backward glances as they walked past. Sophia seemed not to notice the mild sensation she was causing as she donned a leather shoulder bag containing several items of equipment. Indeed, she saw no good reason why the practicality offered by trousers should be enjoyed exclusively by men, and had had several pairs made for investigations such as this, where ease of movement was of paramount importance.

Both Blackwood and Goodman-Brown thought that she cut a very fine figure indeed, but, being unsure as to how to compliment her on her attire without appearing patronising or lacking in propriety, chose not to compliment her at all – which rather disappointed Sophia, especially with regard to Blackwood.

They entered the ticketing hall and were met by the Stationmaster, a plump, smartly-suited man who introduced himself as Miles Hoagland and informed them that he had been told by Mr Exeter to expect them. 'It's a fair walk from here to the chamber, and not a particularly comfortable one,' he said, glancing at Sophia. 'The lady was, er, wise to… er… dress with such appropriateness.'

Flattered, Sophia gave him a broad smile. 'Why thank you, sir,' she said, and, with a somewhat less appreciative glance at Blackwood, followed him across the ticketing hall.

'Have you seen the chamber yourself, Mr Hoagland?' asked Blackwood, as they descended a wide spiral staircase of echoing steel.

'No, sir, I have not,' he replied without looking back. 'Nor would I want to, if some of the things I've heard are even half true.'

'What do you mean, Mr Hoagland?' asked Sophia, who was following immediately behind him.

'The men who have been in there don't like it, ma'am. They say there's something horrible about the place – something *unnatural*. Some say they get a feeling of being watched by someone or something... they say the place should have been left alone, filled in as soon as it was found.'

'Hardly a practical suggestion,' said Blackwood.

'Indeed not, but fear is hardly the province of rational or practical thought, and believe me, I've heard real fear in their voices when they talk about that place.'

'What else do they say – apart from the business about feeling as if they're being watched?'

'All kinds of things. I take a drink with some of them now and then, at the Tapper's Arms around the corner from here. And when they've had a few... well, it loosens their tongues. They talk about having terrible nightmares...' Hoagland hesitated and cast a nervous glance over his shoulder.

'Go on, Mr Hoagland,' said Blackwood.

'I'm not sure I should, sir.'

'Why not?'

'Do you feel you are breaking a confidence?' asked Sophia.

Hoagland nodded. 'Yes I do, ma'am... yes, that's exactly it.'

'But you must understand that we are here to help, to investigate the origin of the chamber, to find out what it means and how it relates to the wider disturbances on the Underground. It would be a great service to the city – to the Empire, indeed – to tell us everything you have been told.'

They had reached the bottom of the staircase and had begun to make their way along a broad corridor faced with pristine white tiles and brightly lit with gas lamps. Their footfalls echoed back and forth along the corridor.

Hoagland sighed. 'Very well, ma'am. As I say, some of the lads have had terrible nightmares since the place was found: dreams of a strange and singular country, with more than one moon in the sky, and the stars shining black instead of white, if you can credit such a thing.'

'Believe me, Mr Hoagland, I can,' Sophia said.

'And they tell of a lake full of clouds instead of water – but clouds which behave *as if* they were water… and strange cities on the edge of the lake. I've looked into their eyes, ma'am, I tell you I have… and I've seen fear there, fear the likes of which I've never seen in the eyes of a man, which can't be dulled by drink the way normal fear can.'

'Interesting,' said Goodman-Brown. 'It would appear that there's a strong psychic link between the chamber and Carcosa.'

'Carcosa, sir?' said Hoagland, glancing back at the psychometrist.

'That's the name of the world the men have glimpsed in their dreams,' he replied.

Hoagland raised his eyebrows. 'Do you mean to say that the place really exists?'

'Yes, Mr Hoagland,' said Blackwood. 'It exists.'

'Good grief!'

They reached the end of the corridor and emerged onto the platform. Sophia was struck by the silence and desertion of the place; she was used to seeing the Underground thronging with people of all classes, but now it was as still and quiet as a mausoleum. It was rather unsettling to be in a place designed and built to be used by thousands of people, but in which no people were to be seen. It was only when the distant rumble of a train came to their ears from somewhere above that she remembered they were in a brand new section of the station, part of the new deep-level Tube line running from Bond Street to Westminster, which was yet to echo with the footfalls of passengers.

Hoagland indicated the mouth of the tunnel to their right. 'The chamber lies in that direction, about a mile or so. Mr Exeter has given me instructions that I am to accompany you.' His tone suggested that he was anything but pleased with his assignment.

'We appreciate it, Mr Hoagland,' said Sophia. She approached the edge of the platform and looked down. 'No tracks?'

'No ma'am, not yet. The metals are not laid until the tunnels are completed... and I don't anticipate that they will be laid *here* anytime soon.'

'That's a fair bet,' muttered Blackwood as he jumped down from the platform. He turned, intending to offer Sophia his hand, but she had already dropped lithely down beside him.

She looked up at Hoagland and Goodman-Brown. 'Shall we, gentlemen?'

*

Dimly lit by freestanding lamps, the tunnel extended perhaps a hundred yards into the distance before curving away to the right. Although the heavy ribbing of the new steel and concrete reinforcing sections was unmarred by the grime of the older parts of the network, they still presented a deeply sinister and unsettling aspect to the explorers as they left the station behind and headed into the gloom.

'Have you had any unusual experiences on the Underground, Mr Hoagland?' asked Sophia.

'Me, ma'am? Why, yes, as a matter of fact I have.'

'What happened?'

'Well...' He hesitated and glanced at her. Her expression clearly indicated that she would brook no refusal, and in truth she was such an uncommonly fine-looking girl that he felt it would be unmanly to refuse to elaborate. He sighed. 'It's not easy to talk about; it was a most upsetting and alarming experience.'

213

'I understand entirely, sir,' she replied in a gentle voice. 'And please believe me when I say that I have had frightful experiences myself. Sometimes… it helps one to share them.'

Behind them, Blackwood looked at Sophia but said nothing.

'About a fortnight ago,' said Hoagland, 'I was working late in my office. I turned away from my desk, intending to retrieve some papers from my file cabinet, when I saw a face emerging from the wall…'

'A face?' said Goodman-Brown.

Hoagland nodded. 'As if someone was standing *inside* the wall and had leaned forward. It appeared to be a man, perhaps in his thirties. I froze upon the spot, and for some moments we simply stared at each other. I was beside myself with fear, I don't mind admitting, but the face continued to regard me. Eventually, I managed to ask him who he was, but he offered no answer. He merely said, 'Help us,' and vanished. I fled from the room immediately, and it has been all I can do to return there every day since.'

'I understand your fear, Mr Hoagland,' said Sophia. 'But you must likewise understand that you had – and have – nothing to fear from any of the poor souls who linger here.'

'That's true, ma'am,' the Stationmaster replied. 'But it's not them I'm afraid of… it's what *they* are afraid of that troubles me.'

'A wise distinction, sir,' said Blackwood.

They continued along the tunnel in silence for a while, and as they walked, Blackwood listened intently for any strange sounds that might herald the reappearance of the lethal abnormality that he and de Chardin had heard the previous afternoon. However, the amulet in his chest continued to tingle only faintly, for which he was grateful.

Hoagland pointed ahead. 'The tunnel comes to an end there, see?'

'Yes,' replied Blackwood. 'But where is the Greathead shield?'

'The tunnelling shield was withdrawn when digging was halted; it's now on the other side of the new station through which we entered.'

They approached the end of the tunnel and saw that it opened into a large cavity, perhaps a hundred yards across, like a subterranean cave. It was clearly not a cave, however, for by the light of a dozen or so free-standing gas lamps arranged around the floor, they could see that it was perfectly circular, its single, curving wall covered with a patchwork of thousands upon thousands of square tiles.

Blackwood stood on the edge and saw that a ladder had been placed there, allowing access to the floor of the chamber, which he estimated to be about twenty feet below. Like the ceiling forty feet above, the floor was covered with the same square tiles as the wall, and from his vantage point, he could see that they all contained the Yellow Sign. Upon the floor of the chamber stood five large blocks of dark stone, each hewn into the shape of a triangular prism, their vertical faces about eight feet high and five feet wide. Each of these prism-like monoliths pointed towards the centre of the chamber.

As he gazed down, Blackwood could feel his amulet begin to stir, but it was like no sensation he had felt before. It was a dull throb, deeply uncomfortable, like a badly-dressed wound that had become infected. The sensation made him feel sick, and his skin crawled as though it had become host to some alien parasite.

Sophia noticed his expression and placed a hand upon his shoulder. 'Are you all right, Thomas?'

'Yes,' he nodded, 'I'm fine.' He looked into her eyes and saw his own pain mirrored there. 'Are you quite sure you want to be here?' he whispered.

She gave him a weak smile. 'No, but neither of us have any choice.'

He stroked her face gently with a trembling hand and then turned and climbed onto the ladder. Sophia and the others followed him down to the chamber's floor, and when they had all reached the foot of the ladder, Goodman-Brown turned and surveyed their surroundings.

'Hard to believe,' he said wonderingly, 'that this place was built by an ancient tribe barely out of the Stone Age.'

'They didn't do it alone,' Blackwood replied as he walked slowly away from the curving wall and looked around. He pointed to the nearest of the monoliths. 'Mr Goodman-Brown, what do you make of these?'

When the psychometrist did not answer, Blackwood turned and glanced in his direction and saw that he was standing still with his eyes closed. There was a deep frown upon his brow.

'Walter...?' said Sophia, moving to his side.

'There is a great and terrible power in this place,' Goodman-Brown said. 'Normally, I need to make direct physical contact with an object in order to apprehend its nature and history. But here... *here* the impressions flow through me like a great tide. Good God! What kind of place is this?'

'We were rather hoping *you* could tell *us*,' said Blackwood.

'It seems that the power here – whatever it is – is amplifying my abilities. It *is* connected to Carcosa... through some mechanism I don't understand.'

'Tell us what you are experiencing, Walter,' said Sophia.

'It's difficult to put into words,' the psychometrist replied. He had put his hands to his temples and was slowly massaging them, as if he were suffering from an intense headache. 'There is space... deep, infinite... a vast swathe of stars... a distant world, ruined and forlorn in the great emptiness, all but consumed by something awful which fastened itself upon it in the dim and distant past. But there is something else...'

'What else?' prompted Sophia. 'What...?' She hesitated and then sank suddenly to her knees.

Blackwood rushed to her and took her in his arms. 'Sophia! What is it?'

'I... can feel the lake around me,' she said breathlessly. 'As if I am back on Carcosa. I can *feel* the waters surrounding me.'

'But you are not there,' he said, taking her face in his hands. Her skin was damp with sweat, and when he placed a hand on her forehead, he could feel that she was burning with fever. 'I'm taking you out of here.'

'No! We can't leave, not now. We... we have a job to do, Thomas. I'm all right – really I am. Speak... speak to Walter.'

Blackwood glanced up at the psychometrist, who was still standing beside them, with his eyes closed and his hands rubbing incessantly at his temples. 'All right, Goodman-Brown,' he said. 'Let's get this over with. Tell us what you are sensing, and be quick about it!'

'A song,' Goodman-Brown said.

'What?'

'I can hear a song, echoing through the infinite vault of space.'

'The song of the Hyades,' Sophia whispered, her head resting against Blackwood's shoulder. '*Songs that the Hyades shall sing... where flap the tatters of the King...* you remember, Thomas...'

'Yes, the Song of Cassilda. But that is just a poem.'

Sophia shook her head weakly. 'No, it's much more than that.'

'Sophia is right,' said Goodman-Brown. 'The stars of the Hyades *are* singing, but it is a song like none I have ever heard before: a sound which is not a sound... an *emanation*, rather, drifting through the void of space, from the stars which look in anguish upon the ruined world of Carcosa.'

'What does all this mean?' asked Miles Hoagland in a tremulous voice, as his eyes darted fearfully about the chamber.

'Quiet!' ordered Blackwood. 'Goodman-Brown, continue.'

'The Anti-Prism is here, somewhere. Even in its dormant state, it is not completely inert. It is waiting... waiting for a connection yet to be made, while the Hyades sing. They are calling for help... yes, I can feel it – *they are calling for help*, as they have done for millennia.'

'If they are calling for help,' said Blackwood, 'who or what are they calling *to*?'

'Something out there,' replied Goodman-Brown. His voice was now as breathless as Sophia's. 'There is something out there... out in the farthest reaches of the cosmos, much farther away than Carcosa... my God, Blackwood. It's something of which even the King in Yellow is terrified!'

'Are you sure?'

'I can feel the abomination's fear and the desperation of the Hyades. They are calling to this... *other*. They are begging it to come and deliver them from the King in Yellow.'

'He's right, Thomas,' whispered Sophia. 'I can feel it now. The King in Yellow is hiding in the Lake of Hali... *hiding*. He is not merely preparing to travel to the Earth; he is preparing to *flee* here!'

At that moment, the air cracked with a thunderous report which echoed around the chamber. Goodman-Brown cried out. Blackwood glanced at him, and saw a dark red patch spreading rapidly across his white shirt directly over his heart. Without another sound, the psychometrist collapsed to the floor and lay still.

'God in Heaven!' cried Hoagland. 'He is shot!'

Instantly, Blackwood was on his feet with Sophia in his arms. Without looking back, he sprinted for the nearest of the black stone monoliths as more shots rang out, shattering the tiles inches from his racing feet. He knew without looking where the shots were coming from. There was only way in or out of the chamber: the newly built tunnel through which they had come. In the instant before he dived behind the stone, he caught a glimpse of a figure standing above, in the mouth of the tunnel.

'Hoagland!' he shouted. 'Take cover!'

He heard running steps, another shot, a cry of pain, and then silence.

Damn and blast! he thought, taking his revolver from his pocket and checking to see that it was fully loaded. He risked a quick peek around the edge of the monolith, and saw that their attacker was now halfway down the ladder. He would have put a bullet through his back, had not two more figures appeared in the mouth of the tunnel, each with his own weapon. One of them fired at Blackwood, and it was only by the merest fraction that the bullet missed his head. He ducked back behind the monolith.

'They're Exeter's men, aren't they?' Sophia said.

'I shouldn't be at all surprised,' he replied. 'Three of them, at least… possibly more.'

'What are we going to do?'

Blackwood considered his options. In another few moments, the man who had shot Goodman-Brown would be across the chamber and upon them, while his fellows remained at their vantage point in the tunnel mouth, ready to fire down upon Blackwood the instant he appeared from behind the monolith.

'I won't lie to you, my dear,' he said. 'We're in a bit of a fix.'

'That much is painfully clear, Thomas. But what are we going to do?'

Blackwood sighed.

There was only one thing he *could* do…

CHAPTER FOUR:
The Servitor

Charles Exeter could feel the thoughts of the King in Yellow stirring in his mind – or at least, those mental emanations which were subtle enough not to cause screaming insanity in the moments before the blood in his brain began to boil. He was still in his Knightsbridge apartments, having left word at the offices of the CSLR that he would be working from home for a few days and should be considered unavailable. He reflected that 'working from home' may have been the greatest euphemism in history, referring as it did to the growing frequency of communications from Carcosa.

The King in Yellow was growing restless: Exeter could feel the impatience in the thoughts worming their way through his mind. The entity wanted to be away from Carcosa and upon the Earth; he was ravening for a new world on which to feed, and Exeter felt a mixture of terror at the form which that feeding would take and elation at the thought of the rewards that would be his when the entity arrived to claim his dominion.

Exeter went to his study, sat himself in his favourite armchair and closed his eyes.

<EXETER.>

I am here.

<THE TIME OF MY ARRIVAL IS FAST APPROACHING, IS IT NOT?>

Yes.

<THE GATE BETWEEN WORLDS WILL SOON BE OPENED. IS THE VOID CHAMBER PREPARED?>

I have checked. The prisms are aligned with the centre. All that is required now is for the Servitor to discharge its contents.

<GOOD. NOW BRING THE SERVITOR HERE, FOR I WISH TO SEE FOR MYSELF THAT IT IS FULLY CHARGED WITH THE PSYCHIC ENERGY OF THE HUMAN SOULS WHICH IT HAS CONSUMED. DO AS I HAVE TAUGHT YOU. SUMMON THE SERVITOR!>

Exeter followed the command. Using a part of his mind which he had never suspected he possessed, but which the King in Yellow had revealed to him and taught him to master, he called out silently to the thing that prowled the Underground, bidding it to leave its subterranean lair and manifest itself before him.

The mental substrates, of which the spiritualistic medium is keenly aware and which she is able to access, flared to life in the dark recesses of Exeter's brain and transmitted the psychic signal. The King in Yellow had taught him the words to use – words which no human vocal chords could enunciate, but which the properly-trained mind could express silently in strange modes of thought, akin to arcane and abstract mathematics. In his more jaundiced moments, Exeter called these modes of thought 'the mathematics of damnation'. He didn't like the phrase, didn't much care for the connotations, especially as they applied to him, but it had stuck in his mind, and in fact it appealed to the same rebellious part of his personality which had brought him into possession of more than one fortune.

Sitting back in his armchair, his eyes still closed, his breath coming in strong, deep draughts, Exeter transmitted the blasphemous mental formulae, and then waited.

*

Outside in the crowded streets of Knightsbridge, those who happened to glance heavenward at a certain moment saw something rather strange in the overcast sky. It was not enough to cause consternation or panic; hardly enough, indeed, to merit a word or two of bemusement to a companion or a fellow passerby, but it did cause several citizens of the metropolis to scratch their heads, figuratively if not literally, and continue about their business marvelling at the complexities of the English weather.

A few might have commented in passing on the curious phenomenon later, to friends or work colleagues, or to their families when they returned home that evening. If pressed for a description, some might have likened it to a small tornado or a waterspout – albeit one which was so tenuous and translucent that it could hardly be said to have been visible at all; a wisp of swirling air that seemed to ripple up from the ground and snake across the sky towards the top floor of a certain large apartment building.

*

Exeter opened his eyes and watched as the air in his study began to twitch and stir, as if with a heat haze. The disturbance gradually grew more pronounced, plucking papers from his desk and whirling them around the room, while the air began to whistle and sing in strange, unearthly tones.

With a mixture of terror and satisfaction, Exeter watched as the miniature hurricane slowly abated, coalescing into something which he could not describe, even though it hung in the air in full view before him. All he knew was that it was vast – far larger than the room in which it had

223

manifested, and yet it was contained in its entirety within the room, as though the three dimensions of space had been stretched to accommodate it.

The thing which had driven Alfie Morgan to madness floated before Charles Exeter, and the railway magnate felt his own mind starting to buckle under the pressure of its alien aspect, its sheer *otherness*. Were it not for the presence of the King in Yellow's thoughts in his mind, reinforcing it in the manner of a scaffold shoring up a sagging building, Exeter knew that he too would have been driven to screaming insanity by the sight of it.

<HOW WEAK YOUR MIND IS, EXETER,> the King in Yellow observed. <HOW FRAGILE, LIKE A COBWEB IN THE HURRICANE THAT IS THE UNIVERSE.>

Exeter didn't answer, for he knew it was true: the human mind *was* like a cobweb, and the Earth was like an ancient house whose atmosphere was perfectly still, perfectly tranquil. Not a breath of wind stirred in the house, while outside in the depths of space and time, storms of alienness raged with such unimaginable intensity that the mind of humanity would never be able to withstand them, would be annihilated at their first touch.

<BEHOLD,> said the voice of the King in Yellow. <MY SERVITOR.>

How arrogant of this pipsqueak race to believe that there was any place for it beyond the confines of its tiny world! Its destiny was not to expand into the cosmos and explore the multitude of worlds rolling silently through the void: it was to provide sustenance for the godlike beings who dwelled there. Beings vast, ancient and ineffably powerful.

Beings like the King in Yellow.

<YES, EXETER,> said the voice within his mind. <THAT IS THE TRUE PURPOSE AND DESTINY OF BEINGS SUCH AS YOU.>

Exeter became aware of vague shapes moving within the thing which floated before him. The shapes moved rapidly forward towards the surface and back into the centre, as though carried by powerful convection currents, and although they were difficult to discern – appearing as little more than disturbances within the churning mass – Exeter could perceive that they were faces, misshapen, anguished, silently screaming.

Part of him reacted with appalled sympathy for their plight, but in truth it was a very small and insignificant part: the sense of human fellow-feeling which had long ago been vanquished by avarice and aggressive self-interest. To be sure, Exeter pitied the imprisoned souls of those who had lingered on the Underground long after they should have departed for the next life, but that pity was small indeed, more an intellectual observation than a genuinely felt emotion.

Nevertheless, it did not go unnoticed by the King in Yellow.

<YOU PITY THEM?> There was a tone of amusement in the voice which made Exeter's skin crawl.

Only a little. And only because they don't realise the higher purpose to which they are to contribute.

<WELL SAID. I HAVE COMPLETED MY ANALYSIS OF THE SERVITOR. IT IS FULLY CHARGED WITH THE PSYCHIC ENERGY OF THE SOULS WHICH IT HAS CONSUMED. IT IS NOW READY TO RETURN TO THE VOID CHAMBER. ONCE IT HAS DONE SO, YOU WILL JOIN IT THERE, SO THAT YOU MAY WITNESS MY ADVENT UPON EARTH.>

I am honoured.

<I CAN TASTE YOUR WORLD ALREADY, EXETER. I HUNGER FOR IT. PREPARE YOURSELF, FOR I AM COMING VERY SOON.>

CHAPTER FIVE:
A Storm of Spirits

Another shot thundered through the Void Chamber, echoing cacophonously in the still air. Clearly, whoever had fired was trying to spook Blackwood and Sophia into making a run for it, allowing them to be picked off more easily.

Blackwood, however, wasn't going to give them the satisfaction. He thrust his head and right arm around the edge of the stone and let off a shot, which narrowly missed one of the men, before ducking back as the replying bullet hurtled past his head. The brief glimpse confirmed his earlier suspicion: the second and third man were remaining in the tunnel mouth twenty feet above the chamber's floor so that they could fire down with ease, while their colleague was steadily approaching the monolith behind which Blackwood and Sophia were taking cover. A pretty good strategy, and one which showed every indication of succeeding... unless Blackwood played what he hoped was his trump card.

'Anne!' he cried out suddenly. 'Anne Naylor! The time is now!'

'Thomas, what are you doing?' said Sophia.

'I suspected that something like this might happen,' he replied quickly. 'So, after taking leave of you last night, I went to Farringdon Street Station, where the ghost of Anne

Naylor has most often been seen. I called to her, and she came... and I asked her for a favour.'

'A favour? What are you talking about?'

'You'll see, if she makes good on her word.' Blackwood called out again, 'Anne! The time is now!'

They heard the men begin to mutter to each other, clearly bemused at what they considered to be a bizarre tactic on the part of their quarry. They only became fully aware of how bizarre when the figures began to emerge into the Void Chamber, first from the curving wall, and then from the floor and ceiling as well.

Sophia gasped as the chamber rapidly became crowded with the ghosts of the Underground – or at least, those who had not yet been taken by the abomination that haunted the place alongside them. The shades of the departed were everywhere she looked, walking across the floor and floating through the air. They were dressed in clothes from a bewildering array of periods, contemporary and historical; there were men, women and children; husbands, wives, fathers, sons, daughters; victims of a thousand tragedies, bearers of a thousand sadnesses, who for years or centuries had lingered unseen, for the most part at least, walking the platforms and tunnels of the railway network alongside the living.

'Good grief!' Sophia whispered. 'There are so many of them... so many who have not passed on.'

'And many more who will *never* pass on, thanks to the Servitor,' said Blackwood bitterly. 'Now watch.'

From their limited vantage point, they could see that the ghosts had begun to whirl around the chamber like a great hurricane, hurtling through the air and screaming in rage. They heard more shots being fired by their would-be assassins, who were now shouting to each other in confusion and panic.

Blackwood risked another look around the edge of the monolith, and what he saw both gratified and terrified him. The air was an indescribable confusion of unearthly movement, a raging gyre of semi-translucent forms which descended time and again upon the man who had been stalking them across the chamber's floor, and who now lay cowering upon the tiles, his arms covering his head in a futile attempt to shield himself from the fury of the spirits. One after another, they plunged through his body, making him shake and convulse and scream with unalloyed terror.

Blackwood glanced up at the mouth of the tunnel and saw that it was empty. The man's accomplices had seen what was happening to him and had clearly given up their mission as a bad job and fled.

'The danger is passed,' he said to Sophia. 'Can you walk?'

'Yes,' she replied. 'I'm all right.'

'Good show! Come on.'

Taking her by the hand, Blackwood stood up and moved through the maelstrom of whirling spirit forms. When they reached the helpless villain, he took a pair of handcuffs from his coat pocket, wrenched the man's arms behind his back and clapped them upon his wrists. The man hardly seemed to notice as he screamed again and again, '*Oh God, make them stop!*'

'Spirits of the Underground,' Blackwood cried. 'Enough! We have him. He is in our custody now, and we will make certain that he faces justice!'

Almost immediately, the raging storm of spirits began to abate, until finally they were left alone in the chamber with the assassin-turned-quarry lying prone and trembling at their feet. The ghosts of the Underground had departed, except for one, who walked towards them and turned her little blue face up to them.

'I did as you asked, sir,' said Anne Naylor.

Blackwood smiled down at her. 'Yes, Anne. And I thank you from the bottom of my heart, as I thank all of the others.'

Sophia hurried to Goodman-Brown and checked his pulse, then turned tearful eyes to Blackwood. 'He's dead, Thomas.'

'And Hoagland?'

Sophia checked the Stationmaster and shook her head.

Blackwood grabbed the man who lay at his feet, turned him over and took hold of him by the lapels of his overcoat. 'You filthy cad! You'll answer for this – you and your employer!'

'Please,' the man replied. 'Please just get me out of here!'

'Oh, I'll get you out of here all right. Next stop for you, my lad, is New Scotland Temple.'

'Anywhere,' the man cried. 'Anywhere but here.'

'What about Walter and Mr Hoagland?' asked Sophia.

Blackwood hoisted the villain to his feet. 'I'll telegraph to the authorities from the station office and make the necessary arrangements…' He was about to say more, but the words stalled in his mouth as he glanced at the bodies of Walter Goodman-Brown and Miles Hoagland, for beside them now stood the shades of the two men, looking down silently upon their physical forms.

Sophia stepped back. 'Walter,' she said, very quietly.

The ghost of Goodman-Brown looked at her, gave her a melancholy smile, and vanished.

Miles Hoagland's shade looked around, fear and confusion clouding his ethereal features. Anne Naylor walked up to him and took one of his hands in hers. Turning to Blackwood, she said, 'Don't worry, sir. I'll look after him.'

And with that, she too vanished, taking the ghost of Miles Hoagland with her.

CHAPTER SIX:
Oberon and Titania

When Blackwood and Sophia arrived at Detective de Chardin's office at New Scotland Temple, they were surprised to see that Simon Castaigne was there. The occultist stood up and gave a small bow as they entered.

'Good to see you again, Dr Castaigne,' said Blackwood, stepping forward to shake his hand.

'And you, sir. I have taken the liberty of bringing Detective de Chardin up to date on our discoveries and speculations so far.'

'Capital,' replied Blackwood.

De Chardin stepped forward. 'Dr Castaigne also tells me that you made the right decision in not pursuing that hellish thing on the Underground.' He offered Blackwood his hand. 'My apologies, sir; I shouldn't have doubted your judgement.'

The Special Investigator gave the detective a genuine smile as he shook his hand. 'Think nothing of it, de Chardin.'

'The detective told me that you have apprehended one of Exeter's men,' said Castaigne.

'That's correct, although at the cost of two lives.'

Castaigne sighed and shook his head. 'That's terrible. Who were they?'

'Walter Goodman-Brown, the SPR psychometrist who had been helping us, and the Stationmaster at Bond Street, Miles Hoagland.'

'Well,' said de Chardin as he motioned his two new guests to have a seat, 'we'll make quite certain that he answers for his crimes.'

'Have you questioned him yet?' asked Blackwood.

'Yes, and we managed to get some interesting facts out of him – along with a fair bit of nonsense, I have to say.'

'How so?'

'It seems that Exeter has lied to his ruffians: the man in our custody babbled about some fabulous treasure that he thinks is hidden somewhere beneath the new chamber. I suppose it's a plausible fiction, and it does make sense for Exeter to keep the truth from his henchmen.'

'Did he say anything more about this "treasure"?' asked Blackwood.

'Only that he was told by Exeter that it would be uncovered tomorrow night...'

'*Tomorrow night?*' Blackwood exclaimed.

De Chardin nodded. 'It seems that Exeter has gathered all his thugs and lackeys together and told them that they will be required to defend the chamber while he secures its hidden contents.' The detective shook his head and gave a humourless chuckle. 'That poor dolt down there; he thinks he's going to be rich.'

'Exeter may be lying to his men about what's really in the chamber,' Blackwood said, 'but he's certainly telling the truth about when the show's going to start. We have very little time.'

'True enough,' agreed de Chardin. 'Did Mr Goodman-Brown manage to glean any information before he was killed?'

'Walter said that he heard a kind of song emanating from the Hyades, the group of stars where Carcosa is located,' Sophia replied.

'A *song*?' said de Chardin.

'A kind of distress signal, you might say,' Blackwood added. 'Goodman-Brown thought that the very stars themselves are calling out for aid… to something…'

'And what is this "something" which they are calling out to?' asked de Chardin, a deep frown clouding his features.

'Something which apparently exists in the profoundest reaches of space… something of which even the King in Yellow is terrified.'

'What?' blurted Castaigne, sitting forward suddenly in his chair.

'It's true, Dr Castaigne,' said Sophia. 'Before he… before he died, Walter said he had the impression that the King in Yellow is preparing to flee to the Earth to escape the thing, which must, I suppose, be approaching Carcosa even as we speak.'

'In that case, our problems are over, surely,' said de Chardin. 'We can sit back and let this space-blighter have at the King in Yellow…'

Blackwood shook his head. 'I'm afraid not. There's no guarantee that this thing – whatever it is – will reach Carcosa before the King in Yellow has embarked upon his journey to Earth – especially if, as now appears obvious, that journey will be undertaken tomorrow night.' He turned to Castaigne. 'We must return to the Void Chamber without delay, find the Anti-Prism and destroy it, before that can happen.'

'Agreed,' replied the occultist.

Blackwood returned his attention to de Chardin. 'And we'll need your help. It's certain that Exeter will have more men there by now. A sizeable contingent of Templar Police will come in very handy.'

'Consider it done,' de Chardin replied.

Blackwood turned to Castaigne. 'I must say I admire your initiative in coming to New Scotland Temple to inform Detective de Chardin of the latest developments, but I'm curious as to what prompted you to do so. I don't recall giving you his name at the Lodge…'

Castaigne and de Chardin exchanged a glance before the occultist replied, 'I was asked to come here to wait for you.'

'By Detective de Chardin?'

'No.'

'By whom, then?'

'By us,' said a deep, powerful voice from a far corner of the room.

They all turned to see Oberon and Titania standing there.

*

As the Faerie King and Queen stepped forward, their iridescent dragonfly wings catching the pale lilac light which surrounded them, the humans felt the breath stall in their throats at their unutterable splendour and beauty, and they felt their heartbeats rising thunderously as the beings' vast yet subtle power flooded their awareness. Without thinking, they all stood up – a sign of deference which caused Oberon and Titania to glance at each other and smile. The last time Blackwood and Sophia had seen them together was during their brief visit to the Faerie Realm a few weeks ago while they were engaged upon the affair of the Martian Ambassador. But the shock of seeing Oberon in his true form was as profound as if Blackwood were meeting him for the first time, and Titania was even more exquisite than he recalled.

'You… are without your disguise, sir,' said Blackwood.

'I am,' Oberon replied.

Titania walked swiftly to Sophia and gently took hold of her hands. 'I am glad to see that you are safe,' she said, 'in spite of your refusal to heed my advice.'

'Part of me wishes I had,' Sophia replied. 'My experience on Carcosa was... unsettling to say the least.'

'I do not doubt it.'

Titania glanced at Simon Castaigne and Gerhard de Chardin, who were gazing at her in unabashed astonishment, for this was the first time that they had set eyes upon her, and they were having a great deal of trouble believing that any creature in the whole universe could be as beautiful as she.

'Sit, my friends,' said Oberon. 'We have much to discuss.'

As quickly as they had got to their feet, the humans obeyed his command (for as such they instinctively took his words) and retook their chairs.

Oberon addressed Blackwood and Sophia. 'Do you recall, at our last meeting, that I told you there were certain pressing matters in the deep Æther which required my attention?'

'Yes,' Sophia replied. 'We were in my office at the SPR. You said you could not linger there for long.'

'And indeed I could not,' the Faerie King replied. 'You, Thomas, suspected that my business had to do with Carcosa, and you were right, for it was to Carcosa that I voyaged as soon as I left Sophia's office.'

'Then you *are* involved in our struggle against the King in Yellow,' said Blackwood.

Oberon nodded. 'As I said to you before, the Faerie Realm is permitted by our Covenant with the universe to intervene, to a certain extent, in the affairs of Earth when the planet is in dire peril. This is one such occasion.'

Castaigne put up his hand tentatively, in the manner of a schoolboy trying to attract his master's attention. Titania giggled, and Oberon smiled at him. 'Speak, Dr Castaigne.'

'May I... may I ask the reason for your journey to Carcosa?'

'Impatient, isn't he?' said Titania to her husband.

'Indeed. Do not worry, for I will explain all to you.'

Castaigne lowered his hand and gave an embarrassed cough.

'I went to that unhappy world to converse with its Planetary Angels, who are mourning the loss of Carcosan life. You, Castaigne, have seen for yourself how the planet has been stripped of almost everything that once lived and breathed upon its surface, leaving it a barren sphere of rock which will drift forevermore through the gulfs of space and time, in silence and death, inhabited by only a few remnants of a once-thriving population.'

'If I may enquire,' said de Chardin, 'what are Planetary Angels?'

'They are the spirits of worlds,' replied Titania. 'They exist on all planets where there is life, and they live in a realm which is coterminous with the physical plane. The Faerie are the Planetary Angels of Earth.'

'I was able to learn much from the Angels of Carcosa,' Oberon continued. 'They were once powerful beings, but Carcosa is far more ancient than the Earth, and over the aeons their strength has waned. Once the King in Yellow had arrived on their beloved world, there was nothing they could do to defend it against his depredations. Gradually, the entity consumed it and its people, and now there is nothing left but barren rock and a handful of cities clinging to the edge of oblivion.

'Walter Goodman-Brown was correct: the Hyades *are* singing a song of distress, as it is written in Cassilda's Song. They have been doing so for many centuries, for stars possess awareness and intelligence – although it is an intelligence which is incomprehensible to the beings living upon the worlds which orbit them. The Hyades became aware that something awful had arrived on Carcosa and responded instinctively to its loathsome presence with their song of despair.'

'And is it also true that the King in Yellow is hiding from something?' asked Blackwood.

'Oh yes,' Oberon replied. 'That is quite true. I also conversed with the stars of the Hyades, and learned much from them. They know a great deal that is forever hidden from the inhabitants of planets, about the secrets of the universe, and some of this information I persuaded them to share with me. The Hyades spoke of something called the Wanderer, which has been pursuing the King in Yellow since before the dawn of recorded time.'

'The Wanderer?' said Castaigne. 'In all my researches I've never heard of it. What is it?'

'I am uncertain, as are the Hyades. They speculated that it is perhaps an entity of some kind, or perhaps the product of an ancient technology, created by a distant and unknown civilisation somewhere in the depths of the Æther, with the purpose of defending our universe against threats from Outside... perhaps a super-civilisation's equivalent of your Bureau of Clandestine Affairs, Thomas,' he added.

'In any event, the King in Yellow *is* afraid of it, and has been moving from planet to planet for countless aeons, feeding and hiding... feeding and hiding... for he has placed Anti-Prisms upon worlds without number throughout this universe, forming a transit network for himself.'

'And that is the fate which awaits the Earth, if the fiend is allowed to come here?' said de Chardin.

Oberon nodded. 'Once he has established himself on Earth, the King in Yellow will begin to feed upon its inhabitants, both human and animal – indeed, all forms of life will be sustenance to him. And humanity will suffer the same fate as the inhabitants of Carcosa.'

'How, precisely, will the thing feed?' asked de Chardin.

'The King in Yellow comes from beyond the edge of ordered space and time,' Oberon answered, 'from a place where the laws of physics are vastly different to those operating in this universe. He is capable of warping the fabric of reality: just as we can dip our hands into a pool of water and create currents within the liquid, so can he create currents within reality itself, pointing them in whichever direction he chooses. In this way, he can open avenues of attraction between himself and anything else on the planet – including the minds and bodies of its inhabitants.

'The Planetary Angels of Carcosa watched this happening, and great was their anguish as they described how the King in Yellow drank the minds of the people, and then the life force animating their bodies. The result was insanity and physical feebleness, swiftly followed by death, and when death came, the victims' bodies dissolved like ice in a hot room, until nothing was left of them.

'This is what will happen if the King in Yellow is allowed to come to Earth. He will choose a place to make his fortress; he will make it impregnable, and there he will dwell, periodically reaching out to feed on all the life which covers the surface of this world.'

'Good God! Then Blackwood is right: we must find this Anti-Prism gadget and destroy it without delay!'

'We must do more than that,' said Oberon.

'What do you mean?' asked Sophia.

'The King's intention is to come to Earth and feed upon its population while hiding from the Wanderer. Eventually, our Sun will begin to sing its own song of distress, but by the time the Wanderer arrives, untold deaths will have occurred, and the Earth will have been irreparably damaged. The King in Yellow will move on to the next world, and then the next. We must make our stand on behalf of all the intelligent beings which are yet to fall victim to the monster's attentions, on worlds as yet unknown to us, in millennia yet to come.'

'And how are we to do that, when so many must have tried and failed in the past?' asked Blackwood.

'The gateway between Carcosa and Earth is actually a tunnel extending through a higher form of space,' Oberon replied. 'The Planetary Angels told me that the King in Yellow has kept a hoard of Carcosan souls with which he will power the Anti-Prism in his castle in the Lake of Hali...'

'While Charles Exeter uses the spirits which have been consumed by the Servitor to power the Anti-Prism here on Earth,' said Blackwood.

Oberon nodded. 'Precisely. When the two devices have been activated, they will resonate with each other through the higher space, and the tunnel between worlds will be opened. But if they are both destroyed while the King in Yellow is in transit within the tunnel, it will be severed from the universe, and he will be trapped within it. Our universe will be free of him forever.'

The humans glanced at each other in silence.

'Oberon,' said Blackwood after a moment. 'You say that *both* Anti-Prisms must be destroyed.'

'At precisely the same moment, yes,' the Faerie King replied.

'And that would involve our travelling to Carcosa... *physically* rather than mentally.'

'It would.'

'How are we to do that? You said yourself that Carcosa is too far away to be reached by our Æther zeppelins.'

'Allow me to worry about that,' Oberon replied with a smile. 'In the meantime, I suggest that you equip yourselves with all that is necessary to survive in an alien environment.'

'I'm sure the chaps at Station X will be able to help out on that score,' said Blackwood.

'Good. Go and speak to them. Titania will go with you and will advise your scientists on the exact nature of the equipment required. I will make the preparations for your voyage. We will require two groups: one to make the journey to Carcosa and the other to descend into the Void Chamber here in London. Each will have but one task: to destroy the Anti-Prism and banish the King in Yellow from this universe forever!'

PART FOUR

The Tunnel Between Worlds

CHAPTER ONE:
The Wanderer

It had roamed for aeons amongst the drifting stars of the island universe known by humans as the Milky Way. Unseen and unsuspected by the beings inhabiting the planets rolling eternally through the galactic night, it wandered and watched and searched... and listened.

It had been created by a great race which had perished in ages long past, on the far side of the vast, glittering disc whose myriad stars sang to each other through the black firmament. It did not know its name, nor even if it had been given a name by those who had created it. It knew only that they were gone forever from the universe, that they had been a noble people, and that their world had been among the first to be visited by the thing that drank minds and sucked the life force from all that lived and breathed.

When the blight first became apparent, their scientists had struggled to find ways to combat it, and perhaps send it back to the ultra-dimensional hell from which it had emerged. But it was impervious to every weapon brought to bear against it. It settled parasitically into the depths of their defenceless world, and then it began to feed.

And the trees withered and died, and animal carcasses littered the land in their millions, and the seas grew thick with noisome darkness and then dried up altogether, and *the people... the people went insane as their minds were consumed, and they screamed things that made their friends and loved ones cover their ears and turn away in anguish, and then they too withered away, and when they died, their bodies melted into the cracked earth and disappeared.*

In their madness, the people raved about a symbol which burned brightly in their minds: a geometrical form which they could not describe, but which some of them drew, sometimes on paper, but more often on the walls of their homes in their own blood:

And while they drew this sign, the people spoke of a thing made of yellow rags which seethed within them, and which they could see in the waking dreams that haunted their collapsing minds.

While their world was being consumed, those scientists who remained alive and sane continued their struggle to comprehend the calamity which had befallen them. The last of their most brilliant minds strove ceaselessly to understand the blasphemous nature of the interloper from beyond space, and to search for a possible weakness.

They studied the weirdly contorted figure, which came to be known as the Yellow Sign; they sent volunteers into the planet's depths to gather whatever information they could, while theoreticians pondered the nature of this and other universes, and the possible forms which intelligence might take in those infinitely distant realms.

But the volunteers never returned, and the theoreticians despaired of ever finding a means to rid their world of the thing which the people had come to call 'the yellow feaster from the stars'.

And then a breakthrough occurred. Through the application of newly-discovered scientific principles combined with Magickal incantations designed to reverse the reality-warping mathematics embodied in the hideous geometry of the Yellow Sign, the theoreticians created an entity of their own.

It was partly organic, partly thinking machine, partly of planetary matter and partly of the Luminiferous Æther. They gave it the power to invert the mathematical blasphemy of the Yellow Sign and thus to undermine the existence of the yellow feaster from the stars.

But it was too late for their world: too much damage had been done; too many people had been lost. All that remained of a once thriving civilisation was a few thousand survivors clinging to the barren, lifeless surface of a withered, sterile globe. The survivors knew what awaited them: extinction through starvation.

When they brought their creation to life, its first act was to communicate to them the fact that the yellow feaster from the stars had departed from their world. The agent of their doom had fled through a doorway in space and time to an unknown destination.

And so the last survivors of that great race gave their creation the means to travel between the stars; they equipped it with vast, membranous wings which would catch the starlight and propel it out into the universe. The instructions they gave it were simple: find the horror and destroy it; prevent it from doing to any other world what it had done to theirs.

They bid it farewell, sent it out into the eternal night, and turned away from the stars for the last time, to await their final destiny.

For millions of years, the entity roamed through the island universe of the Milky Way, searching for the obscene ripples in space and time that would signal the presence of the horror. There were times when it came close, but never close enough, for the yellow feaster possessed a means of instantaneous travel from world to world, a way to open doorways through space. And so the entity had no choice but to continue its search, while the stars watched its passing and sang songs to each other, calling it the Wanderer, for it had no other name.

As the aeons passed, the quest of the Wanderer came to be known by millions of stars, and when the blight appeared on a world, its parent star would begin to sing a song of distress and torment, and the song would be taken up by other stars in its vicinity, and passed on until it was detected by the Wanderer.

And then the Wanderer would come...

But always too late.

And so the Wanderer would turn away from the doomed world, spread its great wings to catch the light from a mourning star, and set off once again, into the endless night, on its eternal quest.

Thus had it been for millennium upon millennium... until a song reached the Wanderer from a lonely star which it was passing. The star had no planetary family of its own, but throughout its long life it had listened to the stories told by others of the Wanderer's quest.

The star sang to the Wanderer of a great calamity which had befallen a distant world and begged the entity to make haste towards that region of the infinite sky.

That world was called by its inhabitants... Carcosa.

CHAPTER TWO:
The Aurelius

Blackwood, Sophia and Castaigne stood on the landing field at Biggin Hill Cosmodrome beneath a heavily overcast sky, like three tourists waiting for transportation to an exotic destination. Beside each of them stood a stout and sturdy suitcase of steel-reinforced leather, courtesy of the people at Station X.

Away in the distance, work was nearing completion on the reconstruction of the cosmodrome's reception centre and support buildings, which had been destroyed three weeks earlier by Indrid Cold, the Venusian *agent provocateur* who had tried to ignite a war between Earth and Mars. Soon the cosmodrome would open again, allowing the arrival and departure of the Martian interplanetary cylinders, but for now the vast concrete launch platform was empty and deserted, its surface still blackened in places from the wreckage of the cylinder which Cold had destroyed.

'I wonder why Oberon asked us to wait for him here,' said Castaigne.

'I wonder how the blazes he's going to get us across trillions of miles of space to Carcosa,' Blackwood rejoined.

'I have a feeling we're about to find out,' Sophia said, pointing into the sky towards the west, where the clouds had begun to billow and churn strangely, like thick cigar smoke disturbed by the slow waving of some vast, unseen fan.

Presently, the clouds parted to reveal a sight which left the three companions speechless and open-mouthed in astonishment. From out of the grey swirl, a ship had appeared: a gigantic galleon, far larger than any that had ever sailed the oceans of Earth. Blackwood estimated it to be more than a mile in length, and he searched in vain for the tops of its masts, which were lost in the clouds above. The main topsail could easily have enveloped the entire Palace of Westminster, and was emblazoned with a vast and intricate design which Blackwood and Sophia instantly recognised as the colossal tree known as the Fortress of Apples, where Oberon and Titania had their home. The great sweeping flanks of the vessel, oak-hued and polished to a lustrous sheen, were decorated with fantastic curlicues of filigreed gold and silver which would have made Beardsley weep with envy, and which were studded with cabochons of luminous gemstones, the smallest of which would have been impossible for a man to lift.

Its vast size was not the only surprising thing about the vessel, however; for at its stern, behind the captain's cabin and officers' quarters common to galleons of Earth, there was a gigantic paddle-wheel similar to those which powered the great riverboats of the Mississippi. To Blackwood's eye, this bizarre concatenation of designs was even more arresting than the ship's colossal scale.

'A floating ship,' said Castaigne, his voice a whisper of awe. 'Gods, what a marvel!'

'Our transportation to Carcosa?' said Blackwood, peering up at the apparition. He shook his head. 'I fail to see how such a vessel – however magnificent – will get us across all those countless leagues of space...'

'Oh, ye of little faith,' Castaigne chuckled.

The great ship loomed above them as it slowly settled upon the landing field. As its vast keel – more than a hundred feet in height – gently touched the grass, the blades barely stirred, as if nothing more substantial than a feather had fallen upon them. The three humans gazed up at the elegantly curved lapstraking of the mountainous hull, like minnows contemplating a whale, and Sophia shook her head and sighed, 'I've never seen anything so beautiful!'

'Nor I, your Ladyship,' rejoined Castaigne.

'I wonder how we're going to get onboard,' said Blackwood.

As if in answer to his comment, a large panel in the upper reaches of the hull slid aside and a wide platform emerged, connected to the vessel by means of a complex arrangement of beams and pulleys. The platform quickly descended to the ground, suspended by copper-coloured chains, and alighted upon the grass a few yards from them.

Castaigne picked up his suitcase. 'Our means of boarding, I should say.'

Blackwood picked up both his and Sophia's cases, and together they stepped onto the platform, which immediately began to rise again into the air. The ground fell away rapidly, and in moments they had a spectacular view of the surrounding countryside, an irregular patchwork of fields and villages stretching to the horizon.

As Sophia gazed across the landscape of southern England, she felt her heart tremble with excitement and trepidation: soon, they would be leaving all this beauty and tranquillity far behind, heading into the depths of space towards a world which might once have looked a little like this, but which was now a blighted sphere, drifting lonely amongst mourning stars, its life almost completely drained by the trans-dimensional monstrosity that dwelled there.

A monstrosity which she had already encountered, and which she would soon encounter again.

Her breath caught in her throat at the thought. Blackwood glanced at her, intuited her apprehension, and placed a comforting arm around her shoulders.

The platform came to a halt, and they turned to see Oberon standing in the hatchway. He was dressed in a tunic of shimmering emerald, black breeches and high boots, much in the manner of a sea captain of centuries past. His great dragonfly wings spread out behind him, and his eyes blazed with the light of Faerie as he smiled at them.

'Sophia, Thomas, Dr Castaigne,' he said, 'welcome aboard my Æther galleon, the *Aurelius*.'

'Thank you, Your Majesty,' replied Castaigne. 'It's quite magnificent... very, er, big.'

The Faerie King's smile grew broader as he beckoned to them. 'Come. You may wish to observe our departure from the main deck, and then I will show you to your quarters.' As he said this, three of the vessel's crew stepped onto the platform and took the suitcases. Oberon indicated them. 'Your equipment?'

'Yes,' replied Blackwood. 'Queen Titania gave very detailed instructions to the chaps at Station X on what to provide.'

They stepped through the hatchway into what was evidently a large reception chamber. The room was furnished with ornate tables and chairs, which gave the impression of having been fashioned from living wood. Large cabinets lined the walls, and on their shelves were arranged numerous objects which might have been ornaments, or perhaps instruments of some kind: it was difficult to tell, so strange were their forms. There was a curious scent on the air, rather pleasing but difficult to identify. Blackwood detected a briny tinge, but in fact it was like no sea-scent he had ever encountered.

Oberon noticed his frown. 'Is something wrong, Thomas?'

'No, not at all – it's just… that smell…'

'Does it displease you?'

'No, it's quite pleasant – I just can't identify it.'

'It is the scent of the Luminiferous Æther, the very atmosphere of Space. This vessel has spent many thousands of years plying the gulfs between the planets and stars.'

'For what reason?'

'For the same reason humans are building Æther zeppelins: exploration. We are as curious about the cosmos as you.'

'If you've been exploring for thousands of years,' said Sophia, 'you must know much more about the universe than we.'

Oberon's smile faded. 'Yes… we do. But come: the ship is ready to depart.'

They followed him from the reception room into a long, wide corridor which led to a vast staircase of the kind one might find on an ocean liner – albeit one that was at least five times larger than any conceived on Earth.

When they emerged on the main deck, they were stunned anew by the vessel's enormous scale. Blackwood estimated the breadth of the *Aurelius* to be more than two thousand feet. The four masts rose from the forecastle, main deck and aftcastle like gigantic trees in a gently sloping field, and he felt himself grow dizzy as he peered up at the crow's nest, which must have been a quarter of an acre in area, sitting atop the mainmast nearly a mile above his head.

'How big a crew is required to operate this vessel?' asked Blackwood, as Oberon led them towards a balustrade of intricately-carved oak running along the length of the main deck.

'On long voyages, the *Aurelius* may carry many thousands,' came the reply, 'but in truth the ship could sail quite easily by herself, for well she knows the ways of the Æther.'

Nonplussed by this rather cryptic response, Blackwood nodded and said nothing.

'And the ship's name?' said Castaigne.

'She is named after one of your greatest philosophers,' said Oberon. 'A man whose genius allowed him a small glimpse of the true nature of the universe.'

A crewman approached and said, 'Your Majesty, we are ready to make way.'

Oberon nodded, and the faerie withdrew.

Immediately, they felt the deck surge beneath them, and the ground, already a thousand feet below, grew more distant as the *Aurelius* rose into the air.

Sophia drew closer to Blackwood, and again he offered her a comforting arm. 'Are you all right, my dear?' he said.

'Yes, I'm fine,' she replied quietly. 'It's just that this sensation reminds me of...'

When she hesitated, Castaigne glanced at her. 'Of your previous journey?'

She nodded.

'I fear that there's nothing I can say to comfort you, your Ladyship.'

'There's nothing I require you to say, Dr Castaigne,' she replied. 'It was my choice... and I must live with the consequences.'

'Consequences?' said Blackwood. 'What do you mean, Sophia?'

'There will be consequences, Thomas. I can say no more than that.'

'Why not?' he persisted. 'Is there something you're not telling us? Something that happened to you while your mind was on Carcosa?'

Her only response was to draw away from him, to walk a little way along the balustrade and stand alone, watching the rapidly diminishing landscape below.

Blackwood was about to go to her, but he felt a powerful hand on his shoulder and glanced back to see Oberon shaking his head. And then Blackwood heard the Faerie King's voice echoing subtly through his mind. *Did you really think she could be in the presence of a being such as the King in Yellow and remain unscathed?*

How could I know? he replied. *I have no idea what kind of being the King in Yellow is. But what are the 'consequences' of which she speaks?*

I am uncertain, came the reply. *But I believe we will find out before this is over.*

*

The *Aurelius* continued its ascent, until the ground was lost beneath the thick, grey clouds, and the sky above, at first bright and blue, gradually darkened into the obsidian blackness of space. As the concept of altitude lost its meaning and became, instead, distance from the planet, the three humans looked out at the unthinkable profusion of stars, which no longer twinkled as they did when viewed from the surface of the Earth; instead, they were diamond-hard pinpoints of crystalline light which shone with a brightness and constancy which was both delightful and unsettling to behold.

Castaigne took hold of Blackwood's arm and pointed to the Moon, which was emerging from behind the Earth's limb. Divested of the atmosphere's impeding effects, the satellite shone with astonishing clarity, as if painted by some ultimate master of depiction on a sheet of glass separating the observers from the infinite gulfs beyond.

'I didn't realise,' Blackwood said to Oberon, 'that the Luminiferous Æther was breathable by humans, for we must be far beyond the Earth's atmosphere by now.'

'We are,' the Faerie King replied, 'and it is not. For your protection, we have cast a shield around the *Aurelius*, maintaining the atmosphere of Earth in close proximity to the ship.'

Sophia, still standing a little way off, caught the exchange and moved to rejoin them. 'What form of propulsion does the *Aurelius* employ?' she asked. 'How are we to cross the trillions of miles of space to Carcosa?'

'We could not do so,' Oberon replied, 'at least, not in *normal* space, for although our Æther galleons can catch the breath of stars in their sails and ride it between worlds, for voyages between the stars themselves, another method is required.'

And then the Faerie King pointed out from the balustrade across the fathomless depths of space, and said, 'Behold the Pneuma.'

As the humans watched, the crystalline stars became warped and twisted, as if a distorting lens had been placed in front of them, smearing them into long, curving threads of light. At the centre of the distortion, something like a hole appeared – if a hole could be said to exist in space – and then it seemed to the observers that it was not so much a hole as the entrance to a great shaft, perhaps fifty miles across, which was lined with mottled silver, and extended not through space, but through something on the other side of space.

Blackwood tried in vain to comprehend this bizarre affront to the laws of geometry and physics, and felt his mind rebelling against the impossibility of what he was seeing. 'What *is* that?' he murmured.

'It is the entrance to the Pneuma: a hypertube extending through non-quotidian space,' replied Oberon. 'It is the means by which we travel between the stars.'

As the *Aurelius* turned her prow towards the vast circular entrance, Sophia asked, 'What is non-quotidian space?'

'A higher dimension: one of the ætherial planes which exist alongside the physical world with which you are familiar,' came the reply, 'and in which the speed of light cannot be exceeded. But inside the Pneuma, the speed of light is meaningless – so meaningless, in fact, that it makes no sense even to say that it can be surpassed: it simply does not exist.'

'A realm in which velocity has no meaning,' marvelled Blackwood. 'Why, it's utterly fantastic!'

Oberon smiled. 'In centuries to come, humanity will learn how to navigate such hypertubes with vessels of their own, and the era of ultimate exploration will begin.'

'Centuries is right,' observed Castaigne with a wry smile, 'for I can't even begin to conceive of the physics required to manipulate space and time in this fashion. How do you do it, Your Majesty?'

Oberon glanced at him, and his smile grew broader as he replied, 'If you cannot begin to conceive of the physics involved, what would be the point in my telling you?'

As the *Aurelius* passed across the threshold and into the mouth of the shaft, the humans looked down and saw that the Pneuma was actually a liquid – or something that behaved as if it were a liquid – which roiled and fizzed, turning back chaotically upon itself like immensely powerful waves vainly assaulting an invisible and impregnable circlet of rock.

Once inside the hypertube, the great vessel descended until its immense keel cleaved the churning cylindrical ocean, and then it settled upon it like a ship of Earth upon an ocean of Earth. Behind the towering aftcastle, the colossal paddle-wheel, fully a quarter of a mile in diameter, began to turn, raising soft mountains of foaming liquid as it splashed into the Pneuma.

The vessel surged forward, its prow slicing through the ocean which roiled and bubbled and undulated around it.

'What's this stuff made of?' asked Blackwood, as he gazed out and up at the monochromatic grey substance arcing over their heads.

'I'm not certain that I could explain it to you in a way that would make any sense,' Oberon replied.

'I'd consider it a great favour if you tried nevertheless.'

Oberon smiled and shrugged, and his great dragonfly wings fluttered briefly behind him. 'Very well. It is the membranous essence of the dividing veil between the material and ætherial planes, warped and liquefied to allow passage through an additional dimension intersecting both.'

'I see,' said Blackwood with all the authority he could muster, which in truth wasn't very much.

Oberon continued, 'It may help you to think of the Pneuma as a transit system, similar to your own London Underground. If you wish to travel from one part of the metropolis to another, you descend into the ground and step aboard a train which moves rapidly through the earth, taking no account of the topography of the surface – the buildings, streets and so on – since they occupy another layer of space which the Underground train never encounters. It is the same with the Pneuma hypertubes, which are unaffected by the topography of normal space and time.'

'Actually,' said Blackwood, 'that *does* help rather.'

'I am glad to oblige, Thomas,' said the Faerie King.

'How long will it take us to reach the Hyades, Oberon?' asked Sophia.

'No more than a couple of hours,' he replied.

'Great God!' Castaigne exclaimed. 'We must be travelling at thousands of times the speed of light!'

'In relation to normal space, we are travelling more than half a million times faster than a beam of light moves,' Oberon said. 'Although, as I have already mentioned, it means little to speak in such terms when describing movement within the Pneuma.'

Blackwood turned to his human companions. 'In any event, we should take this time to unpack and prepare our equipment for use. Oberon, may we be shown to our quarters?'

*

Oberon accompanied his guests to the adjoining cabins which he had ordered to be prepared for them – although to call them 'cabins' was to do them a grievous disservice, for they were more like vast chambers in some exotic palace than any ship's cabin the human passengers had ever occupied. Each room, while furnished in a style which Blackwood and Sophia instantly recognised from its elegant Art Nouveau lines as belonging to the Realm of Faerie, was decorated with artefacts which clearly had no connection whatsoever with Earth, and with paintings depicting scenes of such alienness that their hearts trembled with astonishment and wonder.

'Are these some of the worlds you have visited?' asked Sophia, as she and Castaigne stood in Blackwood's cabin examining some of the paintings, which were executed with such delicacy and detail that they had to stand within an inch from them to establish that they were indeed paintings rather than photographs.

'They are,' replied Oberon.

'I have visited many worlds in non-corporeal form,' said Castaigne, 'but never have I seen anything remotely like this.'

'They are very far from Earth,' said the Faerie King. He indicated one painting, which showed a forest of vast towers, clearly miles high, strung with glittering metallic tubes like hanging vines, their surfaces glowing with iridescent greens and blues and purples and flecked with thousands of lights.

'These are the spire-cacti of Lambda Velorum,' Oberon explained, 'which orbits a star near the edge of the Aquila Rift.'

257

'It looks almost like a city,' observed Sophia.

'That is precisely what it is.'

'What are the inhabitants like?'

'They are gentle and noble.'

'What do they look like?'

Oberon gave a soft chuckle. 'Dear Sophia, were I even to describe them to you, you would be haunted by nightmares for the rest of your life.'

Sophia gave a small start. 'Are they so very different from us?'

'*Very* different.' He turned to Castaigne. 'And you, Doctor, do not know how lucky you have been so far, in encountering worlds and beings whose aspect your mind is capable of withstanding.'

Simon Castaigne paled a little at this, but said nothing.

Oberon indicated another painting, showing a vast cloudscape containing thousands of objects which resembled mustard-coloured puffballs mottled with irregular patches of glowing magenta. 'These,' he said, 'are the singing fungi of Eibon Prime, which orbits a sun on the far side of the Orion-Perseus Discontinuity.'

'The clouds,' said Sophia. 'Why are they so flat along their tops? It looks like someone has taken a huge knife and sliced away their upper reaches.'

'They are flattened by their collision with the Luminiferous Æther beyond Eibon Prime's atmosphere. The singing fungi are highly intelligent, as are the clouds through which they move. Long ago, we established beyond any reasonable doubt that the clouds and the fungi communicate with each other – although we have tried in vain to interpret their cacophonous, radiation-fuelled dialogue. We have never been able to penetrate the meaning of the eternal byplay of information. Some have suggested that they are engaged upon a never-ending discussion on the ultimate nature of the Æther, or perhaps are sharing secrets too strange to be comprehended by any minds but theirs. But that is mere speculation: the true meaning of the conversations between the clouds and the fungi remain for them alone, and probably always will.'

Blackwood listened with interest to all this while he unfastened the sturdy clasps on their suitcases, took out the contents and laid them upon the vast bed at the centre of the cabin.

Oberon came over to join him, followed by Sophia and Castaigne. 'Ah, your survival equipment,' said the Faerie King. 'Fascinating... and rather attractive, I must say.'

'Well,' mused Blackwood, 'I wouldn't wear it to the opera, but I suppose it does have a certain aesthetic appeal... if you like that sort of thing.'

Fortunately, the scientists at Station X in Bletchley Park had been able to accommodate Blackwood's request in pretty short order. They had been experimenting for some time with various means of keeping the human body alive and functioning while on excursions away from the protective atmosphere of Earth – specifically the first lunar zeppelin flight, which was scheduled to depart the following year – and had several working environmental protection suits of various sizes to hand.

The suits were wonders of technological innovation: each was composed of a padded leather overall covered with a thick outer layer of black Martian rubber, which completely sealed it and maintained the body heat of the wearer while in cold environments. Should the ambient temperature rise, a set of frond-like heat exchangers could be extended from the shoulders to maintain a comfortable temperature within the suit. Secured to the back by a combination of brass studs and leather straps was the breathing apparatus, which operated by means of a miniaturised version of the great Vansittart-

Siddeley Ultra-compressors which supplied propulsive power to the new atmospheric system being installed on the London Underground.

The apparatus was connected by a reinforced rubber pipe to the suit's combined helmet and chest-mounted control unit, which was dominated by a large, circular panel of polished brass containing several dials, pressure gauges and switches whose function was to monitor and regulate the flow of oxygen through the suit. The helmet was a tall bubble of specially strengthened glass (tall enough to accommodate a top hat if necessary, according to the suit's designer), on either side of which was mounted a powerful electric light.

When he had first set eyes on the contrivance, Blackwood had been reminded of a deep-sea diver's suit – although this was intended for use in the ocean of space, an ocean far deeper and more perilous than any on Earth...

Blackwood ran a check on the electrical systems of each suit to make quite certain that it was in proper working order. As he did so, he checked with Sophia and Castaigne that they recalled the all-too-brief lecture they had received at Station X on the suits' operation. When he was satisfied that they had absorbed the salient points, he switched off the systems of each suit, and turned to Oberon.

'Now,' he said, 'all that remains is for us to complete our journey to Carcosa.'

CHAPTER THREE:
The Lake of Hali

A pinpoint of blue-grey light appeared in the void above the dying planet. Against the backdrop of infinite, star-speckled night, the point rapidly increased in size until it was tens of miles in diameter. Had anyone on Carcosa been looking in that particular direction at that particular moment, it would have seemed to them that an infinitely deep shaft had appeared out of nowhere; a shaft whose single circular wall was composed of glistening grey liquid.

But no one in Carcosa's last cities was looking up, for the sky held little interest for them: their attention was focussed solely on the slowly-churning waters of the great lake around which Alar, Hastur and Yhtill stood. The King in Yellow, that ravenous, tattered blight from the nethermost regions of space and time, was preparing to emerge from the lightless depths beneath Hali's sweeping cloud waves. The last remnants of Carcosa's once-teeming population knew it – or believed it – for what other reason could there be for the unsettling of Hali's ancient waters?

Their final doom was upon them; the King in Yellow was about to emerge and absorb the silent vestiges of a once-great civilisation: a piece of bread mopping up the last scraps of a meal that had lasted for millennia.

And so the last inhabitants of Carcosa stayed within their homes and did not look out at the moons that had gone insane, or the stars that had turned to black bruises in the sky... or the vast celestial ship whose prow cleaved the thrashing waves of the Pneuma hypertube as it soared out into open space...

*

'This is incredible,' said Simon Castaigne as he gazed down at the planet's surface from the main deck of the *Aurelius*. 'I had never thought to look upon the surface of another world with my physical eyes.'

Oberon looked at his human companions, who were now sealed tightly within their environmental protection suits, and gave the occultist a sad smile. 'Would that it were a happier world you are looking upon, Dr Castaigne,' he said.

'Indeed,' Castaigne replied in a quiet voice, as he continued to watch the blasted grey-black landscape roll past beneath the vessel's great keel. Imagining what this world might have been like before the blasphemous hunger had descended upon it from the stars, he supposed that there must once have been fields and forests, snow-frosted mountains and glittering blue seas, and great cities teeming with people following the complex trajectories of their lives.

Now, though, there was nothing but twisted, ash-coloured rock and scarred, empty plains sweeping silently to each horizon, a place from which light, life, even the laws of physics had been banished. He imagined this happening to Earth and shuddered.

Oberon turned away from the melancholy scene and addressed the platoon of fifty faerie warriors assembled on the deck behind them. Each was dressed in glittering green armour and carried the same type of weapon which Blackwood and Sophia had seen used to such great effect during the affair of the Martian Ambassador a few weeks previously. The faerie carbines looked like long, slender tree branches which ended in many-petalled blooms rippling with strange colours. Their delicate appearance, however, concealed a vast and terrible power, for they were capable of disgorging beams of energy which nothing in the material world could withstand.

Spreading his iridescent dragonfly wings, Oberon said in a loud and powerful voice, 'Today, we go into battle against that which does not belong in the sane universe, against a thing of madness and insatiable hunger which has destroyed countless worlds and threatens to destroy countless more, beginning with our own beloved Earth.

'Beneath us lies the Lake of Hali, which the King in Yellow has made his home. Like a malignant disease, he seethes and writhes within the tortured walls of a once-proud castle that now lies in strange ruin on the lakebed. It is this castle which we must enter, this citadel of madness and chaos which we must conquer, to thwart the beast within.

'It will be a great trial of our strength and courage, for the Planetary Angels of Carcosa have told me of the Servitor of the King in Yellow which inhabits those twisted walls, and which will defend its master to the last.

'Our strategy will be as follows: we shall penetrate the castle first and clear the way for our human friends, who will then destroy the Anti-Prism while the King in Yellow is in transit between this world and Earth. While we are doing battle, Queen Titania, my beloved wife, will lead the assault upon the Void Chamber beneath London and destroy the companion Anti-Prism there. With his entry and exit points destroyed, the King in Yellow will be trapped forever outside the realm of ordered space and time. Am I understood?'

'Yes, my King!' cried the faerie warriors in unison.

'Our human friends well understand the reason we must enter the Castle of Demhe first, and so should you.

The Planetary Angels of Carcosa have told me much of the Servitor which dwells there with its master: a terrible cousin of the creature which haunts the train tunnels beneath London. We will have to destroy it before our friends enter the castle, lest they see it and suffer the same fate as poor Alfie Morgan. Then they will be able to perform their part and destroy the Carcosa Anti-Prism, while Queen Titania directs the attack by Gerhard de Chardin and his Templar Knights on the Anti-Prism installed within the Void Chamber. Thus will humans be the ones to rid the Earth of its approaching doom. Thus will our ancient Covenant with the universe be preserved!'

Oberon gave a signal to the helmsman standing upon the aftcastle, and immediately the deck inclined as the *Aurelius* began to descend towards the churning cloud waves of the Lake of Hali.

The waves parted before the prow of the faerie ship, and with barely a jolt, Oberon's great vessel cleaved the waters of the lake and plunged beneath the surface. Blackwood surmised that the protective shield was still in place, for he had no doubt that he and his companions would otherwise have been swept instantly from the main deck as the ship submerged.

The world was transformed into a green-tinged darkness that pressed horribly all around them, as if it were a living thing, intent on absorbing and destroying this new interloper. The foul murk was, however, short-lived, for at numerous points upon the deck and the vast walls of the forecastle and aftcastle, faerie lanterns were lit, and their illumination, at once powerful and gentle, its hue like luminous mother-of-pearl, banished the gloom in the ship's immediate vicinity.

Carried by radio waves, Castaigne's voice crackled in Blackwood's and Sophia's helmets. 'Can't say that's much of an improvement.'

'Not really,' Blackwood replied, gazing out at the

featureless green void surrounding them. 'Do you have any idea how deep the lake is?'

Castaigne shook his head. 'I'm afraid not.'

'I would estimate it to be about a thousand feet,' said Sophia. There was a distinct tone of displeasure in her voice, and Blackwood quickly understood the reason.

'I'm sorry, my dear,' he said. 'I should have asked you first, since you are the only one among us who has actually plumbed these depths.'

'That's quite all right, Thomas,' she replied, somewhat mollified.

For several minutes they descended through the livid green of the lake, expecting at any moment to be confronted by some slimy denizen. Their descent, however, continued unchallenged.

'This is too easy,' muttered Blackwood.

Castaigne glanced at him. 'How so?'

'I can't imagine that the King in Yellow is unaware of our presence, and yet he allows us to approach. Why?'

'I'll wager it's because he's so cocksure of himself that he thinks he'll be able to dispatch us once we enter his castle.'

'I suspect Dr Castaigne may be right,' said Oberon as he leaned over the balustrade and looked down into the dark depths. 'On the other hand, it may be that he is keeping his minions close to him, their numbers concentrated, so that they can protect him as he prepares to travel to Earth.' After a short pause, he continued, 'In any event, we shall soon find out, for we are nearly upon the castle. Look…'

The others looked down in the direction he was pointing.

Sophia shuddered and closed her eyes, while both Blackwood and Castaigne took an involuntary step back.

'Great God!' said Castaigne. 'Are we really to go in *there*?'

CHAPTER FOUR:
The Doom of Two Worlds

The castle emerged from out of the gloom like the fossil of some vast submarine entity that should never have existed on this or any other world in the sane universe. As he gazed down at it, Blackwood thought he could discern remnants of the castle's original form: a few crenellations here and there, a vague smattering of recognisable masonry, misshapen openings which might once have been windows – although what manner of being now looked through them he couldn't begin to imagine. But these were merely memories of what had once been, for the vast majority of the building (if it could truly be called that) was a hideous tangle of twisted towers and warped buttresses, of bulging walls which collided with each other at strange angles and led the eye in directions the brain was reluctant to follow. The confusion stretched away into the gloom, the bizarre outrages of the castle's malformed architecture eventually becoming lost in the depths of the green-black waters.

'So this is the Castle of Demhe,' said Blackwood.

'It is,' replied Oberon. 'It once belonged to the Royal Family of Carcosa. It was here that Queen Cassilda composed her Song, before she was forced to flee into exile when the King in Yellow took up residence.'

'Does she live still?'

Oberon shook his head. 'She and her family are long dead, as are the great majority of the Carcosan people. Those few who remain now huddle together in the last cities of Alar, Hastur and Yhtill on the shores of Hali, awaiting their final doom.'

'But at least,' said Sophia, 'we may save them, for when we have vanquished the King in Yellow, will they not be able to rebuild their world once it is theirs again?'

Oberon glanced at her and smiled. '*When* we have vanquished him? I admire your optimism, Sophia. In any event, there is precious little of this world left to rebuild.'

'How many are there?' asked Blackwood. 'How many remain alive on Carcosa?'

'A few thousand; a mere handful compared to the millions who once called this benighted place their home.'

'Hmm,' Blackwood said. Sophia glanced at him, but he did not return her look.

The *Aurelius* continued on its course above the warped and smeared form of the castle, propelled by the great paddle wheel at its stern. Looking down upon the vastness of its repulsive form from their vantage point upon the faerie ship's main deck, Sophia wondered aloud if it had originally been this huge.

'Not according to the Planetary Angels of Carcosa,' Oberon replied. 'They told me that Queen Cassilda's castle was large and impressive, its elegant spires rising majestically from a verdant island in the lake. But its size was nothing compared to this, for when the King in Yellow took it for his own, forcing the island to the bottom of the lake, his very presence transformed its fabric, altering its structure and bloating its size, so that it spread upon the lakebed like a tumour ravaging a living body. In fact, I sense that it is growing still.'

As Sophia looked down again, she thought she caught a slight movement in one of the misshapen buttresses strung tendon-like across the castle's surface – although whether this was merely the result of the murky water's distorting effects, she couldn't tell.

'Where are the Planetary Angels?' Blackwood asked. 'Couldn't they lend us a hand in this business?'

'Time was when they could indeed have offered us great aid in our mission,' the Faerie King replied. 'But this world is far older than Earth, and their powers have waned, just as a man's strength and vitality wane with age. But in truth they have already offered us much, for they have divined the way through the castle to the throne room of the King in Yellow, and have shared this information with me. It will save us a great deal of time.'

'How much time?' asked Castaigne. 'I mean, how long do you think it will take to clear the way for us?'

'I am uncertain… it depends on what we find in there.'

A few moments later, Oberon pointed to a large opening which bore an unsettling resemblance to a screaming mouth. 'There! That is where my men and I shall enter, and where you shall too, once you receive word from us that you may do so.'

Blackwood grimaced as he looked down into the ghastly maw. 'Good luck to you, my friend,' he said. 'Good luck to us all…'

*

Midnight in the West End.

Queen Titania sat by herself on one bench in the back of the speeding police carriage and looked across at the five Templar Police opposite her. They were bunched uncomfortably together, like commuters on a crowded omnibus, but found this preferable to sharing a seat with the fabulously beautiful and powerful being who sat smiling before them.

Such was their gallantry, and, truth be told, such was their fear.

Even Detective Gerhard de Chardin, who found little to intimidate him in the world, considered it preferable to stand at the front of the carriage, his head bowed awkwardly beneath the ceiling, his arms reaching out to steady himself, than to share a seat with the Faerie Queen, which he felt would be somehow inappropriate.

Titania was dressed in a suit of armour fashioned from the leaves of the great apple tree, as large as a human city, where she and Oberon had their home in the Realm of Faerie. The leaves were cut and interlaced to form a garment which hugged her body so perfectly that it was easy to imagine her completely naked, which was another reason why the chivalrous Templar Knights chose to look anywhere but at her.

She held in her lap a branch-like faerie carbine, its petalled muzzle glowing softly with a faint ruby hue. Every so often, a Templar cast a quick glance at the curious weapon, unsure as to just how useful it would be in a firefight. Titania caught these furtive looks, and smiled; they would find out soon enough.

The Templars carried their own weapons: each man had a revolver in his hip holster and a recoil-powered Maxim machine gun slung across his shoulders. Beneath their overcoats, they also wore cuirasses of polished steel upon which the cross pattée was etched.

There were five other police carriages behind them, each packed with Templar Knights. As they turned into Bond Street, their wheels clattering loudly on the cobbles, Titania reflected that a faerie detachment would have been so much more elegant and understated in the raid which they were about to mount. She sighed. At least, she thought, what the humans lacked in subtlety they made up for in enthusiasm.

In fact, she had suggested to Oberon that she lead a platoon of faeries into the Void Chamber to neutralise the threat quickly, quietly and effectively, but her husband had gently rebuffed the idea, reminding her that their involvement had to be kept to an absolute minimum. The humans would have to find and destroy the London Anti-Prism; those of the Faerie Realm could not do it for them. For his own part, Oberon was providing transportation to Carcosa for Blackwood, Sophia and Castaigne, and would find and destroy any madness-inducing entities inhabiting the Castle of Demhe, but the destruction of the Anti-Prism on that sad and dying world would likewise have to be effected by humans.

The Earth was under human stewardship now; its protection was a human duty.

The carriage came to a juddering halt outside Bond Street Tube Station, and the Templar sitting closest to the rear door stood and opened it, glancing back at Titania as he did so.

'Your Majesty,' he said.

'Thank you,' the Faerie Queen replied as she moved past him and stepped lithely down to the street.

The metropolis never slept, and even at this late hour there were many people around – late-night strollers, returnees from theatres and restaurants – many of whom cast curious glances at the open entrance to the Tube Station and the two Templar Police who stood guard there, awaiting the arrival of de Chardin and his men.

When they saw Titania emerge from the lead carriage, the passersby stopped and gaped at the exquisite vision, bathed in soft lilac light, which had suddenly appeared before them. They stared open-mouthed at her perfect form, and the glittering dragonfly wings emerging from between her shoulder blades, murmuring to each other in shock, excitement and fear. Even the policemen guarding the entrance to the station forgot themselves and gawped at her, so that it was left to de Chardin to send the people on their way.

'Move along now,' he barked. 'There's nothing to see here. Come on, move along!'

'Nothing to see?' muttered more than one passerby. 'He's joking!'

De Chardin approached one of the policemen standing guard. 'Constable Zafón, your report.'

'We opened the gate five minutes ago, sir,' Constable Zafón replied, consulting his fob watch, 'just as you ordered. We've also apprehended the station's night staff, who are now in custody.'

'Good. We'll question them later, when this business is attended to – although I doubt they're in on Exeter's plan.'

'Yes, sir,' Zafón said, his gaze constantly straying over de Chardin's shoulder towards Titania.

The detective glanced at her, smiled briefly and clapped the constable on the shoulder. 'Good work, Zafón. Carry on.'

'Yes, sir.'

The occupants of the other police carriages had alighted, and fifty Templar Knights now followed de Chardin and Titania into the station.

'You all know the plan,' said the detective over his shoulder as they crossed the ticketing hall towards the escalators, which had been switched off for the night. The station's gaslights were on low and cast a minimal glow, lending the station the look of a vast sepulchre. 'We're anticipating that the Void Chamber will be well protected by Exeter's men, so it'll be a tough job getting along the new tunnel. We'll have to make full use of the boltholes and entrances to maintenance tunnels along the way. Once we gain the chamber, our orders are simple: find the Anti-Prism and destroy it.'

'Sir,' said a tall, powerfully built man at de Chardin's shoulder.

'You have a question, Sergeant Clairvaux?'

'Yes, sir. The creature… the thing that drove that train driver mad. Please don't misunderstand me, sir – I'll have at it given the chance… but what defence do we have against a thing that can drive a man insane at a single glance?'

By way of answer, de Chardin glanced at Titania, who was strolling along beside him. Although not nearly as tall as her burly companions, the Faerie Queen somehow seemed to be keeping up with them with minimal effort. 'Your Majesty?' he said.

'Do not be concerned, Sergeant Clairvaux,' she replied. 'Your part will be to get us into the Void Chamber and destroy the Anti-Prism; *my* part will be to engage the Servitor.'

'But, begging your pardon, Your Majesty,' the sergeant persisted, 'once we're inside the Void Chamber, if the thing is there…'

'You must look away from it,' said Titania, 'even while fighting Exeter's men, if any remain.'

'That will be difficult.'

'Yes. You will be at a serious disadvantage, but you have no choice, for to look upon the Servitor for any length of time will be the end of your sanity.'

'I see,' said Clairvaux.

'Hopefully, however,' Titania continued, 'that situation will not prevail for long: once the Servitor has discharged its contents into the Anti-Prism, I will destroy it. Then, the only threat you will face will be that posed by your fellow humans.'

'Got it, Clairvaux?' said de Chardin.

'Yes, sir!'

'That damned thing,' said de Chardin under his breath to Titania. 'When I think of what it's done to all those poor souls who lingered here, how it's… *consumed* them. I'd like to take that wretch Exeter and feed *him* to the devil!'

'I doubt you'll get the chance to do that, Detective de Chardin,' Titania replied. 'And in any event, that's not what we have come here to do.'

'I understand, Your Majesty…' He was about to say more but then merely shook his head.

Titania glanced at him and said, 'What really bothers you is that our plan calls for us to allow the souls to be fed to the Anti-Prism. Isn't that right?'

De Chardin nodded stiffly. 'That's right, Your Majesty. It seems a terribly callous thing. I don't see why we can't just destroy the Anti-Prism before the Servitor has discharged the souls into it. That would put paid to the King in Yellow's plan to come to the Earth.'

'It would. But you are forgetting two things: one, that the King in Yellow is unthinkably ancient and has seeded countless worlds with Anti-Prisms. If his way to Earth were blocked while he was still on Carcosa, he would simply pick another world to feed upon and continue his depredations in this universe for aeons to come, perhaps for all eternity. And two, the souls which the Servitor has gathered cannot now be saved; they are already lost.'

'What do you mean? Would they not be released upon the Servitor's destruction?'

'They would. But have you given thought to the *manner* of their subsequent existence? If the human mind can be driven to madness merely by looking at the Servitor, what effect would being *inside* the creature have on it?'

De Chardin cast Titania an appalled glance. 'I… don't know.'

'Nor can you begin to imagine. Believe me, Detective, once they have been discharged into the Anti-Prism, their suffering will be at a merciful end.'

They had reached the bottom of the stationary escalator, their footfalls echoing dully on the wooden cleats of the steps. Ahead of them, a long corridor stretched into the barely-lit gloom.

'We'll be terribly exposed while we walk along there,' de Chardin muttered.

Titania smiled and said, 'Wait here.'

She vanished in a puff of fragrant lilac smoke and a few moments later reappeared.

'There is no one at the far end. If you move quickly, you can traverse it with little concern.'

De Chardin threw her a wide-eyed glance, then chuckled and turned to his men. 'You heard Her Majesty. Let's go – quickly and quietly!'

*

King Oberon stood at the mouth of the entrance and looked down into the unrelieved Stygian blackness of the castle's interior. Above him, the *Aurelius* hung suspended in the thick murk of the Lake of Hali, its lights casting multiple halos upon its vast hull and superstructure.

He turned to the faerie warriors who stood beside him on the lip of the abyss. His mind sent a question out to them. *Are you ready, my men?*

We are ready, King! came the reply.

Then let us descend into this place, into its diseased heart, there to destroy the filth and madness that have made it their home. This world, once alive with beauty and light, has been mocked and abused for long enough, aye and more! The time of the King in Yellow is at an end, for we shall destroy all that gibbers and crawls within these chambers, so that our human friends can perform their duty for the sake of the Earth which we all love, though we no longer be its stewards.

We are with you, King Oberon!

Then make ready your arms, and follow me!

And with that, Oberon stepped off the edge and sank through the black water, into the pit.

For several minutes, he and his warriors descended through the darkness, controlling their movements with twitches of their wings, until presently their feet found solid stone, and they found themselves on the strangely inclined floor of what appeared by the light of their chest-mounted lanterns to be a wide, high-ceilinged corridor.

Oberon glanced up at the ragged, chimney-like structure through which they had descended. Away in the interminable distance, he could just make out the lights of the *Aurelius*, shining like a handful of sane stars in a firmament of madness.

He recalled the words of Carcosa's Planetary Angels, the directions they had given him through the twisted innards of the castle, the route he and his warriors would have to take in order to find the throne room of the King in Yellow.

He sent another thought out to his men. *This way.*

With the warriors spread out behind him, their carbines at the ready, Oberon set off into the darkness.

As he followed the twists and turns of the corridor, his feet treading lightly upon the crumbling and flaking stone of the floor, his wings augmenting and correcting his movements in response to the sudden, strange currents which periodically pulsated through the surrounding water, Oberon thought of how dearly he would have liked to take this business out of the hands of Thomas Blackwood and the other humans. Had he been free to decide, he would have led his warriors into the throne room and destroyed the Anti-Prism himself, while Titania did the same on Earth…

But he was not free to make such a decision: he was bound by the Covenant he and his people had made with the universe in the distant past, when the first light of civilisation was stirring in the mind of humanity. No human could truly understand the Covenant, its origin or the need to maintain it – although one day, in millennia to come, humanity itself would be required to turn over stewardship of the Earth to those who would come after.

Oberon recalled the teachings in the ancient texts of Faerie, which told how the Planetary Angels of Earth were born along with the world, how they began their existence not as fully fledged beings, but as motes of potentiality surrounding the molten sphere of the newly-formed world; how they gradually took form and substance according to universal principles of which only the Theosophists had an inkling and evolved, over the course of long epochs, into the great race to which Oberon belonged.

He recalled how he and the others of Faerie had watched the rise of humanity to intelligence and civilisation; how they had been contacted by the Primal Mind of the universe; how a great communion had taken place, during which they were made aware that it was necessary to transfer stewardship of the planet, to leave it in the hands of human beings and retreat to the Realm of Faerie, there to pursue their own destiny.

This they had agreed to do, promising to refrain from interference in the affairs of Earth, save when the planet was in direct and imminent peril. Then, and only then, would they be permitted to act, and at such times, their actions would be limited to helping the humans to save their world, not to saving it themselves, for Earth was now under the stewardship of humanity, not Faerie.

This was the Covenant, the promise they had made to the Primal Mind of the universe that they would observe the guiding principles, the fundamental cycles of eternity, upon which all planetary life was based.

Blackwood had once asked Oberon what would happen if the Covenant were broken, and Oberon had given him a look which made him wish that he had not voiced the question. The truth was that if the Covenant were ever to be broken, if those of Faerie were ever to usurp the role of stewardship and take matters out of humanity's hands, the great cycle would be undermined, thrown out of equilibrium, and the resulting imbalance would bring chaos and destruction upon the Earth and all who dwelled there.

Such were Oberon's thoughts as he and his warriors moved through corridor after twisting corridor, through chambers transformed by alien chaos into bizarrely angled travesties of what they had once been, across the yawning mouths of pits leading to yet deeper regions of the castle from which imponderable moans and rumblings emerged to trouble their minds.

We are close now, he said to his warriors. *Be alert, for the King in Yellow will not lightly give up his plans for the Earth.*

No sooner had he sent this thought than a great shape stirred in the darkness ahead, a shape which filled the corridor with writhing filaments and obscenely bulbous lobes. The thing surged forward as Oberon and his warriors lifted their carbines to their shoulders and fired, and by the intense ruby light of their discharges, they saw something that would have driven a human being to screaming madness, and as he fired his weapon again and again, the Faerie King was glad that he had told Blackwood and the others to wait on the *Aurelius*...

*

Their weapons drawn, de Chardin and the Templars moved quickly and silently along the dark corridor. Titania had once again moved ahead to make certain that no one would be there to meet them when they reached the far end. When they did so, they found themselves in a large, dimly-lit hall from which several more corridors branched off. The entrance to one was blocked by a wooden barrier bearing a sign which read:

TUBE LINE UNDER CONSTRUCTION
LONDON UNDERGROUND STAFF ONLY
PERMITTED BEYOND THIS POINT

The Templars moved past the barrier and into the corridor, the floor of which was strewn with plaster dust, workbenches, pieces of tile and the other flotsam of building work. Walking slowly, his revolver at the ready, de Chardin winced as their boots crunched faintly on the dust.

A sudden movement at the far end of the corridor, and a shot rang out.

Sergeant Clairvaux grunted and dropped to his knees as de Chardin took instant aim and let off two rounds. Two other Templars rushed to his side, their own weapons raised, while a third bent over Clairvaux, preparing to drag him back to the safety of the hall.

'It's all right,' said the sergeant, wincing as he sat up. He drew aside his coat to reveal the dent in his cuirass; the bullet had struck the cross etched upon the steel. 'Once again, the Lord has protected me.' He snatched up his revolver from the floor where he had dropped it and let off a couple of his own rounds.

'Queen Titania!' said de Chardin. 'Can you...? Where is she?'

Titania was nowhere to be seen, but a mere second or two later, the far end of the corridor was illuminated by several bright flashes of crimson light. The Faerie Queen then emerged from out of the gloom ahead and beckoned to them to join her.

'Are you injured, Sergeant?' asked de Chardin as he helped Clairvaux to his feet.

'No, sir, I'm fine,' he replied. 'Knocked the wind out of me – that's about all.'

'Good man. Follow me.'

278

The Templars hurried to the far end of the corridor, which ended in another junction. On the floor, they saw three lumps of something charred and smoking, like joints of meat that had been left in the oven for far too long.

'Our attackers?' said de Chardin.

Titania nodded.

'Good grief,' he muttered, casting an appreciative glance at the faerie carbine at Titania's side. 'I'd had my doubts about the efficacy of that thing...'

'I trust they are now laid to rest, Detective.'

'Indeed, as are my doubts concerning your stomach for a fight, if you'll forgive me for saying so, Your Majesty.'

The other Templars glanced at the carbonised residue of the three gunmen who had ambushed them, then at the beautiful and delicate Faerie Queen who had destroyed them without a second thought, and then at each other.

'You are forgiven,' she said. 'Now, we must make haste, for these were sentries, and the exchange of fire will have been heard.'

'Good point,' de Chardin nodded. 'Come on!'

They moved swiftly to the end of the corridor, which gave onto the Tube Station's new southbound platform. At first glance, the place appeared to be deserted, but Titania was taking no chances. She rushed out onto the platform before de Chardin could stop her and immediately was struck by a hail of bullets from several more sentries who were hiding beyond the platform's edge on the rail bed.

De Chardin and a number of his men cried out in sudden anguish, fully expecting her to be torn to pieces by the gunfire, but the bullets bounced off her armour and clattered harmlessly to the paving stones. Even those which struck her head, de Chardin noted incredulously, did as much damage as butterflies alighting upon her perfect brow.

Titania spread her gossamer wings, and in a movement so swift that the Templar Knights could barely follow it, she flew over the edge of the platform and down to the rail bed. Her faerie carbine flashed again, there were the briefest of screams, and a pale blue smoke began to rise into the air.

After a brief glance each way, she beckoned to them once again.

As they entered the platform, Clairvaux whispered to de Chardin, 'I'm starting to feel somewhat superfluous to requirements.'

The detective smiled and nodded, but his smile faded when he saw the expression on Titania's face as her supernaturally sensitive hearing picked up the comment.

'Do you mock me, Sergeant Clairvaux?' she said in a voice which seemed to be simultaneously as quiet as the patter of rain and as loud as an exploding mountain.

'Indeed not, Your Majesty,' the Templar replied as the colour drained from his face.

'You are anything but superfluous,' the Faerie Queen continued. 'I am getting you into the Void Chamber, but that is all I can do. Once we are there, the task of destroying the Anti-Prism will be yours, and yours alone. Do you understand?'

'Without a doubt, ma'am.'

'And don't call me ma'am.'

'I'm sorry.'

'Very well. Follow me.'

The Templars jumped down from the platform to the floor of the newly-excavated tunnel.

As they made their way carefully through the hot, cloying darkness, de Chardin whispered, 'Queen Titania, may I ask a question?'

'Of course.'

'Why are you wearing armour, when you are clearly impervious to human weapons?'

'My armour is not a defence against anything that humans could make, Detective.'

'Then you really are risking your life to help us?'

'My life?' she echoed, as if the notion confused her slightly. She gave a brief, tinkling laugh and shook her head. 'How little you humans understand.'

De Chardin thought of pursuing the matter but decided against it. Instead, he said, 'Well, at any rate, I would not like to be on the receiving end of your anger.'

'No, Detective,' she whispered. 'You would not.'

*

The time is approaching, thought Charles Exeter, as he stood alone upon the strangely-tiled floor of the Void Chamber.

He had forbidden his men from entering, knowing that they would be far more use out in the surrounding tunnels and corridors. They would prevent any meddlers from interfering with what was about to happen, and in any event, when the Servitor appeared to perform its function, they would best be elsewhere, for only Exeter's mind was shored up by the presence of the King in Yellow.

His advent upon Earth is imminent, thought Exeter, his heart suddenly beating hard with the knowledge. *I am about to betray my species and bring irreparable ruin upon my fellow men.*

<AND WHAT OF IT, EXETER?> echoed the word-impressions from out of the depths of space. <WHAT IS HUMANITY TO YOU, BUT A RESOURCE TO FUEL YOUR AMBITIONS OF POWER AND WEALTH?>

They are... they are my fellow men!

<YOUR FELLOW MEN!> echoed the voice contemptuously. <THEY CARE NOTHING FOR YOU; WHY SHOULD YOU CARE ANYTHING FOR THEM? YOU INSPIRE NOTHING BUT FEAR AND ENVY IN THEIR HEARTS. THEY SEE IN YOU NOTHING BUT THE REALISATION OF THEIR OWN AVARICE, WHICH

THEY HAVE NOT THE WIT TO SATISFY. YOU ARE ABOUT TO RECEIVE MORE POWER AND WEALTH THAN YOU OR ANY OF YOUR SPECIES COULD POSSIBLY IMAGINE. WILL YOU ABANDON THAT FOR THEIR SAKE AND TURN AWAY FROM EVENTS WHICH WILL FAR EXCEED THE LIMITED SPAN OF YOUR EXISTENCE?>

It was true, Exeter realised: what this feaster from the stars would do to the Earth and its people would take thousands of years. Exeter himself might live for five more decades; he would only witness the opening phase of the King in Yellow's reign, but during that brief span...

<YES, EXETER, DURING THAT BRIEF SPAN YOU WILL EXPERIENCE UNDREAMED OF DELIGHTS. ENTIRE NATIONS WILL BE YOURS TO PLAY WITH. YOU MAY POSSESS WHAT I DO NOT NEED, AND WHAT I DO NOT NEED IS MORE THAN COULD POSSIBLY SATE THE GREATEST AND MOST RAVENOUS OF UNFETTERED HUMAN APPETITES. MY REIGN WILL CONTINUE LONG AFTER YOU ARE GONE, BUT THAT NEED NOT CONCERN YOU. WHY SHOULD IT? WHY SHOULD YOU CONCERN YOURSELF WITH WHAT WILL COME TO PASS AFTER YOU ARE DEAD?>

No one ever cared for me. Why should I care for them?

<WHY INDEED? I HAVE EXPLORED THE DEPTHS OF YOUR MIND, EXETER, AND THROUGH YOU I HAVE DIVINED THE TRUE NATURE OF HUMANITY, AND THAT NATURE IS TO *CONSUME!* FOOD, RESOURCES, THE SWEAT FROM THE BROWS OF OTHERS. AND WHEN ALL NEARBY HAS BEEN CONSUMED, THEN TO EXPAND INTO OTHER PLACES, TO CONSUME WHATEVER IS THERE! THAT IS WHAT HUMAN BEINGS ARE, EXETER. A BLIGHT UPON THE FACE OF THE EARTH, RAVENOUS WORMS THAT WILL GNAW

AWAY AT THEIR WORLD UNTIL NOTHING REMAINS. AM I ANY WORSE THAN THAT, BECAUSE I DO NOT HAIL FROM THIS UNIVERSE?>

But we are not all like that, Exeter thought. *There is gentleness and nobility in the heart of man. There is the desire for truth and beauty. How can you judge us all by my example?*

<I DO NOT JUDGE; I MERELY OBSERVE. AND I CARE VERY LITTLE FOR GENTLENESS AND NOBILITY, FOR TRUTH AND BEAUTY, BEYOND THE SAVOUR WHICH THEY ADD TO THAT WHICH I CONSUME.>

Exeter felt a sudden wave of fiendish amusement writhing through his mind.

<DO YOU WISH TO THROW AWAY YOUR REWARD? NOW, IN THESE FINAL MOMENTS, WOULD YOU TAKE THE SIDE OF YOUR SPECIES AND YOUR WORLD AGAINST ME?>

When Exeter hesitated, the voice continued, <YOU COULD EASILY DO SO. WILL YOU?>

You would kill me if I did.

<HOW COULD I? YOU ARE ON EARTH, AND I AM ON CARCOSA.>

But you have power over me. You have influenced my thoughts for months. That is the reason I am here, now, in this place that should have remained buried forever.

<HOW EASILY YOU LIE TO YOURSELF, EXETER! FOR WELL YOU KNOW THAT YOU COULD HAVE IGNORED MY WORD-TRANSMISSIONS. YOU COULD HAVE TURNED AWAY FROM ME AT THE VERY BEGINNING AND BANISHED ME FROM YOUR MIND.>

That's not true!

<IT IS PERFECTLY TRUE. BUT THE ULTIMATE NATURE OF YOUR HUMANITY, THE ESSENCE OF YOUR BEING, FORBADE YOU FROM DOING SO. THE DECISION TO DO MY BIDDING ALWAYS RESTED WITH YOU, EXETER. YOU *CHOSE* TO FOLLOW MY INSTRUCTIONS AND GUIDE YOUR TUNNELLING MACHINE TO THIS PRECISE LOCATION, HERE TO UNCOVER AND REACTIVATE MY MEANS OF INTERSTELLAR TRANSIT. I FELT YOUR SOUL QUIVERING WITH GREED AT THE PROMISES I MADE TO YOU – PROMISES I HAVE EVERY INTENTION OF KEEPING.>

Exeter knew it was true, and now that the crucial moment was approaching, he trembled with the shame of it. The lies he had told himself had been laid bare by this thing from beyond the stars: the lie that he had no choice but to become the most powerful human being who had ever existed on Earth, and ever *would* exist; the lie that his actions were out of his control, that he had no choice but to do the bidding of the King in Yellow.

But it was too late.

Much too late.

And what if I were to turn away from you now?

Again, that hideous amusement. <YOU ARE QUITE FREE TO DO SO. BUT, OF COURSE, THERE WOULD BE CONSEQUENCES.>

Consequences?

<MY SERVITOR IS READY TO PERFORM ITS FUNCTION. ITS APPEARANCE IS IMMINENT. AND WHEN IT APPEARS, YOU WILL FIND THAT I AM NO LONGER HERE TO SHORE UP YOUR MIND AGAINST ITS ALIENNESS.>

You would leave me to be driven insane by it?

<YES.>

That... would be foolish of me.

<CONSIDERING THAT MY SERVITOR WILL CHARGE THE ANTI-PRISM AND FACILITATE MY ADVENT UPON THE EARTH WHATEVER YOU DECIDE... YES, IT WOULD BE MOST FOOLISH OF YOU. YOU HAVE ALREADY BETRAYED YOUR WORLD, EXETER. WILL YOU TURN DOWN YOUR REWARD *AND* END YOUR DAYS AS A GIBBERING IDIOT FOR THE SAKE OF YOUR CONSCIENCE?>

Exeter sighed and closed his eyes. To his great surprise, he started to weep.

No, I will not.

*

In all his thousands of years of life, Oberon had never seen anything remotely like the thing which filled the passageway ahead of them. He had travelled to many worlds on the *Aurelius*, had witnessed many wonders and terrors on the orbs which rolled silently through the star lanes of the island universe which was home to Earth and Carcosa and a hundred billion other worlds, but never had he encountered anything like *this*.

Its shape was nearly impossible to hold in his mind, even though he was looking directly at it: the writhing filaments and pulsating lobes were merely the two most easily describable aspects of it, but there were many others which conformed to no words or concepts which had ever been conceived in this universe.

Oberon and his warriors fired their weapons again and again, and where the ruby beams struck the thing, its abysmal form sizzled and burst, disgorging loathsome, liquid miasmas which instantly recombined to form further extrusions, thrashing madly across the walls, floor and ceiling of the corridor.

How can we defeat such a beast? asked one of the warriors. *We have never encountered anything with such resistance to our weapons!*

Apparently in response to the thought, one of the pulsating lobes split apart to reveal a vast, slobbering mouth which began to mimic obscenely the movements of speech.

<YOU CANNOT DEFEAT IT.>

The word-impressions echoed suddenly through the minds of the faeries.

The King in Yellow! Oberon thought.

<I AM HONOURED BY YOUR VISIT, KING OBERON. I HOPE MY SERVITOR IS AMUSING YOU.>

We know what you are planning to do. We will not allow you to destroy the Earth, as you have destroyed Carcosa.

<AND HOW, PRAY TELL, WILL YOU STOP ME? I CANNOT DIVINE YOUR THOUGHTS THE WAY I CAN WITH HUMANS, SUCH IS YOUR NATURE. TELL ME WHAT YOU ARE PLANNING TO DO, AND I WILL OFFER YOU MY OPINION ON THE LIKELIHOOD OF YOUR SUCCESS.>

My strategy is simple, fiend: I am going to lead my warriors to your throne room, and we are going to destroy you!

<THEN YOU ARE A FOOL, OBERON, KING. DO YOU NOT THINK THAT THE PLANETARY ANGELS OF CARCOSA TRIED TO DESTROY ME ALSO AND FAILED MISERABLY?>

Their power has waned, such is their great age. But Earth is much younger than Carcosa, and we are much younger than this world's Planetary Angels. We will prevail against you!

<WITH THOSE PITIFUL LITTLE TOYS OF YOURS? THEY ARE NO MATCH FOR MY SERVITOR. WHAT MAKES YOU THINK THEY WILL BE ANY MATCH FOR ME?>

Oberon's warriors looked at him, and then at each other. The King had not mentioned the Anti-Prisms on Carcosa and Earth, and such was their faerie nature that their inner thoughts were shielded from the enemy.

<YOU ARE BREAKING YOUR COVENANT WITH THE UNIVERSE,> continued the King in Yellow.

You know of that?

<I KNOW MUCH, FOOL. I KNOW THAT THE EARTH WILL PAY DEARLY FOR YOUR TRANSGRESSION.>

Not as dearly as if I were to allow you to hold dominion there. I will find a way to make amends, even if they involve my own exile or destruction.

<SUCH TOUCHING NOBILITY. IT IS TEMPTING TO ALLOW YOU ACCESS TO MY THRONE ROOM. IT WOULD BE MOST AMUSING TO WATCH YOUR EFFORTS TO DESTROY ME.>

Then allow it! I promise you, you will find our efforts to defend our world most amusing!

<MORE SO, HAD YOU BROUGHT THAT FASCINATING LITTLE CREATURE WHOSE AUDACITY LED HER TO MY PRESENCE RECENTLY.>

You do me a disservice, Yellow King, for I am neither cruel nor stupid enough to bring humans to this place. Their sanity could not withstand it; they would suffer the same fate as the poor wretch whose mind was destroyed by this Servitor's counterpart on Earth. No, you will have to deal with us of Faerie, and us alone!

<NO MATTER, FOR I WILL REACQUAINT MYSELF WITH HER SOON ENOUGH. I WILL DRINK HER MIND SLOWLY, OBERON, IN ORDER TO SAVOUR IT MORE COMPLETELY.>

Allow us entry to your throne room, coward, and we will show you what we think of your intentions.

The slobbering mouth of the Servitor stretched wide as it produced a sickening parody of laughter.

<SUCH ARROGANCE! I COULD ANNIHILATE YOU WITH A SINGLE THOUGHT. BUT THAT WOULD NOT BE NEARLY AS SATISFYING AS TO WATCH YOU RETURN TO EARTH IN YOUR LITTLE BOAT AND SEE WHAT I AM DOING TO YOUR BELOVED PLANET. YOU ARE IMMORTAL, OBERON. YOU WILL BE ABLE TO EXPERIENCE THE ENTIRE SPAN OF MY RESIDENCE ON EARTH. YOU WILL SEE EVERYTHING THAT I DO WHILE I AM THERE. YOU WILL WATCH, HELPLESS, WHILE I FEED FOR TEN THOUSAND YEARS ON ALL THAT LIVES AND BREATHES THERE.

<COME! MY SERVITOR WILL SHOW YOU THE WAY...>

And with that, the foul protuberance that had pretended to be a mouth withdrew into the heaving mass, and the Servitor retreated along the corridor.

As Oberon and his faerie warriors followed, he sent out a single thought across the Æther to Titania:

Make ready, my wife, for we are about to enter the throne room!

*

Nine hundred trillion miles away, the Templar Police were advancing steadily along the tunnel, moving close to the walls so that they could take advantage of the regularly-spaced boltholes and entrances to maintenance corridors, should they come under fire again, while Queen Titania walked along the centre of the rail bed.

The darkness was no impediment to her, such was the vast superiority of her eyesight to that of the humans. She could see right to the end and into the distant Void Chamber, where something appeared to be glowing faintly.

Suddenly, she paused, and de Chardin glanced at her softly-glowing form.

'Your Majesty,' he whispered. 'Are you all right?'

'Yes, Detective,' she replied. 'I have just received a message from King Oberon. He and his warriors are about to enter the throne room in the Castle of Demhe. We must hurry!'

*

Exeter had heard the shots echoing through the tunnels. *They are here!* he thought.

<DO NOT CONCERN YOURSELF,> said the voice of the King in Yellow.

But the Void Chamber is about to be attacked!

<AND WHAT OF IT? AS SOON AS THEY SEE MY SERVITOR, THEY WILL BE REDUCED TO DROOLING LUMPS OF HUMAN MEAT. YOU HAVE NOTHING TO FEAR, EXETER. NOW... BRING FORTH THE ANTI-PRISM!>

The mediumistic substrates in Exeter's brain flared to life, just as they had done when he summoned the Servitor to his apartments. He felt their strange power seeping through his mind, like hot ink through blotting paper, as he called a different set of unpronounceable words into his awareness and transmitted them towards the centre of the Void Chamber.

As he did so, he felt a stirring of the air behind him, and a sound as of something vast heaving itself into existence.

The Servitor had arrived, carrying its cargo of screaming souls.

Exeter shuddered as he felt his mind strengthening under the influence of the King in Yellow. He gave the briefest of thoughts to fleeing the Void Chamber and the horror and madness that were about to be unleashed upon the world... but there was nowhere to flee to, and Exeter strongly suspected that, were he to do so, he would be among the first of those who would fall victim to the ravenous appetite of the King in Yellow.

As he completed the mental incantation, Exeter looked around and saw that each of the bas-reliefs of the Yellow Sign carved upon the thousands of tiles lining the Void Chamber had begun to put forth a sickly, pallid glow.

He looked down at the centre of the floor, watching in horrified fascination as a circular section, perhaps ten feet in diameter, glowed brighter than the rest and rapidly became molten. Like melting wax, the tiles were transformed into a liquid mass which quickly sank into the resulting hole.

Exeter backed away and watched the walls of the Void Chamber warp and twist – while simultaneously remaining perfectly still – to accommodate the ultra-dimensional mass of the Servitor, which approached the edge of the steaming hole.

A maddening, pulsating hum, as of some vast electrical generator, began to thump through the chamber. Exeter felt his bones vibrate with each pulse and put his hands to his ears in a vain attempt to shut out the hideous power of the alien noise.

Something pointed and red began to emerge from the hole at the centre of the Void Chamber: a crystalline spire which surged with a strange interior movement, and whose surface flickered with blue-white arcs of energy.

Exeter gasped and took another few steps back as the spire became a long, slender multi-sided pyramid. As its emergence continued, he saw that its form was mirrored in an identical inverted pyramid beneath – livid red, stirring strangely within, its surface caressed by the crackling arcs of incomprehensible energy.

His familiarity with engineering principles told Exeter that the shape of this thing was a hexagonal trapezohedron, but its shape was the only thing remotely understandable about it.

'The Anti-Prism,' Exeter whispered.

<YES,> replied the voice of the King in Yellow. <WHEN FIRST I ARRIVED IN THIS UNIVERSE, I BROUGHT WITH ME A MILLION DEVICES SUCH AS THIS. BEFORE YOUR EARTH WAS EVEN FORMED, I HAD ALREADY SEEDED A MILLION WORLDS WITH ANTI-PRISMS, TO ALLOW ME INSTANTANEOUS TRAVEL THROUGH YOUR INTERSTELLAR GULFS.>

'How… how does it work?'

Exeter sensed contemptuous amusement from the thing in his mind.

<YOU ASKED ME THAT ONCE BEFORE. I WOULD NOT TELL YOU THEN, AND I WILL NOT TELL YOU NOW. HOW WOULD YOU GO ABOUT EXPLAINING THE PRINCIPLES OF A STEAM ENGINE TO A NEANDERTHAL? IT WOULD BE A POINTLESS EXERCISE… AS POINTLESS AS MY EXPLAINING THE PRINCIPLES OF THE ANTI-PRISM TO YOU.>

As the Servitor surged forward with its awful cargo, the voice of the King in Yellow thundered through Charles Exeter's mind.

<PREPARE YOURSELF, EXETER, FOR THE TIME OF MY ADVENT UPON EARTH IS HERE!>

*

Blackwood was pacing back and forth impatiently upon the main deck of the *Aurelius*, periodically checking the waterproof fob watch which was part of his environmental suit's equipment. Every few minutes, he went to the balustrade, leaned over and gazed into the lightless depths of the castle entrance.

'What the blazes are they doing down there?' he said. 'They must have reached the throne room by now.'

'It's a fair bet that they're encountering resistance,' replied Castaigne. 'We must give them time.'

Blackwood sighed and shook his head. 'Time is not something we have in great supply, Dr Castaigne. If the King in Yellow manages to complete his transit to Earth, it's all up for the human race!'

'I understand, my friend,' said the occultist. 'But there's nothing we can do except wait.'

Blackwood nodded and then glanced along the deck to where Sophia was standing alone. He switched his radio communication device to a private channel. 'I'm worried about her, Castaigne,' he said. 'There's something she's not telling us.'

'About what?'

'Herself – what happened when she encountered the King in Yellow after taking your Taduki drug. Something's wrong, I'm sure of it.'

'Do you think her mind might have been... damaged?'

'No, I don't think it's that – not quite; after all, the symptoms of such a derangement would be quite unequivocal. It's something else... but I'm dashed if I can put my finger on it.'

At that moment, a faerie crewman approached them, and Blackwood switched his radio back to the common channel.

The crewman was carrying something which looked like a large, folded-up sheet of pale green linen, which he handed to Blackwood.

'What's this?' asked the Special Investigator.

'There has been a change of plan, Mr Blackwood,' the faerie replied. 'King Oberon wishes you to bring this to him.'

Blackwood took the sheet, and was surprised to find that it was virtually weightless. 'Then he and his men have gained the throne room?'

'They are approaching it as we speak.'

'Good show!' Blackwood exclaimed.

'Are we ready?' asked Sophia, who had joined them.

'It looks like it, my dear,' Blackwood replied. 'You're sure you're able to guide us through the castle?'

'Believe me, Thomas, every twist and turn is etched in my mind.'

Oberon's voice suddenly flashed through their minds.

I am both gratified and saddened to hear it, Sophia.

'Oberon!' she said. 'Are we to join you now?'

Yes. You must come immediately. Descend from the Aurelius into the castle. By the time you reach the throne room, we will be there. Thomas, do you have that which I instructed my crewman to give to you?

'Yes, I have it,' Blackwood replied. 'But what is it?'

Something without which our mission will most certainly fail!

*

Blown by the wind from distant suns, the Wanderer entered the Solar System. Through the vast outer cloud of comets it flew, and then on through the great ring of asteroids beyond the orbit of the tiny ninth planet, which would not be discovered by human astronomers for another thirty-one years.

It detected the presence, far off in the infinite night, of two ice giants, and further on towards the distant yellow sun which shone brightly, as yet unsuspecting the calamity which was about to befall it, the haloed jewel of a beautiful ringed planet.

Conserving its energy, the Wanderer headed for a larger gas giant whose striated surface was marred by a vast storm of rotating red clouds. Complex celestial calculations were conducted instantaneously in the Wanderer's partly organic, partly mechanical brain, and it swung beneath the vast world, altering its trajectory at precisely the correct moment to catapult it at yet greater speed on a precise path towards the tiny blue mote which drifted serenely through the inner system, which was called by its inhabitants Earth.

The Wanderer scented the Luminiferous Æther in that direction but was unable to detect any trace of the yellow blasphemy from beyond the stars.

It was satisfied: the thing had yet to arrive, and when it did, the Wanderer would be waiting for it, for the Wanderer had received a message from Carcosa's twin suns upon its entry into that system: once again, it was too late to save a world and its people from destruction, but the suns had told it of a conversation they had had with a transmundane being from a nearby system.

This system...

Presently, the Wanderer spread its vast, membranous wings to catch the rays of the sun and began to decelerate in preparation for its final approach to the tiny blue world...

*

The newly excavated tunnel suddenly exploded with a cacophony of gunfire.

'This must be the place,' Sergeant Clairvaux quipped as he and de Chardin hurled themselves into the nearest bolthole, while Queen Titania paused and stood tranquilly amid the storm of bullets. As before, the ones which struck her bounced off and fell harmlessly to the ground.

A Templar Knight behind her was too slow to seek cover and staggered backwards as a hail of bullets struck his cuirass. Before he hit the ground, Titania flew to him in a lilac blur, picked him up and flung him into a bolthole. His grunt of thanks was lost in the continuing thunder.

'Your Majesty!' cried de Chardin. 'There must be a dozen men up there – a score! They've got us well and truly pinned down!'

Beside him, Clairvaux unslung his Maxim and began to return fire. From boltholes and corridor entrances, the rest of the Templar Knights were doing the same, but they were firing into near total darkness, and their expert marksmanship was all but wasted.

'It'll take too long to gain the Void Chamber like this!' de Chardin continued.

'Don't worry, Detective,' Titania replied in a quiet, gentle voice which nevertheless – incredibly – reached the Templar's ears in spite of the thunderous racket. 'I will see to them. You and your men prepare to make for the Void Chamber on my command – and remember, if your gaze falls upon the Servitor for more than a moment, your minds will be undone.'

'Did you hear that, men?' shouted de Chardin.

The Templar Knights shouted back that they did.

Once again, Titania vanished.

Once again, brief screams were heard as the darkness was illuminated by the ruby fire from Titania's faerie carbine.

'By God and all His angels,' said Clairvaux, 'what a fine lady!'

'We'd have been in a deep ditch without her, that's for sure,' de Chardin replied.

In another few moments, the enemy's gunfire had completely ceased. The resulting silence, however, was broken by a sound which made the Templars' relief short-lived indeed.

'What the deuce is that noise?' demanded de Chardin.

'I don't know,' replied Clairvaux. 'I've never heard the likes of it before.'

'Must be that infernal gadget – the Anti-Prism. Exeter must have switched it on!' De Chardin turned to the rest of his men. 'Come on, we've not a moment to lose!'

*

When the gunfire ceased, Exeter glanced up at the entrance to the tunnel leading from the sanity of Bond Street to this chamber of ultra-dimensional nightmare. Could his men have defeated the invading force so quickly? Could they themselves have succumbed?

What's happening? he wondered.

<YOUR MEN ARE PATHETIC, EXETER,> answered the voice of the King in Yellow. <THEY HAVE BEEN DEFEATED BY A GAGGLE OF MONKS AND A FAERIE. BUT THAT IS UNIMPORTANT, FOR THEY ARE TOO LATE TO STOP ME. GIVE THE FINAL ORDER TO MY SERVITOR!>

Exeter turned away from the entrance and transmitted the last of the mental commands he had learned from the King in Yellow.

The Servitor complied immediately. Its hideous, writhing mass seeped through the air to a position directly above the glowing Anti-Prism, and from it sprouted five thick tendrils, like the legs of some gigantic arthropod.

The tendrils descended towards the five stone monoliths which surrounded the central pit. At the instant they made contact, the pulsating electrical sound grew yet louder, the yellow glow emanating from the tiles grew brighter, and the monoliths vibrated visibly, so that to Exeter's eyes they lost focus, becoming hazy and indistinct, as if a sheet of frosted glass had suddenly been placed around them.

And then another sound came to Exeter's ears, a sound he knew would haunt him for the rest of his days, in spite of the power and riches he was about to attain.

It was the sound of ten thousand screams.

It was the sound of the souls held within the Servitor being discharged into the Anti-Prism.

The five thick tendrils pulsated obscenely in peristaltic waves as the psychic energy passed through them from the Servitor to the monoliths, which then directed it in the form of five painfully bright beams of light into the centre of the hexagonal trapezohedron which floated in the air at the centre of the Void Chamber.

The screams grew louder and louder, until Exeter could stand it no more and threw himself to the floor with his hands clasped over his ears. It was useless, however, for that tormenting sound was more than the mere vibration of air molecules; it drove like a lance into his very soul, a single howl of anguish from a profane limbo – desperate, terrified, accusing, *insane*.

'May God forgive me,' Charles Exeter whimpered as he lay writhing upon the glowing tiles of the floor.

<YOUR GOD IS COMING, EXETER,> said the voice of the King in Yellow. <AND HE FORGIVES YOU.>

CHAPTER FIVE:
The Tunnel Opens

The entity known as the King in Yellow was glad to be leaving Carcosa. For ten thousand years it had fed on the minds and bodies of the planet's inhabitants, and now the larder was almost empty. The population had dwindled from more than five thousand million to a mere handful, a few huddled dregs lingering on the surface of a blasted orb that had been drained of all animal and vegetable life. But the King in Yellow had taken its fill, and now it was time to move on to a fresh world, filled with ripe and unsuspecting minds and overflowing with the diversity of biological life.

The need for sustenance was not the only reason to abandon Carcosa, for the King in Yellow had heard the song of the Hyades and knew that the trembling stars were calling out into the galactic night for aid. Its ultra-dimensional mind had scented the Æther, and had detected the approach of its enemy, the biomechanical construct which had been half built, half grown in the aeon-long past by the scientific geniuses of a distant, dead world.

Their eventual understanding of the entity's origin and nature had come too late for them, but they had created a legacy for the galaxy and a great inconvenience for the King in Yellow: a being capable of detecting, enveloping and destroying the invader from beyond space.

That world had been among the first upon which the King in Yellow had descended, and it had made a serious misjudgement in choosing such an advanced race on which to feed. Ever since that time, the entity had been careful to choose only those worlds whose science was not up to the task of offering effective resistance.

Carcosa had been such a world, for although it was well advanced in age, its civilisation had long ago passed through the era of great technological endeavour and had returned to the simplicity of a pastoral existence, its scientific advances abandoned and forgotten. Carcosa was thus at the perfect position in the great cycle of advancement and contraction which seemed to pertain on worlds throughout this galaxy.

And what a galaxy it was! What a universe! Plump with matter and energy and life! An infinite source of nourishment.

The King in Yellow had travelled to many universes upon leaving its own realm beyond the ramparts of ordered space and time, and it had found that most were either empty or contained matter and energy in forms which were unpalatable to it, for what it craved most of all was the delicate psychic energy of intelligent minds, and it had found them in abundance in this universe.

As it awaited the arrival of its Servitor, which would pump the Carcosan souls it had gathered into the Anti-Prism in the throne room of the Castle of Demhe, the King in Yellow thought of the million other Anti-Prisms which its avatars had seeded on worlds throughout the galaxy, and which would facilitate rapid transit between those worlds, and it pulsated in awful anticipation of the feasting to come.

*

Oberon and his faerie warriors followed the Servitor along the warped and twisted corridor leading to the throne room, noting with both compassion and profound distaste the remnants of the lake's aquatic life which moved sluggishly through the tainted water. The misshapen swimming things paused occasionally to inspect them with distorted, gelatinous organs that might once have been eyes, before drifting away into the surrounding darkness.

What a mockery you have made of this once-beautiful world, thought Oberon, as he watched the poor creatures' pained movements.

<MOCKERY?> said the voice of the King in Yellow. <I ENJOY THE WARPING OF THEIR FORMS; THAT IS WHY I HAVE KEPT THEM HERE. MUCH AS I HAVE COME TO FEEL AT HOME IN THIS UNIVERSE, OBERON KING, I FIND THAT IT DOES HAVE A LITTLE TOO MUCH SYMMETRY FOR MY LIKING.>

If by 'symmetry' you mean order, rationality and beauty, then we are in agreement, for they are things of which you clearly know nothing!

<IT IS YOU WHO KNOW NOTHING, FAERIE REGENT! THERE ARE REGIONS POSSESSING A FAR HIGHER ORDER AND RATIONALITY, AND YES, *BEAUTY*, THAN ANYTHING OF WHICH *YOU* COULD CONCEIVE.>

And do you come from one of those regions?

<IT IS TRUE THAT I COME FROM A PLACE WHERE THINGS ARE NOT AS THEY ARE HERE, A PLACE WHERE DIFFERENT LAWS ARE OBSERVED, WHERE A DIFFERENT ORDER OF LIFE PREVAILS. A PLACE WHERE CHAOS IS ORDER, WHERE TRUTH IS FALSEHOOD, WHERE BEAUTY IS UGLINESS, WHERE LOVE IS HATE, WHERE THE VOID IS SOLID AND SOLIDITY IS VOID.>

You speak in riddles, beast. What are you? Why have you befouled this universe with your presence?

Oberon sensed amusement as the King in Yellow replied, <I HAVE COME TO FEED! THINK OF ME AS A

FISHERMAN. WE ARE AT THE BOTTOM OF A LAKE ON THE SURFACE OF A PLANET. THINK OF YOUR UNIVERSE AS A LAKE, ALSO: A LAKE WHICH EXISTS ON THE SURFACE OF A HIGHER DIMENSION – *MY* DIMENSION. LONG AGO, BEFORE YOUR WORLD WAS EVEN A CLOUD OF DUST AWAITING THE GRAVITATIONAL COLLAPSE WHICH WOULD FORGE IT INTO A SPHERE OF ROCK, I LOOKED DOWN INTO THIS UNIVERSE, THIS LAKE, AND SAW THAT IT WAS BRIMMING WITH LIFE. AND SO I CAME TO GATHER THE FOOD WHICH FILLS IT SO ABUNDANTLY. AND BELIEVE ME, OBERON, I WILL CONTINUE TO DO SO UNTIL I HAVE EMPTIED THIS LAKE OF EVERYTHING THAT LIVES AND BREATHES WITHIN IT!>

They had reached a great arched opening, beyond which was the throne room, once occupied by the royal family of Carcosa, but now home to the tattered monstrosity that had brought death and madness and irrevocable ruin to that unhappy world.

And tattered it was, Oberon noted with disgust. Strangely ragged was the outline of the vast thing which squatted at the centre of the chamber. Strangely did the flaps and folds undulate in a hundred putrid shades of yellow. Truly did Queen Cassilda write of 'the tatters of the king'.

For the first time, Oberon fully appreciated the fact that this creature hailed from beyond the ordered universe, that it was nothing which should be suffered to exist among the stars and planets, the light and the life, of known space and time.

<WELCOME, OBERON,> said the voice of the thing.

I can see why they describe you as yellow, but I fail to see why they call you king.

<BECAUSE THAT IS WHAT I AM TO ALL THAT LIVES AND BREATHES AND THINKS IN THIS UNIVERSE.>

I live and breathe and think, retorted Oberon. *And I see you as nothing more than a foul disease.*

<I AM SORELY TEMPTED TO DESTROY YOU THIS VERY INSTANT, FAERIE REGENT, BUT I WOULD RATHER YOU WATCHED THE GRADUAL CONSUMPTION OF YOUR PRECIOUS EARTH. IN TRUTH, THAT IS A FAR MORE FITTING PUNISHMENT FOR THE INSULTS YOU OFFER.>

We shall see, said Oberon, brandishing his carbine.

The Servitor moved quickly, but it was not to attack Oberon or his warriors; instead, it bestrode the glowing object in a far corner of the chamber. Instantly, Oberon swung his weapon around and fired, but he was too late, for the Servitor had already thrown out a gelatinous film to protect both the Anti-Prism and the five monolithic stone structures which surrounded it.

<BEHOLD THE MEANS BY WHICH I WILL DESCEND UPON YOUR EARTH, OBERON. AND SINCE YOUR WEAPONS ARE USELESS AGAINST MY SERVITOR, YOU CANNOT HARM IT. YOU CAN DO NOTHING TO PREVENT MY ADVENT!>

At that moment, Oberon and his warriors dropped their weapons and clutched at their heads as the sound of Carcosan souls being discharged into the Anti-Prism drove like an iron spike into their awareness, while the throne room glowed brightly with the energy being transferred from the Servitor, through the prismatic monoliths, to the transportation device. The pain, terror and anguish was an unendurable agony to them, and they dropped to their knees, their faces contorted, their eyes tightly shut.

The vast, ragged mass of the King in Yellow split apart like a pustulent wound, and as Oberon forced his eyes open and looked at what lay within – at the writhing tendrils whipping and curling around the frothing, bubbling nucleus that was composed of nothing remotely akin to matter – the Faerie King screamed with a terror and despair he had never known, had never even realised he *could* know.

The horror surged forward towards the Anti-Prism.

<FAREWELL, OBERON,> it said. <UNTIL OUR NEXT MEETING.>

*

Slowly, painfully, Charles Exeter lifted himself off the floor of the Void Chamber and gazed up at the Anti-Prism. The Servitor had completed its task: the psychic energy of the souls it had gathered had been fully utilised by the device, which now appeared to be operating at full power.

It began to turn upon its vertical axis, slowly at first, but then rapidly increasing in speed until it became little more than a crimson blur.

The Servitor withdrew and crawled sluggishly to the edge of the chamber, and Exeter had the impression that it was dying.

Exeter staggered back from the whirling Anti-Prism and prepared himself to meet his god.

*

On Carcosa, the Servitor edged away as a perfect circle of darkness opened above the Anti-Prism in the throne room. Framed by a strange distortion of the surrounding water, it expanded to perhaps ten yards in diameter and hovered in perfect stillness.

Like a vast, rotten egg sliding down a plughole, the King in Yellow heaved its amorphous bulk through the opening and was gone.

Blackwood! called Oberon silently.

'We're here, Oberon!' came the reply.

The Faerie King turned to see the three humans standing in the entrance to the throne room.

Shut your eyes! he commanded.

They obeyed him without hesitation as he hurried across the chamber and seized the sheet of green linen which Blackwood was holding. Then he turned and, unfolding the sheet, made for the Servitor which was undulating slowly near the entrance to the tunnel through space. He offered one end of the sheet to one of his warriors, who took it, and together they rose upon their wings and covered the sanity-blasting form of the Servitor.

Instantly, both it and the sheet vanished from view.

Blackwood, Sophia, Castaigne, said Oberon. *Open your eyes and come forward.*

'Where is the Servitor?' asked Sophia as they entered the throne room.

The object I asked you to bring is the Cloak of Invisibility, one of our most precious artefacts, Oberon replied. *The Servitor is still here, but you are now shielded from its aspect, even from its outline. You have your weapons?*

In reply, the three humans unslung their Maxim machine guns, which had been specially adapted by the technicians at Station X to fire explosive rounds in an underwater environment.

Oberon held up his hand. *Do not fire yet, for we must time this perfectly.*

He closed his eyes and reached out with his mind across the nine hundred trillion miles of space separating Carcosa from Earth. *Titania, my love, are you ready?*

*

I am ready, my husband, Titania replied.

She and the Templar Police were standing on the floor of the Void Chamber. As soon as they had descended the ladder leading down from the entrance, two of the Templars had moved to apprehend Charles Exeter, who was standing still, gazing up at the wildly spinning form of the Anti-Prism. He didn't seem to notice their presence until they seized him by the arms. As they did this, they took care not to look in the direction of the Servitor, which now squatted, unmoving, on the far side of the chamber.

'Charles Exeter,' said Detective de Chardin, 'I am arresting you in the name of Her Majesty for the crime of treason against your country and your world...'

He hesitated as Exeter began to laugh.

'You *arrest* me?' said the railway magnate. 'Very well, arrest me. I assure you that you will be releasing me from your custody very shortly, once the King in Yellow has drunk your soul!'

'Yes, well, we'll see about that,' de Chardin replied, glancing at Titania. The Faerie Queen nodded, and in a loud voice which echoed around the Void Chamber, he said to his men, 'Ready your weapons and take aim!'

The Templar Knights, who had taken up positions around the Anti-Prism with their backs to the Servitor, raised their Maxims.

De Chardin looked again at Titania, as a perfect circle of darkness appeared at the centre of the Void Chamber...

Oberon, she said. *Give the word.*

*

FIRE!

Oberon's command was directed both to the humans who stood beside him in the throne room of the Castle of Demhe, and to Titania, who relayed it instantly to the Templar Knights.

Simultaneously, Blackwood, Sophia, Castaigne, de Chardin, Clairvaux and their men all fired at the two Anti-Prisms.

On Carcosa and on Earth, the crystalline structure of the twin devices gave way beneath the onslaught of hot lead.

The Anti-Prisms shattered, and as they flew apart, their jagged fragments hurtled through the throne room and the

Void Chamber and embedded themselves in the walls, and it was only the elevated positions of the devices which saved the humans from being cleaved into a hundred pieces.

And as the Anti-Prisms flew to destruction, a sound came to the ears of human and faerie alike, and all who heard it believed it to be a scream of rage, or perhaps terror, or perhaps a combination of the two, as the entrances to the tunnel between worlds collapsed and flickered out of existence, sealing in that which was in transit between them, excising it utterly from the ordered universe.

CHAPTER SIX:
Back to Earth

The bright glow from the tiles containing the Yellow Sign gradually faded, casting a sullen crimson pall, like the embers of a dying fire, over the Void Chamber.

Although the scream which had briefly emanated from the tunnel between worlds had been cut off, it was replaced by another: a high, keening human screech, which came from Charles Exeter. Titania glanced at him and instantly understood the reason.

Exeter was still facing the Servitor, and although the creature was now all but inactive, its purpose fulfilled, still it stood before him, and with the King in Yellow gone from the universe, Exeter's mind was undefended against the ultra-dimensional horror of its appearance.

Charles Exeter had been driven insane.

'Is that it?' said de Chardin. 'Is the threat to Earth gone now?'

'It is gone,' Titania replied.

The Templar detective glanced at Exeter. Still held tightly by the two policemen, the railway magnate was drooling, whimpering and gibbering quietly to himself.

'Poor wretch,' de Chardin muttered, shaking his head. 'One can't help but feel sorry for him – in spite of what he had planned.'

'It is to your credit that you do,' said Titania. 'What will you do with him?'

De Chardin shrugged. 'Well, it's most unlikely he'll be able to stand trial now. I suspect he'll have to be incarcerated in a suitable mental institution – probably Bethlem Hospital. I suppose there's a justice there – albeit poetic rather than literal – in that he will be in the same place where poor Alfie Morgan is confined.

'But what about that?' he continued, jerking a thumb over his shoulder at the Servitor, which had ceased its sluggish movements and was now as still as a rock on the far side of the Void Chamber.

'The Servitor is dead,' Titania replied, glancing at the abnormality, 'as is the one on Carcosa. I believe they would have died anyway, after channelling so much psychic energy, but in any event, the source of their power, the King in Yellow, is now gone from the universe. It was that being's influence which allowed Charles Exeter to perceive this Servitor without having his mind rent asunder...'

'And when that influence left his mind, it was undefended against the fantastic alienness of the thing,' de Chardin completed. 'Nevertheless, we'll have to get rid of it somehow...'

'Leave that to us,' said Titania. 'You have done well, de Chardin. You have successfully defended your world, at great risk to yourselves. King Oberon will be pleased.'

As she smiled at him, de Chardin felt a great agitation seize his heart, and he looked down in embarrassment. 'Thank you, Your Majesty. We... we certainly could not have prevailed without your help.'

'You are kind to say so. Now, you have some more work to do. Take Exeter into your custody, while I organise the removal and disposal of the Servitor.'

*

308

Although they had avoided injury from the hurtling shards of the Carcosa Anti-Prism, Blackwood, Sophia and Castaigne had been knocked off their feet by the concussive force of the device's destruction, which had spread through the water filling the throne room.

As they stood up, Oberon smiled at them and sent a thought into their minds.

Well done, my friends. The danger is passed; the blight is gone from the universe. You have prevailed, and the Earth is safe.

'It has gone,' said Sophia, and even through the crackle of her radio transmitter, the joy and relief in her voice were unmistakeable.

Blackwood moved to her, and through the tall globes of their helmets, he saw that the brightness had returned to her eyes, and her beautiful face was animated by a smile which was delightful to behold. 'Indeed it is, my dear,' he said.

I do not think that Sophia is referring to the departure of the King in Yellow in quite the way you suppose, Thomas, said Oberon.

Blackwood frowned. 'What do you mean?'

Sophia? said the Faerie King.

'Oberon is right,' she said. 'I said nothing of it, because I didn't want to worry you... but after I took Dr Castaigne's Taduki drug and voyaged here, after I encountered the King in Yellow, I felt that a part of the fiend had stayed with me...'

'*Stayed* with you?' said Blackwood, glancing from her to Oberon. 'Whatever do you mean?'

'I felt that part of its mind was still inside mine – how, I cannot begin to speculate. It was like... like an echo... but it was there, constantly, at the back of my awareness.' Her voice cracked, and she gave a brief sob. 'But it is gone now.'

I suspected as much, said Oberon. *As I said to you on the* Aurelius, *Thomas, no human could be in the presence of a being such as the King in Yellow and return from the encounter unscathed. We must be thankful that the fragment of the entity's mind which remained with Sophia did not cause any permanent damage.*

'I do not believe that was its intention,' Sophia replied. 'I sensed that it was fascinated by me… or rather by my audacity in voyaging to Carcosa alone. I cannot begin to speculate on what it would have done to me, had it succeeded in its plan to take up residence on Earth.'

Nor should you, Oberon said. *The time for dark and fearful speculation is over. Your world awaits your return, although very few will be aware of the great service you have performed.*

'No matter,' said Castaigne. 'I just want to get out of this infernal place and back to Blighty.'

Blackwood gave him a wry smile. 'I thought you were an inveterate traveller, Dr Castaigne.'

'I assure you I remain so, my dear chap, but I feel the need for an extended period of rest and relaxation in pleasantly mundane surroundings.'

A desire I well understand, said Oberon. *Let us return to the* Aurelius *and make for Earth without delay.*

*

As the vast faerie ship lifted clear of the Lake of Hali, Sophia pointed over the edge of the main deck. 'Look!' she cried. 'The cloud waves are breaking up. You can see the water!'

It was true, for just as the King in Yellow had gone from the universe, so the reality-warping effects of his erstwhile presence were likewise beginning to dissipate.

'And look!' added Castaigne, pointing up. 'The moons of Carcosa are regaining their sanity. They are returning to their rightful place in the heavens!'

As he, Sophia and Blackwood watched, the four moons, which had drifted impossibly above the Lake of Hali, appearing in front of the towers of the surrounding cities in an outrageous affront to the laws of physics, began to fade from view, while in the far distance their forms gradually became more and more discernible.

From now on, they will follow their proper orbits around Carcosa, said Oberon. *Dr Castaigne is right: this world is becoming sane again.*

'Although too late for those who remain,' said Blackwood.

The Faerie King lowered his eyes. *Yes, too late for them.*

Quickly gaining altitude, the *Aurelius* passed the shoreline of Hali and flew above the towers of the nearest city. Sophia looked down at the strangely elegant buildings and winding streets extending beyond the great stone ramparts which had shielded them from the constantly moving cloud waves, and she spied the forms of people emerging, collecting in large groups and talking animatedly.

'They know that their world has been set free,' she said, and, peering more closely at them, added, 'They are not so very different from us.'

'No,' Oberon replied. 'They are very similar to humans.'

'Can we not go down to them? Can we not meet them…?'

Oberon gave a soft chuckle. 'I have an inkling that you will be meeting them before very long. But not yet.'

'What do you mean?'

Oberon said nothing; he merely glanced at Blackwood, who was observing the city with a thoughtful expression.

*

The *Aurelius* turned its prow away from Carcosa and its giant red suns and plunged once more into the metallic grey liquid of the Pneuma hypertube. When Blackwood, Sophia and Castaigne had divested themselves of their environmental suits, Oberon gave his guests a tour of his astonishing vessel, from the bowsprit which extended like a vast needle out from the prow (and which itself was longer than any ship sailing the oceans of Earth), past the gigantic forecastle, which was larger than Saint Paul's Cathedral, across the main deck to the colossal aftcastle containing the captain's suite of cabins and quarters for the more senior members of the crew.

From there they descended into the interior of the ship, past the regular crew's quarters (all of which were appointed with an elegant sumptuousness far surpassing the most opulent palaces of Earth), the whipstaff steering mechanism controlling the three-hundred-foot-tall rudder and the engine room powering the great paddle wheel which drove the ship through the higher dimension of the hypertube. Blackwood and Castaigne looked up at the vast and arcane machinery which filled this latter chamber, glanced at each other and shook their heads in befuddlement, for neither could begin to identify any of the components, which had a curiously organic cast to them, as if, like everything else on the ship, they had been grown rather than manufactured.

They were walking through the cargo holds and supply rooms, each cathedral-like in its size, when Sophia stopped suddenly, gasped and put a hand to her head. Her companions regarded her with concern.

'What is it, my dear?' asked Blackwood.

'He is back,' she whispered.

'What?'

'The King in Yellow… *he has returned!*'

'That is not possible, Sophia,' said Oberon. 'He has been excised from the universe; the tunnel between worlds has been sealed off with him inside it. There is no conceivable way–'

'I tell you it's true, Oberon!' Sophia cried. 'I can feel him in my mind again, just as before!'

'Good God!' Castaigne exclaimed. 'If that's the case, then what the deuce are we to do?'

'We are approaching Earth,' replied the Faerie King. 'If the fiend really has broken free of his imprisonment, there is only one thing we *can* do. Follow me.'

Oberon led them back up to the aftcastle, where their guest quarters were located.

'Put on your environmental suits,' he commanded, 'and when you have done so, join me at the helm.'

Blackwood paused at the door to his cabin, and turned to the Faerie King. 'What's your plan, Oberon?' he asked.

'My plan is simple, Thomas. We are going to engage the King in Yellow directly. The *Aurelius* is going into battle!'

CHAPTER SEVEN:
A Deeper Darkness

Blackwood, Sophia and Castaigne arrived at the summit of the colossal aftcastle in time to see the waters of the hypertube dissipate, replaced by the stars of quotidian space. Directly ahead of the *Aurelius* the blue, cloud-strewn orb of Earth hung suspended in the glittering firmament, beautiful to behold and unsuspecting of the calamity which once again threatened it.

'What do you mean you're going into battle?' asked Blackwood as they joined Oberon at the helm. 'If you are directly responsible for the King in Yellow's destruction, you'll have broken your Covenant with the universe. We humans are the ones who must neutralise the threat.'

'There was only one way you could have done that, Thomas,' Oberon replied. 'We tried it, and we failed. There is nothing more you can do. Now... now *I* must take over.'

'And what happens if you succeed?' asked Sophia.

'There will be a price to pay, and I will gladly pay it.'

'What price?'

'I will take full responsibility for the breaking of the Covenant. I will offer myself in payment to the Primal Mind. The punishment will, at best, be permanent exile from the Earth...'

'And at worst?' said Blackwood.

'Death.'

'No!' Sophia cried. 'You cannot!'

'It is a price worth paying for the safety of the world you see before you.'

'There must be another way, Oberon,' said Castaigne. 'There *must* be.'

The Faerie King turned and smiled at the occultist. 'I am open to suggestions, sir.'

'We could… I mean, I…' Castaigne lapsed into silence and shook his head.

'Your Majesty!' cried one of the crewmen from the main deck. 'There!'

They turned their gazes in the direction he was pointing. Off to port, a shape had become visible against the backdrop of stars: a ragged, tattered form of chaos and foulness, still distant, but getting closer by the second.

The voice of the King in Yellow blasted into the awareness of everyone onboard the ship.

<OBERON! DID YOU THINK YOU COULD DEFEAT ME SO EASILY?>

The Anti-Prisms were destroyed, Oberon replied. *You were trapped within the tunnel between worlds… you were trapped outside the universe!*

<FOOL! I *CAME* FROM OUTSIDE THE UNIVERSE! IT WAS SIMPLICITY ITSELF TO BREAK FREE FROM THE TUNNEL! AND FREE I AM – FREE TO SATE MY HUNGER ON THE WORLD BEFORE US. HOW PRETTY IT IS! HOW IT BRIMS WITH LIFE! I WILL DRINK DEEP OF IT… STARTING WITH THE LITTLE CREATURE STANDING BESIDE YOU, THE ONE WHOSE MIND HAS ALREADY COME BEFORE ME…>

'You filthy bloody brute!' Blackwood shouted. 'I'll die before I let that happen!'

<IF THAT IS YOUR PREFERENCE, WRETCH, THEN PREPARE TO DIE.>

At that moment, Sophia screamed and sank to her knees, clutching at her helmeted head with both hands. Blackwood crouched down beside her and took her in his arms. 'Sophia! What…?'

'He is…' she gasped. 'He is… *inside me!*'

She screamed again, and Blackwood looked up at Oberon, his features twisted into a tortured expression of rage and helplessness.

The King in Yellow had drawn close to the *Aurelius*. Unencumbered by gravity, its ragged form now spread out equally in all directions, a vast, amorphous mass which flapped and writhed hideously, like the gelatinous denizens which pulsated in the gelid darkness of Earth's deepest oceans.

Oberon's next words were addressed to his crew, although the humans heard them also.

Ready the cannons, he said.

All along the great flanks of the faerie vessel, vast doors slid aside to reveal pewter-coloured cylinders, each a hundred feet long with a muzzle thirty feet wide.

Fire at will! cried Oberon.

Instantly, the cannons disgorged sun-like spheres of blinding green energy, which struck the monstrosity floating off the vessel's port side. Each ball of green fire found its target unerringly, blasting away huge chunks of the King in Yellow's fetid mass, and with each impact, Sophia screamed louder and writhed upon the deck, her features contorted in unendurable torment.

As he held her wildly thrashing body in his arms, Blackwood looked up at the ragged form of the King in Yellow, which was being torn to further tatters by the impacts of the faerie projectiles. And to his horror, he saw that the thing was recombining after each impact, sending whipping tendrils out to gather up each fragment and draw it back into itself.

'It's not working, Oberon!' he screamed. 'Your weapons are useless against it.'

<BLACKWOOD,> came the voice of the King in Yellow. <I AM SCENTING THE MIND OF YOUR FRIEND THE WAY YOU SCENT A MEAL PRIOR TO CONSUMING IT. HER MIND IS DELICIOUSLY FRAGRANT. I AM GOING TO ENJOY MY FIRST HUMAN!>

'Leave her alone, you bastard!' cried Blackwood. 'If you want a mind to consume, then take mine!'

<I ASSURE YOU I SHALL. BUT NOT YET. FIRST, I AM GOING TO SAVOUR YOUR FRIEND. BUT DO NOT BE CONCERNED, FOR YOU WILL MEET HER AGAIN, WHILE YOUR MINDS ARE BEING DIGESTED TOGETHER.>

Blackwood looked up at Oberon in desperation, but the Faerie King was not looking at him, or at the King in Yellow. His gaze was cast in an entirely different direction, into the depths of space behind the *Aurelius*.

As Blackwood followed his gaze, his eyes grew wide in astonishment.

Against the backdrop of diamond-bright stars... *something* was moving.

'What is that?' he whispered.

Our salvation, Oberon replied.

As the object approached, more of its outline and structure became discernible. It was like nothing anyone on the *Aurelius* – human or faerie – had ever seen. The only components which were remotely recognisable were the vast, fan-like wings, striated with iridescent bands of blue-grey, which emerged from the main body of the thing. The body itself appeared to be composed of a dozen or more flesh-coloured discs, intersecting each other along a single axis, which imparted to it a spherical shape.

Its size was difficult to determine at first, for there was no frame of reference, nothing in the firmament with which to compare it, but as its approach continued… and continued… it became apparent that the thing was of an unimaginable size, completely dwarfing the mile-long *Aurelius*.

'It's the King in Yellow's nemesis!' declared Castaigne, his voice all but strangled by awe. 'It's the Wanderer! It has found him!'

At that moment, Sophia stopped screaming and lay still. Blackwood peered through the globe of her helmet, and then at the gauges on her suit's chest-mounted control unit. *Still alive*, he thought. *Thank God… but what state is her mind in… if she still has one?*

Hold your fire, Oberon ordered, and immediately the seething orbs of faerie energy ceased their battering of the King in Yellow.

<DO YOU THINK THIS IS MY END, OBERON?> said the monster. <I HAVE CONSIDERED ALL MY POSSIBLE FUTURES, INCLUDING THIS, AND I HAVE PLANNED FOR IT.>

And with that utterance, the stars before which the King in Yellow floated grew suddenly warped, smearing around it in arcs of twisted light, at the centre of which was a circular patch of perfect darkness.

The Wanderer must have observed this, for it surged forward towards the phenomenon, but it did not move quickly enough. The King in Yellow vanished into the darkness, and when it had vanished, the stars returned to their normal aspect.

'What happened?' asked Castaigne urgently.

'I don't know,' Blackwood replied. 'But if pressed, I'd say that the beast has escaped, perhaps into some other realm of time and space.'

I would say you are correct, Thomas, said Oberon. *Look. The newcomer has ceased its forward charge. It is remaining still.*

'You are *not* correct, Thomas,' said another voice, and all turned to see Sophia getting unsteadily to her feet.

'Sophia!' Blackwood cried.

'I'm all right,' she said, although her voice was terribly weak and tremulous. 'The King in Yellow is still in my mind,' she added, 'although his influence is much weakened. He has not escaped – at least, not entirely, for he has cloaked himself in a shield of energy...'

A shield of energy? said Oberon. *What kind of energy?*

'I don't know; it is a form of which we know nothing, and it is undetectable... undetectable by us, and by the Wanderer also. It is utterly invisible... but the King in Yellow is still here!'

CHAPTER EIGHT:
Sophia's Sacrifice

The *Aurelius* and the Wanderer floated beside each other in interplanetary space. In comparison to the vast alien device, the faerie vessel was as a grain of rice compared to an orange. Oberon tried to communicate with it, but to no avail; it either could not or would not answer. At the helm, Oberon, Blackwood, Sophia and Castaigne looked at the region of space where the King in Yellow had last been.

'Can you tell if the thing is still there, Sophia?' asked Blackwood.

'It is,' she replied. 'It knows it cannot defeat its nemesis, and yet it is reluctant to leave the Solar System: it doesn't want to wait for the thousands of years it would take to travel through normal space to the next planet on its menu.' There was a tone of bitter disgust in her voice as she said this.

Then we are at an impasse, said Oberon. *I confess I am uncertain how to proceed.*

'I am not,' Sophia said.

Before anyone realised what she was doing, before they could make any move to stop her, she strode past Oberon to the edge of the aftcastle, crouched down and then launched herself into space – directly towards the colossal, winged entity beside which the *Aurelius* floated.

'*Sophia!*' Blackwood cried. 'What in God's name are you doing?'

As her figure tumbled off into the distance, her voice crackled in his and Castaigne's helmets. 'This creature has been tracking the King in Yellow among the stars for thousands of years, like a bloodhound on the trail of its quarry... but the trail has suddenly gone cold. It knows its enemy is still nearby, but it cannot sense the precise location.'

As she said this, Blackwood began to understand what she was about to do. 'Oberon,' he said. 'Get her back. Get her back now!'

The Faerie King looked at him with an expression of immense sadness, and slowly shook his head.

'Do you realise what she's doing?' he cried.

Yes, Thomas, I realise. This is our last chance to rid ourselves and the universe of the King in Yellow. We must let her go.

'No,' Blackwood said. 'For God's sake, no!'

'I don't understand,' said Castaigne. 'Why is she doing this?'

'It's quite simple, Dr Castaigne,' Sophia said, the electrical crackle of her voice increasing as she drifted closer to the Wanderer. 'The entity needs a fresh scent to pick up, and the King in Yellow is still partly inside me. If we make contact, perhaps – just perhaps – the entity will be able to follow the scent to its source...'

Sophia had now diminished to a barely discernible dot against the spherical bulk of the Wanderer, a tiny mote drifting towards something colossal, implacable, silent, incomprehensible.

The others heard her breathing grow more and more rapid as she drifted into the angle between two of the gigantic, flesh-coloured discs of which the Wanderer's body was composed.

Blackwood made to run to the edge of the aftcastle and launch himself into space after Sophia, but instantly, Oberon's powerful hands were upon his shoulders, preventing him from moving.

You cannot bring her back, Thomas. Your environmental suit does not possess the necessary equipment to navigate through the void of space.

'I cannot, and you *will* not,' Blackwood replied. 'She's going to die out there, and I can't let her face it alone. I have to be with her, Oberon, can't you understand?'

I understand perfectly. And you *must understand that if she dies, it will be for a greater good, but if you give up your life simply to be with her at the end, you will have squandered it to no true purpose. It would be a futile gesture, Thomas: gallant, but utterly useless.*

'He's right, Thomas,' said Sophia's voice in his helmet. It was now almost completely drowned out by the crackle of static. 'You are a Special Investigator for Her Majesty. Your destiny is to continue with your task of defending the Empire and the world. My destiny is slightly different.'

'No, Sophia,' he whispered. 'No…'

'Thomas,' she said, her voice barely audible now. 'I want you… to… know… I… you… very much…'

'What did you say? Sophia! I didn't hear all of that. Please say it again!'

But now Blackwood could hear nothing but the crackle of static in his helmet.

'She's gone,' said Castaigne. 'Poor girl. Poor, brave girl!'

At that moment, a flicker of light reached their eyes: a thin frond of pale blue arcing between the two discs between which Sophia's trajectory had carried her.

So great was Blackwood's grief that he barely noticed how the flicker spread across the surface of the Wanderer's body, until the strange entity was completely enveloped within a glittering filigree of blue light. He closed his eyes, sank to his knees and buried his helmeted head in his gloved hands.

It was Castaigne's excited cry that brought him up and forced him to regard what was now happening. A vast fork of blue lightning flashed silently out from the colossal sphere of the Wanderer's body. The fork extended into the far distance before splitting into claw-like branches...

No, Blackwood thought suddenly, they didn't look like claws... they looked more like the bars of a spherical cage...

Like a tendril composed of fizzling electrical light, the blue lightning fork appeared to contract, pulling the cage towards the Wanderer, and as it did so a scream of rage, pain and terror filled the awareness of all aboard the *Aurelius*.

That scream sounded very familiar to Blackwood: it was the same scream they had heard when the Anti-Prism had been destroyed on Carcosa.

It was the scream of the King in Yellow.

*

Like some mysterious, outlandish predator of the deep oceans, the Wanderer continued to reel in its lightning-tendril and the glowing cage to which it was attached. As the cage drew nearer, those on the *Aurelius* saw that it contained a wildly-thrashing mass of ragged, tattered yellow.

The beast's shield has been destroyed, observed Oberon. *It is defenceless, now.*

'What will happen when our friend reels in his catch?' wondered Castaigne.

I have no idea, Oberon replied. *But perhaps it would serve us well not to be too close to it when it does*.

As if in response to this exchange, another fork of energy flashed out from the Wanderer towards the *Aurelius*. As it contacted the ship, the deck heaved beneath them, nearly throwing them off their feet.

Fascinating, said Oberon. *The entity clearly has intelligence and compassion: it's pushing us away!*

The *Aurelius* picked up speed as the lightning fork continued to press against its hull. Soon, the Wanderer had dwindled to the size of the full moon as seen from Earth, and the lightning fork withdrew.

The cage containing the King in Yellow was no longer discernible in the distance, and the filament of crackling blue energy connecting it to the Wanderer appeared as thin as a fishing line.

Oberon, Blackwood and Castaigne watched as it was finally drawn into the vast spherical body of the Wanderer, whereupon the entity's gigantic wings detached from its main body and floated away into the infinite void.

'What is it doing?' asked Blackwood, his voice flat and toneless. In spite of the terrible weight in his heart – for he believed Sophia to be already dead – his natural curiosity would not be denied; still his fascination with the gigantic alien entity pulsed like an ersatz heartbeat in his mind.

It is as I suspected, Thomas, replied Oberon. *It has shed its mode of propulsion because it no longer needs it: the aeon-long search is over; the very purpose of its existence is about to be fulfilled, its mission completed. I am very glad it saw fit to push us away.*

'What do you...' Blackwood began, but the words stalled in his throat as the wingless sphere suddenly contracted like a deflating balloon, and then detonated with the force of an exploding sun.

The conflagration was all but soundless in the rarefied atmosphere of the Luminiferous Æther, but the sight of it filled their awareness, blasting away all other thought save the emotions of awe and terror. It was like no explosion Blackwood had ever seen or even conceived of: a rapidly expanding sphere of mottled blue light and seething energy which hurled itself into space, momentarily obliterating the lambency of the distant stars and filling the observable universe with its power and fury.

As the shockwave from it struck the *Aurelius*, the faerie vessel lurched and spun crazily through the void, so that the stars swam and the orb of the Earth whirled about like a soap bubble in a sudden gale, and it was all Oberon could do to regain control and return the ship once again to an even keel.

When they had recovered themselves and looked once again in the direction of the explosion, they saw that it was already dissipating, the bright, livid blue fading into pale strands of diminishing light which drifted off into the interplanetary night.

It is gone, said Oberon. *And with it, the King in Yellow.*

And with them, Sophia, thought Blackwood.

The Faerie King caught these inner words and turned to the Special Investigator. *She will be remembered forever in the Realm of Faerie. Songs and poems will be composed in her honour.*

Thank you, Blackwood said without words.

Suddenly, Castaigne seized his shoulder and pointed into the void. 'What's that?' he asked.

The others followed the line of his outstretched arm, peering out at the distant stars. Far away, something glinted: a tiny, moving pinpoint of light.

'I don't know,' said Blackwood. 'Oberon, do you have a telescope?'

I'm afraid not: we have no need of them. But my eyesight is far keener than yours, and I can see what it is...

'What is it?'

It is... Sophia!

*

Presently, they saw that the slowly-tumbling form was encased in a sphere of glowing blue energy which, even as the *Aurelius* was brought about to intercept it, quickly faded away to nothing.

Oberon reached out from the edge of the main deck, grasped the suited figure and pulled it aboard, laying it gently upon the deck.

'Good God!' said Castaigne. 'You were right to say the entity was compassionate, Your Majesty. It must have thrown a shield around her, protecting her from the explosion.'

His mind in turmoil at this sudden turn of events, Blackwood looked over the suit, checking the gauges on the chest-mounted control unit. He could not yet bring himself to hope that Sophia might still be alive, for she had been at the very centre of that colossal detonation, and there was no guarantee that the shield had been effective.

The glass on the gauges was cracked, the needles twisted out of position, so that they were completely useless as indicators of the suit's integrity or its occupant's physical condition. He checked the helmet and saw that it was intact. Beneath it, Sophia's face was completely still, her eyes closed. He checked the rest of the suit for ruptures which would have allowed the life-preserving oxygen to leak away into space, but there was none.

Then another thought occurred to him, and he turned to Oberon. 'We must get her out of the suit this instant: the oxygen supply may have been interrupted. Can you raise the shield around the *Aurelius*, as you did before?'

'But what good will that do?' cried Castaigne. 'Even with the shield in place, we are still in vacuum!'

'Damn!' Blackwood swore. 'I didn't consider that.'

Do not be concerned, said the Faerie King. *I have already put the shield in place, and am filling it with oxygen from the ship's stores.*

Blackwood and Castaigne felt themselves buffeted by the sudden presence of air where there had been none before.

Blackwood undid the clasps around the suit's neck-ring and lifted the helmet away. 'Sophia,' he said. 'Sophia, can you hear me?'

There was no response, and Blackwood gently brushed away the hair that had fallen about her face. 'Sophia… please wake up…'

And then Blackwood heaved a great sigh of relief, and a single tear slid down his cheek, as Sophia's eyelids flickered.

EPILOGUE

Thomas Blackwood sat in Queen Victoria's private office at Buckingham Palace. The room was silent, save for the subdued hiss and gurgle from Grandfather's steampowered artificial legs as he sat on the chair next to him. The Queen herself was seated at her desk, reading Blackwood's report on the affair of the King in Yellow. She had read it once already, as soon as Blackwood had completed it upon his return to Earth, but so singular were its contents that she could not resist perusing it once again, having summoned the Special Investigator and the Director of the Bureau of Clandestine Affairs for a private discussion.

Blackwood shifted uncomfortably in his seat. He did not enjoy being in the Queen's presence, not only for the quite natural reason that he was in no small part intimidated by the redoubtable monarch, but also because her unnatural youth, artificially recaptured through the use of Martian rejuvenation drugs, unsettled him.

Although she was eighty years of age, Victoria had the appearance of a woman in her twenties: her skin was pale and flawless, her dark hair lustrous, while her eyes burned brightly with the vital fire of youth. She had accepted the gift of the rejuvenation drugs when it was offered to her by the Martian Parliament in the months following first contact between Earth and the Red Planet six years ago, and during that period her body and mind had drawn back from the approaching abyss of death, while the sunset which all had believed to be upon the Victorian Era had been transformed into a new dawn.

Victoria gathered the pages of the report together and placed them on her desk. A little way off to the right, another desk stood with nothing on it save the writing accoutrements which had belonged to her beloved husband, Albert. It was still the Queen's habit to dress in black, for she had let it be known that however long she lived, she would never stop mourning his passing.

'You are quite certain, Mr Blackwood,' she said, 'that this singular enemy of ours is utterly defeated?'

'We need entertain no doubts on that score, Your Majesty,' the Special Investigator replied. 'The King in Yellow has been completely destroyed by the alien entity.'

'And nothing remains of either?'

'Nothing, Ma'am.'

'And where is Lady Sophia?'

'She is recuperating from her ordeal in the Faerie Realm. King Oberon took her there as soon as we had returned to Earth. He says that she will be fully recovered in a short while.'

'We are most gratified to hear it. Her brave and selfless actions will not be forgotten.'

'Thank you, Your Majesty.'

Victoria paused before continuing, 'And now, Grandfather tells us that there is something you wish to discuss.'

Once again, Blackwood fidgeted uncomfortably. 'Yes, Ma'am, there is…'

Victoria spread her hands and raised her eyebrows. 'Come, sir, don't be shy! What is it?'

'It concerns the people of Carcosa. Their planet has been utterly ruined by the depredations of the King in Yellow, and while it is true that their nemesis has gone forever, still there is not enough left of the animal and plant life on that unhappy world to sustain the survivors. I was wondering…' He hesitated.

'Yes?'

'I was wondering whether we might offer them a new home here, on Earth… in Great Britain…'

'Do you think they would come, if we made such an offer to them?'

'I'm not sure. It may be that the fight has been knocked out of them, that they no longer have the strength to continue, on their world or ours. All I know is that if they stay on Carcosa, they will become extinct.'

Victoria glanced at the report and shook her head. 'We cannot even begin to imagine the horrors that have befallen them, the ruin that has overwhelmed their world. Indeed, had it not been for you and your colleagues, Mr Blackwood, those very same horrors would now be afflicting the human race. But tell us, how would they travel across the countless leagues of space from Carcosa to Earth? We are informed that even our new Æther zeppelins cannot travel such distances.'

'I have taken the liberty of discussing this already with King Oberon. He has agreed to place several of his Æther galleons at our disposal to bring the last Carcosans to Earth. But of course, the final decision is yours, and yours alone.'

Victoria's youthful, limpid eyes met Blackwood's. 'The decision is already made,' she said. 'You have our permission to offer the people of Carcosa a new home in the British Empire.'

Blackwood let out the breath he had been holding. 'I'm grateful for your generosity and compassion, Ma'am. I will let Dr Castaigne know, for he would be the perfect choice as an ambassador.'

'Do you think there are any more like him?' asked Grandfather suddenly.

Blackwood turned to him. 'I beg your pardon, sir?'

'That King in Yellow blighter. Are there any more of his kind sniffing around out there?'

'I'm not sure – although I must admit that it's a distinct possibility.'

'I'd like to get my hands on one of those Anti-Prism contraptions,' Grandfather huffed. 'Instantaneous travel, by golly! Think of the advantages that would bestow upon the Empire!'

'I hope I never see one again,' Blackwood rejoined vehemently. 'Especially considering the means by which they are powered.'

'Point taken, Thomas,' said Grandfather, 'but I'm sure that if we ever managed to find one and give it to the chaps at Station X, they'd find another way to power it…'

'With Vril energy, perhaps?' said Blackwood bitterly, and a little too loudly.

Victoria raised her eyebrows again, while Grandfather reddened somewhat.

Blackwood realised that he was in danger of overstepping the mark. 'Forgive me,' he said quietly. 'I meant no disrespect, sir, Your Majesty; it's just that I believe there are some things which mankind is not meant to know – at least at this stage of our technological development.'

'Hmm,' Grandfather murmured.

'We fully appreciate and understand the strength of your opinions, Mr Blackwood,' said Victoria. 'We still have nightmares about our attempt to harness the power of

Vril.' She shuddered visibly. 'Let us hope that those infernal devices remain forever hidden wherever in the universe they have been seeded.'

She glanced at Grandfather, who nodded. 'Quite so, Your Majesty, quite so.'

'And what of the ghosts on the London Underground?' the Queen said. 'Will they be less disruptive, now that the monster which had tormented them is no more?'

'I believe so,' Blackwood replied. 'Queen Titania is there as we speak. She is reassuring them that the horror has departed forever…'

'She's also supervising the disposal of the thing,' added Grandfather. 'She's doing a splendid job down there, and jolly pretty she is, too!'

'Really, Grandfather! You surprise us!' Victoria chuckled.

'Oh, I… I do beg your pardon, Ma'am.'

The Queen returned her attention to Blackwood. 'And what of the little ghost child who gave you so much help in your assignment? What was her name…?'

'Anne Naylor. Oberon and Titania have decided to adopt her.'

Victoria's face brightened. 'You don't say!'

'It's true, Ma'am. Anne once told me how she loved faeries but had never seen one. Now, she will spend eternity amongst the gentle miracles of the Faerie Realm.'

'How delightful. Well, it only remains for us to congratulate you on another job well done, Mr Blackwood. And please do pass on our best wishes to Lady Sophia when you see her. Tell her it is too long since we last took tea together!'

'I certainly will, Your Majesty,' said Blackwood as he and Grandfather stood up to take their leave.

*

Three days later, Blackwood received a message from a runner, inviting him to Sophia's home. Without delay, he left his apartments and hailed a cab for Kensington.

Sophia's housekeeper opened the door, bid him good day and asked him to go straight through to the sitting room. The look of happiness and relief on her face was plain as the sun, and Blackwood gave her a warm smile, along with his hat and coat.

'Thomas!' cried Sophia, rising from her armchair and rushing across the room to hug him.

Her housekeeper caught sight of their embrace, blushed a bright shade of crimson and hurried off to prepare some tea.

Blackwood himself was a little embarrassed by this show of affection; nevertheless, he held her close. 'How are you, my dear?'

'Very well. Come, take a seat.'

They sat together on the *chaise-longue,* and Blackwood took her hand. 'You're quite sure?'

'Indeed: the faerie physicians took very good care of me. It was so wonderful to spend a few days in their realm. You can't imagine the healing power of simply being there!'

'I have no doubt of it.'

'But tell me: what's been happening while I've been gone? Did you see the Queen?'

'Yes, and she asked me to give you her best wishes… and I suspect you'll be receiving an invitation to join her for tea at the Palace before too long.'

'How splendid!'

'And the Bureau is going to handle the demolition of the Void Chamber in preparation for the completion of the new tunnel from Bond Street to Westminster.'

'And what of Charles Exeter?'

'De Chardin was right: he has been incarcerated in Bethlem Hospital. Apparently, he has about as much chance of regaining his sanity as poor Alfie Morgan – which is to say, not very much.'

Sophia nodded. 'Well, we certainly helped the detective to investigate the disturbances on the Underground... although not quite in the way I had expected.'

'Indeed not!'

'What will the Bureau do with all those thousands of tiles lining the Void Chamber?'

'They will be taken to Station X for further study. Our chaps suspect that the Yellow Sign is some form of mathematical symbol, perhaps with strange attributes. Some are already theorising that it is capable of aiding in the warping of time and space which the Anti-Prisms performed.' He shook his head. 'You would think that by now they'd have learned to leave such things alone.'

'Are you surprised that they haven't?' Sophia asked.

'Not in the least.' Blackwood felt his mood darkening, which was not what he wanted today. 'In any event, I think we could both do with a holiday, don't you?'

'I do indeed, Thomas!' Sophia beamed and then furrowed her brows playfully. 'And yet... don't you think it would be awfully unseemly for us to take a holiday together?'

Blackwood shrugged. 'I don't think so; after all, we are professional colleagues. Why should we not enjoy some well-earned rest and recuperation in each other's company?'

The playful frown disappeared as Sophia cried, 'You've convinced me! Where shall we go?'

'I don't know. Where would you like to go?'

Sophia glanced through the sitting room windows at the dense fog outside. 'Somewhere bright and warm. Atlantis is very pleasant at this time of year.'

Blackwood smiled at her. 'Very well. Atlantis it is!'

THE END

ACKNOWLEDGEMENTS

Many thanks to Anna, Emma and Rob at Snowbooks for their continued encouragement and support, and to Anna in particular for her vigilant and judicious editing.

Thanks also to the shade of Robert W Chambers, who inspired this book with his marvellously sinister and eerie creation, the King in Yellow. I should point out that the beautiful 'Cassilda's Song', quoted several times in the text, is not my work (would that it were!), but his.

Finally, to mum and dad for their love, support and encouragement, and to all my friends who continue to inspire me, a very big thank you.

A sneak peak from...

The
Gods of Atlantis

A BLACKWOOD & HARRINGTON MYSTERY

...coming soon from Snowbooks

CHAPTER ONE:
A Coincidence and a Conversation

Thomas Blackwood, Special Investigator for Her Majesty's Bureau of Clandestine Affairs, stood on the promenade deck of the Royal Mail Dirigible *Randolph Churchill,* looking down through the panoramic windows, at the great sweep of the blue-green Atlantic and the distant edge of the island clutching the horizon ahead. Luncheon had just finished, and the diners filing slowly out of the restaurant and into the long chamber, which followed the shallow curve of the skyliner's vast gasbag, chatted quietly and amiably to each other of the largely inconsequential matters which invariably exercise tourists at the start of their holidays.

The pleasant nature of his surroundings notwithstanding, Blackwood was somewhat out of sorts. Lady Sophia Harrington, Secretary of the Society for Psychical Research and his trusted colleague, should have been with him. They had arranged to take a well-earned break in Atlantis following the conclusion of the affair of the King in Yellow, which had placed a near-intolerable strain on Sophia. At the last moment, however, the SPR's President, Sir William Crookes, had asked a favour of her, and she had informed Blackwood that she would join him in the island's capital city of Chalidocean as soon as she were able.

This had darkened Blackwood's mood considerably, for he was anxious that Sophia should take some rest without delay: she had been driven to the point of insanity and death in their struggle against the hideous extra-dimensional entity which had set its hungry eyes on Earth, and which had only been vanquished with the help of King Oberon and Queen Titania of Faerie.

Although the SPR routinely provided advice and help to Her Majesty's Government on matters pertaining to the occult and supernatural, Sophia's contribution to the affair had gone far beyond the call of duty. She needed a break, and every day her recuperation was delayed put an additional strain on her. Blackwood didn't like it and would have had words with Sir William had Sophia not dissuaded him, giving her assurance that, once her responsibilities had been attended to, she would join him in Atlantis, and they would put all their cares behind them – at least for a week or so...

Blackwood's thoughts were suddenly interrupted by a voice behind him. 'Is this your first trip to Atlantis?'

Startled, he turned to see a tall woman standing a few feet away. She was attired in a fashionable dress of purple silk, which was complemented by the plum-coloured feathers adorning her toque hat.

'I beg your pardon, madam?' said Blackwood.

The woman smiled, revealing perfect teeth. To Blackwood's eye, she looked to be of Far Eastern origin; in fact, there appeared to be something of the Tibetan in the roundness of her pretty face and the bright yet impassive intelligence in her brown eyes.

'I was enquiring,' she said, with an accent which was more redolent of the plains of Hampshire than the Himalayas, 'as to whether you have been to Atlantis before, or if this is your first trip.'

'No, it is not,' Blackwood replied, in a tone which, while polite, was nevertheless intended to dissuade his interlocutor from any further attempt at conversation.

She paused, clearly waiting for him to say something more. Blackwood returned her gaze, hoping that his expression would tell her what his tone of voice had not: that he didn't want to be disturbed. In fact, he was rather surprised that she had approached him unannounced in the first place. Was she travelling alone? If not, where was her companion?

Her attire suggested that she was well-to-do, and Atlantis was certainly the place to be at this time of year: the fierce heat of summer had long since released its sweaty grip on the island, and the average daytime temperature was a pleasant seventy-five degrees Fahrenheit. Blackwood was willing to bet that the majority of the people here in the First Class section of the *Randolph Churchill* were like her: wealthy and bored, and ready to spend a few weeks on the beaches of the south, or to take in the sights of Chalidocean and the other large towns.

The young woman stepped forward and stood beside him at the railing. Looking through the angled windows at the steadily-approaching island, she said wistfully, 'I do so adore Atlantis in the winter... my favourite country, my favourite time of year...'

'I am truly delighted for you,' Blackwood muttered. 'The beaches are quite superb.'

She laughed, and Blackwood had to admit that he liked the sound: it was easy and rather sensuous in a subtle kind of way, and he barely managed to suppress a smile. 'I am not speaking of the beaches!' she chided. 'I mean the towns and villages, the architecture, the history of the place. Chalidocean, the Temple of the Ages, the Great Hypogeum...' She hesitated. 'Perhaps I should introduce myself.'

I'd rather you didn't, thought Blackwood.

'My name is Athena Lee, but you may call me Athena.'

Great Scott!

'In that case, I shall call you Miss Lee, and bid you a good day,' Blackwood replied, and with that, he gave her a curt bow and withdrew from the observation deck.

*

As he retired to the First Class lounge, Blackwood felt a twinge of regret at his less-than-gallant behaviour. The fact was, however, that he was in no mood for casual conversation with unaccompanied and unaccountably forthright young ladies, no matter how exotic and intriguing their ancestry.

He sat in one of the burgundy leather armchairs scattered around the lounge, ordered coffee from a passing waiter and withdrew a letter from the inside pocket of his frock coat. The letter, which had arrived at his rooms in London two days earlier, was from Professor Thorfinn Skalagrimsson, Director of Antiquities at the University of Chalidocean.

17th November 1899

Dear Thomas,

I write to you with news of an astonishing discovery which we have made in the Great Hypogeum. As you know, for many years it has been suggested that there is a hidden chamber directly beneath the Main Depression. I had always assumed such speculation to be little more than wishful thinking (and I know that you are of the same opinion).

However, following a minor earth tremor which occurred a week ago, I led a small party into the Hypogeum to assess any damage. We were mortified to discover that the plaster beneath several frescoes in the corridors had been shaken loose and immediately began an operation to retrieve the pieces and attempt to restore them.

However, this dreadful happenstance had an unforeseen and fascinating consequence, for beneath the plaster in the third quadrant of Corridor 1 spotted what appeared to be a large stone plug.

We partially removed the plug as soon as we were able, whereupon we discovered a passageway leading deeper into the ground at a steep angle. As I am sure you have already guessed, this passageway led more or less directly into a hitherto unknown chamber!

You were always my brightest student, Thomas, and I still recall with great affection our many fascinating conversations during our time at the Sorbonne. For this reason, I would like to invite you to participate in our examination of the chamber – and its contents, which I will not mention here. Suffice to say that this may well prove to be the most significant archaeological discovery ever made in Atlantis – indeed, anywhere on Earth.

I hope you will come at your earliest convenience, and join us at the outset of what I believe will be a new era of historical study and research.

Yours, etc.

Skala

Blackwood folded the letter, replaced it in his pocket and took a pensive sip of his coffee. Skala (for thus was the professor known by his friends) was not fond of needless exaggeration, and yet the letter was almost breathless in tone. *The most significant archaeological discovery ever made in Atlantis – indeed, anywhere on Earth.* What had they found in the newly-discovered chamber?

At any rate, it would be good to see Skalagrimsson again: Blackwood had fond memories of studying with him at the Sorbonne in the early 1880s, long before he had been recruited to Her Majesty's Bureau of Clandestine Affairs.

Skala had occasionally acted as a consultant to the Bureau on matters pertaining to ancient history and was one of the very few people who knew of Blackwood's position as a Special Investigator.

It was a curious and welcome coincidence that the recent discoveries should have occurred so shortly before Blackwood's and Sophia's decision to take a holiday in Atlantis; and Blackwood looked forward to telling his colleague about them. Perhaps Sophia would agree to join their investigation. He certainly hoped so, for a little intellectual recreation might be just what the doctor ordered.

Once again, Blackwood's thoughts were interrupted by Athena Lee, who sat down in the armchair opposite and gave him a broad smile.

'We meet again,' she said.

'Indeed we do,' Blackwood huffed.

'If you will forgive the observation, sir,' said Athena, 'I have introduced myself to you, but you have yet to return the courtesy.' Her tone of voice suggested amusement rather than offence.

Blackwood sighed. 'My name is Thomas Blackwood, and I am delighted, just *delighted*, to make your acquaintance.'

Athena hailed a waiter and ordered a cup of green tea. 'So, Mr Blackwood, may I ask why you are going to Atlantis?'

The question was casually phrased... *a little too casually*, Blackwood thought. He regarded his unwanted companion more intently. 'I'm taking a holiday. Why do you ask, Miss Lee?'

She shrugged. 'Just making conversation.'

I wonder, the Special Investigator thought, returning her smile.

The waiter brought her tea, and Athena gave Blackwood a long look as she sipped it daintily. 'I couldn't help noticing, as I approached, that you were reading a letter from someone called Skala. Could that possibly be Professor Thorfinn Skalagrimsson?'

Well, really! thought Blackwood. *The nerve of the girl!*

'Forgive me, Miss Lee, but while I admire your perceptiveness, I must say that the contents of my letter are none of your concern.'

'Oh, indeed not! And I assure you that under any other circumstances I would not have made such an observation. It's just that ... well, Professor Skalagrimsson's name is well known in academic circles; and with the recent discovery in the Great Hypogeum, I'll wager that he is about to become world-famous.' She leaned forward suddenly. 'Are you an archaeologist, Mr Blackwood?'

'No, I am not, although I did study the subject in my youth.'

Athena looked disappointed, and although he really shouldn't have cared, Blackwood found himself slightly offended.

'I for one am fascinated by the mysteries of the remote past,' she said. 'And I have to say that I can't help wondering whether the new discovery might shed some light on the legend of Lemuria...'

'Lemuria!' Blackwood couldn't help laughing. 'Surely you're not one of those poor benighted souls who believe in lost civilisations and the like!'

'I do indeed, Mr Blackwood!' Athena returned with a sudden smile. 'Let us not forget that ten thousand years ago, Atlantis was the greatest civilisation on Earth. Surely it must have had an antecedent, a mother civilisation: it didn't just pop up fully-fledged out of nowhere.'

'No, it didn't. It developed, like all civilisations, from hunter-gatherer, through the development of agriculture, to city-based living. There's no mystery there, I assure you.'

Athena then followed what to Blackwood's mind was the typical tactic of the crank: having had her misconception dispelled, she immediately shifted course and pounced upon a related topic in an attempt to buttress her already-failed assertion.

'Well then... what about the *decline* of Atlantis? Surely you're not going to deny that there is a genuine mystery there. Why did the classical Atlantean civilisation end?'

Blackwood sighed, although this time he could not resist a genuine smile. Having resigned himself to the impossibility of avoiding this attractive but insistent young lady, he decided to allow himself to be amused by her. 'Very well, Miss Lee; why do *you* think it ended?'

'Some historians think that the ancient Atlanteans practised black magic, which was originally the source of their success, the reason for their attaining such a high level of sophistication when everyone else on the planet was wearing loincloths and living in mud huts. But then, something happened: the Atlanteans went too far along the path of dark power. The keepers of the Universe's ultimate secrets saw what they were doing and punished them, destroying their civilisation. Plato says as much.'

'Ah!' Blackwood rejoined. 'Actually, Plato says that Poseidon deserted them when they began to worship other gods. But you mustn't place too much confidence in ancient writers, however great their stature. The Atlanteans have always been romantics, lovers of strange stories and tall tales. I suspect that when Plato travelled there, he fell in with a few leg-pullers.'

'Madame Blavatsky doesn't think so...'

Blackwood shook his head in a fashion which he hoped would be condescending enough to send Miss Lee on her way. Had he known a little more of the marvellous intricacies of the feminine mind, he would have realised that this could not fail to have the opposite effect. 'Blavatsky!' he exclaimed contemptuously. 'My dear Miss Lee, Madame Blavatsky is a poseur and a fantasist of the worst kind: one who doesn't have the decency to market those fantasies as what they undoubtedly are – pure, unadulterated make-believe. If you want to learn something about Atlantean history, I advise you to read people like Mithridas and Zacks – not Blavatsky.'

'I assure you I have,' Athena replied. 'And I suspect they may have to modify their positions somewhat, once the Central Chamber has been fully explored and its contents examined.'

It occurred to Blackwood that Miss Athena Lee might not be a bored socialite after all. 'What, precisely, is your interest in all this, if you don't mind my asking?'

Athena Lee's smile grew broader. 'As I said, I'm fascinated by the mysteries of the past... and I'm a special correspondent for the London *Times*...'

'Ah! A journalist,' Blackwood muttered in a tone which made Athena pout. So much of his work was performed in the utmost secrecy that the Special Investigator was never comfortable around journalists; while he understood that it was necessary to keep the public well informed of events both national and international, he frequently found their inherent inquisitiveness irritating to say the least.

'I have been commissioned by my editor to write a piece on the new discovery,' Athena continued. 'Perhaps you might secure for me an introduction to Professor Skalagrimsson...'

'Perhaps,' Blackwood smiled humourlessly. 'Then again, perhaps not.'

*

As the *Randolph Churchill* made its final approach to Chalidocean Aerodrome, about a mile south of the capital, Blackwood put his fob watch back three hours to Atlantis time and joined the other passengers in the disembarkation lounge, one deck below the promenade. Many were standing at the windows, watching the island's southern regions move swiftly by, and Blackwood couldn't resist joining them. As he looked down at the gentle greens and ochres of the ancient landscape, and the glittering blue lakes scattered here and there like sapphires cast aside by fickle gods, he began to feel a deep and soothing contentment.

He had been away from Atlantis for far too long.

Contrary to his expectations, Athena Lee made no further attempt to engage him in conversation; in fact, she was nowhere to be seen, which he found vaguely puzzling, since all of the hundred or so passengers had arrived in the lounge in preparation for landing.

He put the question from his mind as the sixteen propeller engines mounted along the sides of the gasbag rotated in their gimballed stanchions to face aft. There were a few exclamations of delighted surprise as the deck lurched a little under the sudden reverse thrust and the great vessel began to decelerate.

Like a vast silver whale gliding through a deep ocean, the skyliner made a leisurely descent towards the hundred-foot-tall mooring tower. Guided by cogitators in the control gondola, the small thruster propellers dotted across the surface of the vessel whirred into life, correcting its attitude until the mooring gear in the nosecone connected with the masthead, and the RMD *Randolph Churchill* came to a halt. Guy ropes were instantly thrown down, to be gathered up by the ground crew and attached to cast-iron hitching posts embedded in the ground around the mooring mast.

The doors of the disembarkation lounge slid open, and, travelling case in hand, Blackwood followed the other passengers out onto the lush grass of the airfield, where half a dozen horse-drawn omnibuses waited to take them to the Aerodrome's reception hall.

As he took a seat in one of the omnibuses and the vehicle set off across the landing field, Blackwood glanced through the rear window at the colossal bulk of the dirigible, fully a thousand feet long and two hundred wide, the Union Jack emblazoned upon the gigantic rudder at the stern. Already, maintenance crews were swarming towards the vessel with the intention of preparing it for its return flight to London.

Presently, the omnibus emerged from the shadow cast by the dirigible and clattered swiftly across the landing field, coming to a halt outside the elegant, whitewashed building which housed the Reception Hall and Customs Office.

Blackwood had been expecting Skalagrimsson to meet him in the arrivals lounge; instead, he found a fresh-faced young man holding a small sheet of card with his name neatly handwritten upon it. He was tall and well-proportioned, with smooth olive skin and shining black hair. His cheekbones were high and well-sculpted, and his chin was delicately pointed. A native Atlantean.

'I'm Blackwood.'

'Mr Blackwood,' the young man smiled broadly, shaking his hand. 'I'm very pleased to meet you. My name is Marko Piritas; Professor Skalagrimsson sends his apologies for not coming to meet you personally. He said you'd understand.'

Blackwood returned the lad's smile. 'Of course I do, Mr Piritas. I'll wager he's in the Hypogeum right now – I would be too, if I were him.'

Marko Piritas took Blackwood's suitcase. 'The professor tells me you've booked a room at the Hotel Agartha on the Inner Ring Island. Would you like to go there now, or...?'

'Actually, I think I'd like to go directly to the Hypogeum.'

'You're not too tired?'

Blackwood shook his head. 'Thank you for your concern, but the flight was eminently comfortable, and I'm anxious to see the new discovery as soon as possible.'

They made their way through the bustle of the arrivals lounge and out into the parking area, where several hansoms waited patiently for passengers. To Blackwood's surprise, Piritas walked past them all and led him to a combustion-engined motor car, which Blackwood recognised as a Karl Benz Velo.

'Yours, Mr Piritas?' asked the Special Investigator as he admired the richly-lacquered wood of the vehicle's bodywork and the polished brass of its pistons, lanterns and steering column.

'Oh no!' Piritas laughed. 'I couldn't afford one of these. It's Professor Skalagrimsson's: he loaned it to me to pick you up.'

'How thoughtful of him.'

Blackwood climbed aboard while Piritas secured his suitcase on the luggage rack above the engine compartment and then cranked the four-cylinder boxer engine to sputtering life. He then jumped up onto the bench seat, manipulated several levers and guided the vehicle away from the curb.

'So,' Blackwood said as they chugged away from the aerodrome, 'are you involved with the excavation?'

'Yes,' Piritas replied. 'I'm working towards my doctorate. Professor Skalagrimsson is my supervisor.'

'You've got the best.'

'I think so. The professor mentioned that you studied with him in Paris.'

'Indeed. That was a very happy time in my life. What's the subject of your doctoral thesis, if I may ask?'

'Changes in Atlantean eschatology during the Late Period. I'm halfway through my first year, but I'm tempted to change, in view of...'

'In view of what's been found in the Hypogeum,' Blackwood completed. 'May I offer you some advice, Mr Piritas?'

'Of course, sir.'

'Don't switch subjects in midstream. Regardless of the reason, it never looks good, and besides, you can always do post-doctoral studies on any new discoveries.'

'I suppose that makes sense,' Piritas said, his voice sounding oddly relieved.

'Besides,' Blackwood added, 'you may well find you're able to integrate these discoveries into your thesis.'

Piritas glanced at him. 'Do you think so?'

Blackwood shrugged. 'I'd say it's a fair wager. You're studying classical Atlantean beliefs about the end-times of the Universe – and they've just discovered a secret chamber beneath the most sacred of burial sites. I'm sure that'll be worth an extra chapter!'

Piritas nodded. 'I confess that the thought had occurred to me.'

'In his letter to me, Professor Skalagrimsson mentioned the contents of the chamber, but he didn't elaborate. What, exactly, have they found?'

Piritas's reaction was surprising: he tensed visibly, and his knuckles grew white on the Velo's steering column. 'I think... it's best if you discuss this with the professor.' He gave Blackwood a sidelong glance. 'No offence, Mr Blackwood.'

The Special Investigator shrugged. 'None taken.'

Marko Piritas became unaccountably quiet and withdrawn for the rest of the drive north. Blackwood wondered at the reason, but decided not to press him further, and instead contented himself with taking in the lush countryside passing beneath the bright blue sky.

*

The drive to the Great Hypogeum took just under two hours. Part of the route took them past the outermost circle of the capital, Chalidocean, which had once been known as the City of the Golden Gates – although they had long since been stripped of their gold by the numerous peoples who had invaded Atlantis over the millennia.

In the far distance Blackwood could see the central Acropolis, the gargantuan cylinder of marble-faced granite which rose nearly five hundred feet above the city. On top of the Acropolis stood two equally impressive buildings: the Royal Palace (now home to the Atlantean Parliament) and the Temple of Poseidon. In the winter months, when dawn's damp mists hung over the city, the two buildings seemed to float in the air without any means of support, as if they had materialised out of the mythological realm that had first inspired their builders in remote epochs. That mythology told how Poseidon had shaped the land around his home into three great circles, divided by canals fed by the glittering blue waters of the River Sturla, the 'Sighing River', which tumbled from the mountains to the northwest. Its nickname came from the gentle sounds it made as it followed its upland course towards the flood plain on which Chalidocean stood, which gave rise to the legend that the waters sighed with wonder at the prospect of entering the beautiful City of the Golden Gates.

Looking at the Acropolis, which was said to have inspired Bruegel to paint his miraculous *Tower of Babel* in the sixteenth century, Blackwood wondered whether the great civiliser-god of Atlantis had indeed taught his worshippers the principles of this monumental architecture. He knew it was not so, of course; but it was a pleasant conceit nonetheless.

Amid the ruins of the Outer Wall, he could just glimpse the outermost of the vast concentric canals encircling the Acropolis. Beyond stood the Copper Wall, then the Tin Wall, and finally the Orichalcum Wall which surrounded the Acropolis itself. Many people described Chalidocean as the Venice of the Atlantic. Blackwood certainly believed them to be the two most beautiful cities in the world; however, much as he admired Venice, he preferred to think of it as the Chalidocean of the Adriatic. It certainly made more sense, given the Atlantean capital's vastly greater age.

The last third of their journey took them through the southern half of the Pallasar Forest, the dense swathe of woodland which dominated the island's central region. Blackwood breathed in the cypress scent, relishing its fresh tang, while Piritas guided the Velo along the gently winding road. Gradually, his feeling of irritation at Sophia's absence diminished, and the excitement and anticipation he had felt upon receiving Skalagrimsson's letter returned.

Presently, the forest grew less dense, and then the trees gave way altogether to the large central clearing with its well-preserved archaeological remains and discreetly-positioned visitors' centre. The car chugged slowly past the five small subsidiary temples and came to a halt beside the roofed megalithic circle enclosing the Great Hypogeum. At the main entrance, a sign read:

UNIVERSITY OF CHALIDOCEAN
ARCHAEOLOGICAL DIG IN PROGRESS
NO ADMITTANCE WITHOUT WRITTEN
PERMISSION FROM THE DIRECTOR

As Blackwood and Piritas climbed down from the car, the Special Investigator felt his heart quicken. Finally, he was about to find out what, according to Skalagrimsson, might possibly require the rewriting of Atlantean history...